The Inquisitor

A Novel

HUGH WALPOLE

Doubleday, Doran & Company, Inc.

Garden City 1935 *New York*

PRINTED AT THE *Country Life Press*, GARDEN CITY, N. Y., U. S. A.

FOR
ROBERT GIBBINGS
Friend and Artist

... State of rest which they call Yin ... state of action which they call Yang. The play opens with a perfect state of Yin. When Yin is thus complete it is ready to pass over into Yang. The impulse or motive which makes a perfect Yin-state pass over into the new Yang-activity comes from an intrusion of the Devil into the universe of God.—ARNOLD TOYNBEE, *A Study of History*.

Men in the pressure of their daily business forget the examiner. . . .
This spiritual world may at any moment break in upon the material world, causing a general disorder which men, in their blindness, attribute to casual accident.—HENRY GALLEON, *Essays Civil and Otherwise*.

... I was just going to tell Pa if there was any errands he wanted run my chum and me was just aching to run them, when a yellow cat without any tail was walking over the minister . . .—GEO. W. PECK, *Peck's Bad Boy*.

PREFATORY LETTER

LONDON, 1935

MY DEAR ROBERT:

Whenever I have in the past written a dedicatory letter to a novel, I have been reproached by my friends who tell me that it is a very old-fashioned and otiose thing to do. Whether that be so or not, I see little harm in it, especially if one wishes, as I do in the present instance, to make a certain point clear.

First I would like to acknowledge with what extreme pleasure I dedicate this book to you; modesty forbids my mentioning in public the reasons of my gratitude to you. You well know what they are.

There is something, however, that I have been wanting for many years to say, and this is, I feel, a fair opportunity. *The Inquisitor* is the fourth of a series of stories about a cathedral town that I have called Polchester. The three that precede it are, *The Cathedral, Harmer John* and *The Old Ladies*. The fact that I have written these novels about a cathedral city has persuaded a number of critics, friendly and otherwise, that I have been attempting to rival that wonderful portrayer of Victorian life in a cathedral city—Anthony Trollope. I had, you scarcely need to be told, never any thought of such absurd rivalry. Had I the genius to create characters so masterfully actual as the Bishop, Mr. Slope and Mrs. Proudie, I would wear my hat at an angle and challenge with confidence all the present realists of the English novel. In truth, the aim of my four cathedral novels has been exactly opposite from that of the creator of Barchester, and their ancestor, if they have one, is the author of *The Scarlet Letter* and *The House of the Seven Gables*.

These four novels of mine are, of deliberate purpose, novels of event. There are in the course of them murders, suicides, abductions, riots—not that I would have Polchester supposed to be a town of violence—far otherwise—but there have been in its history, as in the history of all towns, moments of drama, even of melodrama. And these I have deliberately chosen as illustrations of my one continuous theme. In fact, I would hold my breath and declare most dangerously that I am not afraid of melodrama. I think that possibly the contemporary English novel is written too frequently in undertones. Many of the cleverer novelists in England at this present instant seem to myself to talk in whispers. I do not defend melodrama, nor do I think that these cathedral novels of mine are melodramatic, but their violences are deliberate, and the scenes at the close of this present novel are true history.

> With every good wish,
> Yours, dear Robert,
> HUGH WALPOLE

Contents

CONTENTS

INTERLUDE

PART III

MICHAEL FURZE

PART I

Boanerges

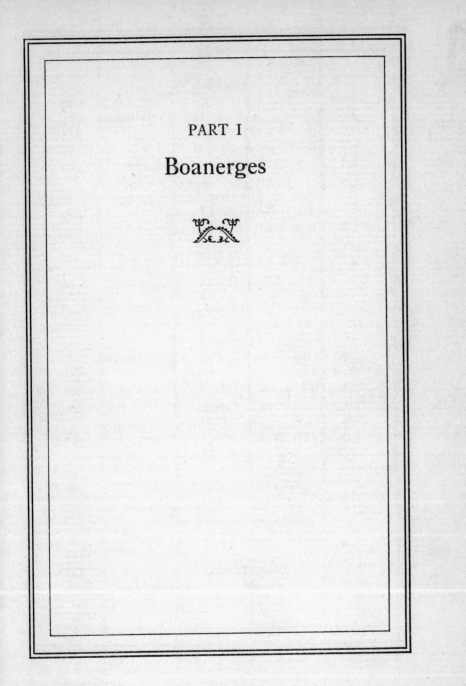

CHAPTER I

Another Citizen—The Cathedral Is Filled—The Cathedral Is Empty

THE THIN PAPERY SKY of the early autumn afternoon was torn, and the eye of the sun, pale but piercing, looked through and down. The eye's gaze travelled on a shaft of light to the very centre of the town. A little scornful, very arrogant, it surveyed the scene. The Cathedral had chimed at three, and at once the bells began with their accustomed melody to ring for Evensong. The town, bathed in a smoky haze, clustered about and around the Cathedral, Cathedral Green and Arden Gate, dropping through the High Street, then lower to the Market-place, then sharply over the Rock to Seatown that bordered the river. Slowly up, beyond the river, sloped the quiet autumn fields to the hills that spread, like dun cloths, to the sea. For the moment, while the sun's eye gazed its last on that afternoon, the huddled town, the long fields, the wide band of sea caught a pale glow of light, looking up to the sun with the timidity of a girl reassured by her lover's unexpected attentions.

Men lolling in Riverside Street, said: "There's the sun!"

At the St. Leath Hotel on Pol Hill beyond the town, windows stole a glimmering shade. In Canon's Yard the old houses with their twisted shapes and crooked chimneys grinned, for an instant, like toothless old men. It was market day and in the Market-place the huddled sheep, the wide-eyed cows, the barking dogs, the farmers, the old women were mistily gold-lit as

3

with a divine dust. The frock-coated statue at the top of Orange Street was illuminated at the nose; in the yard of the old Bull a weary maid rubbed her eyes; Hattaway, the architect, standing in the door of Bennett's bookshop, looked up to the sky and smiled; two of the old ladies of 10 Norman Row, starting out for their walk, said together: "Why, there's the sun!"; Mr. Stephen Furze, alone in his cobwebby room, saw the sun strike ladders of light through the air and shook his head at them; young "Penny" Marlowe, arranging chrysanthemums in the drawing room at St. James's Rectory, smiled mysteriously as though surprised in a secret.

The King Harry Tower caught the light, then seemed, with a proud gesture of disdain, to toss it away.

The eye of the sun, having seen everything, withdrew.

Mists were rising from the river.

The Reverend Peter Gaselee, young and ardent, was crossing the Cathedral Green, to Evensong. Halfway over he was stopped by a bent figure, shoulders wrapped in a grey shawl, hat shabby and shapeless, that said in a sharp and piercing voice: "Ah, Mr. Gaselee—sun came out for a moment but it's gone in again." Peter Gaselee was annoyed by this interruption, for he was in a hurry and old Mr. Mordaunt was a fool. However, it was his policy to be agreeable to everyone—it was also the obligation of his cloth. So he said brightly:

"Ah, Mr. Mordaunt—been sketching?"

"Yes, I have. I've stopped now because the light's too bad. If the sun had stayed I'd have had half an hour more." He drew his grey shawl closer about his shoulders. "Like to see what I've been doing?"

"Delighted," Gaselee said, but thought: Silly old ass— always must be showing his mad sketches to everyone. His fine thin nose twitched as it always did when he was irritated, but his smile was genial as the old man, with a trembling hand, drew out a sketchbook.

"There—the light's bad. But you can see it all right, I dare-say." He opened the book and showed, his fingers tapping against the paper, a double-page drawing. Gaselee flattered himself that he had a fine knowledge of the Arts. He and old Ronder, and possibly Hattaway, were the only men, he told himself, who cared for such things in Polchester.

There was no doubt that old Mordaunt could draw. The Cathedral rose from the paper like a living thing, the King Harry Tower like the proud head of a triumphant giant.

"Those lines in King Harry look like teeth," he said, for he must say something.

"Well, they do sometimes. In certain lights."

"And who's that standing in the West Door?"

The old man peered more closely. "Oh, you see someone there, do you? So did I. But there wasn't anyone there really. At least, I don't think so."

"He's too large for life anyway."

"Yes, long and thin and black. That's how I saw him."

"How do you mean—you saw him—if there wasn't anyone there?"

The old man began eagerly: "Oh well, light does strange things. But I've often thought I've seen him. Very thin, in black. He never moves even when the light changes."

"Shadows, I suppose."

"Yes, shadows."

Gaselee smiled and nodded his head. "Good-afternoon, Mr. Mordaunt. I must be getting on. Going to Evensong."

"Good-day to you, Mr. Gaselee. I must be getting on too. Yes, I must. Good-day to you."

Gaselee walked on. He passed in at the West Door.

Old Mordaunt drew his shawl very closely about him indeed and slip-slopped along, hugging the sketchbook closely to him, the sketchbook that was more to him than wife or child or any human being.

Gaselee walked rapidly through the Nave and up into the Choir. He found his favourite seat, the end one but two on the left towards the Altar, knelt down and prayed, then settled himself with comfort and looked about him.

The lights were lit because of the duskiness of the afternoon;

the curtains had not been drawn and he could see, beyond the misty candlelight that hovered, like a benediction, over the choir seats, into the dark colours of the Nave. A deep, comforting silence, made more peaceful by the distant rhythm of the bells, brooded at the heart of the building. A choir-boy was moving in and out of the seats arranging the service papers.

Once the place had blazed with crimson and gold, paintings of extravagant colour on the walls, marble pavements, the windows shining in the pageantry of coloured glass. Behind him to the left was the Black Bishop's Tomb, the Tomb itself made of a solid block of dark-blue stone, the figure of the Bishop carved in black marble. . . . Ah, there is Mrs. Braund, wife of the Archdeacon, stout, comfortable, and a strange lady with her. There would be very few people today.

A thickset man came stamping along, head up as though he commanded the place, Lampiron, the sculptor, but he never would show his work to anybody—a rude man of whom Gaselee was secretly afraid. . . .

The bells stopped. The organ began. The procession came in. Only Canons Dale and Moffit today—Dale, young, thin, with a face like a hawk, old Moffit hobbling along on a stick.

"Dearly beloved brethren . . ." The service began.

After a while Gaselee lost himself in reminiscence.

Although he was only twenty-eight he seemed to himself to have led already a life of surpassing interest and excitement. He was to himself a figure of quite extraordinary interest. Everything that happened to him was wonderful, although not so wonderful as the things that were going to happen to him.

The first thing that astonished him was that he had been able to do so much for himself. Nothing could have been more ordinary than his parentage, his birthplace. His father had been rector of a Wiltshire parish, miles from anywhere, lost in rolling down and country lane. He had been the only child, and his parents had, from the very first, thought him exceptional. His mother had adored him and he had for her all the condescending love of a favoured only child. His father was a saint, an old stout man now with dishevelled white hair, a passion for gardening, for cricket, for dogs and the people of his village. Gaselee felt for him a stern protective affection, the feeling that one has for someone who knows nothing about life, who may be taken in by anyone or anything, who is so simple as to be not altogether sane. When people spoke to Gaselee of his father and said that he was one of God's saints and a very merry man, adored by his people, Gaselee agreed, but with an implication that it was kind and generous of them to say so. . . . Dear old man. . . .

From a very early age his parents had been astonished at their son's ability to express himself, for they themselves had never found words easy. They wondered, too, at his appetite for reading, at the things that he knew and, as he grew older, they listened with loving attention to his opinions about everything. He told them, affectionately, how old-fashioned they were, and they agreed absolutely with his opinion.

Because they were poor they could not send him to one of the larger public schools. He went to Taunton.

He did very well there, though not brilliantly. He knew a little of everything and was popular because he behaved to everybody as they would wish him to behave. He made no very close relationships because he never gave himself completely to anybody. He had no time for that because he was so busy organizing his own progress. This with one exception. Much to his own surprise and even to his chagrin he developed a passion for a boy called Radcliffe. He was not accustomed to passion and it made him uncomfortable. He could not help himself. Charlie Radcliffe was a quiet, good-natured boy with nothing at all remarkable about him. He could be of no use to Gaselee in any way. At first he returned Gaselee's friendship; then he quietly withdrew, giving no reasons. This was the greatest trouble in Gaselee's school life. He was baffled and bewildered by it. Everything else went well and he won an Exhibition at Jesus College, Cambridge. At Cambridge he lived carefully—he never threw money about. He rowed for his college, was popular exactly as he had been at school and made no close friends. He went to a Clergy Training College at Drymouth and did well there too. Then he had a curacy near Exeter; two years ago he

7

became curate of St. James's, Polchester, whose rector was the Reverend Richard Marlowe.

He had come to Polchester because he felt that it was a good stepping-stone for him. Bishop Kendon was an old man now but famous in the world for his books, his energy, his strength of character. Many remarkable men had been at Polchester—Bishop Purcell, Archdeacon Brandon, Wistons of Pybus St. Anthony. The Pybus living was famous for its incumbents, the majority of whom had been moved to great preferment.

During his two years in Polchester he had, he was sure, made a real mark. He was popular, considered intelligent, and as a preacher increasingly in demand. He was an excellent preacher, modern, easy, well informed, sometimes eloquent, always sensible. He took part in many of the town's activities, played golf, sang in an agreeable light tenor, was considered better read than anyone in the town save old Canon Ronder.

With Ronder he had made a strong alliance and here there was something genuine and real. Although the old man was seventy-five, disgracefully stout and exceedingly lazy, he had a mind that delighted young Gaselee's—sharp, cynical, brilliantly instructed, keen as a dagger. Gaselee's two years had been very happy and successful ones. He had a right to be pleased.

He realized that the time of the anthem had arrived. He looked at a printed sheet that had been laid in front of him and murmured, "Another of Doggett's experiments." It was like Doggett to write a new anthem and perform it for the first time at an ordinary daily Evensong when there would be no audience.

Some people said Doggett had genius, and Gaselee, who loved music and knew when it was good, thought that he might have, but the man was so silent, so retiring, did so little for himself and his future—a little mousy man with a large round head and a face like an egg, who seemed not to care whether one liked his music or no. Gaselee had been kind to him, but Doggett didn't seem to know it.

This was a setting of a poem of Christina Rossetti's.

Gaselee read the poem:

BOANERGES

"Love is the key of life and death,
Of hidden heavenly mystery:
Of all Christ is, of all he saith,
Love is the key.

As three times to His Saint he saith,
He saith to me, He saith to thee,
Breathing His Grace-conferring Breath:
'Lovest thou Me?'

Ah, Lord, I have such feeble faith,
Such feeble hope to comfort me:
But love it is, is strong as death,
And I love Thee."

The second verse was sung by a boy unaccompanied.

That's young Klitch, the son of the man with the curiosity shop, Gaselee reflected. In the third verse seven bars were repeated, reminding him a little of the close of the adagio in Mozart's "Jupiter" symphony. I'll tell Doggett that. I bet he never thought of it. There's something ridiculous, he thought, in an ugly little boy whispering into space "Lovest thou Me?" even though—— Then something pulled him up as sharply as though his face had been struck.

Deep shame held him. They were kneeling and he buried his hands and prayed. It was his soul that had risen from some deep chasm where too often it was hid, and clearly, quietly, faced him. For he cared for beauty and all lovely things, goodness and high conduct and the nobility of man. He believed in God, but life was forever offering him alternatives, pride and wit and self-advancement and the good opinion of his fellows. Soon, very soon, when he was walking through the lighted town to his lodgings, the world would surge back again—"Because Christina was a poet, because a boy sang unaccompanied, because Doggett is a musician, I was sentimentally moved as old stout Mrs. Braund has been moved. A boy sang, a poet wrote, a musician played, and I believed in God. . . ."

THE INQUISITOR

But the mood had not quite passed. His eyes were closed behind his hands, but it seemed to him that the Cathedral slowly filled. The great empty spaces of the Nave had been cold, but through the West Door they crowded in, hundreds upon hundreds, silently. They formed now a serried mass, flowing out into St. Margaret's Chapel, into King Henry's Chapel, under the shields of Henry V and Warwick the King-Maker, over the ledger stones of the Priors, beside the tomb of Henry Quair, the Franciscan friar, with its trefoil canopy, into the Lady Chapel with its carvings of angels, into the King's Chapel with the lovely "Virgin and Children" windows, into the Northeast Transept where is the tomb of the Saxon bishop Wilfred, along the South Aisle that has the tombs of Prior Edward of Barpledon and the great Bishop Holcroft, into the Chapel of All Angels where the famous Emily, daughter of the Earl of Glebeshire, lover of the poor, heroine of the battle of Drymouth, lies, yes, up into the King Harry Tower, down into the Norman Crypt, and, at last, behind him, crowded about the Tomb of the Black Bishop itself, like a mist from the sea, an invasion, an army, a mighty breathing, watching, waiting multitude.

The fantasy was so strong that he scarcely dared to raise his eyes, and when at last he glanced about him, piercing the wavering light of the candles, he still could not be entirely resolved. In his ears and in his eyes there was a conviction of a pressing multitude and he felt that thousands of eyes were bent upon himself.

He was apprehensive; he was suddenly afraid. It was like a nightmare that he sometimes had of making some fearful blunder before a critical company. In his dream he realized that pause, that look of wonder and that awful certainty within himself that he had, in a moment of incautiousness, made a mistake that nothing now could undo. Slowly his eyes cleared. The Cathedral was empty save for the little gathering of human beings about him. Only, as he looked towards the Altar he fancied that one high, thin figure remained, black, motionless, solitary. Then that illusion also passed. The Choir was filing out, Broad the verger preceded Dale and Moffit—old Moffit, his head bent, tap-tapping with his stick.

Gaselee was himself again. On the way out he smiled at Mrs. Braund, nodded to Lampiron, and felt with pleasure the keen evening air blow about his forehead.

Now it so happened that at the moment of the singing for the first time of Mr. Doggett's setting of Christina Rossetti's poem, Polchester received a new citizen. The 3:45 from Drymouth steamed into Polchester Station, gave itself a little shake of appreciation and slumbrously stopped.

Out of one of the third-class carriages stepped a large stout man. The first person in Polchester to have a real conversation with this man was Mr. Herbert Klitch, who had the curiosity shop, No. 11 Norman Row.

Norman Row is a line of small and rather ancient shops and houses that abuts on Arden Gate, facing the Green and the Cathedral. Just behind this row of buildings is Canon's Yard. Some of the houses of Norman Row date back to the sixteenth century. There are a number of shops—the Cathedral Shop that has all the postcards, the guide books, Canon Moffit's book on the Cathedral, cheap imitations of the knocker of the West Door, the carvings of the angels in the Lady Chapel, little replicas of Henry Quair, the Black Bishop, Bishops Wilfred and Holcroft, religious books and, most popular of all, small bronze copies of the Harmer John Memorial. Next to the Cathedral Shop is the Glebeshire Tea Shop, and next to that the Woollen Shop which is run by the Association of Glebeshire Industries. Also in Norman Row live Broad the head verger, Mr. Doggett the organist, Mrs. Coole who has a lodging-house for old ladies.

Mrs. Coole's house is No. 10, the Cathedral Shop No. 3, Mr. Doggett's No. 8, Mr. Klitch's No. 11.

Herbert Klitch was a round, rosy-faced Pickwick sort of man, very jolly, not a fool, with a great affection for his wife and his boy and girl. Especially he had a passionate love of his boy, Guy, who, besides having a fine treble and being head boy in the Choir School, was a nice child with a real talent for mechanics.

THE INQUISITOR

As the Cathedral chimed four o'clock Klitch turned on the electric light. The shop had been dark for some time now, but Klitch had not troubled: he had been alone there, sitting in his back room, glancing out of his back window, which, through a space in the houses of Canon's Yard, looked away on the left to fields and a thin line of graceful hills. He always said he had one of the best views in Polchester, for his back window gave him green fields on one side and the town and the drop to the Rock on the other, while the front shop commanded the whole of the Green and the Cathedral in its complete splendour.

"The whole of Life, Nature, Commerce, Religion—and in Canon's Yard itself the daily humours of the human animal." His shop, he considered, was the true centre of the town.

He was, himself, broad-minded, tolerant, looked on everyone with humour and was an enthusiastic gossip. One of his weaknesses perhaps was that he could keep nothing to himself. He knew everything about the Town, what the St. Leaths were doing at the Castle, old Ronder's present pulling of intricate strings, why Lady Mary Bassett had quarrelled with Mrs. Cronin, what Humphrey Carris had up his sleeve. Especially did all the life of the Cathedral—clerical, human, musical, official—pass under his eye. And because he had money enough, a good wife, good children, a fine digestion, and was able to laugh at his enemies, he was a happy man.

His shop was crowded with things good, bad and indifferent —furniture, pictures, suits of armour, a stuffed crocodile, silver, china, rugs and old books. There were always some valuable things to be found there by those who knew. He had no conscience at all about cheating anyone who was ignorant enough to be cheated. His theory was that anyone who wished to buy old things should learn something about the job. He dealt with an admirable "faker" in Drymouth who could provide you with a Chippendale chair, a piece of Lowestoft, a Girtin water colour in no time at all. He made his living, in the main, from the junk that was in his front window. He was clever at arranging his window, and would have there some delicate china, an Indian shawl, some Toby jugs, and a piece of carving from a Spanish cathedral, so tactfully placed that they all gave lustre to one another.

When someone came to the shop who had true knowledge, he brought out his real things. This was his happiest time, for he had a great and genuine love of the true and the beautiful. He would surprisingly lower his prices for a connoisseur, feeling that here was another artist like himself. One or two things—a Bonington drawing, a small Chippendale table, some Waterford glass—he loved so much that he kept them to himself. He himself painted water colours and very bad they were.

Not only was his face round and rosy but his skin was very smooth and he was a pattern of cleanliness. He always wore a rather high wing-collar and in his tie a gold pin. He liked loose pepper-and-salt tweeds in the winter time, and on his thick gold watch chain was a masonic sign. He was a high official in the local Lodge. His short thick legs were quick, impatient, impulsive, and the rest of his body seemed to move with slow good-nature behind them as though it said: "Hold on, legs. You'll wear me out one of these days, but I'm proud of you all the same." He thought a pretty girl one of the nicest things in the world and I would not say that he had been always faithful to Mrs. Klitch. "In spirit—always," he would say, and Mrs. Klitch said, "What I don't hear about don't worry me."

He went into the front shop, and, looking about him, thought that he would soon close, for it was not likely that there would be any more customers today. He was filled with pride and satisfaction. The front shop looked nice, very nice indeed. He arranged a few things, humming "Raindrops on the Roof" as he did so. He stopped and patted his Chinese Warrior on the shoulder. He was very proud of his Warrior, a big figure in red-and-gold lacquer, carrying a sword. He had a black hat and black boots and in his eyes there was a stare of cold arrogant brutality which Klitch greatly appreciated.

Then (Klitch often afterwards remembered the exact circumstances) his shop bell rang, the door opened and a man came in. He was tall, broad and stout. He was wearing an ulster and carried a shabby brown bag. This last he at once put down

on a sham Chippendale chair and said: "Mr. Herbert Klitch?"
His voice, even as revealed by those few words, was remarkable.
It had a resonance quite unusual, so that you felt that it was
carried on in a series of reverberating echoes. Nevertheless, its
tone was tunefully deep and true.

"Yes, that's me," said Klitch ungrammatically.

"Ah," said the man. Then he took off his ulster. "Just as
though," Klitch said afterwards, "he meant to stay for the
night." He smiled a broad and beaming smile. This should have
been friendly and yet was not altogether so. As Klitch very
quickly noticed, the man was in many ways a series of con-
tradictions. He was big and should have given an impression
of great strength, but there was too much flesh on his bones.
His head was finely shaped, but the cheeks were flabby, the
mouth too small. The eyes were large and friendly but also a
little sly. His most remarkable feature was his nose, which was
unusually long, fleshy about the nostrils, and gave the impression, as some noses do, that it had a life independent of the rest
of the face. His colouring was fair and he had an untidy light-
brown moustache.

The moment that Klitch really looked at him he said to himself, "Now where have I seen that nose before?"

The stranger stood with his legs apart and began to talk.

"I've just arrived in your town and left my bag at the station," he said. "The fact is that I have only a few shillings in
my pocket. Don't be afraid," he went on, laughing, "I'm not
going to beg; no, and I'm not going to hold a pistol at your head
either. I was looking all the way along for a curiosity shop,
somewhere to sell a very pretty thing I've got in my bag here.
I thought I was beat and then I came on your shop." He smiled
in a friendly, intimate way. "You see, I only landed at Drymouth this morning and there were one or two things I had to
buy there. I'm staying with relatives here in Polchester, but I
don't want to arrive without a penny to my name. I'll be getting a cheque from America in a day or two, but that will take
a week or more to clear." He looked around him. "You've got
some nice things here."

"Yes," said Klitch, "I have—and I don't know that I want any more. Times as they are, we're all trying to sell things rather than buy them."

"Perfectly," said the stranger. "I fully appreciate that, but when you've seen what I've got here I think you'll like it."

He turned to the shabby bag, opened it and, from the middle of a pair of not-too-fresh pyjamas, produced something in brown paper. Klitch, who was a good observer and liked to say, with his head on one side, that nothing was too small to be important, noticed that the hands were big, podgy, and the backs of them covered with brown freckles. I'd know those hands again anywhere, he thought. The man, with great care, his face puckered with child-like seriousness, unwrapped the paper and then held up something that made Klitch exclaim, in spite of himself, "Ah!"

It had been his habit for many years to assume complete indifference if he was a purchaser and show a friendly eagerness if a seller. He was disgusted with himself for saying "Ah!" The man said nothing. He simply held up his prize against the light and his whole big body was taut with pride.

He was holding a crucifix of black marble. The Christus was carved in white ivory. It stood on a pedestal of brilliant green ivory.

"You may well say 'Ah,'" he remarked at last. "You won't see another like this in a hurry. Spanish—seventeenth century."

No, Klitch wouldn't. He realized that. Moreover, the artist-demon in him was stirring, gripping his heart with its talons, urging him on, spiteful vindictive little animal, to perform some egregious commercial folly.

"Yes. It's fine," Klitch said. "I won't deny it." He examined it more closely. He took it into his expert hands. The figure was exquisitely carved and it was no absurd fancy of Klitch's that, with its dignity of suffering, its abnegation of all pride, its poignant authority, the room and everything in it should be aware of a new presence.

Klitch placed it on a table. Both men looked at it.

"Of course," said the man, "it's worth I don't know how much. If I waited I could get anything I like for it in London."

"Perhaps," said Klitch, "you could and perhaps you couldn't. It's amazing these days what low prices fine things are fetching at Christie's and Sotheby's."

"Oh, *that's* not the way," said the man. "The thing to do is to find somebody who wants it, somebody who must have it. But I haven't the time. That's the damnable part of it. Fact is," he went on, growing more confidential, "I don't want to part with it—if I can see a way out."

"What's its history?" Klitch asked.

"I got it from a man in New Mexico. He said it came from Toledo. It's seventeenth-century Spanish all right though."

"Probably stolen," Klitch thought, and told himself to be careful.

The man went on: "Now this is what I thought you might do. Let me have fifty pounds or so. Give me three months. If I can pay you back with interest in that time I take it back. If not, at the end of three months, you keep it. It's worth three or four hundred if it's worth a penny."

"Staying in Polchester?" Klitch asked.

"Well, to be honest with you I don't know. Depends how I like my relations and how they like me. But you're safe enough any way. If I abscond in the night you've got the thing for keeps. I'll give you a paper saying that if I'm absent from this town a month without redeeming it it's yours. Nothing could be fairer than that."

Yes, Klitch thought, that was fair enough. He knew where he could sell it tomorrow for a hundred. But he didn't want to sell it. The longer he looked at it the more he liked it. Fifty pounds was a lot of money, but he had done well that summer.

"I'm not a pawnbroker, you know," he said, smiling.

"This is different," said the man.

Yes, it was. Klitch hadn't seen so beautiful a thing for a long time.

"All right. I'll do it," he said suddenly.

"Cash," said the man.

"I think I've got enough. Come into the back room."

He sat down and wrote out a declaration. Then he jumped up.

"Wait a moment," he said. "I'll have a witness if you don't mind." He went to the little staircase and called out: "Maria! You there?"

Someone answered, and presently a little woman with grey hair and a mottled face like a strawberry came down.

"Here, Maria! I want you to witness this."

Mrs. Klitch stared at the big man with great interest, but she was a discreet woman, did her business and retired up the stairs again. Then the man sat down and, holding the pen very clumsily in his big hand, signed his name.

"Why!" Klitch cried. "Furze? Michael Furze? Any relation of Mr. Stephen Furze?"

"I'm his brother," said the man.

That, thought Klitch, is where I got the nose from!

"His brother!" Klitch said. "Stephen Furze's brother! Well I never!"

They went back into the front room.

"Yes, my name's Michael Furze. My friends call me Mike." The man, smiling, stood swaying slightly on his big legs.

Klitch gave him three ten-pound notes and the rest in ones.

"So you're going to stay with him?"

"I suppose so. I haven't seen him for twenty years. What's he like now?"

"What was he like twenty years ago?"

"Oh, thin as a stick and mean as hell."

"Well, he's just the same now. He's not liked in the town. Too many people owe him money."

"Ah—same old Stephen." Furze's eyes narrowed. "He had a girl of ten when I last saw him. She still with him?"

"Oh yes."

"And Sarah?"

"Mrs. Furze? Yes, she's still there."

"They don't know I'm coming," Furze said, grinning. "It'll give them a bit of a surprise."

17

"I expect it will." Then Klitch added: "I doubt if you'll stay there long."

"Why? What's the matter with them?"

"A bit miserly, the old people. You won't get much to eat."

"Oh, won't I?" Furze smiled again.

"You'll find the town a bit quiet too," Klitch said.

"Just what I want—some quiet. I've roamed the world over. Moscow, Tokio, Honolulu, New Zealand, Paraguay, Colombia—anywhere you like. I could tell you some stories. . . . But I've always fancied a place like this. I'm a religious man."

"You're what?" asked Klitch.

"Religious. Does that sound odd to you?"

"No. Not odd," said Klitch. "Only precious few people are these days."

"Well, they ought to be." The voice began to boom again. "They'll find it mighty uncomfortable for themselves one day. The soul—what's more important than the soul? Here for seventy years or so, then—eternity. Eternity! Just think of it, man! When I was in Paraguay once . . ."

He then proceeded to tell an amazing story with dragons and witch-doctors and tortured old women and a large black snake in it. The story was wonderful and most unconvincing. Furze stopped with a click.

"Well, there—I could talk all night. I must be getting on and give my dear relations a shock. A miser is he, dear Stephen? Always was. Grown on him, I expect."

"I expect it has," Klitch said gravely.

"I hate to leave that with you. May I come in and look at it sometimes?"

"Why, of course."

"I'll buy it back from you in no time. You'll see." He shook hands and Klitch was astonished at their soft pudginess. "Good-night. Many thanks." He picked up his shabby bag and went out.

Klitch looked, from the open door, after him. There was no sign of him. He had been swallowed up as though he had never been. A thin, vaporous mist had come up, but above it stars shone out and the Cathedral, like a black ship, sailed against the pale sky.

"That's a rum bloke," Klitch thought. "Never met a rummer."

He looked at the Cathedral. Empty now and silent. Not a soul there. He wondered sometimes what it felt at night. Did the spirits of the old priests and warriors and monks come out from their tombs? He had thought sometimes that he would invade that silence. What would he discover? A foolish, fantastic thought, but then he had for so long lived with old, discarded things, chairs and tables and pictures and suits of armour that seemed to him to have a life of their own. Well, if chairs and tables had, why not knights and bishops?

He went back into the shop and looked at the Crucifix. Yes, it was lovely. He hoped fervently that that fellow would not find the money.

He called up the staircase: "Maria! Come down and see what I've got!"

CHAPTER II

A House Like a Bone, Set for Two Antagonists

MICHAEL FURZE, when he had taken some strides into the thin evening mist, remembered that he had not asked Klitch where brother Stephen's house was. But that did not matter. He had the name of the house—the Scarf—and there must be plenty who knew it.

He was greatly pleased with himself, as, in fact, he very often was. To call him conceited would be to call him mature: he had the vanity of a child, of an animal, of anything not old enough to make mature comparisons. His own idea of himself was that he was a wonderful fellow for bringing things off. His boastfulness—he was a tremendous boaster—did not come from the nervousness of self-suspicion nor from the blindness of a fanatic. He was like a boy who thinks his school the whole world. He forgot instantly his mistakes, follies, ignorances, exposures. A varied and adventurous life had taught him nothing. In the same way he lied continually because, as soon as he said a thing, it became at once for him a truth; because of his physical size, his voice, his laugh and something attractively naïf in his personality people laughed at him indulgently. He was not mean nor revengeful; desire for revenge *might* be stirred in him and it would have then all the determined purpose of a limited nature; as yet, in his life he had been treated on the whole well.

And now he was thinking that he was a wonder. Here he was, arriving in a town altogether unknown to him, without a penny in his pocket, and behold, within an hour he had fifty quid! Had fifty quid as he wanted it too!

Oh yes, Mike, my son, you're a marvel. You go from place to place, all the world over, and land on your feet and get what you want, have money and food and friends for the asking! What is there about you, Mike? Hasn't God got some special purpose for you? Didn't He make you as you are that you should do some wonderful thing? Then, when the clock strikes, at the exact moment, there you will be, the world, astonished, at your feet, all glory to God! Weren't you a marvel in the war, Mike?—never once hit, never ill save for that bit of dysentery in Palestine. And weren't you a marvel in America and in Constantinople and in China? Aren't you a marvel with women too? Don't they all fall for you and, when you're sick of them, don't you just leave them as a real man should?

And now you've come to the right place, Mike, my son—a cathedral town. Haven't you always wanted a cathedral? Haven't you in Venice and Toledo and Paris and Cologne stared open-mouthed at those wonderful places just as though you had some special right to them, some personal relation with them? Haven't you said, since you were a baby: "There's nothing so wonderful, nothing I, Mike Furze, want so much"? And hasn't it been a kind of wonderful coincidence that your stinking, parsimonious, bread-scraping brother should choose, fifteen years ago, of all places in the world a cathedral town to live in? Choose it *and* stay in it! There's a kind of miracle for you!

He had reached the Arden Gate. He turned for a last look, and there it was, its black mass raised above the mist against the stars. Clutching his brown bag, his legs apart, he stared at it, wondering whether, in full light of day, he would be disappointed in it. This wonder came freshly to him on every fresh occasion, for after all, what could this passion of his for cathedrals be but an illusion? One day—he expected it to come at any time—he would say to himself: "Well, now—think of that—

whatever did I see in the thing?" and he knew that, when that moment came, he would suffer some loss, the kind of loss that he would suffer were he never to see his black marble crucifix again. This sense of what he would lose led him to yet further appreciation: "No, indeed—I am no ordinary man. The ordinary man cares nothing for cathedrals."

Through Arden Gate he walked and started down the High Street. Now he must consider the Town, about which of course he knew nothing at all.

He could not, as a visitor returning after several years might do—Shade, thin bony Shade of Miss Midgeley, are you there?—wonder at the many improvements and possibly lament them—at the up-to-date splendours of the St. Leath Hotel; at the fine sprouting of red-brick villas up the hill above Orange Street; at the renovation of the Bull with its bathrooms and handsome garage; at the parking place off the Market; at the reclamation and renovation of Pennicent Street, that once abominable heart of Seatown, now Riverside Street, at the excellent and justly famous eighteen-hole golf course carved from part of the St. Leath domain (the St. Leaths, poor things, no longer wealthy as once they were); the two splendid cinemas, the Arden and the Grand, forgetting the little cheap one, the Majestic (vulgarly known as the Dog), down in Riverside Street.

Yes, so modern are you, might that sparse and bony Shade exclaim, that you are contemplating (you, James Aldridge, Mayor, and you, Humphrey Carris, solicitor, and you, Fred Hattaway, architect, and you, Dick Bellamy, universal provider), a flying-field, on the other side of the river towards Pybus.

So far in the one direction: and in the other might that Shade —universally present, for whom time has no meaning—marvel also that so little is changed, that wildness still runs in Riverside Street (what of the Dog and Pilchard? Is Hogg's stout shadow not hovering there yet?), the Market-place has not lost its scented country air, nor the Bull its dark and tallow-candled passages, nor Canon's Yard its mysteries, nor Norman Row the dignities of its tempestuous Abbot. . . .

And the Cathedral? Here the Shade pauses, waits, and enters to find a great company in attendance. . . .

Michael Furze asked no questions. He passed down the High Street through the lighted town. Everything was alive and bustling. Motors pushed and hooted through the narrow street; the St. Leath motorbus, having met the last train of the day, jigged its way up the hill; farmers (for it had been market day) stood solidly gossiping, moving contemptuously at the last possible instant from the path of intolerable cars; opposite Bennett's was the lighted hallway of W. H. Smith's (and oh! the rivalry and hatred that this opposition had created) and, two doors below it, the brilliant flaunting electric-lit windows of Bellamy's main store! Here surely was promise of life and adventure for Michael Furze. Furze with his brown bag and his fifty quid!

He stopped.

"Would you mind telling me," he asked the policeman at the corner, "where the Scarf is? It's the name of a house. I don't know the street. Belongs to a Mr. Stephen Furze."

The policeman directed him.

He turned to the right and down, finding himself then in an unexpected quiet, passing some railings that guarded a drop of sheer black-fronted rock. He stayed there a moment and looked downwards, to the life and lights of Seatown. He knew nothing of Seatown as yet nor of the spirit that informed it, but he had the sharp sniffing apprehensions of a child or a puppy and he realized that there was, down there, some world very different from the High Street just as the High Street was different again from the Cathedral. So small a place and three distinct worlds in it—or were they distinct? These speculations, however, were not for him, whose whole instinct was towards self-preservation and self-glory. Nevertheless, he was apprehensive. The mist came up from the river and with the mist a sea tang, a breath of the unknown. He translated this, as he moved forward, into a new nervousness as to how his brother would receive him. He was not afraid of his brother. Oh no, not he! They had never cared for one another—but who *could* care for Stephen? Michael had left the home in Hull—their father had been a shipping merchant—at a very early age, apprentice to the merchant service, and after that it was only at odd moments that they had met. Stephen had moved to London, had been some sort of broker in the City. Twenty years ago Michael had spent a week-end with them at Tulse Hill—on his own invitation needless to say. And what a week-end! Poor Mike had emerged on the Monday a starved man: every mouthful had been grudged him. Stephen's meanness had become a mania—yes, with the intensity, the preoccupation, the watching, waiting lust of madness.

Wasn't it crazy, then, after such an experience, to return? The notion had come to him on the ocean, travelling from America without a penny in his pocket. He had been idly turning over the pages of some magazine when he had been confronted with a magnificent photograph of Chartres. There it was just as he had last seen it, glorious, triumphant, flattering him with the appeal that it made to him, so that his throat contracted, his fingers curved. How many others on the boat with him would feel that delighted pleasure? He remembered then that Stephen, his wife and child had gone, fifteen years ago, to live in Polchester in the south of England. He remembered even the name of the house—the Scarf, Polchester, Glebeshire, England.

It hit him then like a blow in the stomach. Stephen must be rich by now: twenty years of miserly saving. There would be results of that. Stephen was ten years older than himself and, even twenty years ago, had been a lanky pale-faced skeleton. And there was the Cathedral, one of the most famous in England. In that moment of time, staring at the pictures of Chartres, his mind was made up, his destiny settled.

Now the child in him, part roguish, part malicious, part friendly, part fearful, anticipated the meeting.

He came to a house, isolated, not far from the church of which the policeman had told him. He could see it very dimly, but he knew it to be the one, for on either side of the gate were stone pillars surmounted by misshapen stone animals. What they represented he could not, in that light, tell. He pushed back the gate that screamed on its hinges; his feet crunched the

gravelled path. Before the door he hesitated. Not a sound came
to him save the rustling at his feet of a few autumn leaves
taunted by the evening wind. Then, most unexpectedly, across
the whole extent of the town, the Cathedral struck the hour.
He waited until the full total of the five strokes that followed
the chime had ended. Then, as though that had decided him,
he pushed, with all his force, the bell. He heard it peal as though
through an empty house. He waited and with every second of
pause his impatience grew. It was as though he felt a personal
insult, and he pushed the bell again; he might have been mutter-
ing: "You'll keep me out, will you? Well, I'll show you."

He heard someone approaching; light spread behind the fan.
The door opened and an old woman stood there, peering out
into the dusk. He knew that she was Sarah Furze.

"Who's there?" she said.

He stepped forward, but she did not move.

"Don't you know me?" he cried, and his voice boomed into
the house. "I'm brother Mike!"

She stared at him, pushing her head forward. He could see
that she was very much older than when he had seen her last.
Her face was dry, faintly yellow, seamed with wrinkles, and her
eyes dull and strained with the defeated gaze of someone very
short-sighted. Then he realized with a shock that she was more
than short-sighted: she was blind.

The voice must have told her who it was, for she stood aside.
He passed by her into the house.

"Michael!" she said, her voice quavering with astonishment.
"I can't see. . . ."

"It's myself sure enough," he shouted at her as though the
knowledge of her blindness made him think that she must also
be deaf. "Turned up again like a bad penny." Then he caught
her by the shoulder, pulled her towards him and kissed her. Her
cheek was dry and powdery. She was a little old woman wearing
a faded black silk dress, her grey hair plaited in old fashion but
very neatly above her wrinkled forehead.

"There's no one in the house," she said.

He stood there, staring about him. He realized a number of

things—one that the place was lit by gas, another that the hall, the stairs were dry and clean like an old yellow bone. Yes, dryness and cleanliness and a faint, a very faint odour in the air of mortality, as though far away, in the heights or depths of the house, someone were lying awaiting burial. It was not altogether unpleasant, this very faint odour; it was chemical perhaps rather than corporeal. Yes, the odour of a chemist's shop, many degrees rarefied. He was sharp and observant in any new place because he had, in his life, travelled so far and encountered so many adventures. He noticed that once the wall-paper of the hall and staircase had been a bright yellow with crimson roses. Now the walls were dim as things are that have been kept underground away from the light. The only furniture of the hall was an umbrella stand, very ancient, leaning a little away from the door as though it feared the draught; above this a looking-glass and at the side of the glass some coats hanging like corpses. Only one picture hung on the wall, a photogravure of Father Christmas arriving in a family of excited, clapping, laughing children and pouring from his sack a multitude of gifts. One other thing he noticed, and that was that at the head of the stair was a high window, its glass of yellow-and-green lozenges.

Plenty of time for looking at things, he thought, for there he was and there Sarah was, motionless, staring in front of her with her sightless eyes. There was no sound at all save the faint hiss of the gas jet in the globe above his head. He must be doing something about this. The silence was twisting his nerves.

"Stephen out, is he?" he cried heartily. (His voice seemed to drive up to the green-and-yellow window and back again.) "When will he be back?"

"Soon—very soon—any minute now."

"I've come to stay the night."

"You must talk to Stephen," she said, rubbing her lip with her fingers.

"Aren't you glad to welcome me, old girl, after all this time?" he said, feeling that something must be done.

"Yes, yes." Her lips moved in a smile. "Where have you been all this while, Michael?"

"The world over, old girl. Places you've never heard of, I'll be bound. And now I've come home."

"Yes. Stephen *will* be surprised."

"I bet he will." He wondered whether she were still uncertain of his identity. She stood there with indecision. And yet she could not be uncertain. Once you'd met him you'd recognize Michael Furze again anywhere, in the very confines of the deepest darkness.

However, he could not stand there forever, so he said:

"What about sitting down, old girl, and waiting a bit? I've been travelling all day."

"Yes, of course."

"I only left the boat this morning."

"The boat?"

"Yes. I've come from America. Come straight here to see how you were all getting along."

It seemed that she had made up her mind, for again with that smile which came and went as though she herself had nothing to do with it, she moved down the hall. She moved with the concentrated certainty of the blind and, coming to a door on the left, opened it.

"You can make yourself comfortable here perhaps. Stephen won't be long, I'm sure."

He moved in, taking his brown bag with him. He was at once struck with the icy coldness of the room.

"My God!" he thought. "I shan't be able to stay here a week."

He saw things that he recognized. The old clock on the mantelpiece with the grumpy face, faint yellow marks of discoloration that gave it a pouting mouth and a twisted nose. It was not going; the hands pointed to quarter-past eleven. Two large china ornaments, country girls in wide-brimmed hats carrying baskets of flowers; two armchairs of horsehair; a white wool rug with black lines on it; a glass-fronted cabinet containing some very mediocre china, a Swiss cowbell, a carved wooden box. All these things he remembered from his childhood. On that same rug Stephen had, in one of those dry, bitter tempers of his, rubbed his knuckles in his brother's eyes until he screamed again. His mother had slapped him for opening the cabinet without permission. The clock made a noise, when it was going, like an old man in a wheezing hurry. He had been all the world over and had returned to these same things. He could fancy that they recognized him and he half expected the old clock to start off again on its wheezy way to show him that it remembered him. But no—everything here was frozen into silence.

The gas was already lit. The room was bare in spirit and irreproachably clean.

Sarah had left him then, so he sat down on one of the horse-hair chairs, his bag at his feet, and wondered what would come next.

He had not long to wonder, for the door opened without a sound and Stephen stood in the room.

"I believe he was in the house all the time," Michael thought. But he went cordially to his brother, shook his hand with almost extravagant warmth and cried:

"What about this for a surprise, old boy? Delighted to see you."

Stephen had not altered very greatly in twenty years. He was sparser, sparer; his body had a *preserved* look, as though he had been kept all this time in some kind of spirit. He was as tall as his brother, and his big white nose, projecting from his gaunt face, suggested a possibility, like Michael's, that it had a life of its own. It was a peering, active, probing nose with its own knowledge, its own discoveries, its own conclusions. He had scanty grey hair, wisps of it brushed carefully over the white domed skull; pale shaggy eyebrows; eyes mild, sleepy; a mouth uncertain, rather tremulous.

In truth, had it not been for the nose and a curious lithe active movement of the long thin body, Stephen Furze might seem a gentle, sluggish, easy man, kindly of intention, noninterfering. He wore a black frock-coat of ancient cut, a high white collar, a black bow tie. His garments were old but scrupulously brushed and neat. When he spoke all Michael's childhood and youth rushed back to him, for Stephen's voice had a soft, gentle ring about it that distinguished it from all others.

When he spoke he gave an impression of great politeness but of firmness too. There was nothing humble in his tone, and he had a way of suddenly protruding his eyes from under the heavy white lids so that they looked at you as a candle shines when the cover is lifted.

He gripped his brother's podgy hand and it was then that his body seemed to rise, hover and hang forward.

"A surprise! I should think so! We thought you the other end of the earth. We'd no idea *where* you were, and naturally, for you haven't written to us for years."

Michael removed his hand and stepped back.

"I was always hoping to write and tell you that I was a millionaire," he said. "Thought my luck would change, but it didn't. Then in New York I was suddenly homesick, felt I must see old England again. Before I died, you know." He laughed.

"Died!" said Stephen. "We are both far from that, I hope."

"I only landed at Drymouth this morning and came straight here."

"Well, sit down, sit down," Stephen said with a kind of warm gentleness. "You'll stay and have something to eat with us? You can't refuse us that after all this time. Where are you stopping? The Bull?"

(This, thought Michael, with my bag staring at him!)

Michael squared his shoulders.

"I've come straight here," he said. "Can you give me a bed for the night?"

Stephen gave a quick apprehensive look round the room. He looked at the china ornaments, the cabinet, the table. It was as though he were guarding these things, protecting them from attack.

He stood by the fireside. He rubbed his nose.

"The fact is, Mike, we're not prepared for you. You should have given us warning. Poor Sarah—I don't know whether you noticed, but she's blind, poor thing—a terrible deprivation. And at the moment we have no maid——"

"Oh I'm used to roughing it," Michael broke in heartily. "I'll sleep anywhere. If I stay for a bit I can look around——"

At the word "stay" Stephen Furze straightened his body, then turned with a gentle twisting movement towards his brother.

"Stay? Well, as to that . . ."

This short conversation had brought his childhood back to Michael with an amazing vividness—for always, from the very beginning, the relations of the two brothers had been like this: they had never wasted time over preliminaries, had been at once in opposition, Michael with the blustering vehemence of his simple egotism, Stephen with the quiet resolve of a monomaniac.

Stephen always had his way. But now—and how curious that it should be so late postponed!—they were meeting for the first time in serious contact as grown men. Michael had the obstinacy of his naïf selfishness, Stephen the driving determination of his monomania. But, as yet, there was no battle, for Michael said:

"Look here, Stephen. I didn't mean to spring this upon you. Truly I didn't. I should have written, but I only made up my mind at the last moment. I'm like that, you know. A rolling stone. Never know where I'll be tomorrow. I just said to myself: 'I must have somewhere quiet in England for a week or two after rolling round.' Then of course I thought of you. And then the Cathedral—I like cathedrals, I don't know why. . . . I'll be no trouble to you. I only want a room and my breakfast. And of course I'll pay for my keep."

Stephen said gently, "Yes."

"Only a room and breakfast. I'd want a fire in my room though. I feel the cold. . . ."

"Well," said Stephen, "what . . . ?"

"Oh, about twenty-five bob a week, don't you think?" Then from his breast-pocket he took his roll of notes and laid them on the table in front of him. "I'm in funds just now," he said.

Stephen looked at the money. His hand moved quietly forward and he touched them. He murmured, "There's a lot of money there."

"Yes. Fifty pounds."

"What are you going to do with it?"

"Oh, I've got to live on that until I've found something to do."

He was uneasy, even frightened. The cold dead room seemed suddenly charged with life as a dark place is filled with light. He had the sense that his brother was drawing him in with his long arms and holding him in an embrace; some instinct made him take the money and put it back in his coat; as he did so he heard Stephen draw a long breath, like a sigh, something poignant and sad, a deep murmur of regret.

"Yes—I think we could manage that, Michael. We have no servant, as I told you. Only Sarah and my daughter. But I *think* we could manage. It will be pleasant to have you after all this time."

Michael stood up. He knew that they had achieved, in that moment, a relationship different from any that they had ever known—closer, more intimate. At the same time he realized that he had a kinship with Stephen that he had never suspected. He had always liked money, but only for the things that it bought him. Now he felt that there was something in money itself, the look of it, the feel of it. When Stephen had touched those notes he had wanted to cry out: "Now you leave that alone!" Stephen must have saved a lot, being the miser he was. There must be plenty hidden away in the house somewhere, he wouldn't wonder. . . .

With this thought he was also uncomfortable. Something said to him: "Get out of this. Leave the house, the town. Don't come back. You're not such a bad fellow. You were safe five minutes ago. Be safe again."

But of course he liked risks. . . . He liked risks. The two brothers stood facing one another. They had never been friends, and Stephen, being ten years older, had always had his way. But now. The ten years were gone, didn't count. Stephen was thin and worn. He didn't look well. He mightn't live so very long.

They moved upstairs.

THE INQUISITOR

The room that Stephen showed him had an old canopy bed with faded crimson hangings. On the wall was a text, with painted flowers: "Thou God seest me." The washstand, two chairs, a wardrobe were shabby and it was very cold.

"You won't forget about the fire," Michael said.

"No, no. It may not burn very well at first. There hasn't been a fire for some time in here. I'll tell Elizabeth."

Michael put the bag on the floor.

"Well. . . . That's good. I'm glad we've come to an arrangement. Look here, I'll pay you in advance for the first week." He took out the money. "Here's a pound. I'll give you the five shillings tomorrow when I get change."

"Oh, I think I can change another pound." Stephen took from his pocket a strong black purse with a steel clasp. He found ten shillings and then brought five shillings in silver from his trouser pocket. Michael gave him another pound. Stephen put them in his purse; the clasp shut with a snap.

He stood rubbing his long hands together.

"We live extremely simply here. Very quiet."

"That's what I want—quiet. I've been bumming around too long." He bent down to his bag. Stephen watched every movement with such intentness that Michael longed for him to go. He wanted him out of the room.

"When's supper?"

"Half-past seven. There'll be a friend of ours, a Major Leggett."

Oh, so he entertains, does he? Not too mean for that. What's this smell in the room? As though everything had been washed with some antiseptic soap. He took out his pyjamas, a small battered case with razors and brushes. Stephen's eyes never left him.

"I'll be down for supper."

Then Stephen did an odd thing. Michael's broad stout body was bent over the bag. He felt his brother's hand rest on his back; then his fingers touched his neck where the short bristly hairs stood out.

"See you later then," Stephen said softly and went away.

* * *

BOANERGES

When his watch told him that it was half-past seven he went downstairs. In the sitting room he found a man and a girl. The man he disliked instantly. This antipathy, which in the end was to affect a great many others beside themselves, was at once mutual. It was not odd that Leggett should dislike Michael, for it was his lot in life to be like an animal with his back to the wall, frightened and defiant at once, fawning and snarling, driven almost crazy by fear, distrust, malice, consciousness of his own brilliance and the injustices under which he suffered, judging others by himself so that he thought everyone capable of the mean, false, violent actions that belonged to his own character.

Physically he was a short stocky man who looked as though he had to do with horses. He was bald, of an unhealthy complexion, streaky, sometimes grey, sometimes bloody like uncooked beef. His mouth was both hard and conceited, his eyes small and suspicious, but, in spite of these disadvantages, there was something pathetic, alone, driven, about him.

Something spiritual in him warned him of inevitable defeat. He had played, it appeared, many different rôles, had once kept horses, had run a shop in London, had been a journalist, had married a Spanish lady who had died and left him a small fortune which he had soon spent. He was, it was understood, quite hopelessly in the hands of the Jews. He insisted that he should be called Major, although it was one of those ranks that the war had bestowed and that gentlemen had long discarded. He was a lively, bitter, spiteful talker with wide knowledge of men and affairs. He was an enemy of society; there are always one or two of these in every community. They are the jungle animals of social life.

The girl was of course Elizabeth Furze, the daughter of Stephen and Sarah Furze.

Michael's first idea of her was that she was a plain, gaunt woman of no attraction whatever.

She was tall, thin, pale, with large grey eyes, prominent cheekbones, a high pallid forehead. Her clothes were simple, old-fashioned in cut; her dark hair was dragged back from her forehead as though to accentuate her plainness. On this first evening she scarcely spoke. She had the self-eliminating air of a woman who, whether from shyness or a sequence of unhappy experiences, had decided long ago that she would offer fate no chance to hurt or shame her. She busied herself during the meal, handing things, taking plates away, and Michael observed that her movements were exceedingly quiet and even graceful. By the end of the evening he thought that she was not so plain, for her eyes were gentle and she had dignity.

The meal, as he had expected, was very meagre. There was some thin, tasteless soup, a piece of cold beef which Stephen carved, some potatoes in their jackets, a blancmange. It's a good thing, Michael thought, that I shall be taking my meals elsewhere. He himself talked much and loudly. He always did so when the atmosphere around him was silent and still. It was as though he was conscious of a void which he must fill. He boasted a lot of the things that he had done and the places that he had seen. He told many stories, booming away, thinking himself excellent company. When he talked like this something pleasantly simple appeared in his character. He trusted those around him because he was pleased with himself. When he was not attacked he was ready to be kind to everyone. Leggett said very little and, when the meal was ended, departed. A little later Michael went up to his room because there was nothing else to do. He found a fire lighted there and he sat in front of it, smoking his pipe.

He hadn't done so badly, he reflected. He had established himself in the house and so in the town. He had an idea that things would happen to him here. Perhaps he would find a rich wife. He would like to settle down and have a child or two.

There must be money in this house. He would become Stephen's confidant, his partner in his affairs perhaps. He had done the right thing; he had come to the right place. . . .

But in the night he had a dream which, unlike many dreams, he remembered in every detail on awaking. He was standing outside a cathedral: a magnificent façade, with a great rose window, carved stone figures, a glorious pattern of leaves and animals above the vast door. This cathedral stood at one end of a Market-place which was filled with people, talking, buying and selling, all busy and happy. As he watched, thinking how happy they were, the sun disappeared and the air was cold; the hearty chatter died down to a sound like the twitter of birds. Everyone gazed about apprehensively. Then there was a great silence as though a door closed and shut them off from him. He himself felt a trembling expectant fear. Then, as the sky darkened, he looked about him and saw that the market was emptied. The booths were there, the piled fruit, the gaily coloured flowers, clothes hanging, brass pots and pans, china —not a human being anywhere. Absolute silence. Something told him that he ought to run for his life but he could not move.

The leather apron in front of the great door was pushed back and a little procession came out. First two men in black appeared carrying an empty stretcher. They were followed by a small group of persons, also in black and quite silent. Behind these, walking by himself, was a tall figure. Michael saw, with a shudder, that the head of this man was twisted on one side as though his neck were broken. The little procession advanced without a sound and it seemed that the softly shod feet made no contact with the pavement. The air now was bitterly cold and the silence held a kind of crowded emptiness as though, near him, hundreds and hundreds of people were watching and holding their breath.

Michael saw that the procession was making directly for himself, and he knew that if it reached him something appalling would follow. But he could not move. The stretcher, the followers, the man with the twisted neck advanced nearer and nearer. He was in an agony of terror. Then he heard arise on every side of him, like a wind getting up among trees, the whisper: "The Inquisitor! The Inquisitor!"

With a great cry he awoke. He found that his pyjamas were damp with sweat. He lit a candle. There was still a faint colour in the ashen fire. The text looked down on him from the wall. He could hear someone snoring in a distant room.

CHAPTER III

The Marlowes, Although Not At All Rich, Give a Nice Party

IT HAPPENED THAT, on that same evening of Mike Furze's arrival in Polchester, the Marlowes were at home to their friends only a few doors away from Stephen Furze's house.

The Rectory of St. James's was one of those houses squeezed together on the edge of the hill known as the Rock. The house commanded a wonderful view—below, Seatown, the river, the fields, woods and hills beyond it; and from its upper windows the Upper Town and the Cathedral. The Rock itself was full of history: from the river, up the rocky street, across the Market-place, up the hill again, across the flat beyond Arden Gate, into the Cathedral, the enemies of the Black Bishop had fought their way; there is a sharp, jagged piece of rock known as the Tooth, whence, visitors to the town are told, some of the Bishop's enemies were thrown, in full armour, down, many feet, into the Pol.

The Rectory was beaten upon by all the heavenly winds, but it was a strong old house with some dramatic memories. It had had some notable incumbents: Dr. Burroughs who wrote a book once famous, now forgotten, *Happy Polchester Days;* Morris who, in 1897, caused such a scandal by running away with Archdeacon Brandon's wife, and, Marlowe's predecessor, William Rostron, now famous as one of the leaders of the Buchman movement.

36

BOANERGES

Marlowe had been rector for ten years now. The queer thing was that, although he and his family were very good people, they were greatly liked, and almost everyone who was anyone came to their At Home on this evening. People liked old Marlowe—he was between fifty and sixty but looked older because of his white hair and absent-minded untidiness. He was one of those simple-minded saints who are frequent in novels and infrequent in real life.

People in fact were able to patronize the whole family, which was one reason of their popularity. They were not modern at all, and Mrs. Marlowe said the most comic things at times. Also they were very poor, another example of the scandalous way in which our clergy are treated. St. James's Rectory was one of the old, rambling houses, far too big for anyone with small means, and it was well known that Mrs. Marlowe did most of the housework herself. It was said that she did not dare to allow her husband to carry a penny in his pocket because he gave it away instantly to anyone who begged of him. It was said also that she had to supervise his exits and entrances, that it was a wonder that he did not appear naked in the Market-place. This was of course greatly exaggerated, as most things are apt to be in cathedral towns. Mr. Marlowe had a good intelligence, preached an excellent sermon, talked often with much wisdom, but he had a habit of thinking of three things at once, would lose himself, quite like Dominie Sampson, in his quaint and curious reading, and lived, often enough, in a world very far from this one. They had one child, Penelope, known as "Penny," now nearly eighteen years of age and, beyond question, prettier than any other girl in Polchester. Mrs. Marlowe was broad and stout, with soft untidy brown hair, a strong sense of humour and a passion for gaiety, hospitality, any kind of fun. She loved gardening, the "Pictures," dances, picnics, anything that was going. It is obvious that there was nothing unusual, interesting, modern, exciting about the Marlowes.

A famous novelist declared the other day that it is ridiculous in these times to pretend that anyone is good or bad. Human beings are so complicated a mixture of glands, atoms, electrons and the rest that a neutral scientific grey is the only modern colour.

But you could not call Mr. and Mrs. Marlowe grey. No one denied but that they were good people, that is, if generosity, honesty, courage and love of one's fellows combine to make goodness. You could patronize them and pity them and laugh at them but, mysteriously, you could not despise them.

Everyone went to Mrs. Marlowe's parties, although everything was most homely. The cakes were baked in the house, the tea and coffee were not as good as they should be—no one attempted to entertain. Perhaps it was that people felt safe in this house. The Marlowes thought the best of everyone, most foolishly. Mrs. Marlowe enjoyed gossip like any other woman, but she flushed and became embarrassed if you told her a real scandal. And yet she was not a prude. She knew more about life than you might suppose. It was amazing, as Lady Mary Bassett often said, that having such a pure mind she was not more of a bore. But she was not a bore: she was gay, merry, easily pleased and always, so far as one could tell, happy.

It was, in fact, a very happy house.

Peter Gaselee explained all this and a good many more things as well to the Reverend James Bird, the new curate at St. Paul's, Orange Street, and Mr. Bird listened with his mouth open. James Bird had been in Polchester a little over a month and this was his first Polchester party. While dressing for it, in his lodging halfway down Orange Street, he had been so extremely nervous that, had it not been for his fear of his rector, Mr. Porteous, he could not have ventured. But one fear, as he found was so often the case, was greater than the other.

He was a small man with brown eyes and brown hair; he was very timid, often said the wrong thing out of nervousness. He had not as good an opinion of himself as his character demanded.

He was exactly the kind of person whom Gaselee could appreciate and value on an evening like this. His admiration of Gaselee's cleverness was extremely obvious; he looked up to

Gaselee as a wonderful creature, and of course Gaselee liked that.

Gaselee at a party always watched and waited. His plan was to sit in the background until he was sought for. He trusted that his personality would be noticed soon enough. It was much wiser to be sought for than to do the seeking.

So he sat in a corner with little Mr. Bird and told him all about everybody.

"You must be beginning to know people by this time. All the same, I'll give you my idea of one or two of them. You've made up your mind about your commander, Porteous, I expect. Do you play games well?"

"No, I'm afraid I don't," said Mr. Bird.

"Well, that's a pity. To be a friend of Porteous you've *got* to play games. Don't be shocked when I tell you that he has an advantage over the other clergy in Polchester because he was at the same public school as Jesus Christ—a very fine public school, one of the best. He was in the same cricket eleven. You'll have noticed how, in his sermons and elsewhere, cricketing terms are those that serve his purpose best. 'Play the game,' 'Play for your side,' 'Play with a straight bat,' 'It's the team spirit that counts.' Christ to him is a good fellow with whom he has been on intimate terms all his life. That makes him very jolly and happy and sure of himself. 'All that Christ wants,' he says to us, 'is for you fellows to be sportsmen, never forget that Christ is Captain of the team and knows how best to win the match.' What he can't bear is for anyone to be a bad sportsman. Judas was one and there are several in Polchester just now. The Bolsheviks are bad sportsmen, and the Americans just now because they want us to pay the War Debt and all Methodists and Roman Catholics and Scientists and immoral writers and the Bishop of Birmingham. 'Mens sana in corpore sano.' I hope you don't think I'm unfair. He's an excellent fellow, and when he greets a fellow sportsman you can hear him from one end of the town to another. I'm afraid you'll have to learn some game or other—even ping-pong would be better than nothing. . . . Do you see that large lady over there with an auburn

permanent wave and a fine firm bosom? That is Mrs. Carris,
wife of Humphrey Carris, solicitor. The Carrises are very important people here. Mrs. Carris was a Miss Polly Lucas at
St. Earth. Good Glebeshire family. She is very intelligent socially. She knows just who is worthy and who is not. She gives
many parties. She is always giving parties, tennis parties, cocktail parties, dinner parties—not so much because she likes
parties as because she keeps the social register. It is a little
difficult for her in these democratic days, but she manages to
mark the line. Her daughters help her. You are asked first to
luncheon and if you are all right you move on to dinner. There
is a deep and very eloquent rivalry between herself and Mrs.
Braund, the wife of the Archdeacon, who leads the Cathedral
set. They are allies at one time, enemies at another. Mrs. Carris
is an excellent bridge player which gives her an advantage, but
Mrs. Braund is related—rather distantly but still related—to
the Howards. Mrs. Braund speaks sometimes of the Duchess of
Norfolk with considerable familiarity.

"That's Mrs. Braund—but of course you know her—talking
to Lady Mary Bassett. Lady Mary is the intellectual head of
Polchester. She is the daughter of old Lord Pomeroy who was
once the Colonial Secretary. When she was a little girl in London
she was most brilliant. At the age of ten she startled men like
Henry James and Augustine Birrell with her witticisms and
French phrases. She grew even more and more brilliant and
made so many epigrams that people kept notebooks simply to
record them. Then she married a rich young man called Bassett
who had a place near Drymouth. She wrote two novels and
then unfortunately he ran away with an actress and she had to
divorce him. People in London got tired of her because she
talked so much and was always scratching her left ear——"

"Her left ear?" said Mr. Bird bewildered.

"Well, it wasn't always her left ear. She has restless habits.
She came to live just outside Polchester and is a great addition
to our society. She's a little eccentric now, but what can you
expect when you begin to be brilliant so young? Now I'll show
you someone nice for a change. Do you see that tall slim woman

in black? That's Mrs. Hattaway, wife of Hattaway the architect. She's one of the kindest, most natural women in England.
Hattaway is very clever and knows more about the Cathedral
than anyone here. Mrs. Hattaway is good and kind and has a
fine sense of humour. If you're ever in trouble she'll be a good
friend and give you excellent advice.

"Do you see that elderly man with the broad shoulders and
the big head? That's Lampiron, the sculptor. He's one of the
most interesting men here."

"I noticed him at once," said little Bird. "A very remarkable-
looking man."

"Yes, he is, isn't he? If he were a bit taller he'd be very handsome. He lives here because he loves the Cathedral. Up to five
years ago he was quite a good painter—of the old-fashioned
kind, you know. He had pictures in the Academy that you
couldn't tell from coloured photographs. Then quite suddenly
he was converted—like Gauguin."

"I don't know about Gauguin," said Bird.

"Gauguin was a business man who gave up everything and
went to the South Seas to paint. In the same way Lampiron gave up his photographs, which he sold quite well, and
took to sculpting. Everyone here thinks that his sculpting is
awful. Worse than Epstein they say, knowing of course nothing *about* Epstein. Lampiron struggles along and never finishes
anything and never earns a penny. No one knows how he lives,
except that they say he is deeply in debt to an old usurer in the
town called Furze. He is a man of violent temper and has a
most generous nature. He must be nearly seventy, lives alone,
is a fine fellow if a little wild at times. The town likes him, but
looks on him with alarm and wouldn't be surprised at his murdering someone if the fancy took him."

Gaselee looked about him. He had seen that Mrs. Marlowe's
eye was upon him and that his time for instructing Mr. Bird
was nearly over.

"Then there are your fellow clergy. I'll leave you to find out
about them for yourself. But we have almost every variety in
this room at the moment. There are two saints, Marlowe and

old Moffit in the chair there. Moffit is over eighty and walks with God. That the Archdeacon can scarcely be said to do: he thinks too much about ceremonies and ordinances to have time for anything else. Dale there, the tall fellow with the black eyes, will be a saint one day, I shouldn't wonder. He is a modernist and spends his time showing that science has aided and abetted religion rather than hindered it. That fat fellow there, Cronin, on the other hand, won't let a miracle go, and is as nearly Roman as not to matter. Then there is your Porteous, who is a sportsman, and you and myself. The most remarkable of us all is not here yet. He told me that he was coming—Ronder. Have you seen Ronder?"

"I've seen him in the distance," Bird said.

"Yes—well—he's been the dominant church figure here for thirty-five years. He and Wistons divided the place between them until Wistons went. He's old now, and fat and lazy. He thinks of his latter end—but his brain's as sharp as ever."

Gaselee paused. Mrs. Marlowe was talking to a newcomer; he had a few minutes to spare.

"You know, Bird, one thing is very remarkable to me. Here are all these people in this room, representative of the town; you will meet the same types in any cathedral city. We are all talking gaily, easily, lightly. But there is not one here, except little Penny Marlowe perhaps, who has not known all the terrors and distresses of life, physical, spiritual, financial. We are all of us in peril every moment of our lives. We live in a cathedral town—yet nine out of ten of us think of religion scarcely at all. There is a man I mentioned just now who lives only a few doors from here. His name is Furze. He lends money at exorbitant interest; you would be astonished if you knew how many of those here have had some dealings with him. You'd be amazed if you knew the whole truth about Humphrey Carris or Hattaway or Lampiron. Once this was a town where religion mattered. In Brandon's day, for instance. You know about Brandon? No? He was Archdeacon here once—he died in 'ninety-seven—the year Ronder came here. He stood for the old type of churchman, powerful, arrogant, God's vice-gerent. Then he fell. His wife ran away with the rector of this church here, St. James's, and his son married the daughter of a vulgar publican. He died of it and Ronder took his place. From that moment, as I see it, religion has mattered less and less here. I suppose that the years since the war have been the most godless in the world's history. The heathen themselves believed in *something*. In the Dark Ages the Church had tremendous power. Now in every cathedral in England what do you find? A handful of people, empty ceremonies, persons quarrelling about minute dogmas, mocked by the rest of the world. Sometimes, when there's an anniversary or something, the kind of thing we're having here next year, there's a stir because people like pageantry. And of course there are good devout clergy still and emotional movements like the Buchman Groups. But the Cathedral itself is left for dead. All the same it isn't dead." He got up. "There's a life there stronger than any of us. We're a silly, conceited, stupid lot —missing the only thing that is real, the only thing that matters. And one day God will come down from the mountain and strike us with leprosy as he did Miriam, and we shan't have any Moses to plead for us either. . . . How are you, Mrs. Marlowe? What a delightful party. This is Mr. Bird of St. Paul's. He's only been here a month or so and I've been telling him who everybody is."

All who were present in the house that evening afterwards remembered the occasion because of what shortly occurred. But two persons were especially concerned, and they were, in all probability, the two happiest human beings there. Penny Marlowe, who was just beginning life, and old Canon Moffit, who was just leaving it.

Penny Marlowe had, only last month, left the Polchester High School for Girls. Now she was to help her mother at home. Not long ago I saw, in Jamaica, a water colour by Koren. It showed three negroes worshipping a lily, or rather the angel in the lily. In the centre of the drawing the lily rises from its grey roots, snow-white on its green stem. About it, in obeisance, are the ebony faces of the kneeling negroes. Their bodies are clad in their smocks of faint rose and the pale colour of young lilac. It is a drawing of exquisite strength, purity, simplicity, sincerity. Penny Marlowe was like that. She was not very tall, but slim and straight, with the natural suppleness of a young green-stemmed flower. She had dark hair, curly about the nape of the neck, parted like a boy's. Her colour was delicate in shadow of rose and in the strong unmarked whiteness of her high forehead. She had no affectedness anywhere, but was as natural as are all the girls of her generation.

Her skin was not yet spoilt by rouge, and if her nose had shone she would not be in despair. But her nose did not shine. When she was hot and excited, little beads of perspiration gathered on her brow; her legs were slim and strong, her breasts as yet very small and firm. She laughed a great deal, was scornful and impatient and angry and forgiving and intolerant and loving, all very quickly.

She was a representative young girl of her age in that she was sure that she knew everything about life but in reality knew very little. She knew how to drive a motorcar, how to mix a cocktail, how to play contract badly, how to deal with men. About this last she especially prided herself; she thought that she knew everything about sex, because girls talk so much at school, and Helen Marsden had lent her *Married Love* and Katherine Becket possessed a copy of *Lady Chatterley's Lover* and they had read pieces from it together. She had never told anybody that she hated both works and that she never felt the same to either Helen or Katherine again. She was determined to be shocked by nothing, because that was the attitude of all the older girls—and now it was not so much that she was shocked as that something inside herself held itself aloof from this, would not be touched by it.

But of course she allowed neither Helen nor Katherine to perceive this. She was as jolly with them as ever but now gave them no confidences. She felt, however, almost intolerably wise. There was no situation that she would not be able to meet. She could go out into the world at any moment and be a nurse or a secretary or even a Member of Parliament. Only, after the things that she now knew, she wanted to have nothing to do with men. She would go through life a virgin. She would devote herself to the suffering, the unhappy, perhaps lepers or prisoners.

One evening Anthony Carris, at the end of his first year at Oxford, tried to kiss her, and she laughed at him so convincingly that he was greatly surprised. Whatever he might be he was sure that he was not comic. Penny Marlowe was a very pretty girl, but she was a little country schoolgirl and should be flattered that he took notice of her. He resented her behaviour and thought, for a week or two, that he was in love with her. Then he found to his comfort that Helen Marsden took him seriously.

The fact that made Penny different from some of her contemporaries was that she loved her home and her parents. She thought that there was no place in the world so beautiful as Polchester, no home so charming as the old St. James's Rectory, no two people as lovable as her father and mother. She told no one these things, because in her world the one emotion that you must never show was sentiment. However, she did not patronize her parents in public, as many of the girls did. It was true that she found them old-fashioned in their ideas, but she had the wisdom to suspect that her mother knew almost as much about life as she herself did, and it wasn't her mother's fault that she had been brought up in those absurd Victorian days when a girl could go nowhere without a chaperon and did not dare to mention a baby.

She liked to look nice, was excited over a new dress, loved to drive Mabel Carris' car when Mabel allowed her, but she was not vain; to be alive was splendid. She meant to have a magnificent life. . . .

Now she was talking to the two Miss Trenchards, Miss Katey Trenchard and Miss Dora Trenchard. These two ladies were elderly and had lived in Polchester all their lives. Their brother, who had been a canon of the Cathedral, had died some five years ago. They were both tall, wore black and each had a beautiful long necklace of emeralds for her only ornament. Their hair was white, and they were English ladies of the old type, quite unself-conscious with dignity and kindliness, representatives of a caste that is now almost vanished from the world, greatly to the world's loss. They seldom left Polchester, were always together, did not play bridge or drive motorcars or talk scandal, but were not dull to their friends, who were quiet people like themselves—Lady St. Leath, the Marlowes, Mrs. Hattaway, Mrs. Braund. They did not read modern books very much, but felt that they were in touch with the literary world because their cousin Millie Trenchard had married a well-known novelist, Peter Westcott, and Millie's brother Henry was a considerable dramatist. They thought that there was no country like England and no cathedral like Polchester Cathedral. No one knew much about their affairs, and they had lived for so long in the little house just inside Arden Gate that everyone supposed that they were comfortably off. This was not true, for, recently, the investments on which they depended had shrunk in the most alarming manner. Dora, also, had a weak heart, from which she suffered sadly at times, but they would have thought it the worst manners in the world to speak to anyone either of their financial affairs or their bodily complaints.

They stood now beside Penny and thought what a lovely child she was.

"I hope you're enjoying yourself, dear," Dora said, looking mildly at Lady Mary Bassett, who was close at hand, declaring to Canon Cronin that Proust must be taken with caution because intellectual snobbery was bad for the stomach. Canon Cronin, who thought that Proust was some sort of food or medicine, began to explain that a cousin of his had recently become a vegetarian with disastrous results, and Dora, looking at Lady Mary, decided that she was laughing at the poor Canon, felt sorry for him and disliked Lady Mary (whom she and her sister privately thought very common) even more than usual.

Penny said that she was enjoying herself enormously.

"That's right, dear. I'm sure you deserve to. You must come and have dinner with us one day now you're out. But, dear me," she went on, "how easily girls come out these days! Katey and I were quite twenty before we went to our first ball at the

Castle. What a fine one it was! You never see balls like that these days. Do you remember, Katey, how handsome Archdeacon Brandon was and how fast we thought poor Mrs. Combermere because she smoked a cigarette!"

Both ladies laughed and looked at Penny, their eyes beaming love and benediction.

"I've another reason for being excited," Penny went on. "I'm to act in the Pageant. I've just heard——"

"How splendid! What are you going to be?"

"I don't quite know. It is being written by Mr. Withers, the poet. He lives at Boscowell, you know, and he's been over this week and shown the Committee his scheme, and Mr. Carris has just asked me if I'll take a part. He says I may have to ride a horse——"

"Dear me, how exciting it will all be!" said Miss Katey. "I do hope the weather will be fine. Like the 'Ninety-seven Jubilee. You weren't born then, dear, of course, but we had the most *beautiful* weather. . . ."

Mr. Lampiron came up and joined them. Penny knew him only by sight, but now, as she looked at him, she thought that he was very handsome. His great head with its jet-black hair, his face so strong and rugged, his broad shoulders, his air of honesty and not caring what anyone thought, and independence and courage, all greatly impressed her. Besides, he was the only artist she had ever met, and she thought that it must be wonderful to be a sculptor. People said that the things he did were hideous, that he never finished anything and never sold anything, but that only made him the more wonderful in her eyes. So, under the benignant protection of the Misses Trenchard, they met for the first time.

He, on his part, was surprised at her beauty. He was not conscious that he had ever seen her before, and for a moment he was puzzled as to who this lovely child could be. Then he remembered: this must be old Marlowe's little girl who had just left school.

Almost at once, as though they had some message for one another, they drew a little apart from the others.

47

"You are Miss Marlowe, aren't you?" he asked her.

"And you are Mr. Lampiron."

"Yes, I'm old Lampiron—sixty-eight years of age, who tries to carve hideous faces in stone, hasn't a penny, loses his temper and is a scandal to society." He looked at her fiercely under his black jutting eyebrows, but laughing at the same time. "That's the way you've heard me described, isn't it?"

"I don't know. I don't think I've heard you described. You see, I've only just left school." Then she thought that that wasn't quite truthful so she added: "I *have* heard you mentioned, of course." Then she added still further: "I'd love to see your sculpture."

"Why?"

"It must be wonderful to *make* things. To write poetry like Mr. Withers, to build a chapel in the Cathedral like Mr. Hattaway, or to carve as you do."

They were sitting down in a corner behind the piano. He sat forward, his hands pressing on his broad knees.

"The trouble today is that too many people are making things—imitating other people. Too many books, too many pictures. Too much of everything. The best of my work is that nobody likes what I do, nobody wants it."

"Doesn't an artist work for other people?" she asked.

"An artist works for himself," he snapped at her quite angrily. But she wasn't in the least afraid of him.

"Oh, I see. . . . But when hundreds of years ago they made the towers and the pillars and the windows for the Cathedral, that was for other people, wasn't it?"

"They believed in God," he said. "Have you ever seen the Carolus Missal?" he asked her.

"No, I haven't."

"You should. It's in the Cathedral library. It's a small book with twenty pictures on vellum. Every page is illuminated with borders of birds and flowers in gold and crimson and blue. One monk took twenty-five years doing it. He didn't care whether anyone ever saw it or not. He was a happy man."

"Then you should be happy too," she said, smiling at him.

"I am sometimes," he said. "But I was lying to you just now when I said that I don't care whether anyone likes what I do or no. I'd be beyond myself if wise people liked my work and said I was a great sculptor. I've had pictures in the Academy, you know, and ladies said they were sweet."

"Weren't you happy then?"

"I was miserable. The Academy is the abode of the lost, and the ladies were idiots."

"It seems very difficult," she said.

"My dear child, life wasn't meant to be easy. But still there's a limit. . . . Now tell me about yourself. What do you want to get out of life—fun, babies, friends?"

They looked at one another. His heart was greatly touched by her confidence and trust.

"I haven't thought about it yet. I've only just left school and I'm enjoying every minute."

"Yes, that's right. I feel as though I were twenty sometimes and could do *anything*. But I'm not twenty. I'm sixty-eight. I get tired and people bother me for money. I see visions, but the stone won't do what I want it to. And then I lose my temper and say things I don't mean. People are good to me and I want to bite them. People are bad to me and I want to kill them. I trust people and they deceive me. But I don't want you to believe these things. It's all my own fault; everything is always your own fault. Remember that when you get older. Have a grudge against yourself but not against life."

"You don't look as though you had a grudge against anything."

"Don't I? That's very sweet of you." He looked very proud and pleased. "The more you say nice things to me the better it is for me. Flattery never did anyone any harm in spite of what people say. Everyone wants encouragement, and of all the types in the world the worst is the sort that goes about telling you truths for your good. Life will do that without anyone assisting it."

"You don't look," she said, "as though you'd mind in the least what people think."

"Ah, don't I? That's all you know. Everyone minds. We all live in glass houses and we all throw stones. I don't want you to be false to me. If I ask you for an opinion I want you to give it me honestly. But if I don't ask it I want the things you say to me to be *nice* things, so that I may have a little encouragement."

"*I* can't encourage *you*."

"Oh yes, you can. You have already. Very much indeed." He held out his hand. She gave him hers. "Are we friends?"

"Yes—yes," she said eagerly.

"Will you come and see me one day?"

"Of course I will."

"You won't like my sculpture."

"What does it matter what I like? I don't know anything about anything yet."

"Oh, taste begins from the beginning. If you have a little you can educate it. If you have none, you'll never know it."

They seemed like very old friends, and it was a good time for them to shake hands. The party was at its height and everyone was talking, laughing, making that loud and insincere party-noise that can cover so much intense concentration on private affairs. No one saw them. Lady Mary was scratching her ear and wondering, as she often did, how people could be so stupid, why she lived in the provinces, whether a visit to London wasn't due, whether intelligence wasn't rather a curse after all—and all this time explaining to Mrs. Braund that in a letter that she had received last week from our Ambassador in Paris he had said that France would never leave the League of Nations whatever Germany did, and Mrs. Braund said what a good thing while her eyes watched Mrs. Carris, who was surely never at her best in purple, and Mrs. Carris, chaffing Canon Dale in her deep hearty voice, thought out a nice little luncheon party for next Tuesday, a few *real* friends, when they could settle a number of details about next year's pageant to their own private satisfaction.

She had her eye on Mr. Gaselee, surely a coming man— clever, discreet, with an eye for the right people—A kind of

Canon Ronder in the making, she thought. Would she be able
to persuade Humphrey to buy that new Alvis upon which she
had set her heart? And Mrs. Braund giving herself all those
airs just because her great-grandmother's second cousin had
married a Howard. So she smiled on young Canon Dale like a
mother and didn't ask him to luncheon.

She would invite Mr. Gaselee. It was then that Canon Ronder arrived. For thirty-five years his entrances into Polchester
drawing rooms had made ever the same impression. No one
knew how he did it. He was old now and remarkably stout, but
his black silk waistcoat was as creaseless, his collar and shoes
(the last with silver buckles) as shining, his coat as perfectly
cut now as then. Only now he gave the impression of being a
little sleepy. His round gleaming face was a mask on which the
round gleaming spectacles were an added mystery. He seemed
apart now, aloof. Hattaway said the Chinese god had retired
back into his temple. If you wanted an answer from the Oracle,
you must ring the little golden bell, beat on the brazen gong
and, above all, bring offerings, peach blossom, a young kid, a
bowl of jade. By that Hattaway meant that Ronder only went
out now to houses where there was a perfect cook, and appreciated greatly a new addition to his collection of books of the
'nineties—he had an especial interest in the author of *Hadrian
VII*—or his pieces of red amber.

There were certainly no peach blossom, no red amber, no
unpublished writings of Fr. Rolfe at the Marlowes'. Why had
he come, then? He had come partly because he liked the Marlowes and partly because he liked, once and again, to watch,
for a brief moment, the movements of Polchester society. In
spite of his half-closed eyes he was as quick as ever he had been
at seeing what was afoot. His old passion for inserting his fingers
in every pie had not deserted him; only his body sometimes
betrayed him. There was a pain under his heart; there was a
dragging weakness in the left leg. There was never absent from
him the haunting fear of death.

He had also his own unprejudiced unselfish liking for a saint.
Whether he believed in God who could say but God Himself?

He was wise enough to know that men like Wistons, Bishop
Kendon, Moffit, Marlowe, Dale had discovered for themselves
the only secret worth discovering. He admired them, even
envied them—the only men on this earth he envied. And his
cynical spirit expected that at the last they might discover that,
after all, they had been deceived.

He made an odd contrast with Marlowe now—old Marlowe
whose vest was sadly wrinkled, whose white hair needed cutting,
the cuffs of whose shirt were frayed. But he liked the old man
who beamed at him with his bright blue eyes, who chattered
eagerly about his chess, which he was for ever playing, in which
he would never improve. "Dale is pretty good, you know. It
was an excellent game. Another move and my knight and
queen would have done the trick. But that pawn of his—I'd
overlooked it. If I'd moved my bishop my king would have
been all right, but he brought his rook down. . . ."

"I expect Canon Ronder would like something to drink,
dear. There's iced coffee, Canon, and tea and lemonade."

"Where's that pretty girl of yours? She shall give me something——"

"Pretty girl? What pretty girl?"

"Why, your own, you old ass." He put his hand affectionately on Marlowe's shoulder. "Ah, Mrs. Braund. . . . How do
you do, Lady Mary? How about Sainte-Beuve? You remember
I told you to look up that bit about Grimm and Rousseau——"

Lady Mary, giving her high vibrating cackle, said that
Sainte-Beuve was the showman of the mediocre—a Cook's
guide to the writing bureau of Mme de Sévigné, a Napoleon III.
Plutarch. . . .

Ronder said: "You're too clever for me, Lady Mary. My
only author now is Dorothy Sayers——"

He caught sight of little Penny Marlowe and moved towards
her. He moved slowly, pushing his big stomach forward as
though he would deceive the world by his insistence on his
grossness. He had heard of Hattaway's comment. A Chinese
god, squatting, brooding on his navel, death in the shape of a
suspended dull-leaved lotus flower. There was the pain beneath

his heart. He exercised his customary control that he should not place his hand there. . . .

Penny saw him and came forward. Then it happened. No one, for the last quarter of an hour, had noticed old Moffit, who, sitting in a chair, his white beard on his chest, smiling took his last look on the world.

For he half rose. He put out his hand, caught Penny's, fell forward, then crumpled at her feet, his head against her dress.

He looked up. She heard him say, "The Cathedral bell. Time——"

She cried out, knelt down, gathering him in her arms.

Old Moffit's death at the Marlowes' party was always afterwards considered the first of the sequence of events. . . .

CHAPTER IV

Some of the Things that Can Happen between Three and Four on an Autumn Afternoon

WITHIN A FORTNIGHT of his arrival in Polchester Mike Furze had made a friend of almost everyone in the town. Everyone does not, of course, include the Aristocracy, the Cathedral set, the Upper Ten. They were not, as yet, the most of them, aware of his existence. But these were not of the Town. The Town, in fact, resented the airs that the Cathedral assumed. Even Carris and Hattaway, even James Aldridge, the Mayor, who considered themselves part of the Aristocracy, fought the Cathedral whenever there was opportunity of a fight; the lesser men—Bellamy of the stores, young Mr. Bennett the bookseller, Crispangle the W. H. Smith manager, Browning of the St. Leath Hotel, Merton Mellock, pastrycook, Clapton, owner and manager of the Arden and Grand cinemas—these men, their wives, children and dependents, considered the Dean, the Archdeacon and Mrs. Braund, Lady Mary Bassett their secret enemies, although they made money out of them whenever possible and bowed, smiled, conversed in the most friendly fashion on all public occasions.

Below these again were the Outlaws, the dominants of Seatown, the riffraff of the Dog and Pilchard, men and women known well to Leggett, the unemployed, the army of rebels, the descendants of the sea rovers, the smugglers, the pirates, constant to Polchester for the last thousand years.

Lord and Lady St. Leath, simple, unassuming, generous-hearted, were the only two human beings popular throughout all Polchester.

It was to the Town and not to the Cathedral that Mike Furze became very soon familiar. It was Klitch, the curiosity man, who nicknamed him Boanerges, and the word became universal.

Boanerges was a good fellow when people liked him and things went well with him. His large fat body, his smile and laugh, his loud reverberating voice, his friendliness with everyone, man, woman, child and dog, made him welcome, his stories made him popular. And *what* stories!

It seemed that there was no part of the world that he did not know, no adventure that had not been his. He had wrestled with lions, strangled gigantic snakes, taken the lead in revolutions, starved in deserts, been wrecked in mid-ocean, defied witch doctors, been left for dead by savage natives, known Al Capone in Chicago, explored dead cities, navigated unknown rivers.

He was a fearful liar—that was taken for granted. He admitted himself that he had a gift for narrative. But behind the exaggerations there must be truth. To intimates he bared himself and showed the marks of the tiger on his thigh, the tattoo round his middle with which a priest of a Chinese temple had decorated him, the scar on his right leg where a lion had clawed him. All this with the greatest good-nature. You could not call him a conceited man, although he was certainly a boastful. He called himself a failure in life. To Crispangle's young boy, sixteen years of age, a day boy at Polchester School, he remarked very gravely: "Take me as a warning, my lad. I've seen the world, but what have I got from it all? A rolling stone gathers no moss. Stick to your job, Ronald, and make your father proud." But young Ronald thought that moss was a dull uninteresting vegetable and that to be clawed by a lion was worth all the settled jobs in the world.

In spirit Polchester has not changed very greatly since the days of Harmer John. In spite of the motor coaches that come every day up and down from London, in spite of the garages and the radio and the cinema it is as provincial today as it was in 1897.

Bellamy went often to London; Aldridge and Crispangle and Browning had their motorcars. Their children learnt, twice a week at the Arden, all there was to learn about the splendours of Hollywood, the vice and wickedness of New York and Chicago, the absent-minded melancholy of Garbo, the lovely body of Dietrich, the rough humours of Laurel and Hardy. All these boys could not change the essential *separateness* of the town, it was a world apart from other worlds, even as it had been when the Black Bishop thundered from the Cathedral altar, Colonel Digby defended its walls against the Round-heads, and the young men and maidens gallantly marched out Somerset-wards to be massacred at Sedgemoor.

Therefore Boanerges was an event even as Harmer John had once been. But he did not preach at them as Harmer John had once tried to do and been murdered for his pains. No indeed. Very much the opposite. He had no gospel of Beauty unless you can call jollity and careless adventure, and a drink with the man nearest you a gospel of Beauty. Boanerges was no saint, no hot-gospeller, no preacher of virtue. A liar, a braggart, come from God-knows-where, but good company, a teller of excellent stories (especially when the women were not present), a man who knew the world.

There was, moreover, one element in his situation that was most especially intriguing—that he should be the brother of that miserly, slave-driving old skin-flint, Stephen Furze.

Everyone in the town knew the truth about Furze, that he had half Polchester in debt to him, that he drove the wickedest bargains, that he was relentless, that, in his own home, he was so miserly that he was said to live on potato parings and bread crusts and force his wife and daughter to do the same.

What a situation, then, that a man like Stephen should have a man like Michael for a brother—the two of them under the same roof!

Further than this, Boanerges himself was a man of an in-

genious and diverting curiosity. In his hearty blustering way
he asked questions of all his friends and, strangely enough,
remembered the answers. There is nothing that man (and
woman too) enjoys more thoroughly than a listening friend to
whom no small detail is wearisome.

How unique is our history, how apart from all other experience! How fearful was that gastric ulcer, how obstinate our
daughter's passion for the worthless young motor expert, how
inexplicable the vagaries of one's wife! The tragedy is that we
have, all of us, these unique experiences, and listeners are rare.
We are all eager to tell, so few of us ready to listen! But Boanerges *was* ready to listen. He had, as all the town knew, his own
wonderful stories and he could talk, without drawing rein,
for hours at a time. But also he was ready to sit, his hands on his
knees, his pipe in his mouth, his long nose eager and expectant,
his stomach comfortably protruding, eager to insert the proper
note of surprise, the ingenious question, the grunt of sympathy.

In this way he discovered very quickly a world of private
affairs. Bellamy, a little shrewd man of business, declared himself. He was doing all right, very well indeed, but the shop in
the High Street was cramped. There was land behind it that
would do the trick, but in these depressed times it wasn't wise
to venture too far. Mrs. Bellamy wished it, but Mrs. Bellamy
was ambitious—socially ambitious. Mrs. Carris made her
restless. She was every bit as good as Mrs. Carris. Who, after
all, *was* Mrs. Carris, even though she did give parties every
minute of the day and night? He, Bellamy, thought this social
business bloody rot—that's what Bellamy thought it. But these
women—well, you know what women are. Never satisfied. He
gave Mrs. Bellamy everything in reason, but there it was, night
after night. . . . She never left him alone. If they'd had a child
things might be different. Mrs. Bellamy hadn't occupation
enough. . . .

With Crispangle it was another path. He was a large, red-
faced fellow, with his secret anxieties. His heart was centred
round his boy Ronald—no anxiety there, for the boy was as
jolly and healthy a lad as you could find. No, *his* trouble was

Mrs. Crispangle, a pretty little blonde with innocent bright-blue eyes. Mrs. Crispangle, as the whole town knew, liked men. She *adored* men. Whether there was really anything wrong no one exactly knew. Crispangle himself didn't know. He gave her her liberty. What was a man to do? She would take it just the same whether he gave it her or no, but she liked such *worthless* rotters! That scoundrel Leggett, Mellock's young waster of a son (she was old enough to be his mother), commercial travellers staying at the Bull. The trouble was that Crispangle loved her, loved her and despised himself for loving her, than which there is no more miserable state. And what an example for his boy! Well, there it was; there was danger hovering over the Crispangle roof, and Crispangle himself, arranging the latest novels in the centre of his shop, decorating his windows with the latest Priestleys and Galsworthys (his eye on the classical decoration of Bennett's bookshop opposite), would wish sometimes that he had the courage to put his head in a gas oven, that he did not love Mrs. Crispangle any more, that he might escape with his boy to the South Sea Islands and drink his fill to the tinkle of the ukulele.

Yes, Boanerges learnt many things—of the excellent energy but unhappy sensitiveness of the Dean, of how sadly henpecked the Archdeacon was, of the greed and wisdom of Ronder, of the goodness and decency of Canon Dale, of the penniless condition of the Marlowes, the airs and affectation of Browning of the St. Leath Hotel, the brilliance and haughtiness of Hattaway, the hideous sculpture of Lampiron, the learning and wisdom of Bishop Kendon at Carpledon.

He learnt these things and many more. But especially he learnt the surprising power of his brother Stephen in the town. Rumour, as usual, exaggerated, no doubt, but in the fifteen years of his residence here Stephen Furze had become money-lender-in-chief in Polchester. His clients ranged, it appeared, from poor old dreamers like Marlowe and gentlemen like Lampiron to any wastrel at the bottom of the town. He did not care where he fixed his talons, but once he had his grip he did not let go. Boanerges was surprised at the hatred with which his brother was regarded. He was almost a legendary figure; it was said that he had been seen in two different places at the same time. His manner of walking, quickly, silently, his long nose pointing the way, his soft and gentle politeness (he was not obsequious), the stories of his wealth (he was made into the exaggerated villain of the miser legend, boxes of gold pieces under his bed, stockings of specie up the chimney, and the rest), the tales of his relentless iron-gloved firmness—all this Boanerges learnt and wondered at.

For he was compelled to confess that his first fortnight under his brother's roof had revealed him as anything but a figure of melodrama. It is true that the food was sparse, the house bare and cold, the atmosphere far from gay, but Stephen himself was quiet, decorous and, in his own fashion, friendly. The truth is that Boanerges at first saw but little of him. After his breakfast he took his walk; he had his midday meal at the Bull; in the afternoon he often attended Evensong, looked in for a chat with his friend Mr. Klitch, watched a game of football; he supped at the Bull, played a game of billiards, talked with his friends. He knew that it would not always be thus; his fifty pounds could not last forever.

He was determined, however, to remain in Polchester. No place had ever suited him so exactly; he had friends here and the Cathedral; something in the character of the little place appealed to the childish simplicity of his character. He would, perhaps, have children, settle down. He might one day be Town Councillor or even Mayor. Who could tell?

Then he discovered a queer thing. Something drew him back to the house. He found that he would return to it, during the daytime, for no reason at all. He would be talking to some friends in the Bull, happy, contented, telling the tale or listening to some pleasant little urban scandal, and suddenly he would laugh, nod, say "Cheerio" and turn homewards. He would let himself in, stand in the hall and wonder why he had come. He would listen, sniff the dry antiseptic air. The house would be as still as the grave. It might be that everyone was out, and then he would walk stealthily, almost on tiptoe, from empty room to empty room. There was nothing to see, nothing to find. His brother's room was orderly—a roll-top desk, a green-and-white safe, a table with some neglected books, a large fern in a blue pot in the window, some chairs. The roll-top desk was locked. The room was dusty because no one was permitted to touch anything there. A big cabinet with drawers was also locked. And yet the room was not dead. Some life haunted it, and Mike felt that he was watched. One window looked over the Rock down to Seatown, the other to a confusion of climbing roofs and the Cathedral. Heavy curtains of a faded brown hung on either side of the windows, and it was a trick of Michael's, when he had made sure that his brother was not there, to look behind these curtains. He did not know why he did so. Sometimes Stephen *was* there. Mike would knock and enter. His brother would look up from his desk and smile.

"Yes—what is it?" he would ask gently.

Mike would apologize and withdraw. It was a fact that this room drew him with increased fascination. It must be here that Stephen kept all his secrets—in the safe, in the roll-top desk, the locked drawers. He did all the work himself. He possessed no secretary or clerk. "Perhaps, in a little while," Mike thought, "I can persuade him to let me help him. He must need someone. He can pay me a small wage." And at that thought he would smile angrily to himself, for he realized that Stephen would never pay anyone anything. Mike was beginning to understand what this lust might be. He was even himself sharing in it. No one could live in that house and *not* share in it. Mike began, out of sheer devilment, to play a game. When he was sitting talking with his brother he would, as though absent-mindedly, first jingle the loose coin in his pocket, then he would take a penny, a sixpence, a two-shilling piece in his hand, shake them together, look at them, lay them on the table in front of him. While he did this he would laugh cheerily but look, out of the corner of his eye, at his brother. He saw the long thin body stiffen. Stephen had a prominent Adam's-apple, and this now seemed to swell like a live captured thing in his throat. It was as though it would burst the dry skin in its efforts to escape.

The eyes would brighten, the long nose deaden at the tip. Then the hands would come out, would move forward, the fingers spreading, each long bony finger with a life of its own. The hands would rise, would catch the lapels of his coat, or descend slowly to the table, or close with spasmodic twitching. Then the whole body would bend forward and the sharp eyes fasten on the coin. All this would be subconscious, the inner self rising and dominating the external self which still smiled and spoke like an automaton.

Mike knew well how men will, without realizing it, watch a woman pass in the street, will continue their conversation, go about their business—but their real self is completely driven and dominated by the desire for this woman's form. The woman vanishes; with a sigh of frustration the real self sinks, as an animal cheated of its desire, subsides again into the muddy depths of the stream. That was a lust that Mike knew and recognized. This was kindred with it as all lusts are kindred. He would pick up the coins and replace them in his pocket.

But, in playing this game, he himself began to be caught. Sometimes, when he was alone, he would take coins from his pocket and examine them, turn them over, study their dates. He parted from them reluctantly. Some of them were of recent date, fresh and shining and the image of the King sharp and brilliant. At night, when undressing, he would pile the coins in a little heap on the table and gaze at them.

What a fortune Stephen must possess! Mike began to share the general superstition and to fancy that there must somewhere be boxes packed with bright and shining coin. His curiosity began to stir also around Stephen's clients. How did he deal with them? How did he behave when they asked for time or some remission of sentence? How were that smile and that gentle voice?

On one smoky autumn afternoon he had a brief interesting contact with one of Stephen's visitors. The Cathedral had struck three. He was standing in the hall when in great haste Lampiron the sculptor came down the stairs.

What had occurred?

About two-thirty on that afternoon Lampiron had rung the bell and Sarah Furze had admitted him.

"Is Mr. Furze at home?" he had asked.

"I will find out."

The blind woman, as always, touched him deeply. He was touched, as he knew, too easily by pitiful things, doing often enough nothing about them, for what *can* an artist do?—and then doing, suddenly, too much, foolish, extravagant things beyond his means. He followed her into the house, standing four-square there on his stout legs, his head back, as though already on his guard against his enemy—for Furze *was* his enemy as he well knew.

She moved in darkness but with certainty, and he thought— how awful to be blind, to see beautiful things no more, the moon rising in a clear sky, the clean, smooth petal of a flower, the white resilience of a stone waiting to be carved. She was imprisoned in this horrible house as in a grave. He never entered it but he wanted instantly to leave it again, and his impatience which, old as he was, he had not yet learnt to command, drove him even now although he knew that he must not leave this place until he had got what he wanted. The thought of how serious things were made his heart hammer under his double-breasted blue jacket. No one would know how nervous he was; he looked like a sea captain standing, his legs spread, his hands behind his back, as though in command of his ship and telling anyone to go to hell; but that was not at all how he felt. He took out a large silk handkerchief and wiped his forehead. His hat dropped to the floor and he bent to pick it up. How he hated to feel this fear, but there was something about this man of which he was deeply afraid. The man had no bowels. He was a devil, and it would be kindness to everyone to knock him on the head and bury him.

Sarah Furze returned. She came down the stairs with her hand against the faded yellow wall-paper. At the bottom of the stairs she stopped and said: "Please come up, Mr. Lampiron."

When he was in the room he stared defiantly from under his thick black eyebrows at the man at his desk. He knew that defiance was the last thing that he should show. He had come to placate the man, to ask a great favour, to beg him to be merciful. But he could not beg of any man nor pretend to be what he was not.

Stephen Furze was most agreeable. He asked Lampiron to sit down near to him. He looked at him most friendlily—for why should he not? This broad, strong, thickset man with the fine black head of hair, the strong shoulders, the grand body for a man of his age could crush him, Stephen Furze, with one hand—and yet it was Stephen Furze, who had no bodily strength at all, would do the crushing!

"I'm glad to see you, Mr. Lampiron. What can I do for you?"

Lampiron plunged at once into the matter. He would waste no time but would get away from this beastly house as soon as might be. He was never very good at explaining things: he had not at all an orderly mind. However, what he wanted to say was clear enough. He pulled a rather shabby little notebook from his deep pocket, found a piece of paper on which he had made calculations. On January 3, 1928, Furze had lent him, on certain terms, one hundred pounds. On June 5, 1930, Furze had lent him two hundred pounds. Three hundred pounds in all. At various dates he, Lampiron, had paid Furze certain sums. In all he had paid Furze three hundred and twenty pounds. Nevertheless, as he understood it, he still owed Furze one hundred and thirty-five pounds, part of which must be paid at the very latest three weeks from that present date. He was afraid that, owing to unforeseen circumstances, he would be unable to pay anything on that date. He wished to point out that he had already paid Furze more than his original debt. He wondered—and here, in spite of himself, he stammered a little—whether Furze might not see his way to excuse him the rest of this debt or, at any rate, to postpone the payment until times would be better with him. Times, as Furze undoubtedly knew, had not, during the last few years, been good for artists. He was finishing a piece of sculpture which he had every hope of selling in London.

If in three weeks' time Furze insisted on payment he would be forced into bankruptcy, which would seem to him an intolerable disgrace. He would have to leave the town, and at his age that would be for him a great tragedy. Indeed, he did not think that he could easily begin life again anywhere else. He hoped that Furze, in consideration of all the circumstances . . .

It had been terrible for him to have to say all this—as though he had been forced to strip himself naked—but, as he spoke, although he knew the nature of his opponent, he could not help but put himself in the other man's place. If someone had come to him thus how gladly he would have said: "Why, of course, old chap, wait until times are better for you. . . ." He could hear his own voice uttering these words, and as he ended he looked up with a broad smile and felt as though his cause were won.

Stephen smiled too and very genially said: "Wait one moment, Mr. Lampiron. I'll see how we stand."

And Lampiron said: "Yes, that's right. I think you'll find the figures correct, though."

Furze opened a drawer of his roll-top desk and produced therefrom neat bundles of papers tied with pink tape. He also found a big black-covered ledger. He turned his back to Lampiron, bending over his desk and considering the papers.

Lampiron looked at that back and considered how, were clothes absent, he would be staring now at a long knotted spine bone, very prominent as a cord holding together that thin grey-white body. That spine bone would be curved and the curve would suggest that, with strong fingers, it might be snapped. And Lampiron saw Furze, bending forward as though he were bare to the waist. The grey-white spine bone, knobbled and bent, offered itself to his strong hands. . . . He choked; he coughed; he put his hands to his throat. He reflected that he had recently read somewhere that there was such a thing as reality and that it was the writer's business to deal only with that. As soon as his critical readers beheld the writer abandoning reality they sighed for him and were ashamed. They would be ashamed now, thought Lampiron. This is not real. And yet

64

this *is* real—this dusty room and Furze's spine bone, grey in colour, knobbled and bent, that I wish to snap with my hands. ... I do wish it. I should like to see him fall to the floor, broken, lifeless, nothing. ...

"You see, Mr. Lampiron," Furze having swung round in his chair towards him was saying, "business is business. I know well how you feel about it. We all know that artists are not the best business men. No one sympathizes with them in that more than I do. But looking at my papers I find that everything is perfectly in order. You wrote your signature to these arrangements realizing fully what they involved. ..."

Lampiron stared at Furze as though by so staring he would turn him into thin grey paper which he then could tear at will. But what he was really thinking was: How have I got myself into this mess? How is it that I have any relations with that swine? I was a decent fellow once and safe and no one could have any power over me.

And he thought of a studio that he had had on the river—Putney—the water flowing swiftly with little friendly encouraging slaps against his garden wall, and the smell of mown hay from some neighbouring field, the omnibuses going over the bridge, and an old aunt, alive then, having tea in his studio, saying, "I never *can* resist gingerbread." It had been all right then. It was all wrong now.

He heard Furze say:

"I'm afraid these things are not altogether in my own hands, Mr. Lampiron. And on the whole I think you will agree that I have always tried to meet you. In difficult times like these it is not easy to find someone as accommodating as I have been——"

Anger was rising in Lampiron's breast and he knew that it must not. But the same exhalation rising from it dried his throat, and his voice was hoarse when he said:

"I've paid you my debt and more."

"Yes, that is perfectly true. But it is I that have been forced to take the risks. I lent you the money on no security whatever."

"You had security. You knew that I was here, that I would not run away——"

"Well—no. Everyone in the town knows that you are a man of honour, Mr. Lampiron. And that is why—if you will allow me to be perfectly frank—I am a little surprised that you should be unable to meet the obligation in three weeks' time. It is a matter of—let me see—" he consulted his papers—"forty-three pounds, seven and sixpence—and then, after that, only two more payments."

Lampiron could beg of no man, but, that he might silence the restive growling monster—so familiar to him, so dangerous, the creature that, chain it as he might, seemed, when it wished, to break any chain—he began to attempt conciliation:

"You see, Mr. Furze," he said, "I'm not young any more. It would be quite different if I were. Rightly or wrongly I've dropped popular art and am trying to make something that I can believe in. Sculpture takes time and is expensive. You have to get the material long before you see any financial return. I don't want much. I live very simply, I assure you. Give me some time. I can't work properly if I'm harassed by money worries. Let me work and I'll pay off the whole debt—by God, I will— and I'll take care not to get into the hands of a miserly swine ——" He stopped short. The words had come of themselves. It was not he that had said them. Again his cursed lack of control! He rose to his feet, his hands trembling, dismay in his heart, for he knew now that he had ruined everything.

Furze looked at him.

"Well, Mr. Lampiron," he said. "After that——"

And that look from those half-lidded eyes ended the matter.

Lampiron moved forward. His hand shot out and caught Furze's shoulder. "And that's what you are. Doesn't the whole town know it? Someone will be ridding the place of you one day, and a fine thing too. . . ." He turned. He was choking with his cursed temper that was always ruining his chances. . . . He saw that that beef-faced little stable-jockey, Leggett, was standing just inside the doorway.

He stormed at both of them: "Have me up for assault and

battery, the pair of you, and go to hell where you both belong.
. . ." He banged the door behind him, tumbled down the stairs
almost into Michael Furze's arms—and so out of the house.

When the hall door was closed silence settled on the house
again. Mike Furze thought—Fancy that now! Lampiron was
in a fine temper about something! My dear brother has been
tiresome. Or perhaps it was that Leggett, who only five minutes
ago had gone upstairs as though he had known that he would
be wanted. There was a mutual dislike between Mike and
Leggett. Leggett behaved as though Mike did not exist, barely
spoke to him. He regarded Mike, naturally enough, as an inter-
loper. Mike could understand that. But what did he need to be
so superior for? He was nothing to look at with his bald head
and unhealthy red-and-white complexion and thin mouth. He
looked as though he should be standing, sucking a straw, outside
a stable. But he talked as though he were the best-educated
man in the world, quoting French books and claiming to be an
authority on everything. . . . No morals either—no woman safe
from him.

Mike, looking up the stairs, wondered what those two would
be discussing now. Planning some devilry, no doubt. He'd find
out some of their secrets. He'd have Mr. Leggett at his feet
before he was done. Now that he was in the house they'd find it
no easy matter to get him out of it again! He might make a
friend of Lampiron, discover what his trouble was. There were a
thousand things he could do!

Then he heard steps and he saw coming down the stairs his
niece Elizabeth, dressed for going out. He did not understand
that girl. He had, as yet, achieved no relationship with her at
all. She was reserved, that was what she was. Did not seem to
want to have anything to do with anybody. And yet he could
not say that he disliked her. She was plain but she had dignity.
It occurred to him suddenly that she must know about many
things. It was certain that she shared some of her father's
secrets and he thought that he would make friends with her. He
liked her; he admired her. She had a dull time of it, poor girl.

"Going out, Elizabeth?" he asked.

"Yes," she said.

Her clothes were shabby but neat. He thought that she mightn't look so bad if she were well dressed—a little colour to her cheeks. She had a fine figure, good eyes. She carried herself well. Her voice was soft in tone.

"May I come with you a little way? I'm going up into the town myself. . . . I'll get my hat and coat."

So they went out together into a town veiled in smoky haze. The sky above their heads had an undertone of red fire, felt rather than seen. The Market-place and the High Street were full of life, cars coming and going, people shopping, dogs barking, and there was a pleasant frosty nip in the air, a scent of the sea; the Cathedral bells had been ringing for Evensong. Now they had ceased, but the echo of their tune seemed to linger in the air. Mike talked, making himself agreeable.

"You know, Elizabeth, I'm a little afraid of you. I fancy you find me an encumbrance. I'm sorry for that because I would like us to be friends."

She looked straight in front of her.

"You mustn't think that," she said. "I don't make friends easily."

"I've noticed that and I think it's a pity. You seem to have an awfully dull time. You stay in the house too much. Why not come out with me once and again? I'm not such a bad old stick once you know me."

"There's a lot to do at home. Mother can't do very much. We can't afford a servant. Only Mrs. Wilson coming in twice a week."

"But that's absurd," he said eagerly. "Your father's one of the richest men in the town."

"We like it better—not to have a stranger in the house living with us."

"But now that I'm staying with you it means extra work." She turned towards him and smiled.

"You don't give us much extra work, Uncle Michael."

"Well, I'm glad you think so. All the same——"

They were walking up the High Street now and Michael found friends all the way. He called out to one, waved his hand to another. Mrs. Braund, in her car, passed slowly up the hill.

"Let's go into the Cathedral for a moment," he said.

"Service will be going on."

"We can sit in the back of the Nave for a little while."

She did not dissent and they passed under Arden Gate into the Precincts.

As he pushed the heavy door with his hand and stepped in he felt his expected thrill; it did not lessen with custom but rather increased. It was a thrill both of excited expectation and of some sort of gratified vanity. He *must* be an unusual fellow to feel thus about a cathedral. Bellamy and Aldridge and Crispangle never bothered their heads about the Cathedral save on state occasions. He had spoken to Crispangle about the way he felt, and Crispangle had said that he didn't look like a chap who would go batty, but you never could tell. There'd been a painter chap once—Davray was his name—before the war, and that Swede, Harmer John, and there was old Mr. Mordaunt now who was always drawing. You could see him sitting in the Precincts in every kind of weather. What was there in the Cathedral after all? Of course it didn't serve *him* too badly. Books about the Cathedral were the soundest stock he had. They sold *all* the year round. And of course the Cathedral *did* bring tourists to the town, but for his part all it did for the people who lived in the place was to start a lot of snobs turning up their noses at the *real* people who made the town what it was. What purpose did the Cathedral serve any more? Nobody went to the services unless perhaps young Canon Dale was preaching—but the place was dead, anyone could see how dead it was!

But it wasn't dead for Michael Furze! Now, as he sat down quietly with Elizabeth on a little chair at the end of the Nave, it seemed to him tingling with life. The Nave itself was lit with electric light. The Choir, hidden now from their view, threw up the misted light of its candles. Dimly the service came through to them. Someone was reading a lesson. The vast Nave was deserted save for two isolated figures, seated at the very front under the round carved pulpit to the right. Mike knew by this time much of the Cathedral's history and, leaning forward, his elbows planted on his knees, it seemed to him that figures were still, after these many hundred years, busied about their daily work. The monks were singing: "Under the shadow of Thy wings, O Lord, protect us," the seventh service of the day, Vespers followed by Compline. There were the Pilgrimages. The pilgrims were crowding there listening to the last service. Many of them had walked all the way from London, taking weeks on their journey. They still showed you at the Bull one of the walls that had belonged to a great Pilgrim Dormitory containing one hundred and fifty beds. Now they would be looking about them, the painted glass of the windows glowing in the faint candlelight. They had visited all the Cathedral sights, but especially the Black Bishop's Tomb. They had waited. Then the silver bells sounded and the canopy was raised and the Shrine with the Black Bishop's relics revealed. . . .

He wondered what the girl beside him was thinking. She too was leaning forward, her long legs drawn up, her head cupped in her hands. He stole furtive glances at her; he felt kindly, protective. The Cathedral made him a little mad, heady and irresponsible. Other things in other places had excited him thus, and when such a mood was on him he wanted to shout, to throw his body about, to make love, to force a fight on someone, to make a disturbance—children, when they are excited, feel like this and their elders rebuke them. When the elders themselves yield to such a temptation it leads often enough to the lock-up. Boanerges had been locked up, and more often than once. When he was excited he could be either murderous or generous. Now he felt generous, with the pillars rising into darkness like trees in a forest. The Choir was singing the anthem, and the organ beat into the stones, transmuting them, and the beat changed to a liquid rhythm as though fire ran on the wall and tongues of flame licked the pillars. The anthem died away. A voice recited prayers. Then the organ began again, but very slowly like a wind that blows petals from the orchard trees, the curtains were drawn back, and before a shimmering dance of candlelight the Choir moved down the steps and away into the darkness.

Then he was surprised: he looked at his niece and saw that she was crying. . . .

He had always prided himself on his wonderful social tact, and especially with women. He was in fact not subtle enough to be tactful, nor had he that natural instinct towards good manners that makes up for subtlety. His theory about himself was that he knew in every situation exactly how to behave with women. He believed further that when he wished to be socially attractive no woman could resist him. When women did resist him, as was quite often the case, he persuaded himself that it was because he had not been really interested. Now he felt most kindly towards Elizabeth, so he thought that he would leave her alone for a little. He whispered: "I won't be five minutes. Just going to look at something." The Nave had sprung to life. Some visitors who had attended Evensong were moving about. Several had seated themselves to listen to the last notes of the organ.

Broad, the verger, came majestically down the centre of the Nave. Broad was one of the many friends that Mike Furze had made in Polchester. White-haired, stout and most majestical, he had been verger here only ten years, successor to young Lawrence, old Lawrence's son, but you would suppose that the Cathedral owed its very existence to him. He was a man whose majesty was only equalled by his self-confidence, his nice sense of social distinctions, his tyranny towards obsequious persons, and his real passion for forms and ceremonies.

He was a good man and kind to his small round wife, his girl and his boy when he had time to attend to them. But the Cathedral was his life; he existed in only a faint half-hearted way when absent from it.

"Would you let me up into King Harry for a moment, Broad?" Mike asked him.

"It's after hours, you know, Mr. Furze."

"I know, but I won't be five minutes."

"Here's the key, sir. I'll be waiting for you."

Mike took the key, crossed the Nave, passed up a side aisle until he reached King Henry's Chapel. This was on the right of the Choir, and on the delicate screen that defended its privacy there hung a notice saying that this chapel was dedicated to private worship and meditation. It was hoped that no one would disturb any private worshipper. Mike reverently crossed the flagged floor; he felt the quiet of the little place, the intimacy of the group of chairs, the dark purple and gold of the altar cloth, the two silver vases containing bronze chrysanthemums, and above the Altar the sixteenth-century painting in dark red and green of the martyrdom of St. Sebastian. All the colours here were faint in the dusky twilight of the great church.

At the corner of the chapel Mike found a little wooden door. He started up through black darkness, his fat body having bare room between the thick stone walls. Halfway up he stopped and listened. He was now in utter darkness; the silence was part of the darkness. He wondered what sudden impulse it was that had made him come. When he had seen Elizabeth's tears he had said to himself: "I must get away. I'll go up King Harry." But why? Now, pausing in that chill and dumb blackness, some sort of foreboding seized him. That was not unusual. He was full of forebodings, the child of superstition. He would not walk under ladders, nor look at the moon through glass, nor sit down thirteen at table. He counted blocks of pavement as he walked, and lamp-posts and the numbers of houses. A fortune teller in Mexico had warned him that the seventh, the fifteenth, the twenty-ninth and the forty-seventh years of his life would be his dangerous years.

It was true that he had had scarlet fever when he was seven, been bitten by a dog when he was fifteen, abominably treated by a Spanish lady when he was twenty-nine. He would be forty-seven next year. And now he wanted to go back. He was afraid of something, the dark perhaps. A whisper, as though from the stone walls, seemed to tell him that this was a bad place for him. He was so superstitious that he was capable of imagining that it was the Cathedral itself that was warning him.

However, he went on. There was a glimmer, then a grey shining of light, then, with relief, he stepped up onto what was known as the Whispering Gallery.

This was a railed platform that ran above the King Henry Chapel and then on, above the Nave, to the opposite tower. Mike went on and up, knocking his knees against the little winding stone stair, sometimes in darkness, then benefited by the dim light of a narrow window, then in darkness again. At last he came to a square, empty little room with a wooden floor. One side of this room had no wall but was open and strongly railed in. Here visitors, having paid their shilling, paused on their long journey to the top of the Tower, leaned on the rail and looked over—a dizzy sight, down, down, into a great depth that shone mistily, that was the Nave. Out of the Nave, up into heaven, soared the buttresses and pillars. Here you could realize the proud and contemptuous life of the Cathedral; at such a height man was nought, and the life of the great building, stirring, never still, was the true life of undying beauty. The lines and curves, so strong and yet so delicate, formed a beauty that man could not destroy, for he might pull down stone upon stone, scatter the fabric into space, and *yet* the building would be there, immutable, indestructible, stronger than material man, having kinship only with the spirit.

Looking down, Mike could see points of light, specks of gold on St. Margaret's screen, the brass of the Black Bishop's Tomb, the gold of the figures on the great white reredos.

He turned and walked across to the thin slit of a deeply bedded window in the further wall. Through this the cold evening air beat upon his face. He was now a great height up and, were it full daylight, he would be able to see Polchester stretched like a pattern in a rug below him, on all sides of it the chequered shape of fields and, on a clear day, the sparkling band of sea.

The little room itself was very dark, and he must be careful to avoid the space where the wooden flooring failed to cover a big drop against the wall. In the daytime he had noticed this and wondered why no one had extended the wooden flooring.

The drop must be some twelve feet at least, and, peering over, looking down into dust and fragments of paper, he had thought that here would be a good place for someone to be hid or to conceal a treasure. For, even on the brightest day, this corner under the wall was obscure and you could not see what lay there. The hollow must be part of the stone pillar that had, for some purpose, once been cut away.

So now very carefully he avoided the place where he knew it to be, found the stair and cautiously climbed down. Why had he come? But why did he do so many things without reason? Perhaps there was a reason after all. He was not, he complacently reminded himself, like other men.

Elizabeth Furze, meanwhile, knew why he had gone. He had seen that she was crying. She was ashamed and wiped her eyes with her thin glove. It was not often that she cried, but today her loneliness, her ignominy, her isolation had swept upon her, carried with the music, the majesty of the dimly lit building, and the attempts at some sort of clumsy kindness on the part of her uncle. She was not a weak or a sentimental woman. She had long ago faced her destiny, which was to be the plain unwanted daughter of a man detested by all mankind. Had it not been for her mother she would long ago have left the town where she was so hatefully conspicuous—but, as she could not leave it, she had set her countenance, with cold hostile resolution, to show them all that she too was proud and would surrender her will to no one.

She refused all offers of friendship because she was sure that these must be prompted by pity. Only sometimes in her lonely walks she would talk to a child, give it some pennies or ask it questions about its life, its home, its pleasures. This was one of her two sources of happiness—she discovered that children were not frightened of her but liked to be with her. The other was her love of this place, the town, the Cathedral, the country round it. Especially the country, and when she was standing on the high ground above the Pol, saw the wind bowing the corn, or the rich colour of the newly turned earth upon whose surface, maybe, the sea gulls had gathered—then she would draw a deep breath and smell the soil and the sea, rain in the air, sun scents in leaves, and forget, for a time, the imprisoning shame of the house where she lived.

She had become, in these years, almost fantastically self-conscious. She imagined that with every step that she took people watched her and whispered about her father. She could have forgiven him, however, this and other worse things. One thing she would never forgive him. Because of his miserliness her mother was blind. An operation would have saved her, and her father had refused the cost of it. Her mother said nothing. She did not complain. She showed no emotion of any kind. Whether she cared for her daughter at all Elizabeth did not know, but, on her side, Elizabeth loved her passionately, perhaps because she had no one else to love.

But, above all, the centre of her character was stern. Not only circumstances had made her so. The tears that she had shed now had been forced from her by a sudden realization of a beauty nobler and more eloquent than any in which she herself could share. Because of her isolation she had wept, but at once her pride returned, doubly fortified, and rebuked her weakness.

She got up from her chair and moved quietly about the great church. She stopped in front of the window near the King's Chapel—the Virgin and the Children.

It was for these windows that she came most often to the Cathedral. She knew every figure, every detail by heart.

In one of the Cathedral Guides they are thus described:

"In the window on the extreme right the Virgin Mary in a purple gown bends down over a field of lilies to watch the infant Christ at play. Next to it, the Christ and St. John paddle in a stream bordered by thick grasses, while the Virgin watches them from the window of a crooked house set in a cup of purple hill. In the centre window children are running in a crowd after a white kid, and the Virgin Mary holds back her Son, Who stretches out His arm after His playmates; in the lower half Joseph is in his workshop. Jesus, seated on the floor, looks up at him while the Virgin, in a dress of vivid green, stands near Him, guarding

Him. In the third window, on the left, they are walking, father, mother and Son, up the steps of the Temple, watched by a group of grave old men. In the lower panel Jesus is playing at His mother's feet, while an ox, an ass, and three dogs seem to be protecting Him."

She could see it now only faintly, but knew every aspect of it so well that light was not necessary for her.

She was startled because someone spoke to her.

"Are not these windows of the Virgin and the Children beautiful?"

She was startled; it was so rare that anyone spoke to her. She turned and saw that it was a little clergyman. There was something about him so simple and inoffensive that she could not be offended.

"Yes," she said. "But the light is bad now. You should see it in the daytime."

"There are so many things in the Cathedral," he said. "It will take a long time to know them all. But even in this light the colours are lovely. I'm glad I'm living here. I can come often."

She wanted to move away now that she knew that he lived in Polchester. It was only because the light was dim that he had spoken to her, not seeing who she was.

But he could see her clearly. The light above the King's Chapel illuminated her. He looked at her and thought that she had a fine strong face. There was something reserved and independent that he admired.

"Do you live here too?" he asked.

"Yes," she said shortly.

"I hope you won't think me impertinent, but I'm the new curate at St. Paul's, the church at the top of Orange Street. I have just been attending Evensong. What a beautiful service, and how strange that there should be so few people present."

"Many people in Polchester have never been inside the Cathedral—and never will be."

"Really? Is that so?" He looked at her with a smile, and in spite of herself she smiled back at him.

76

"Good-evening," he said, and went away.

Directly afterwards her uncle joined her and they went out of the church.

"Look here," he said, when they were outside, "would you like to see something very beautiful, Elizabeth? It's only a step away."

She walked beside him across the Green. They went into Klitch's shop. She drew back as she entered, hating to be looked at by Mr. Klitch. When they were gone he would say: "Do you know who I had in my shop this evening? Furze's daughter. The old scoundrel starves her, I'll be bound. She hasn't a penny to clothe herself with. . . ." Oh, she knew well enough!

Her uncle was very jolly with Klitch. He talked to him as though he had known him all his life.

"Come on, Klitch, let's see it! I'll be buying it back from you next week. Anyone tried to take it from you?"

Then Elizabeth Furze saw something very lovely—a black marble crucifix.

Klitch placed it on a table, and it stood in all its separate dignity and beauty, remote and apart from the gilt chairs, the carved tables, the needlework of green and purple, boxes with coloured pictures, and high mirrors with gold leaves and flowers. It stood apart. The Figure suffered and was triumphant.

"Come on, Klitch, who's been trying to buy it from you?"

"It's been much admired, Mr. Furze, I can tell you. An American gentleman was enquiring. I'll be sorry to see it go."

"If anyone robs me of it I'll break his neck," Mike said.

He touched it, bade Elizabeth come close to it.

"Ever see anything like that? I'll say you haven't."

Klitch smiled and was very friendly.

"That's mine," Mike Furze said as they walked out of the dusk into the lighted town. "I wouldn't lose it for a million."

"It's very beautiful," said Elizabeth.

CHAPTER V

Beginning of the Battle of Lady Emily—Also Some Hours in the Life of Mr. Bird

M<small>R. BIRD</small> did not forget the lady with whom he spoke in the Cathedral and very soon he discovered her identity.

He was walking through the Market-place with Gaselee and she passed them. He took off his hat, and she bowed; he fancied, however, that she did not recognize him.

"Do you know that lady?" he asked Gaselee.

"That is Miss Furze—the daughter of the world's worst moneylender."

He was surprised and greatly interested. Poor lady! How terrible for her! No wonder that she should appear reserved and on her guard. He felt that he would like to meet her soon again and show her that he was her friend. How foolish! He had only spoken a few words to her. She did not even remember him. But he felt a warm sympathy because she was in all probability lonely, and he was lonely too.

After two months in Polchester he was very lonely indeed. His character being what it was, it had been unkind of Fate to send him to Mr. Porteous, who was exactly the wrong person to give him the confidence that he always so badly needed. Porteous did not understand diffidence, nor did he know the cure for it. He was a kind man, although not quite so kind as he thought he was. Mr. Bird's smallness of stature, his shyness in company, his inability to make the best of himself, seemed to Porteous something of a joke, a great deal of a pity, and the kind of thing that Jesus Christ deplored. He talked to Bird as an elder brother who is captain of his school eleven talks to his younger brother who has ink on his fingers, dust in his hair, and an apprehensive walk.

"We are all Christ's soldiers, my dear friend. We are in His service. He is our Captain. Nothing must dismay us. With Him at our side we must have no fear."

He gave Bird a great deal of work because he was himself busied about so many public affairs. "Let us see. There is the Guild of Work at eleven-thirty. I can't be at that because of the Friends of the Cathedral meeting. At two-thirty there is the Mission at Polcreath. You should be back at five for the Young Men's Holiday Fund. Don't let Botchett have his way over that. He wants us to go to Newly Sands this time. Quite absurd. We went to Newly three years ago, and there were so many people that both the cricket and the bathing were spoilt. Stand up to Botchett."

This thought of standing up to Botchett was quite enough to spoil Bird's whole day. Botchett, who was one of the church-wardens at St. Paul's, was loud-voiced, red-faced and obstinate. A most difficult man.

There was the further trouble of Camilla Porteous. Camilla was the only one of Porteous' three children still remaining at home. She was over thirty now, a tall, strong, athletic-looking creature who should be excellent at hockey and at golf. Unfortunately this was not the case. Her looks belied her; in spite of her athletic form and jolly masculine voice she had the nature of an unrepentant sentimentalist. She was all woman and wanted a husband. It seemed that there was no one in Polchester destined for that appointment, time was passing, and her father's last two curates, Mr. Enderby and Mr. Salt, had been, with feminine wile and intrigue, attacked and invaded. They had both escaped, for Mr. Enderby detested women and Mr. Salt loved a girl in Lancashire. So she discovered that she liked Mr. Bird immensely. This was quite genuine. She cared for all small and defenceless things—all animals; even leaves and flowers seemed to her to have a life of their own and need protection.

On Mr. Bird's side there was something so peculiar in the softness and tenderness that proceeded from that masculine and athletic personality that he was struck quite dumb by it. She paid him visits in his Orange Street lodgings and, to his horror, talked to him about his underclothes.

"Take care of the cold. Wool next the skin is the only thing in this treacherous climate. I know what you poor bachelors are—no one to look after you—all your socks in holes. Don't mind asking me, Mr. Bird. Nothing is too much trouble."

He murmured his thanks.

"We must all help one another. Oh dear! Doesn't it seem to you, Mr. Bird, a strange thing that when it should be so easy for us all to love one another, we don't?"

She stood up, her legs widely planted, her arms extended as though she were swinging a hockey club.

"This beautiful world! The birds know better how to live in harmony together than we do! The robins, the wrens——"

Mr. Bird murmured something about the cruelty of Nature.

"Oh no! I can't agree! Of course there's the cuckoo and one or two more, but that's simply because they don't know better. We *do* know better. Life's meant to be all harmony, and what do we make of it? . . . Well, I must be getting along. Forgive me for talking as I feel. But I know that you understand. I feel that we are friends. Father's not been fortunate in his curates lately—Mr. Enderby was so very unsympathetic. I hate to say anything against anybody, but everyone felt the same. And Mr. Salt—well, Mr. Salt was always wanting to take the train to Bradford, if you know what I mean."

She smiled and moved a step towards him. He felt terror in his heart. She gave him one long look and departed.

Then came a day when, for the first time, he began to realize some of the undercurrents that were driving the town's course. It was this meeting—the first meeting of the Pageant Committee—that did two things to him. It showed him that he himself, insignificant as he was, belonged to the whole move-

ment of local events. It showed him also that these local events
involved hostilities, jealousies, drama far beyond his own
personal history. From this afternoon he was included in
everything that afterwards occurred. Porteous had been made
chairman of the Pageant Committee for two reasons: one that,
beyond anyone else in the town, he was a man who got things
done; two, that he held a proper and decent balance between
the interests of the Cathedral and the Town. The Committee
consisted of the Bishop, Lady St. Leath, Mrs. Braund, Canon
Ronder, Gaselee, Mrs. Carris, Mr. Withers, the author of the
Pageant Book, Aldridge the Mayor, and Mr. Nigel Romney.
Of Mr. Romney a word must be said. He was an important
member of Polchester society. He was a bachelor of middle
years, wealthy and eccentric. His appearance was odd, for he
was tall and thin with a very long neck and auburn "waved"
hair. He had a high shrill voice, and did not deny that his nature
was feminine. Indeed, rather than deny it he proclaimed it
everywhere: "My dear, it was nothing to do with *me!* My
mother wanted a girl. She thought it would be so much nicer
for Father. And so there you are!" He was very clever at
tapestry and took his work with him when he went out to tea.
He lived in a little house on the hill above Orange Street, had
an Italian manservant, an excellent cook and some excellent
pictures. His rooms were famous—his dining room that was
entirely in white, white curtains covered the walls, the tables
and chairs were white, and there was a large bowl of white
carved fruit at the table's centre. Then there was his bedroom
in purple and green—an odd combination, you would think, but
rather agreeable in fact. He collected jade and rock crystal. He
had a small white dog called Titania, very hairy and impertinent.

He knew everyone in the town. That was his real importance.
Although he was intimate with the Canons, Lady Mary, Mrs.
Carris, he was friendly also with Aldridge and Bellamy. Even
in Seatown he had friends, very rough ones some of them.
He had the kindest and most generous of natures. He was
always giving presents and helping the needy; he subscribed

to everything. The ladies loved him and confided their dearest secrets to him, and this was natural, for he understood exactly what they needed. Ordinary men were very selfish, thought only of themselves, and when they did make a fuss of a woman it was because they wanted something. They were tactless too, would talk about their silly business when they should be silent, refused little attentions when little attentions were requested, and went to sleep with their mouths open at the very time when they should be courteous. Mr. Romney did none of these things. He would listen by the hour to the most trivial nothings, would understand with real kindness how a look, a word, a movement might hurt. And naturally, because it was just these little things that hurt himself.

He was, at the same time, very indiscreet. He said so everywhere. "Oh no, you *mustn't* tell me!" he would cry. "I'm simply not to be trusted. I can't keep a thing to myself, my dear. It's too awful. I don't know what reticence means."

Then he was very changeable, very suspicious, very easily offended, and he showed that he was offended like a child. He would simply pick up his tapestry and go. There would begin then a very elaborate correspondence. The Italian man-servant would arrive with notes. He must be wooed, and wooed he always was because of the many intimate private things that he knew.

He had a strong if rather feminine sense of humour and should, people said, have been an actor. He was excellent at imitating the idiosyncrasies of his friends—Mrs. Braund at bridge, Lady Mary when she sneezed, the Misses Trenchard speaking to their cook. He was most amusing too when he caricatured himself, himself gardening, himself losing his soap in the bath, himself running for shelter in a shower of rain.

But his real value was in his social omniscience. He knew *everything* that was going on in the town, everyone's weakness, when there was a quarrel, when a reconciliation. His curiosity was insatiable.

But his great *gift* was for colour. He helped people with their curtains, their pictures, their furniture. His taste was quite marvellous. And in all this he was most unselfish. No trouble was too much for him.

That was the reason of his presence on the Pageant Committee. Mr. Porteous did not wish it, for Mr. Porteous disliked him extremely. He knew that Romney mocked him. No one was cleverer than Romney at mocking you with the completest good-nature. Porteous did not like to be mocked. Porteous had once said to him: "You're looking a bit pale, Romney. What you need is a little healthy exercise. A game of golf once and again."

That was tactless of Porteous, for Romney was sensitive about his appearance, which was, he considered, unusual and distinguished.

So after that, when he met Porteous, he always spoke about sport.

"Fine cricket they're having," he would say, "at Lord's. I see someone's been batting for a week, and is sleeping on the ground in a tent so as to be up and ready in the morning."

And Porteous would say in his most cheerful manner: "Not brought your sewing today, Romney?"

No, they did not like one another at all, which was a pity.

On this first meeting of the Pageant Committee, Porteous wished Mr. Bird to be present to take notes. So present he was. He did not enjoy the occasion. He was afraid of everyone there. Only Romney took any notice of him. The Bishop and Lady St. Leath could not be there.

Everyone was given a copy of the Book of Words.

"What I suggest," said Porteous, "is that we all take this home and study it." (He had a trick of emphasizing certain words, and he said "study" as though he were ordering them to charge the foe.) "It is clear to me from a first cursory reading that the two principal parts are the Black Bishop and Lady Emily. Indeed the scene when Lady Emily harangues the citizens is most stirring—very noble and stirring indeed." (Here he bowed to the author.) "I perceive that Lady Emily has to ride a horse. She was also, at the time of the battle of

Drymouth, some forty-five years of age, so the part must be taken by someone—well, someone no longer a child."

Here, as Mr. Bird noticed, both Mrs. Braund and Mrs. Carris looked up self-consciously.

"I would make an excellent Lady Emily," Romney said, and everyone laughed. But everyone also knew that the matter of casting this part was going to be no jesting affair.

Romney, looking quickly at the book, saw many fine opportunities for pageantry. His heart began to beat. His pale cheeks flushed. Whatever else he was or was not, he was an artist. This was utterly sincere to him. He would fight to the death for the hang of a curtain, would, in olden times, have been tortured rather than yield on the principle of colour or symmetry. And here was this fool Porteous who knew nothing about anything. He saw battles ahead.

Ronder, seated back in his chair, his hands folded on his belly, watched them with curiosity.

Once upon a time (and his younger self was so alive, so friendly, standing now at his side!) how deeply the intrigue, the pulling of strings, the influencing of events all involved here in this coming pageant would have excited him! Even now he could feel, as though faintly fanning his cheek, the warm breath of that urgent flame!

But now he was spectator—spectator even of himself! His great bulk made all chairs, save those in his own house, uncomfortable for him. He sat back now, his hands crossed over his stomach, his thick neck uneasy, his short legs aching beneath the table. His eyes were half closed. His clothes were perfect in cut, his high white collar gleamed, his shaven cheek had an almost Chinese smoothness. He did not move. He had not yet spoken.

He seemed to see into the very hearts of all those present. How well he knew the almost boyish eagerness with which Porteous was taking charge of this affair, his blindness as to the psychology of others, his complete self-assurance, his real religion, his real confidence in God's approval of himself. How well he understood Mrs. Braund, her good heart, her sense of fighting in a vulgar world for the old order of decency and class, and the pathos that came from that kind of out-moded snobbery; he knew that she saw in Mrs. Carris with her vulgarity, parties and pushing daughters, something as ill-smelling as onions, as common-tasting as tripe.

How well he understood Mrs. Carris and her vitality, her lack of taste, her social jealousies, her picture of herself as buoyant, brilliantly coloured, the only alive person in Pol-chester.

But best of all he understood Romney almost as though that queer creature were part of himself. For there had always been in himself a feminine streak. It was that, he thought, that had in reality so fatally antagonized Brandon all those years ago. And, as he thought of that old battle, the consequences of which were not ended yet, he wondered whether he had not been a little in love with Brandon, in love with his splendid masculinity and vigour and health.

Yes, he understood Romney, and could see how the creative fire was now burning in him at the thought of the coloured fantasies to be drawn from the heart of this pageant; he under-stood too the sensitive antennæ now quiveringly extended; a word, a smile, a gesture, and Romney would be elaborating intrigues, taking sides, forcing issues just as he had once done. But not with the same result. Romney was weak as he himself had never been, weak and passionate in his personal contacts as he had never been, and standing always on the razor edge of personal disaster. Oh yes, he understood it all!

And as he saw these human beings he found them all so touching, so human and, above all, so small, turning like little toy figures around the great battlement of the Cathedral.

Soon he must leave this. Soon he would be—where? A curious trembling seized his body. His fingers tapped on the table. He would go as old Moffit the other night had gone before his very eyes. In the face of that great imminent fact everything faded to nothingness. He sank into darkness. He felt a horrible decay in every bone of his body.

"Yes," Porteous was saying, "this will undoubtedly be a

very great event in the history of the Town and the Cathedral, and what I feel, ladies and gentlemen, is that we all have an immense *responsibility* in this matter. We must not think of ourselves, but must work as a *team*—one for all and all for one."

"What I want to know, Mr. Porteous," said Mrs. Carris, "is how we come to final decisions. There will undoubtedly be differences of opinion——"

"Then of course we vote."

"Oh, I see. But if we vote about every point it will take a very long time——"

"About many things we will, I trust, be unanimous."

"And what about the finances?" (It was clear that Mrs. Carris intended to take a leading part at these meetings.)

"Well, as to the finances . . ."

It seemed that the Cathedral will contribute, and the Town will contribute. . . .

"Exactly. If the Town is to contribute, then in my opinion it is not represented sufficiently on this committee. The Mayor, myself, Mr. Romney—we, I suppose, represent the Town. I hope everyone understands me. I'm the last person to make any trouble, but I know things will be said and questions asked——"

"We have the right to invite persons especially concerned——"

"The Town seems to me very adequately represented," Mrs. Braund said in her deep voice.

"Well, we'll see." Mrs. Carris tossed her auburn head ever so slightly. "I *know* that questions will be asked. . . ."

It was here that Gaselee, very modestly and with a smile that he knew to be charming, played his tactful part. "May I say just this? Isn't this a matter greater than any question of Town or Cathedral? Speaking for myself I am very proud that I have been asked to be on this committee. I think Mrs. Carris is so right in wishing that we should do nothing to rouse outside criticism, but if we all act together, as one man, as Porteous says, there *should* be no criticism. Or if there is any we will meet it all together. All of us—well, we want this pageant to be one of the finest the west of England has ever seen. And it will be, I know."

(That young man, Ronder thought, will go far here. Perhaps he will take my place. But he's more ambitious for himself than for anything else. Was I? I can't be sure. I have never been sure.)

"Of course there's the weather," the Mayor said unexpectedly.

"The weather?"

"Well, there's always the weather, isn't there, in England? Everything will depend on it. A wet week and everything will be ruined."

Aldridge—who was a tall thin man with purple cheeks and a pale, pointed nose—was alternately optimist and pessimist. His moods went with his digestion. His sufferings from dyspepsia seemed to him simply the most important item in the universe, and he regarded his stomach as a battleground in which the issue was epochal. His symptoms—the nausea, the headache, the heartburn and the rest—were personal to him like the members of his family.

He was not so well today, and throughout the meeting he had been considering whether a small portion of duck, eaten by him on the previous evening, was responsible. This bird hovered over his head and blinded his eyes. When he was well he was like Wellington after Waterloo; he had settled the fate of Europe.

Today there was little more to do. Next week they would consider the distribution of the parts. . . .

"Well, well," said Porteous, rubbing his hands. "A good beginning, I think, an *excellent* beginning." But he considered the long thin back of Romney, who was just leaving in the company of Mrs. Braund. He was telling her a story that amused her very much indeed—about himself possibly. How he wished that that fellow was not on the Committee! A ridiculous mistake. He would speak to the Bishop. Perhaps it was not too late for something to be done. Bird, fearful as always that his lord and master would seize upon him and give him some new job to do before morning, nevertheless managed to escape. He would take a little walk in the evening air. He felt greatly distressed. It seemed to him that everyone on the Committee hated everyone else. Mrs. Braund and Mrs. Carris frightened him. They were so large and so self-assured. How was he ever to do his duty successfully in this town? He formed in his mind his favourite picture of a quiet country parish where no one alarmed him, where he would have silence and peace so that he might think about God and feel God near to him.

Lovely weather! As he walked down Orange Street beauty closed him in. The sky was softly blue and patterned with rosy cloud. Everyone moved gently. The street was as it might have been fifty years ago. No motorcars. The Georgian houses, each with its neat stone steps and shining knocker, let the evening light fall quietly on the grey stone. The air was sharp, fresh, sparkling. At the bottom of the street, where the river flows under a bridge, a barge, painted a brilliant red, moved slowly seawards. The water, in grey shadow and then suddenly sparkling with the evening glow, stirred gently as though a kind hand stroked it.

Standing on the bridge, he saw the Cathedral towers rise above the roofs in black silhouette. Birds flew, more peaceful than the sky that they traversed.

"Good-evening, Mr. Bird," a voice said.

He turned and saw the sculptor Lampiron at his side. He was greatly pleased. He had met the sculptor on one or two occasions of late and he felt that they were already friends. He was not afraid of Lampiron in spite of his gruff voice, his independent opinions, and the name that he had for carving monstrosities.

"Taking a walk?"

"Yes. Five minutes in the air. I've been sitting indoors all the afternoon."

"Come in and see my place. It's just round the corner here."

"Well, really——"

"Oh, nonsense! I'll take no denial."

Lampiron caught him by the arm and Bird gladly submitted. It would be interesting to see those abominable sculptures!

Lampiron had a little house looking over the river. He took Bird upstairs into a room that was in complete disorder, newspapers on the floor, an empty beer bottle on the table, books on the chairs. . . .

"Never mind this. Here's where I work." He led him down some stairs at the room end, pushed open a door, and they were in the studio. When Lampiron switched on the light the first thing that Bird saw was a great block of stone, and from this stone projected two gigantic female breasts. He gazed at this, hoping that unexpectedly a face might emerge from that grey mass—or if not a face, at least a hand or a foot, something that he might recognize.

Giving a little sigh he raised his eyes timidly to Lampiron's. Then they both laughed.

"You don't like it, eh? Of course not. But you don't understand it. A thing like that can't come to you all in a moment. The stone itself is practically a phallus—and then the breasts . . . Now don't be shocked. I won't have you shocked."

"I'm not shocked," Bird murmured.

"That's right. People in this town faint if you mention the generative organs. Anyway, this is the grandest thing I've done yet—and it's not Asiatic like Epstein. My God, no! It's universal. The life of man. But probably you don't believe in the life of man or think it's important. No, you believe in God and think that says everything. But it doesn't. Not by a long chalk. God's all right, but only if you believe in Creation——"

"I believe in love," little Mr. Bird said, most unexpectedly to himself. Then he went on rapidly: "I know that sounds silly. It's what every sentimentalist who beats his wife says. No, but I mean it. And I'll tell you why. Because I've been sitting on a committee for hours this afternoon with everyone hating everyone else. It made me very unhappy. And frightened too. Because if we've learnt nothing after all these years, perhaps we're worth so little that we'll all be swept up and thrown into the dustbin."

He looked wildly about him, his eyes staring at the obscure shapes—here a rough head, there gigantic thighs and bending knees, and there again more female breasts. He was near to tears, although he did not know it.

"I can't think why I'm talking like this. As a rule I'm afraid to open my mouth. But it's coming here, seeing all these terrible things you're making. . . . I like you so much, and surely these things are *frightful*——" He raised his hands as though appealing for forgiveness. Then dropped them. "I beg your pardon. I've been terribly rude when I know you so slightly. . . ."

Lampiron saw that his eyes were full of tears. He led him to an old shabby armchair with a large hole in it.

"There you are. Sit down there. Have some tea—or a whisky-and-soda—will you?"

"Yes. Thanks. I think I *would* like some tea."

Lampiron pushed a bell. "If only that old bitch isn't out. . . . Here, I say, I'm sorry. But no, I'm not. We're going to be friends and it will never do if I have to pull myself up and apologize for my language every moment. It will do you good anyway—a counter to old Porteous and his gang. But look here——"

He pulled a chair close to the one in which Bird was sitting.

"This is important. This is hellishly important. We've got to have this out. You come in here and think these things hideous. So does everyone else in the town except the Hattaways. Not that that matters. Neither you nor anyone else here know anything about art. It's a thing you've got to learn about, you know, like engineering or banking. People look at a painting or a piece of sculpture and say: 'Oh, I don't like *that!*' and think they have finished with it. Bloody fools! What you've got to do is to find out what the artist is getting at, and then, when you're fairly sure, you can say whether you think he's got it or not. And then there's nothing final in it. You're limited as critic by everything you've been and are. What *you* are. What the *artist* is. What *art* is. Three separate things.

When for you they coincide, then for *you* the creator has done his job. But only for *you*, mind. . . . Come in. Yes, Bridget. Some tea, please, bread and butter, jam, cake."

"I don't want any cake," Bird murmured.

"Oh yes you do. Do you good. Well, look here. I'm nearly seventy; I've only been working at this thing for five years. I know nothing at all about it. But when I'm working I'm so happy I wouldn't exchange places with anyone alive or dead. My health and my work—my two good things. Everything else is rotten. I've hardly a friend in the place. I haven't a bean. I owe that swine Furze a hell of a lot and he'll turn me out of here if I don't do something about it. Take my sculpture too in part payment. I wouldn't wonder if I murdered him one day. I'd kill him tomorrow if I could think of a way that wouldn't be detected. Oh yes! I mean it. Don't look so shocked. I'd be doing a kindness to humanity. He has most of the town under his thumb.

"And then sex. I'm nearly seventy, as I told you, but I'm strong as a horse. I could sleep with three women a night. I don't, but I walk this bloody town at two in the morning to cool my passions. Ludicrous, isn't it? An old man with passions. Disgusting too. I tell you it's neither ludicrous nor disgusting. It's life—teeming, fructifying, careless, casual, procreative life. I've energy enough. Look here. Feel that arm."

Bird felt his arm.

"Muscle there, isn't there? But it's all working up to an explosion. I'm like a man chained. I don't ask for much. Enough money to do my work in peace. A nice quiet mistress who wouldn't think of me as an old man. Peace to work. That's all. And I can't get it. I can't get it. There's no peace in this town. That's working up for an explosion too because no one here thinks of what's real. Beauty."

"God," said Bird.

"It's the same thing. The thing in the centre. You can't go on neglecting it forever. It's damned patient, but it won't wait forever."

He strode off to a corner and returned with two or three

pictures that had been standing with their faces to the wall. He showed them to Bird. One represented cows in a field grazing, another the moon rising over an oily sea, a third the street of a village.

"But they're beautiful!" cried Bird.

"No, they're not. They're hideous. Or rather they're nothing at all. They don't exist."

"Do you mean to say," said Bird, "that when you could paint like that you gave it up and—and—did *those?*"

Lampiron laughed. He took the paintings and placed them once more with their faces to the wall.

"Can't you see——?" he began. But he broke off. "No, I see that you can't. The difference between life and death. Well, well."

The tea came in.

"Here. This is a fine cake. It's gingerbread. I'm sure where you are they don't give you enough to eat. Now I've been doing all the talking. Tell me a little about yourself."

"Yes, I will," Bird said suddenly. "I haven't talked to anyone about myself for years. Nobody's asked me. There's nothing much to tell though, except that I'm a coward. I'm frightened of everyone and everything, myself included."

"Why?"

"I don't know. I've no confidence. Only when I'm alone and God seems very close to me I'm comforted. Sometimes then I feel that I could face anybody."

"This business about God," Lampiron said. "I don't understand it. You're a parson, so you have to put up a show, but in your inner self, when you're alone, do you really believe it? Believe that Christ was divine, that there's another life after this one and the rest of it?"

"I think I believe in a sixth sense," Bird said slowly. "Non-material. I *know* that there's another world. Often I'm in touch with it. And when I leave my physical body I shall understand it more fully. I *could* understand it more now if I were not so physical, if I loved people more, thought less of myself."

"I see," Lampiron said. "I don't believe in your spiritual world, but I do believe in my creative one, and maybe they're the same. Perhaps we're both right. But your *physical* self. I shouldn't have thought you were very physical. Do you mean women?"

Bird blushed.

"Of course I'm like other men," he said. "But I've never had relations with a woman——"

"My God! How old are you?"

"Thirty-two."

"Thirty-two? And never slept with a woman! Your passions can't be very strong then."

"They are—sometimes. But it wouldn't be right—for me. One day I hope I shall marry." To his own surprise he thought of the woman whom he had seen in the Cathedral, Furze's daughter.

He went on: "I've never spoken to anyone of these things before. I've been too timid. Of course as a clergyman I've had to warn boys about sex and I've encountered it many times in my work—very sad it's been sometimes. But I've always managed. It's only since I've come here that I've felt everything difficult. There's something about this town . . . You know, it seems so quiet and ordinary on the outside, but when you get to know it a little, there's something underneath. . . . But I don't think I shall be quite so nervous now. It's helped me like anything talking to you."

"And it's helped me!" Lampiron cried. "Life isn't all jam for me just now. I put a bold face on it but, between you and me, I'm frightened myself sometimes. Waking up at two in the morning, hearing the Cathedral bells strike, knowing I'm nearly seventy and am in debt to that swine and am not earning a penny . . ."

"You could sell those pictures," Bird said.

"No, I couldn't. Not here. No one in Polchester buys pictures."

"I—" Bird began shyly—"I—if you didn't ask too much— I should greatly like to have one."

"Bless your heart!" Lampiron cried. "Would you really? And so you shall. But you shan't pay me for it. I'll give you one and it shall illuminate your lodgings. Here—which will you have?"

He dragged them over again.

"Oh no, I couldn't."

"Of course you can. You shall help me sometime if I'm in a real hole——"

Bird was dreadfully embarrassed. That wasn't at all what he had intended. Suppose that Lampiron thought . . . So he chose one—the picture with the cows in a field.

"Good! That's been making me feel sick for years. You've done me a service. I'll send it up to your lodgings tomorrow."

"I'd like to take it with me."

"Would you? All right. I'll wrap some paper round it."

When Bird stood up to depart Lampiron put his hand on his shoulder. "You're right," he said, "to be celibate—if you can. Then when you marry—— Only don't wait too long. To be married, you know. And if she's the wrong woman I'll strangle her!"

Bird smiled, shook hands, and departed.

It was dark now. A wild wind blew down Orange Street and knocked the picture against Bird's legs. What a fine man! I've made a new friend! But how violent! I do hope he won't do anything in a sudden passion. . . . But whatever he did I'd stand by him. I've made a friend. . . .

He entered his lodgings with a brave heart.

CHAPTER VI

Heart and Soul of an Idealist

No man thinks himself a villain. There is no melodrama about Stephen Furze: only thus far has he the right trappings for melodrama—that his voice is gentle and his movements quiet. There is a stillness where he is, a stillness so profound that violent spirits like Lampiron are compelled to break it.

Furze's own view of himself was that he was a man of justice, who hated untidiness. This passion for *bareness* was a growing passion. There was dust in his own room because he allowed no one to touch anything there, but for the rest there was a shining bareness everywhere. A scrap of paper on the floor was to himself a personal insult. As he bent his long legs to pick it up, a rage bubbled in him. How *dare* it lie there? He had the acquisitiveness that leads to sitting naked in a naked room— a cell, at last, perhaps, padded, for he could not feel so surely a possessor of great fortune as when there was no detail before his eyes to insist on his limitations.

The collector with his Aldine, his Fourth Folio, his small Turner water colour, his "Edinburgh" Burns, must be aware of the other Aldines, the Second Folios, the thousands of Turner water colours, the "Kilmarnock"—but, alone, in his hired lodging with his sixpenny Shelley and mug of beer, he can possess the world.

So Stephen Furze was forever adding to his riches both in

fact and in imagination. But he did not wish to *see* his wealth. Looking on a blank wall he appeared to own the whole world.

This was one edge to his passion and it led to constant paring away of material and physical things. The weekly bills were examined ever more closely; in the rooms of the house there were things day by day found to be superfluous. He moved, blinded by his vision of all the things that were *not* there and that were his, and his wife moved at his side seeing in *her* darkness all the things that she had loved when she had sight—tables, chairs, pictures—that were for her still present.

And the other edge to his passion was his almost divine consciousness of justice. No man alive was more honest than he. When, as Lampiron had done the other day, someone came to him and accused him of injustice, a cold abiding hatred of that man stirred in his heart. He was capable of real hatred, a very rare capacity in man. He hated because he was wronged. He was a benefactor to the town. Times had been bad these last years, and there were many he knew who would have been ruined ere now had it not been for the services he rendered. The interest he asked was a fair interest. Because he was a man who looked after his own and took what was his due, was he therefore extortionate? From the world of his desires, just as from the world of his vision, he had banished everything that was unnecessary. Sexual passion had never meant anything to him; he did not care what he ate, nor what he drank, nor where he slept, nor for friendship. He needed no one in the world but himself. Every energy, every thought, was concentrated on this purpose of possession. The love of it had two bases: one the actual fact of possession so that he would sit in his room and make his calculations and think, This day last year I had so and so much. Today I have this much more. And after that the *power* of possession. He thought, All these people are in my hand. I, Stephen Furze, who once was nothing. Bellamy, Marlowe, Lampiron, Browning and many more. When they see me coming they tremble. I have the Town in my hand. I am just, I am powerful. I am almost like God.

For, like all men who care about the spin of a coin, he was superstitious.

Until he owned God as he owned these others he would be afraid of Him. God had escaped his grasp and he had a vague, undefined fear and hatred of the Cathedral with all its gold and brass and marble and painted windows. He went there sometimes and wondered how much it had cost to build the Nave and what a fine tomb with plenty of decoration would fetch if it were sold. He spoke of the Cathedral with contempt—an old empty collection of junk. But he did not *feel* contempt when he was there. He stood in the Nave and knew that the place hated him—another instance of injustice.

Into this world of his there had come his brother and, whoever else he might wish to destroy, it was his brother who came first on the list.

He had all his life despised and loathed his brother. Mike stood for everything that he scorned—noise, riotous living, boastfulness, rashness and, most of all, dissipation of possession. Mike had never kept a thing—wastrel, wanderer, vagabond. When Mike appeared Stephen's first impulse had been to turn him at once from the house. But then there had been the money. Fifty pounds dangled before his eyes. After that had come the desire for power. He would make Mike his slave, keep him in the house to do his bidding, reduce him gradually to a wretched subservient dependence. Here too there was justice, for the thought of Mike had, all his life, taunted and mocked him.

He waited for the moment when the fifty pounds would be gone. His moment arrived. One evening Mike came to him and suggested that he should stay in the house and, for a weekly wage, perform certain services. Stephen quietly agreed. He laid his hand on his brother's shoulder, and his long, cold fingers possessed his brother. He knew that Mike was spying about the house. He read Mike's purposes as though he saw, through a glass, into his brain. Mike, his money spent, could no longer be the jovial boon companion about the town that he had been. Stephen gave him a pound a week.

"It's only till I've found a job."

"Quite. Quite. Meanwhile there are things you can do. . . ."

He stopped the fire in Mike's bedroom.

Elizabeth came to him with the weekly bills. He read the items through one by one.

"Hutton's bill is too large."

"But Uncle Michael has all his meals with us now."

"Yes, yes, I know."

"And he complains that he is not getting enough."

"Oh, he complains, does he? He need not stay. No one is keeping him here."

She surmounted her fear of him as a swimmer surmounts a gigantic wave.

"Father, we are none of us getting enough. I do my best, but now that there are four of us——"

"Eh, my dear, my dear—so you are complaining too?"

"Yes!" she cried passionately. "You are mean to us, Father. Why? You are one of the richest men in Polchester. I can't stand it much longer, and if I go——"

"Leave your mother?"

"Mother would come with me."

"No, she would not."

Elizabeth knew that that was true and that while her mother was there she must be there too.

He took her hand in his.

"Isn't this a lot of trouble about food, Elizabeth? I manage very well, don't I? I don't complain. But have it your own way. Buy what you like. Buy what you like."

But she knew what would happen if she did. Her mother would be made to suffer. He would pierce her blindness with stabs of pain. He knew so well how to make his own sense of injustice her distress, for oddly enough, as Elizabeth thought, her mother loved her father. That, at least, was how it appeared to Elizabeth.

She would put out her hand in the darkness and touch him, and then, when she felt the cloth of his sleeve, she would smile, as though she had now all the happiness that she wanted.

Elizabeth looked at her father, then turned away. But at the door she looked back.

"Uncle Michael has changed everything," she said. "Don't forget that." Then she came nearer to him. "Do you know how old I am? I shall be thirty next month. For years I haven't said a word. You've thought that I've noticed nothing, minded nothing. But I have my own life that you can't touch. Mother is blind because you were too mean to have her cared for. That I'll never forgive you even though Mother does. We've been shut up in this hateful house as though we'd been buried. But someone has come in now from outside. I've been so deeply ashamed of you that I couldn't hold my head up in the town, but I'm not responsible for you any longer. Although I stay here for Mother's sake I'm free. I'm a woman with a life of my own from now on."

And she went slowly out.

He was greatly surprised. Elizabeth had never spoken to him like this before and he had not thought her capable of it. He recognized in her for the first time something of his own character. She too felt a sense of injustice and, although her complaints were absurd, he liked her independence.

But this was another thing that his dear brother had been doing—stirring his daughter to rebellion. He sat there, pleased with his isolation. Nobody understood him and he did not wish that anybody should. His contempt for the human race was profound. After thousands of years of civilization they had not learnt how to manage sensibly their affairs. Less than twenty years after plunging into a war of unprecedented horror, a war from which no one had gained anything, they were all busily preparing for another. All men were enemies—all men were fools. He smiled. All the better for himself. He would not have it otherwise. He remembered that he had left two shillings and a sixpence in the trousers that he had been wearing yesterday. With a sudden fear lest someone—his rascal of a brother maybe —had taken them, he hastened, quietly, to his bedroom. . . .

Later he walked out. Out of doors he wore at all times of the year, whatever the weather might be, a bowler hat with a very large brim, and a long overcoat, dusty grey in colour. This over-coat was now old-fashioned in shape. It hung straight down from his shoulders to his boots. The collar was faded. Neverthe-less, clothed in this garment he did not appear shabby. The bowler hat was also out of fashion with its large soup-plate brim, and on wet days he walked under an umbrella that was really enormous and quite green with age. So that he was always seen, when abroad, either as a grey shadow that melted into the walls of the houses, the sky, the pavement itself, or as a vast green umbrella that moved above a grey coat, silently, from point to point.

It was not until you were face to face with him that you were aware of the countenance with the long white nose, the arms that ended in grey gloves, and the eyes that moved with a gentle but penetrating motion, taking in the world.

Again and again Polchester citizens, in the half-light, en-countered this figure as abruptly as though it had risen there and then from the paving stones.

"Good-evening, Mr. Bellamy."

"Oh!—good-evening, Mr. Furze!"

And the bowler hat and grey coat, or the umbrella and grey coat, as the weather might dictate, would disappear around the corner, or vanish into mist as though it had never been.

On this particular afternoon a wet mist blew about the town. It came from the sea and was raw and penetrating. Therefore Furze had his umbrella. But his first visit was not far distant. He wished to spend five minutes—five minutes only, for he had much to do—with Mr. Marlowe of St. James's. The Rectory was, of course, only a door or two away.

Hidden beneath his umbrella, the wet mist blowing about him, he waited for the opening of the door. It was opened by young Penny Marlowe, who, seeing that umbrella and coat so motionless on the step, seeing no face and hearing no voice, gave a little cry. Then, as the umbrella lifted and the long white nose appeared, she realized who it was.

"I beg your pardon, Miss Marlowe. May I speak to your father for a moment?"

"Oh, you gave me quite a fright, Mr. Furze—I didn't see who it was. Won't you come in? I'll see where Father is."

She always felt sorry for Mr. Furze. She knew that he was very unpopular in the town, but to her he seemed delicate, uncared-for, wearing shabby clothes. She blamed that daughter of his because she did not look after him properly.

Stephen Furze came in and stood in the warm hall that was overcrowded with things. He stood there, his hat in one hand, his umbrella in the other.

Her father, as Penny knew, was playing chess with Canon Cronin in the study. His two great passions in life were reading and chess. He played chess with anyone whom he could find. The happiest night of the week for him was the meeting of the Polchester Chess Club at the Bull. Like so many of the happiest chess players, he would never be any good, but always hoped that he might. He had brilliant ideas. He read books of instruction. He played out International Games that were printed in the newspapers, and often said that he wondered at Tcherzki of Czechoslovakia for moving his Bishop, or that Ellis of Sweden must have been dreaming to allow that Passed Pawn. He dreamt often of brilliant moves with the two Knights, arm in arm, so to speak, stepping gallantly up the board together, or of a great occasion when, before assembled multitudes, his Queen and Bishop cut diagonally into the very heart of the enemy, transfixing him with surprised terror; but, in actual fact, he could not keep his head. He would grow so desperately excited as he saw his plans maturing, as he moved a Pawn here, a Bishop there, that he was utterly unprepared for the sudden dash of the opposing Queen on to his own front line, his King, alas, pinned in by his own Bishop and three attendant Pawns.

"Oh! But it's impossible! Another two moves and I would have had you! I *can't* understand . . ."

So, alas, it was again and again. Cronin, with whom he mostly played, was not a good performer, but he was calm and collected. He never did a brilliant thing nor was he ever transcendently careless.

"If you'd only show a little emotion!" Marlowe would cry.

"What is there to be emotional about? You get too excited, Dick. It's not only bad for your chess, it's bad for your heart too."

So they were now engaged when Penny opened the door and said that Mr. Stephen Furze would like to speak to Father for just a minute.

Dick Marlowe's face was distorted. He got up, almost knocking the chessboard over in his agitation.

"Hullo, Dick—what is it?" Cronin asked.

"It's nothing." Marlowe, who was stout, rubicund, young-looking in spite of his white hairs for his years, had suddenly aged. "Would you go into the drawing room, Ned, and wait? It's only five minutes. We'll finish the game afterwards."

Cronin went out. He was distressed. He knew, as everyone save his own family knew, that Dick Marlowe, who was a fool about money if anyone was, had had dealings with this fellow. Why? What had induced him?

Stephen Furze came in.

He stood there not obsequiously, not sycophantically, in his grey coat that fell to his boots, with his bony skull under the thin grey hair and his hands in their grey gloves.

"Oh, Mr. Furze. How are you? Good-afternoon. Won't you sit down?"

Marlowe rubbed his hands, smiled, sat down, himself, in one of the armchairs by the fire. But his heart was hammering. What was this man here for? He had paid him something only a month or two ago. When was it? How much had it been? He could remember nothing. But it could not be much that he owed him—only a pound or two now. How had it all begun? By his overhearing, at a Chess Club meeting, someone say, "There's always Furze. He'll lend to anyone—*and* want it back again with increase."

The thing had remained in Marlowe's mind. He was always wanting money. They were so desperately poor, and then there were his own extravagances about books! His secret vice. Crockett's, the second-hand bookshop in Myre Street, lured him again and again.

When about to pay one of his visits there he felt all the pride and excitement of a gay buck about to court a handsome young lady. The Rectory attics were piled high with dusty volumes. The study walls were lined with books—and there poor Hester, his wife, was scarcely able to make ends meet!

He knew how wrong it was. Every night and morning he prayed to be delivered from Crockett's as a man might pray to be delivered from drugs or drink. He salved his conscience a little by paying Crockett's cash, but to obtain the cash—yes, that was why he went to Furze.

Furze came out of his door one day as Marlowe came out of his. Some words were exchanged, Marlowe spent ten minutes in Furze's room and the transactions were begun. That was three years ago! Now Marlowe did not know where he was. How deeply he was ashamed that a clergyman should be in this position, but behind the shame was growing an almost nightmarish fear. The sum of his debt seemed ever to grow, pay as he might. He was always resolving to have the matter bravely out, to demand that Furze should go with him to Symon, the old lawyer in Bury Street, and have the thing settled, whatever it cost him.

But he was frightened. He did not wish anyone to know of his folly. Moreover he very easily lost consciousness of his troubles. When he was playing chess or reading one of his beloveds, Jean Paul Richter or Gibbon or Donne's Sermons or, greatest and best of all, Goethe, who seemed to him both the priest and king of all mortal men, he would settle down, and his lips would smile and his gentle mild eyes cloud with pleasure.

It had been always so, but now his enemy—for so he felt Furze to have become—was closing in upon him. There were times when even his adored Siebenkäs would fade before that long thin figure. He would wake and fancy that Furze was standing beside his bed. He would start and cry in his sleep. . . .

So he looked up now, smiling, and said: "Won't you sit down, Mr. Furze?"

"Oh no, thank you very much, Mr. Marlowe. I only looked

in for a moment. The fact is that a small sum is due—*was* due, in fact, on October the twenty-seventh. I thought that you might have overlooked it."

"Why, no, Mr. Furze. Of course not. How much is it exactly?"

Furze took from his pocket a small dog-eared pocketbook bound in faded green cloth. This pocketbook was very famous in the town.

"The amount is eight pounds, five shillings and sixpence."

His manner was dignified, kindly and reserved, but, as he looked around the room, he felt disgust in his heart. How crammed with unnecessary lumber the place was! Those leather armchairs would fetch quite a price and the marble clock on the mantelpiece was worth something. That was a fine table the old man worked at, with its leather blotter and the photographs of his wife and daughter in silver frames. As to the books that reached from ceiling to floor, they made Furze feel quite sick. There was an extravagance for you! No one could read all those books. What was the use of them, gathering dust, hiding clean bare walls . . . ?

Marlowe cleared his throat. "Certainly you shall be paid, Mr. Furze. In a day or two. I don't quite know how I stand at the bank."

"That's perfectly right, Mr. Marlowe. I know that times aren't easy, especially for the clergy. Any day within a week or two. I thought you'd prefer to be reminded."

"Certainly. Certainly." Then Marlowe made a great effort. "I wonder whether you could tell me what my total debt is to you. I hope to be able to clear the whole thing off very shortly."

"Why, of course. With the greatest pleasure. I think I have the total here."

He looked at the little green book again. There was a long silence broken only by the marble clock, which chirruped, "*Cheer*-up . . . *Cheer*-up . . . *Cheer*-up."

"Yes," said Furze at last. "I make it, Mr. Marlowe, just seventy-one pounds, four shillings and threepence. The total debt deducting the ten pounds that you paid me in July last."

Seventy pounds! The room darkened. Marlowe put his hand, for an instant, to his cheek and pinched it.

"Dear me! That is more than I had supposed. But I have never had anything approaching that amount from you—and I have paid you——"

Furze consulted the book. "You have borrowed from me, in the last three years, eighty-three pounds in all. You have paid me thirty-one pounds, ten shillings. I charge, of course, a slight interest, as everyone does."

"I quite understand." Eighty-three pounds? Could it be possible? But this must be stopped, ended, done with. He would go to Cronin or Braund or Hattaway, all good friends, and borrow the whole sum. . . . This thought cheered him.

"I had no idea it was so much. I think I can promise you, Mr. Furze, that you shall be paid in full very shortly."

"Thank you, Mr. Marlowe. But pray don't put yourself out. I only wish to oblige you. . . . Good-day. Nasty wet afternoon, isn't it?"

In the hall he found his hat and umbrella and quietly vanished. His business was in Seatown: thither he departed.

Seatown had never been beautiful. Once upon a time, perhaps, when a few cottages had clustered under the Rock, it had its romance, but the Pol can never have been a fine river here, and at low tide it must ever have been the thin grey trickle of a stream that it is today. Mud was the basis of this world, slime oozing to the foot of rock. But who can tell? There were stories that hundreds of years ago the river had been so deep and wide that ships sailed along it to the Polchester port and, on its farther banks, wild forest stretched to the border of the sea. Thirty-five years ago it had been a shabby place, its streets haunted by loafer and vagabond, slatternly women at its doors, the children the worst cared for in the south of England, and Samuel Hogg doing a nefarious trade at the Dog and Pilchard. Then in 1906 Harmer John had come to Polchester, later been murdered in Pennicent Street, and in 1913, as a shame-faced tribute to his memory, all Seatown reformed, rebuilt. On October 7th, a memorial to Harmer John had been unveiled by the Mayor, and Pennicent Street had become Riverside Street. The delighted citizens on that day beheld, instead of disgraceful slum, a row of houses of a drab, grey stone. Each little house had grey chimneys, neat windows, bath (h. and c.), indoor sanitation and a square of garden. A neater, uglier street was not to be found in the whole of England.

Satisfaction was general. And after that? After that the war. And after the war a strange return to Seatown of its old inhabitants—if not the originals, then children of the originals as close to their fathers as might be. For blood will tell. The spirit of Seatown was stronger than the spirit of its reformers, and back they came, the scallywags, the castaways, the wastrels. Sam Hogg was dead, but his true successor, Lanky Moon, a long cadaverous fellow with a glass eye, ruled the Dog and Seatown with it.

During the post-war years the citizens of Seatown became a fine collection of down-and-outs and unemployed. No cathedral town in the whole country had a finer. Decent enough many of them were, but mingled with the decent were the indecent, rebels against society, some remnants of the old gipsy bands, drunkards, pickpockets and loafers. Communist orators found Seatown a good ground for development, and with justice, for there was grinding poverty here, hardship, disease and sickness.

It had been, it appeared, nobody's business to keep the new Seatown of 1913 in repair. Bridge Street and Riverside Street soon brought those smart grey houses into dirt and disorder. Furze himself owned some of the property. Moon some more. The gentlemen of the Town Council never visited it. Harmer John's memorial was overgrown with weeds.

Furze himself was at home there. As now he descended Bridge Street he felt that this was what he liked—no extravagance here, no flummery of silver photograph frames and leather armchairs.

Many of the Seatowners were in his debt as were their grander fellow citizens—little debts, a pound here, ten shillings there, but he knew them all to a penny and the power that the small debts gave him here was the equal of any power he might have above the Rock.

As the misty rain swirled against his umbrella he noticed everything: the small shabby Bridge Street shops glowing with their lights through the murk, M'Canlis the tobacconist, Lugge the old-clothes man, Mrs. Murphy's sweet-shop (here the street paused, elaborating a little square in which most incongruously there was a misshapen statue of Queen Victoria), then, as the street fell downwards again, Ottley's billiard saloon, Locke's Family Hotel, and, at last, at the corner of Bridge Street and Riverside Street the Majestic picture-house, scene of many a scrambling riot.

Round every one of these places and persons hung a family history, every detail of which was known to him—old M'Canlis and his wastrel of a son; Mrs. Murphy, whose daughters were no better than they should be; Ottley's billiard saloon, the principal seat of the wilder Communists; Locke's Family Hotel, a brothel first and a hotel after—he knew them all. He looked in for a word with Mr. M'Canlis, paid Ottley a brief visit, and then, stepping into the rain again, ran full tilt against the broad stout bosom of Gurney, police inspector. Gurney started.

"Why, Mr. Furze, is it? I never saw you."

"Rotten weather, Inspector."

"Rotten it is. . . . Well, so long then, Mr. Furze."

Gurney's round red face with its innocent blue eyes, the broad thick body, the heavy plodding walk—these were perhaps more humorous to Furze than anything else in Polchester. For Gurney was weak, kindly, devoted to wife and children, consciously inefficient, amiably tolerant—all things that Furze despised most deeply. So long as Gurney was Inspector of Police in Polchester, men like Moon and young M'Canlis and Ottley had nothing to fear.

(Later that evening Peter Gurney, seated in front of his fire, pipe in mouth, his youngest child on his knee, confided to Mrs. Gurney: ". . . I was in Bridge Street and there he was, right upon me as you might say, hidden by his old umbrella—I never knew a man for making no sound like that Furze. . . .")

But Furze's business this afternoon was with Moon of the Dog and Pilchard.

The Dog was, and had been for many a year, a place of great importance in Polchester history. It was now approaching the moment of its greatest importance. You would not suppose so if you looked at it. You might, in fact, in this swirl of misty rain, pass it by altogether. The sign, placed there years ago by Hogg, painted by that mad fellow Davray, who had haunted the place too much for his good, still swung there, almost invisible in this dusk, creaking like a crying baby through the confused chatter of the river, which fell in a kind of waterfall over a stone ridge just at this point. The sign showed a brown dog gazing despondently at a heap of silver pilchard, brown and silver faded by now, and a brave splash of crimson sky almost fallen to darkness.

For hundreds of years there had been some kind of drinking place on this very spot. Murder had been committed here, the story ran, in Elizabethan days, when some poor vagrant had been robbed and his throat cut. But he was not the only man who had died here. . . . Its life had been thick, tortuous, dark and sinister. So it was still. No one could bring light into that main central room. Once there had been candles, then gas, now electricity, but still the murk and steam and fog hung there, and behind the bar Lanky Moon watched the world that he governed.

High above the town the Cathedral, at its bottom the Dog. Some power in common between the two? A power, at least, of history, a force gathered through time from the passions and furies and prayers of men. And at last the two forces were to meet. . . .

Within the central room there was always the sound of the tumbling river and the low voices of men. Often the voices would rise, laughter, quarrelling, a sudden shout, and with the voices the sound of the river also seemed to rise.

To Furze it was all exceedingly familiar. He entered now, sat down in a corner and waited for Moon to come over to him. The bar was closed and the tables cleared, but some of Moon's regular customers were still keeping him company. He noticed young M'Canlis and a girl, Fanny Clarke, a wild, loose, good-looking young ne'er-do-well, and Tom Caul. Caul was a bruiser, over six foot, thick and broad, a boxer of some Glebeshire and Cornish fame until evil habits had rotted his body. A man with a brooding sense of injustice, given to passionate tempers, with some gift of speech. He called himself a Communist, having as his only desire a general robbing, burning, destruction of all and sundry. Behind his wildness there was a certain dim philosophy.

Moon came over to Furze and sat down.

"Well, Mr. Furze, how's yourself today?"

But Furze wasted no time.

"Look here, Lanky, what about the Foster house in Bridge Street? Is that woman turning out or isn't she?"

"I don't know. She's very sick."

"Will she die, do you think?"

"I shouldn't wonder."

"We could get another family in there with a little squeezing. The Benches would move in."

"It's a bit crowded as it is, Mr. Furze."

"There's that room at the back. There's only old Foster there. If Mrs. Foster goes the old man would have to go too."

"Yes, that's right, Mr. Furze."

"I passed Gurney as I came down."

"Yes, he's been in here just now. He told us to clear."

"What was he wanting?"

"Oh, I don't know. Looking around. He's a bloody bastard, he is."

Furze went on: "I heard last week that there's talk again in the Upper Town of looking into things down here."

"The hell there is!"

"Yes. Once every five years or so they get a fit of it."

"Who's behind it now?"

"Hattaway chiefly. He's always talking of pulling the whole place down. He's been talking to Carris and one or two more."

"What he wants," said Moon darkly, "is a knock on the head one night—interfering bastard."

They both looked up and gazed, speculatively, at Caul, who lounged his great bulk over a table, murmuring to the beautiful Fanny, who was yawning and picking her teeth.

"There's a lot of discontent down here," Moon said in the tone of a benevolent philanthropist. "Things are bad. What the hell? Do they think their bloody dole makes the world a Paradise? That's what *I* want to know. Running about in their Rolls-Royces." He dropped the philanthropy. "See here, Mr. Furze, can you let me have ten quid?"

"Yes—on conditions."

They talked for a while, then Furze got up.

"I'll be moving. Let me know about that house in Bridge Street." He went across to Caul. He stood there, his broad-brimmed bowler dominating them.

"Well, Caul, how is it?"

"Bloody bad, Mr. Furze."

"Why don't you get something to do? There's some work up at the St. Leath. They're making a new tennis court. I could put in a word for you."

Caul stretched his huge arms.

"No thanks, Mr. Furze. None of their bloody tennis courts for me."

"I hear you were speaking out at Goston the other night."

Caul raised himself. A look of pride and almost of nobility came into his dark stubbly countenance.

"Yes, Mr. Furze—I talked a bit."

"Good. I must come and hear you some night."

Furze put out his hand and touched the man's shoulder. Caul remained passive, submissive.

"Good-evening, all. I must be getting on."

When he came out the rain had ceased. With that cessation everything had changed. The November afternoon was sinking into dusk, but above the river and rising fields a pool of pale gold light, cupped like a mountain tarn between two crags of dark sky, suggested deep upon deep of colour. Very faintly the reflection from it lay upon the river and feebly lit the windows of the Dog. The street glittered like steel from the rain. Trees on the opposite bank were softened at the heart of their darkness. Behind him the town piled up, undistinguishable in detail, like a fortress above the Rock.

He had no eyes for beauty, which was a thing beyond price and therefore worthless. Nor, when he reached the Market-place, did he feel the contrast between the silent disorder of that Lower Town where he had just been, and here where all was bustle, noise and business. Lights were springing up like flowers behind the windows; in the half dusk, under this same pool of gold, now fainter, dimmer, gold upon white now, a hud-dle of sheep were moving out of the market, two motorcars panting impatiently behind them.

He wished for a word with Crispangle, so he turned into the Smith bookshop. Crispangle mentioned Furze's brother; coming out of the shop Furze stayed for a moment and thought of him. It was at this moment that his austere idealism was more abruptly offended than at any time during the afternoon. Crisp-angle had spoken of Michael as a friend, and this disgusted Furze. And now he must return to find that fellow lounging about the house, eating his food, spying on him. . . . Mingled strangely with the disgust was a suggestion of fear. He did not doubt but that Michael would do him a harm had he a chance, but it was more that Michael was forever talking. For years there had been silence in that house and now it was con-tinually broken with that waster's chatter.

He said things that broke Furze's concentration on his own affairs. For example, a dream that he had had about a yellow-faced man with a broken neck emerging from the Cathedral door in silence upon a listening town. Nothing in it, but for some reason it had remained in Furze's mind.

Another thing had caught his attention. Chatter about a crucifix that he had sold to Klitch, that he hoped shortly to redeem, something that he loved most in the world. . . . For some reason this selling of the crucifix and the yellow-faced man with the twisted neck remained together, connected uneasily in Furze's mind. He had a mighty brain for detail—nothing was too small for his retentive memory—he remembered all that Michael had said about that crucifix. The thing that he loved most in the world. . . .

A thought struck him. He had started down the High Street homewards, but now he turned. He would see this crucifix. Something pleased him. A thin pale smile gave him, for a brief moment, the semblance of a shadow against the wall brought into solidity by a joke. The bowler hat moved upwards to Arden Gate.

He paused and looked at the Cathedral before he turned into Klitch's shop. The Precincts were quite silent; the evening light cast one frail cloak of pallid glow on the Cathedral walls before darkness swallowed them. Staring contemptuously—for he despised the Cathedral as an outworn worthless collection of junk—he was conscious, unexpectedly, of a discomfort, a dis-ease. In this half-dark you could fancy that a figure emerged, a small and silent procession. . . .

But imagination of this sort was not his fashion. He dealt in facts, facts that could be bought and sold.

He knew that Klitch disliked him. He knew, too, that here was a man over whom he would never have any power, so that his visit was brief. He said that his brother had told him about a crucifix that he had sold. Might he see it?

Klitch produced it. Furze studied it. How much would that be now? Klitch told him. A large sum. But it would keep its value, it was a fine piece? Klitch reassured him. Even in these poor days it would always fetch a good sum. A magnificent piece. Furze touched it. Cold to the touch. He disliked the figure of the Christ—Christ, a lamentable charlatan. . . . How long before the crucifix passed into Klitch's possession? Not so long now. And then Klitch might sell it to anyone he pleased? Yes, that was the bargain.

"I ask because I might myself be the purchaser. It would give my brother great pleasure. I should be distressed if he lost it."

The notion that Stephen Furze would be distressed at such

a thing seemed to Klitch very comic, but he gave no sign.

"Will you be so good as to let me know when it comes into your possession?"

Klitch promised.

"What's the old swine after now?" he thought. "Surely he will never pay such a price?"

"Good-evening, Mr. Klitch."

"Evening, Mr. Furze."

CHAPTER VII

Christmas Eve: I. In the Town

CHRISTMAS EVE was on a Saturday this year. The weather was bright, sharp, with a suggestion of warmth behind it.

Although the sky was a winter's blue and the sun shone through a faint mist, yet you could be reminded that, not so very far south, palm trees grew in the open, and that in the Scillies there would be, in a week or two, a soil covered with flowers.

Everyone, of course, was busied with the last purchases. There was a kind of Christmas fair in the Market-place, all according to custom, and, as the clouds turned to rose above the river, the lights came out in the shops, flared on the booths, the candles burnt on the High Altar.

Polchester, although a staid country town, had often known moments when it appeared to be driven by some corporate movement—of joy, of fear, of wonder, of commercial ambition.

A very happy and cheerful spirit drove it now in spite of hard times, threatening politics, world disorder. It was still able to withdraw itself and create a life altogether its own, as though it were the solitary body of living men rolling along on the surface of a dark naked planet. For an hour or two at least it had its own mood, its individual life.

Penny Marlowe, working her last on her Christmas gifts alone in her room, was so happy that a modern cynic would have considered her thoroughly wicked.

BOANERGES

Being very young and having, as yet, travelled abroad but
little, she considered her bedroom simply the most beautiful
in the world. It was lit with candles, the electric light having
fused only the evening before. There were two on the dressing
table, two on the writing table and one beside her bed. The room
had known little change for many years. It was furnished with
one of the very earliest and one of the most beautiful of the
Morris wall-papers, the "Daisy" pattern; this was faded
now, but it still had the freshness of early spring flowers. There
was an old dark clothespress, a screen pasted with pictures from the illustrated papers, a bookcase that held books
very queerly mixed, for there were the loves of her childhood,
The Pillars of the House and *The Chaplet of Pearls*, Tennyson's
Idylls and Dickens and Scott—these innocents keeping company with *Sons and Lovers*, *Vile Bodies* by Mr. Evelyn Waugh,
and T. S. Eliot's *Waste Land*. Penny did not understand a word
of *The Waste Land*, but it had been given her last Christmas by
young Stephen Braund, who was in his second year at Oxford
and was himself a poet.

Penny was wearing a frock of bright apple green and, kneeling
on the floor, made parcels, tied string and sang while she did
so. She was happy because she loved Christmas, because it was
enchanting to be given presents, yet more enchanting to give
them, and for one more reason, which will be, in a moment, apparent. She thought that she had chosen well: a new book on
Chess for her father, and a pair of warm gloves; a piece of old
lace for her mother and a water colour of the Cathedral that
she had bought at a bazaar; handkerchiefs for the servants; one
thing and another thing for her various friends (these she would
shortly herself leave with her own hands at the doors of her
friends)—and one thing more.

This last was her most serious consideration. It was a small
replica of Donatello's David. She had seen this, a few weeks
earlier, in the window of Klitch's shop and had at once entered
and purchased it, although it was more than she could afford.

It was intended for Mr. Lampiron.

As she knelt, her hair illuminated by the candlelight, she

looked very beautiful and very young. The sleeves of the apple-green dress fell forward and encumbered her and she shook them back with an impatient gesture. The flowers on the wall stirred in the shifting candlelight. The room was chill, for there was no fire, but she was not cold. Bending forward, working so busily warmed her, but her face was flushed too with a delicate colour because she was thinking of Mr. Lampiron. Would he be angry with her for her gift? Would he consider it bold of her? She was a modern girl and knew that women must feel no inferiority before men, must say what they think just whenever they please, but she had talked to him only four times in all; he had been very kind to her. He was the grandest, most splendid person she had ever met. . . . But . . . *would* he be offended? Her hands trembled, white against the green of her dress, as she picked up the David. Then she did something very unmodern indeed. She kissed it. The flowers trembled on the wall.

In the house of the Furze family, only a few doors away, Elizabeth Furze was dressed for going out. She carried in her hand two small parcels. She had been looking for something in the bare and chilly dining room. She had realized how chilly it was and had stood there, for a moment, trembling in a great passion of distaste and resentment. Then many years of training brought her control. She stretched up her arm and, with her thin grey-gloved hand, turned the gas down to a crimson beady eye.

As she did so she felt her arm touched and saw that her uncle Michael was standing at her side. He closed the door behind him and they stood close together in the cold dark.

"Look here," her uncle said. "Have you got any money, Elizabeth?"

"No," she answered. She was telling a lie—in her own defence. "I spent it all in this morning's shopping. At least," she continued, "I have a few shillings. But there's collection at the Cathedral and——"

"Oh, a few shillings! That's not what I mean!" She could

feel that he was breathing furiously. He gripped her arm. "No, it's pounds I want. Enough to get away from this bloody hell! Here!" He turned up the gas. "Do you see how I've changed?"

Words began to pour from him while she stood motionless, her grave pale face lit with a kind of beauty of patience and consideration.

"Do you remember what I was when I first came here? You do, don't you? Stout and jolly and red in the face—I was, wasn't I? Didn't everyone like me? Wasn't I the friend of all the town? And now my clothes hang on me! The same suit I had when I came. I haven't had any money to get another. And I haven't had enough to eat. *You* know that I haven't——"

"That hasn't——" she began.

"Oh, I don't blame *you!* It's not your fault nor your mother's. It's that foul, bloody miser your father. That's who it is. Haven't I tried to get jobs everywhere? Haven't I told them all I'm ready to do anything? But will they have me? Not they! Ready enough to drink with me when I was in cash. But now . . . They won't help *his* brother out of a mess, won't have *his* brother hanging round—and I don't blame them either. What did I ever come to this house for? Didn't something warn me what it would be? And here he's got me, got me right at his feet—so that he can torture me and mock me and starve me. . . ."

"Why," she said, "do you stay?"

"Stay? What else can I do? I haven't a penny. He sees to that. I haven't anything to sell either. I might have gone, all the same, if I'd been younger. And this house—it does something to you, or rather *he* does. He saps your strength, your vitality. He's a bloody vampire, that's what he is. Doesn't all the town know it? Doesn't he hang over the whole town like a great shadow? You feel it yourself. I know you do. You wouldn't stay here a day if it weren't for your mother. You can't kid me." He stopped, still gripping her arm. "There! Don't you hear something? He's coming downstairs."

They both listened. No, there was nothing, no sound.

He went on:

"I haven't asked you for money before, have I, Elizabeth? I'm not a bad sort. I'm not really. But he's got me down. I don't know what I won't be doing. He starves me and laughs at me with that damned quietness of his and makes me work. He's *got* me. He's got his fingers digging into my very vitals. Oh, God! I shall do him in one of these days, I know I shall!"

He was trembling. She could feel his hand quivering on her arm. She looked at him and felt a great pity, for her heart was tender and soft. Yes, he *had* changed! His big frame looked weak and unbalanced. His cheeks that had been round and red were now puffy and streaked. His eyes were red-rimmed as though he had been weeping. She knew, too, that it was true what he had said.

They had been speaking with lowered voices. Now it was with little more than a whisper that she said:

"Go away, Uncle Mike! Go away! Even though you haven't any money. I could give you a pound or two perhaps. Then take a train to somewhere—some place where they don't know us. They'll give you work, I'm sure they will."

"Yes," he said eagerly. "I will. You're right. That's what I'll do." He dropped his hand from her arm and patted her shoulder. "You're a good woman, Elizabeth—one of the best I've ever known. I'll never forget——"

But he stopped. He was listening again. He shook his head.

"I don't think that I *can* get away from this damned house. It seems to hold you. I don't feel that I've any strength left." He went on: "Do you know what they called me when I first came here? Boanerges. That means Son of Thunder. Not much like a Son of Thunder now. Not much."

He shook his head.

"I'll see you again. Where are you going now?"

"I'm leaving a few things. Then I'm going to the Carol Service at the Cathedral."

"Oh yes! The Carol Service. I'll see you there."

In St. Paul's Rectory Miss Camilla Porteous and Mr. Bird were hanging holly over the pictures. That was not at all what

Mr. Bird wanted to be doing. He had presents that he wished to deliver—one present in especial—and he was in quite a fever of agitation lest the Rector should give him some work so that he would not be able to be present at the Carol Service at the Cathedral. He was wondering, as he stood holding the steps for Miss Porteous, whether *this* time he might not be strong enough to defy the Rector. He had been growing bolder during these last weeks. Two things were strengthening him—one of these his friendship with Lampiron. While he stood there he was going over the conversation in his mind:

"I'm very sorry, Rector, but I'm going to the Carol Service. . . ."

"Oh yes. Quite so. But what about DUTY, Bird? DUTY— DUTY—and especially at this time of the year——"

"I'm extremely sorry, Rector, but I'm going to the Carol Service. . . ."

The last thing that he wished was to make trouble at Christmas. Nevertheless, Lampiron told him that rebellion must come *some* time—and why not now?

"I'm extremely sorry, Rector, but I'm going——"

Miss Porteous stood, with firm strength, on the little steps, her grand legs like towers. She patted the very ugly oil painting of her grandfather, an old red-faced gentleman with white whiskers and a blue, staring eye.

"There! I think that will do!"

She came down from the steps and stood looking at Mr. Bird tenderly.

"There, Birdie!" (How horrible to him was this diminutive that of late, when they were alone, she had adopted!) "We're nearly done!" How supremely unattractive she was, he thought. Like a man in woman's clothes—and he had a wild notion that she and Romney ought to change garments!

"What do you say to a moment's pause?" She sat down in an armchair, spreading her legs. "You know, I like you so much. Do you like me?"

Mr. Bird stammered.

"That's one of your charms—your modesty. I was saying to

Mrs. Braund the other day that you are one of the most modest men I've ever met! But don't be shy of *me*. I'm the last person to be shy of. Confide in me. Tell me your secrets. I often wonder —I'm queer that way—wondering, I mean—I have thoughts that no one would suspect—why we don't trust one another more, why we're not more tender with one another. I feel sometimes that I want to put my arms round all the world and give it a great hug. Do you never feel like that?"

"No, I can't say that I do," said Mr. Bird.

"And yet I'm sure that you must be full of kindness. We're very alike in many ways. You're like me. You wouldn't hurt a living thing!"

He felt suddenly in a morose temper.

"I don't know. There are mosquitoes and red ants and slugs."

She laughed in a tender brooding kind of way. "Ah, you take me too literally. Of course there are *some* things. What I mean is that we love our fellow human beings. Now tell me. Haven't you felt while you've been here that we have a great deal in common?"

"I don't know," he stammered. "I don't know you, Miss Porteous."

"Don't *know* me!" She stared at him with large reproachful eyes. "Why, Birdie—and whose fault is that? I *want* you to know me. I feel that you, more than anyone else in Polchester, would understand me. Ask me anything you like—*any* question —and I'll answer it. That's what friendship is. And we *are* friends, aren't we?"

"Yes, of course."

"*That's* right. We'll take a long walk one day, Birdie, and talk about *everything*—the loveliness of nature and *everything*. Tell me, Birdie——"

But fortunately at that moment Porteous came in—with a rush of energy, as he always did.

"Well, well—oh, THERE you are, Bird. I was wondering where you were. Not doing anything especial?"

"We are hanging the holly."

"Ah, fine, splendid! Have you finished, because there's a

little thing—Camilla, my dear, have you taken that parcel to Mrs. Abrahams? No? Well, if you *wouldn't* mind . . . And, Bird, I want you to go over to the Probyn Schools and tell Axminster . . .Wait a minute. Come into my study and I'll give you some papers for him. And while you're there you might help him out with the Boys' Evening. I know he's short-handed. . . ."

Now was the time. Bird cleared his throat.

"I thought of going to the Cathedral Carol Service——"

"Cathedral Carol Service? Ah, yes. Of course. Very nice. I'd like to have gone myself, but DUTY—DUTY comes first——"

Bird looked at Miss Porteous, and her bony affectionate face gave him courage.

"You'll have to forgive me," he said. "I saw Axminster last night and he really doesn't need any help. He told me so himself. I'll take the papers over, of course. The Carol Service doesn't begin till eight."

There was a silence. Porteous was quite bewildered as though, captaining England against Scotland in the Calcutta Cup, his best wing three-quarter had suddenly said that he must go home.

"Well, really——" Then he stopped. "All right. I'm a little surprised, Bird. It isn't MY idea of work. Very well. Come to the study and I'll give you the papers."

He strode off, greatly displeased. Mr. Bird followed. This was his first victory.

As Miss Porteous was hanging the holly, Penny Marlowe leaving her parcel at Lampiron's door, the carol singers from St. James's banging the knocker of old Dr. Montefiore's house, a small boy stealing a sugar pig from the Market-place stall of Mrs. Plaice who had once had triplets, young Broad, the verger's boy, trying on long trousers for the first time, the two Miss Trenchards putting the last touches to their Christmas tree (tonight they were having a children's party), Mike Furze plunged downwards to Seatown, not reckoning whither he went.

Had something told him that that moment when he spoke to his niece under the gas in that chilly room was his last instant of security? Did he know that when she said to him "Leave the town!" and he realized that he could not, he was thereafter a doomed man?

It seemed to him as he walked down the hill that everything now was different. He was caught. He was a prisoner. Every direction of escape was closed to him as though he had been snatched by the scruff of his neck and shoved into a cell. It had been coming to this for many a week past, and like a man who has been dreading a doctor's sentence of death he found some relief in certainty. He had not the will power. That was what had left him. It was as though his brother had drawn it from him in a long bloody thread from the centre of his body. Sitting there in his chair, spinning this out of Mike's carcase.

I'm like a rabbit—fascinated by the snake.

He was filled with self-pity. I'm not a bad fellow. I've never done anyone much harm. I can be jolly, I've had heaps of friends. I was cursed the moment I came to this town. The Cathedral—that's what's responsible. And selling that crucifix. But I can get that back. If I could get a job and save . . . But if I *did* get a job my brother would come after me. He'd draw me back into the house again. Where's his power? Filthy swine . . . oh, filthy swine! To do him in, to close your hands round that skinny neck, to press and press, to watch the tongue protrude, black, they say it is. . . . But then that would be murder. They hang you for murder. . . . No. Better if someone else would do the swine in. Plenty of people hated him. Oh, plenty! They'd all murder him if they were sure of not being found out. It would be doing a kindness. He was a pest in the town, a sort of Inquisitor like that figure with the crooked neck he'd dreamt about. He'd read in some book somewhere that everyone had his or her Familiar, a shadow that accompanied you everywhere, knew your most secret thoughts, watched and judged your every movement. So the Cathedral might have an Inquisitor. Ah, but he would be no ordinary spirit, but something tremendous, God's Inquisitor judging all men. He would be immortal. But miser Stephen—*he* was not immortal! One squeeze of the fingers—one hard, hard, HARD squeeze of the fingers . . .

He was, in fact, a trifle light-headed because he had not had enough to eat, poor old Mike! Poor old Mike. Thin tears welled up. He bit his lip for sorrow. No food, no drink, no women, no one to love. Only his brother to hate. . . . Yes, if the Inquisitor looked into *his* soul he would find nothing but an empty impoverished place, and hatred, like a starved black cat, lurking. . . .

Yes, he was light-headed. He lurched a little on his feet. He was in Seatown.

There was M'Canlis' shop. Tobacco. Then he passed Ottley's billiard saloon; now he paused before Locke's Family Hotel.

He knew this was a bawdy shop. He had been there once or twice in his wealthier days. Now there were lights in the window; someone was playing a piano. They were singing. Oh yes, it was Christmas Eve, when everyone must be jolly! He went in and his fantasy continued, for he could not tell you what, during the next hour, his speech and his actions were.

There was Fanny Clarke. She was sitting on his knee. He put his hand inside her dress; she rubbed her cheek against his. Someone gave him sausage and bread to eat. They were all eating bread and sausages. Someone gave him whisky to drink. They were all drinking. There was mistletoe hanging from the lamp in the centre of the room, the room where the oilcloth had yellow and black squares, and the big black cat reared on its hind legs spitting; and Fanny's breasts were warm and firm and he would kiss her under the mistletoe, but it was Tom Caul's unshaven cheek that he touched—Tom Caul, who, standing in open shirt and trousers, was spitting out pips from the orange that he was eating, and they struck the hard shining oilcloth, and Tom's hairy chest was bare, sweat gleamed on it, for the room was very hot.

But Mike was sober enough. Oh yes, the Inquisitor with the broken neck could find nothing to criticize here, so he led Caul aside and, very seriously, his hand on Caul's shoulder, dropping his voice so that no one should hear, said: "The best way to kill him is to press your fingers into his neck. It wouldn't take much to throttle him."

"Sure," said Caul. "That's a good way."

"A dam' good way."

"Sure," said Caul. "I was telling you."

"And no one but you and the Inquisitor knowing anything about it."

"Who the hell . . . ?"

But Caul stank. He can't have washed for a month, and the sweat running down his body . . . A big man, with mighty arms. What hands and what fingers! They say he speaks finely—and the smell of Caul became familiar to Mike, and friendly, and their arms were about one another's waists, swaying, their bodies were on the table covered with oilcloth. Oilcloth everywhere. . . .

"It's Christmas Eve," Mike said.

"A bloody fine Christmas Eve," Caul said.

So at that Mike knew that he must go to the Cathedral for the Carol Service. He laid his hand for a moment on Caul's damp thick strong neck and went out.

The little station at Carpledon had been once (when for instance in Jubilee Year, '97, Archdeacon Brandon had taken the train to have luncheon with good Bishop Purcell and had quarrelled so unfortunately with Canon Ronder) nothing more than a wooden shed. Now there is an important-looking station and a hotel, the Carpledon, and the long level fields above the Pol will be, they say, very shortly a flying-ground.

But the Bishop's palace is still guarded by its woods, fronted with its broad shaven shelving lawns—old, thickset, the tiled rosy-red roof, the bell tower, the high doorway with the carved arms and the two shaggy lions, above all the oaks, the great historic one to the right of the lawn magnificent and proud as ever—all this is here and will be ever here, even when outer forms are destroyed, for its spirit is immortal.

At the moment when the oilcloth of Locke's Family Hotel stirred Boanerges to bewildered confidences, Bishop Kendon was standing in the dining room watching Coniston the butler and Alfred the boy hang the holly over Driver's Knight and the

Lady. The room was little changed from Bishop Purcell's day, the high-ceiled dining room, the red-brick fireplace fronted with black oak beams. There was a glass bowl with Christmas roses on the long refectory table, and from the white walls the Bishops, starting with Bishop Sandiford of 1670, ending with Bishop Rostron who succeeded old Purcell, looked smilingly, austerely, pompously down on the long spare body of their successor. Kendon was well over six feet and as thin as a stick. He was seventy-three years of age, but straight of body and hair still jet-black. He had a thin hawk-like face, with eyes singularly soft and beautiful. He suffered from severe cardiac trouble and had been, only last year, in bed for six long months—a stern discipline for his ardent restless spirit, and he had borne it with marvellous patience and humour. Dr. Montefiore had warned him that the days left to him on this earth would be few. He loved life with a passion, but he was ready to go, for he thought that his work here was done and that the next world would be a fine place to labour in.

He was watching Coniston's efforts with a twinkle, for Coniston was short and fat, breathed through his nose, and made little noises like "Dash it!" and "Bother!" when the holly was pugnacious and hostile, as holly often is. Coniston was a bachelor and had been with the Bishop for forty years.

The Bishop was his whole life, the beginning and middle and end of it.

"There, Coniston. That will do. You've told Frank to have the car round at quarter-past seven?"

Coniston came down from the ladder.

"Chut, Alfred," he said as the ladder wobbled. He turned a round, red, anxious face to his master. "You think you ought to go, my lord?"

"Of course I ought to go. When have I missed a Carol Service?"

"Certainly, my lord. But last year it didn't do you any good, and you *will* stop talking afterwards, and there are all the services tomorrow——"

"That's all right, Coniston."

"Very good, my lord."

The Bishop knew that the end might come for him at any moment. But why not? Where could one die better than in the Cathedral? Hadn't dear old Moffit been lucky the other day, passing over as he did in one instant of suspended breath? There was an hour before supper and he would enjoy himself. He crossed over to the library, humming and thinking what a good time Christmas Eve was, with the smell of holly and the sharp air, good things cooking in the kitchen, the Christ Child in the manger, the shepherds watching the Star, the Kings with their gifts. . . .

In the library he put on some records of the *Winterreise* cycle. Schubert had been, his whole life through, his intimate devotion. It was as though he had been his friend and companion. The brilliant "Biedermeier" world of Vienna he knew as though he had been part of it. He had been surely present at the first performance of *Sappho* at the Burgtheater, had admired Grillparzer's pale honey-coloured curls, had drawn his breath in astonished delight as Fanny Elssler danced before him, had laughed at Meisl's farces, shouted applause at Raimund's *Diamant des Geisterkönigs*, marvelled at Nestroy's acting, when, with the lifting of an eyelid, the humorous, scornful curl of a lip, he filled with emphasis the empty spoken word, best of all, danced (oh! how he had danced!) on the Kahlenberg at the Feast of Violets. But Schubert, with the low forehead, the snub nose, the dark curly hair, the eyeglasses—he was his brother, his friend, his constant companion. How often he had watched to catch that sudden genius-fire flash from behind those glasses! How well he knew the loneliness, the dark despair, the longing for love, the struggle, the poverty, the passion for friendship! Yes, with Schwind and Schober, with Joseph von Spaun, with Mayrhofer and Sauter, with Hüttenbrenner and Randhartinger, he had been and was Schubert's friend. Now, as he listened to the Wanderer's, "Gute Nacht," tears filled his eyes. Beyond the pain comes consolation. The spring will follow the winter. The post-horn sounds, the day breaks in storm, the world is awake again and the organ grinder, his empty plate at his side, grinds out his wheezy melody. . . .

The record ceased. The only sounds in the library were the dim rustle of the fire and the little friendly "check-check" of the clock. The past? The present? We are all in God's hands. God, Who knows nothing of time, Who holds us in His arms, knowing that our sorrow is only prelude to deeper knowledge of His love.

The Bishop smiled and, bending forward to the cabinet, found the "Gloria in excelsis Deo" from the E flat major mass.

"I see God's beauty burning through the veil of outward things."

The hour, seven o'clock, sounded from the Cathedral. Then the chimes began, softly carrying the town forward with them. The shops were still open. In Orange Street and Myre Street, up the High Street through the Precincts, in Canon's Yard, in Pontippy Square, by Tontine Bridge, at the Three Feathers and the Bull and the St. Leath, along Norman Row, every house was busy with preparation.

Behind many windows the blinds were not yet drawn, and you might see, if you wished, like sparkling pictures, rooms with fires burning, holly bristling on the walls, life everywhere moving and stirring to the event. Flame burning within the stone, stars scattering the sky where there were no clouds, the air listening and still as though it caught its breath. . . .

Lampiron stepped into Smith's before going on to the Cathedral. Here then was quite a gathering—Hattaway the architect, Bellamy, and, of all people, old Mordaunt, his shawl over his shoulders. Crispangle, the business duties of the day over, was host, looking as though he had himself written all the books in his shop and knew that they were good.

"Here's Lampiron," Hattaway said. "We'll see what he thinks about it."

"Thinks about what?" Lampiron said, picking up a book here and a book there. He could never see a book without wanting to touch it. Then he went on: "Look here, Crispangle, I want a book for a girl. I'm glad you're still open. I thought I'd be too late."

"It's Christmas Eve. What kind of a girl? What kind of a book?"

"Oh, modern—and not too modern."

"That's helpful. Do you want a novel?"

"No. Not a novel——"

He found a pocket edition of Norman Douglas' *South Wind.* "That's good, isn't it?"

"Very good—but it's a novel—or sort of."

Lampiron began to read, his broad body rocking a little on its stout legs. Soon he was lost.

"Here—come out of it, Lampiron," Hattaway said. "Crispangle's been cursing this pageant. He says that it's a monstrous imposition on the town, that it's a mockery to give Mrs. Braund the chief part, that the Committee's ridiculous, that the Town has to pay and will get nothing for it, that the unemployed are going to make a row because of the expense, that——"

"Well, I don't see why *he* need worry," Lampiron said. "The shop people are going to benefit more than anybody. Think of the trade it's going to bring."

"Oh, will it?" Crispangle said scornfully. "Supposing it's wet? And who's going to come and see a pageant so mismanaged that it will be a scandal all over the south of England? Anyway, why should the Cathedral people run it? Blasted snobs the lot of them! We're among friends here and I can tell you that Ma Braund will look a fine sight on a horse! And there's the Archdeacon, so above himself that he'll scarcely condescend to speak to you." He imitated the Archdeacon's rich and solemn tones. "'Ah, Crispangle, how are you? I want Stephens's on *The Creeds*. What! Not got Stephens? Impossible! I thought you were a bookshop.'"

They all laughed.

"No. This won't do," Lampiron said, putting *South Wind* down. "She wouldn't like this."

"What about Masefield or Noyes or Barrie or Milne?"

"Nonsense!" Lampiron stood, sniffing like a dog at the shelves. "Ah, here's a book!" He had found Samuel Butler's *Notebooks*. "Here's the very thing, even if he does say Handel's better than Beethoven."

"If you want to know what I think," Crispangle went on, "this damned pageant is going to do nothing but make ill-feeling and then be a financial failure on top of it. This town will never move forward until the Cathedral people know their place. They stop every improvement. They belong two generations back, the whole lot of them. There's something wrong about this town, with Seatown in the state it is and that swine Furze with half the place in his debt——"

He stopped, as men so often did when Furze's name was mentioned. Lampiron thought, That devil—he keeps me hanging like a fish on a line. . . . From week to week. . . . It's fiendish. . . . Crispangle looked about him. "Why, that man's a devil! See what he's done to his brother. He was a cheery, jolly sort of ruffian when he came here. *Now* look at him! Down at heel, hang-dog——"

"All the same," said Bellamy, "I don't see what Furze has to do with the Pageant."

"He has to do with everything. It would be the best thing ever happened if someone wrung his skinny neck. Why, even decent old souls like Mr. Marlowe, they say——"

Here, to everyone's surprise, Lampiron broke in, violent as he often was:

"All right, Crispangle. Keep the Marlowes out of it. They're friends of mine. There's enough gossip without your adding to it. Here—what do I owe you for the Butler?"

Then old Mordaunt most unexpectedly came forward and, poking his nose into Hattaway's face, said:

"The Cathedral won't like it, you know."

"Won't like what?" Hattaway asked.

"All this play-acting. Making fun of them all. They're not so dead as you think they are."

"What! The Black Bishop and Lady Emily and the rest?

They're not making fun of them. They're going to glorify them! It's in their honour."

"Mr. Mordaunt's right," Crispangle said. "It's desecration, that's what it is! Mrs. Braund on a horse pretending to be Lady Emily, and the Boy Scouts, their heads sticking out of sacks, thinking they're monks. But that's not what I object to—Lady Emily and the rest can look after themselves. It's the airs the Cathedral lot give themselves that I object to—and so will plenty of other people too!"

"I know what it is, Crispangle," Bellamy said, laughing. "It's all because they haven't asked you to play a part."

"Oh, to hell with them!" Crispangle answered. "I wouldn't take a part if they asked me!"

"Oh, wouldn't you! But you needn't worry. They haven't asked any of us either. And there's Lampiron there, who'd be a perfect Black Bishop——"

"As a matter of fact," Lampiron said quietly, "that's what I'm going to be."

"What!" they all cried.

"Yes. I had a note from Aldridge two days ago. I don't mind. Perhaps someone will buy my sculpture when they see how fine I am in armour!"

"Well, I'm damned!" Bellamy said. "Can you ride a horse?"

"Of course I can ride a horse!" But he had turned away from them and, sitting on a chair in a corner behind the popular novels, he took out his fountain-pen and wrote in the Butler:

FOR PENELOPE MARLOWE
from her friend
JOHN LAMPIRON.
Christmas 1932.

He stared at the book.

"Put that in paper for me, will you, Crispangle?"

"I'm surprised they've asked you, Lampiron," Crispangle said, taking the book. "I should have thought you were too much of a pagan."

"If you ask me," Bellamy said, "the old Bishop was nothing but a pagan himself."

"I'll tell you what, Lampiron," Crispangle said darkly. "This will bring you nothing but trouble."

Hattaway went out, and through the opening door the Cathedral chimes floated into the shop.

From Locke's Family Hotel to the Dog and Pilchard is a short step. Mike Furze took it. He even sat in that same corner where his brother had but lately sat.

Lanky gave him a drink for Christmas-time. What he did there, what he said there, he did not himself know; it would later have its proper significance. It is probable that he boasted, that he raged, that he snivelled. It is certain that he danced on the rough uneven floor with two women from Portoloe, and seeing, through a mist of smoke, drink and misery, the big body of Caul (who, maybe, had followed him down) once more, danced with him too.

"Yes," says Caul, holding him, "and what was it you was saying about twisting the old bastard's neck?"

But he knew nothing of what happened at the Dog. Afterwards he found himself at the riverside in the sharp air, a net of stars that like silver fish swam in a great inverted bowl above his head. So it seemed to him. He heard the rush of water tumbling over the weir, a song from behind a lighted window, smelt tar, dung, drainage, stale clothing—Seatown's smell. . . .

And then his head cleared. In an instant. Through the chill refreshing air the Cathedral peal rocked to his feet. He knew where he was. He knew what time it must be. He knew that he must go to the Carol Service.

He climbed up crooked, stinking Daffodil Street, that was the quickest way, steep and cobbled though it was, into the Market-place. He had always had the capacity to clear himself, in a moment, of the fuddle of a debauch. It was not that in these last hours he had been debauched. He had been drunk on unhappiness and loneliness more than on any liquor; but now, as he climbed slowly the dark hill, edging that famous Rock from whose height once so many mighty men-at-arms had been pushed, blaspheming, he was sober with a cold intensity of miserable desolation. Here it was, Christmas Eve, a fine Christmas Eve, the sky packed with stars and everyone within doors enjoying themselves. And he was in worse case than having no home at all. He clenched his cold fists and vowed that he would not return to that house. He would sleep in the street rather. He would never set eyes on his vile brother again. He would go to the Cathedral, listen to the singing, pray for safety to that all-powerful Inquisitor—guardian, tyrant, like that old sea captain he had once sailed with who must poke his crooked nose into everyone's affairs, so that he had seen the ship's cook . . . No, like his beloved crucifix rather, the patient Figure stretched on the Cross—a Figure, at least, so tall and so dark, watching at the Great Door, or, with broken neck, issuing forth while the multitude, hidden, waited . . .

He was in the Market-place, where the Fair was ended; most of the booths were gone. Here the Cathedral bells were very loud, echoing from house to house, ringing with such gaiety, such kindliness, inviting, persuading. . . . He all but tumbled into William Caul, the elder blind brother of that ruffian in Seatown. William Caul had been blind from birth and for many years had kept a stall of odds-and-ends in the Market—second-hand books, cheap pictures, scraps of brass and old silver. He was a widower and was cared for by his girl, a child of fourteen or so. He was a thin, grey-faced little man with a pale wispy beard. The light was still burning above his stall. He was standing there alone. He heard Mike's step and lifted his face, gazing with intent watchfulness.

"Evening, Mr. Caul," Mike said, feeling, he knew not why, a sudden comfort. The bells cheered him, and this blind man, at least, would neither know nor care that evil times had fallen on him. "I'm Mike Furze," he said, touching the man's sleeve. He had often enough stopped at his stall, turning the books over, examining the scraps of silver. "You're after the rest," he went on. "They've gone home, all of them."

"Why, Mr. Furze, it's you, is it? Mr. *Michael* Furze?"

"Yes," Mike said roughly. "Can't you tell my voice from my brother's?"

Caul put out his hand, touched Mike's sleeve, then caught his hand and held it.

"Why, of course," he said. "But it's by the touch of the hand I can tell best. There are some hands I would tell among a thousand, and yours is one of them, Mr. Furze."

Caul's hand was chill and bony.

"Why, what is there especial about my hand?" Mike asked.

"It's hard in the middle of the palm and soft and warm the rest. Strong and soft both together. And you have a scar on your thumb. First time I ever held it I noticed that scar. You have freckles on your hand."

"Why," said Mike, "you ought to be a detective."

"So I oftentimes think," Caul said with a chuckle. "And so I warn my young brother. He'll get himself into trouble one of these days."

"Trade been good?"

"Oughtn't to complain, but it's Christmas-time of course."

"I must be getting on. I'm going to the Carol Service."

"And I'm going in to my supper. Ah, here's my girl." His ears had detected her step, but to Mike it was as though the child, hidden in a shabby black overcoat too big for her, had appeared from nowhere at all. "Ellen, you're late."

Mike detached his hand.

"I must go on or I shan't get a place. The Carols are very popular, I hear."

"Aye, it's a sort of old fashion. Never been myself. My wireless is good enough for me. They have a fine music-hall show Saturdays."

"Good-night, Mr. Caul. Happy Christmas."

"And happy Christmas to *you*, Mr. Furze."

Mike went on, up the High Street.

Ronder was entertaining a friend or two to a meal before the Carol Service. Gaselee, Romney, Cronin were his guests. The drawing room where they sat, waiting for the announcement of supper, was exactly as it had always been. The chair cushions, the curtains of the mullioned windows, were of the same warm dark blue. The low bookcases were white, and in his corner still stood the pure white Hermes on his pedestal, his tiny wings outspread. Still there was only one picture, the copy of Rembrandt's Mother.

The difference between now and thirty-five years ago was that the room today was clothed with an old-fashioned charm.

"I'm a trifle excited this evening," Ronder said; his hands were comfortably folded over his paunch. "I received from my London bookseller the rare postscript to Rolfe's *History of the Borgias*. A great rarity——"

"Why is it rare?" Cronin, who was fat, good-natured, extremely High Church, loved to ask questions. He hoped to entrap the interrogated, having a very high opinion of his own intellectual astuteness.

"Well," Ronder said, tapping the tips of his fingers together, "the publishers wouldn't print it with the book because of its subject—the rather savage affection some of the Borgias had for their page boys."

Gaselee felt uncomfortable. He detested in his secret heart anything likely to upset the settled order of society. So long as society was properly ordered, his own career would decently progress. Either Communism or Fascism was repulsive to him; disorderly morals, also, perhaps because he remembered Charlie Radcliffe long, long ago at school.

"It must have been simply *too* wonderful," Romney said, picking up a very perfect copy of John Gray's *Silverpoints* that lay on a table at his side. "The Borgias. All purple, frosted silver, a page painted in gold-dust from head to feet carrying a crimson macaw. There's to be a scene in the Pageant when Henry Quair, the Franciscan, interrupts the fair on the Cathedral Green. The Knights come out of the West Door, and I want them to be in gold armour and a page carrying a crimson macaw. . . ."

"Oh, yes," said Ronder, lazily. "What about the Pageant? How do *you* think it's getting on?"

"Quite well, I think," Gaselee said. "But it's a terrible lot of work. We seem to meet every day, don't we?"

"I hear there's a good deal of feeling in the town. None of the townspeople appear to have been given good parts. Isn't that rather tactless?"

"I don't know. Lampiron is to be the Black Bishop."

"Lampiron is, is he? That's interesting. He's a bit old. And he's scarcely a townsman."

"What about that old miser Furze for Henry Quair?" Cronin asked, laughing.

"Now it's an extraordinary thing," Ronder said. "Remind me, Romney, to show you Lord de Tabley's *Poems*. The cover is really very fine. . . . What was I saying? . . . Oh yes, it's an extraordinary thing, but I never go anywhere without hearing about that man. He seems to have cast a kind of spell over the town. Why?"

"He's hated," Gaselee said. "As though he's the devil himself. It does happen sometimes. I remember when I was at Drymouth for a while there was a hunchback there who was said to be a sorcerer, used to throw spells on people and that sort of thing, you know. He was quite harmless, I believe, but a lot of roughs took him and threw him into the sea one day. Quite mediæval. However, this Stephen Furze *isn't* harmless if all I hear is true. As bad a usurer as they make them."

"Why doesn't someone catch him out and have him up before a magistrate?" Ronder asked.

"Oh, he's as clever as can be. The report is he's pretty well a millionaire, but he starves his wife and daughter and brother quite shockingly. His wife's blind."

"Oh, he's got a brother, has he?"

"Yes—arrived from somewhere in September. Quite a noisy, cheerful man then. Now he moves about as though he had a murder on his conscience."

"Have I seen the miser?" Ronder asked. "I must have, I suppose."

"I expect so. A thin, cadaverous man, often with a green umbrella. He steps about like a ghost."

"I also hear," said Ronder, "there's a lot of trouble breeding down in Seatown. The unemployed think money ought to be spent on *them* instead of a pageant!"

"What nonsense!" Gaselee said. "Why, the Pageant will be the finest thing for Polchester there's ever been. The best advertisement the town's ever had."

"It's had quite a lot in its time," Ronder murmured.

For he was suddenly bored, in a way that was common with him these days. What did pageants and misers and Borgias and rare books and conversations like these amount to at the end? At the end? He moved in his chair. He heard the Cathedral bells chiming beyond the window. He looked at the Hermes. Did *that* also amount to nothing? There was a taste, salt and dry, in his mouth.

Supper was announced.

"Ah, come along. Hope you're hungry . . ." He looked at the holly perched precariously above the Rembrandt. Christmas Eve. What a terrible number of Christmas Eves he'd seen by now!

As Mike Furze started up the High Street his niece Elizabeth had but just left a small parcel at the door of No. 32 Orange Street. The parcel contained a pair of warm lined gloves and was addressed to the Reverend James Bird. On the top of the gloves was lying a card, and on the card was written:

THE REVEREND JAMES BIRD.
With best Christmas wishes from Elizabeth Furze.

This was the boldest action of all her life. Indeed she had thought that she would never have the courage to deliver it. It was not that she knew Mr. Bird very well. Their meetings had been, in the last weeks, frequent and very brief, always in some public place. She did her meagre shopping between eleven and twelve of a morning; most of it was at Bellamy's general store, for Mr. Cutts, one of the assistants, was always kind and attentive to her; she shrank from entering any place where her desperate sensitiveness might be alarmed. It happened often that Mr. Bird was passing up the High Street as she came down it. He would stop and speak to her; once or twice he turned and walked with her a little way. He was always very quiet, unobtrusive. He seemed to be glad to speak to her. It was a fact that she had no friends at all in Polchester and hitherto had thought that she wished for none. One or two were kind to her when they met her—that nice Canon, Mr. Dale, the Misses Trenchard, one funny old lady, Mrs. Dickens, who lodged with that fearful woman, Mrs. Coole—but she felt always that they must be ashamed to be seen speaking to her. "That dreadful man's daughter . . ."

Instinctively she knew that Mr. Bird was not ashamed, and after a while she fancied (although this was of course absurd!) that he was pleased to be with her, and once he had seen her from the other side of the street and hurried across to her. She liked him so very much. She had had no one all her life to love save her mother, and her mother had, within her, a dumb hard resistance to approach that came from hard experience and deep-abiding sorrow.

But Elizabeth's heart was as warm and ardent as her independence was fierce and stubborn. She would *seek* love from no one. She would go on to the end alone, as many other women must do, and would ask for help from no human being. But the point about Mr. Bird was that he himself wanted help. He told her very little of his circumstances, but she knew that he was almost as lonely as she, that he was timid and shy and afraid of women. He told her once that he had made friends with Lampiron, the sculptor, and what a fine man he was and how many troubles he had; but this made Elizabeth nervous and frightened, for she knew whence Lampiron's troubles came and that he was one of her father's most unhappy debtors. She had wondered then for a moment whether *this* could be the reason that Mr. Bird had sought her out; soon he would ask her to plead with her father on Mr. Lampiron's behalf. But no; he never made any allusion to her father. He seemed to understand with wonderful tact and sympathy how not to frighten and alarm her.

She had soon to confess to herself that she looked out for him, and that it was a happy moment for her when she saw his neat little figure, felt the touch of his hand, and caught the smiling generosity of his brown eyes as he greeted her. She was not at all a sentimental woman. She hated demonstrations. She had a great sensitiveness to being touched by strangers or anyone for whom she did not care. She thought most novels foolish and that women were silly to surrender to men, to be subservient, to ask for favours. She disliked most men and could be infuriated often by the airs that men gave themselves. But Mr. Bird was lonely, and she was sure that he must be most unhappy with that noisy self-confident Mr. Porteous and his long-legged masculine daughter.

Nevertheless, she would never confess to herself how very glad she was to see him.

As Christmas approached she thought of him very much and of what a lonely time he would have. Why should she not give him something? It would do no harm. If he thought it bold of her she did not care, and, in any case, women in these days were every bit as good as men, if not better!

She had a very little money of her own, some twenty pounds or so which she kept hidden away, under her clothes in a drawer. It was one of her constant fears that one day her father would discover this store! So she was bold. She bought the gloves, she wrote the card, she left the parcel!

She stood for a moment before turning on up Hay Street into Green Lane, which was a short cut to the Cathedral. The street was well lit, and overhead a fine mesh of stars burned in the sky. She sighed, shook her head at her daring, then, a grave solitary figure, started up past the Statue.

Someone passed her and paused.

"Why, Elizabeth, good-evening!"

It was her father's jackal, Major Leggett, his bowler hat cocked on one side of his head, a smart light overcoat and a green silk muffler with white spots decorating his ugly body. Yes, ugly to her he was and detested by her!

She said good-evening.

"And what are *you* doing here?"

"I am going to the Carol Service."

"Leaving Christmas gifts on the way. Who can the happy man be? I shall have to tell your father of this!"

He was always facetious with her, always spoke to her as though she were a little girl of ten. One of his chief pleasures was to try to shock her with indecent stories, and sometimes he would pretend to make love to her, hating her as she very well knew he did. But she smiled. It amused her to think that she had a friend unknown to him, unknown to her father, unknown to all the world.

"Wouldn't you like to know!" she said, and went on.

Only in the dusky silence of Green Lane she was sorry. She would hate her father to be told. And now he *would* be. It was Leggett's business to keep him informed of everything.

The Cathedral bells now were pealing loudly. The whole town rang with them and the whole town responded, for the Carol Service was an institution; it was the right and proper way to begin Christmas. For many people it was the one and only occasion of entering a church during the year.

Up the High Street they all hurried, laughing and talking, greeting to left and to right. Lampiron and the Crispangles; the Bellamys; Inspector Gurney and Mrs. Gurney and the little Gurneys; Penny and her father and mother; Humphrey Carris and Mrs. Carris and Mabel and Gladys; Mr. and Mrs. Aldridge; Symon the lawyer from Bury Street; Mrs. Porteous and Camilla; Lady Mary Bassett and Miss Pringle, who was staying with her; Mrs. Hattaway; even one or two, and perhaps more than one or two, from Seatown. Across the dark Cathedral Green stepped Klitch and Mrs. Klitch, proud and eager to hear the singing of their son; Cronin and Romney and Gaselee with Ronder; the Misses Trenchard happy because their children's party had been so delightful; Mrs. Coole's old ladies from No.

10 Norman Row; Mr. and Mrs. Browning, grand and pompous from the St. Leath Hotel; Lord and Lady St. Leath and their son Robert arriving in a high old-fashioned Daimler; lastly, old Mordaunt in his grey shawl, stepping through the West Door as the bells ceased.

Mike Furze too was there.

CHAPTER VIII

Christmas Eve: II. In the Cathedral

IT HAPPENED on this evening that between the hours of six and seven no living human being was to be seen within the walls of the great church.

Evensong was over; no lingering tourists paced the Nave. Broad and his assistant, Titchett, had gone to their homes to have a bite and a drink before the evening service. Beyond the Precincts all the town was alive. Within the Cathedral there was life also.

Outwardly there was a great peace and silence and a half dusk, half dark, through which fragments of gold, of purple stone, of coloured glass, shimmered.

Soon Broad would be here to switch on the electric light and a glory of colour would shine; now the light and colour were of another kind.

No one can tell us what is life and what is death. We are certain of nothing save of the life of our bodies, which is the least of all our lives. It *is* sure, however, that no stone is raised to the glory of God that has not, because of that glory, life. Much preparation therefore was going forward now within this building and a great multitude was at work.

The centres of activity in this cathedral are the Tomb of the Black Bishop, the King's Chapel with the Virgin and Children windows, Harry's Tower that has seen so many great and fearful deeds, Bishop Wilfred's Tomb in the North-east Transept, the Tomb of Bishop Holcroft, the Chapel of All Angels where Lady Emily lies, and the War Memorial Chapel at the end of the South Aisle.

These—Henry Arden the Black Bishop, Gascon Bishop Wilfred, Simon Holcroft, Emily de Brytte—are the four great human figures of this church. They are all known, in face and body, by a happy chance, as well as though on this very day they walked the Polchester streets. Arden from Clerk Thomas's book: "He was mighty-chested, a dark hairy man, short and thick of the leg, with wrathful eyes and a smiling mouth. No man dare cross him and he was beloved of all men." In the Hunticombe Chronicles, preserved from Hunticombe Abbey, there is this picture of Bishop Wilfred: "A slender man, very tall, fair-coloured, with a bright blue eye. He was lame of one leg, but had a fiery spirit."

In the same Chronicles but, of course, later in date, there is much mention of Simon Holcroft: ". . . his stoutness hindered him. . . ." "He was in stature a bull and could roar like one . . . red-bearded." Simon Holcroft was one of the greatest of all mediæval bishops; he gave all that he had, money (he was exceedingly wealthy), energy, all his life to the beautifying and increasing of the Cathedral. He was a master craftsman himself and could make anything with his hands. He loved craft and all craftsmen of whatever kind.

Emily de Brytte was big-boned and fierce; more like a man than a woman. In the battle of Drymouth (Temp.: Wars of the Roses. She was an ardent Lancastrian) she charged on her white horse, herself armoured from head to foot, turned the battle and lost her right hand in the mêlée. She had very fair hair that she cut short like a man's, and she loved the common soldier, drinking and swearing with him and always ready to listen to his grievances. She in her later years did very much for the Cathedral with gifts of money and personal attention; the last, if legend is to be believed, often gave umbrage and she is said to have smacked the face of the then Bishop, Lancreste.

Those four had ruled this church for many a day, and so will for many a day to come.

BOANERGES

There are many things that Arden must remember—the day that the monks, angry for some trivial thing, marched round the church "widdershins," carrying their crosses upside down; or the riot in the infirmary when the old and sick and those recently bled, all together rebelled, showing most unexpected energy because of the protest of one of them against his bleeding, he defying the rule that monks, because they ate so largely, must be bled five times a year; or the anger that he was in one summer morning because the "rere-dorter," or latrines, stank so abominably; or the winter morning, a cold wind blowing, when he led the soldiers out to the hill beyond Arden Gate and turned the enemy back tumbling to the Rock; or that last blood-red afternoon when the setting sun shone through the coloured windows and he on one knee before the Altar felt the sword at his throat. And he would remember, too, the little things that he loved—the slab of alabaster from Nottingham from the High Altar (he was proud that day and stroked the alabaster again and again with his hand), a church-service book whose margins were gay in green and purple and gold with country dances and children riding hobbyhorses, monkeys at school; or a day in the country when, before a still and golden sky, he would watch the oxen slowly drag the harrow with its rows of wooden teeth across the patient field.

And Holcroft—his hands must be itching at the handicrafts again—ironwork on the doors, fine work on a silver or bronze seal, a painting on the wall, St. Michael holding a pair of scales on one of which is a little naked soul, the Devil, tugging at the scale to drag it down, St. Michael in silver armour and the Devil a flaming red—or maybe something as simple as a lock on an oak chest, not too simple, though, to have all the beauty that loving hands could give to it.

And Emily de Brytte? She would be thinking of war, of her great white charger, of her "basnet," of her padded doublet of cloth lined with satin and sewn with diamond-shaped gussets of mail—of the reek and the heat and the noise of the "bombards," of the little miniature cannons on long wooden stocks, of the cries and the trampling of the horses and the shout of victory.

Or maybe a softer life, the hall of the great house above the Pol (ten years after her death destroyed by fire), with the oiled linen stretched across the windows, the bright painted pictures on the walls, the display of gold and silver vessels, the solemn ceremony of the dinner—and the kindly stout body of her Humphrey beside her, cutting her meat for her because her right hand was gone.

If Time has no place here, Death has none either. What of the men of the Fabric Rolls—sawyers, smiths, plumbers, bell founders, painters, carvers in stone? You can see for yourself how they were in the corbels of Henry Sainte, above the seats in the Chapel of All Angels, with the master painter and his two cats, one black, one white, or the pleasant picture of the bell founder seated at his mew beside the great bell. There is the carved stone of Humphrey Whitten who acted with Burbage in London, the glorious monument of Henry, 8th Marquis of Brytte, with the divine laughing babies and the sinister shadow of young Simon Petre behind him.

But the darkness stirs with figures. This same darkness has no property more wonderful than the shadowed movement of life within it. A figure, shadow upon shadow, watches, nay, commands that movement. The armoured men, the monks in their hodden grey, the common craftsmen have *their* light so that darkness is unknown to them. A splendour of blazonry! Colours on stone, gold, purple, violet, stalls of the Choir gilded to a fine light, the battle flags hanging in brilliant procession blazing with the contrasted shades and grand designs of their armorial bearings. The flames of the tall candles blow in the wind; the thick smell of incense clouds the air; trumpets from the great West Door ring out.

Henry Arden, his vestures thick with gold, his giant ring gleaming on his finger, marches to the High Altar. . . .

"Yes," says Broad. "We have plenty of time."

There is nothing about this church that he does not know, but his knowledge rouses no sense of wonder in his breast. Facts are always facts to Broad. One thing has been ever manifest in his world—that there is one great man in it. He is often in a dream of wonder at himself, at his handsome figure, at the things that he knows, at his ability to deal with any kind of situation. He likes proverbs. "Handsome is as handsome does" he will say to a mystified tourist who has wanted to find Henry Sainte's corbels, or "Least said soonest mended" when a visitor enquires the history of Lady Emily. This cathedral, he created it. But the wonder is not with this cathedral—with himself rather, whose work it is.

With him, this evening, under sufferance, is his young son Timothy, to whom, unlike his father, all the world's a wonder. He must ask endless questions to which his father seldom gives a reply. Now this evening, alone save for that fine and pompous figure in the great church, he draws a great sigh.

"How many is there buried in this place, Dad?" he asks, and sticks close to the great man because figures on tombstones can sometimes unaccountably move.

Young Titchett appears, hurrying. Seven has struck and the pealing of the bells has begun. Mr. Doggett comes down from the choir stalls. The heavy leather apron of the great door is slowly pushed back and old Mrs. Dickens from Mrs. Coole's arrives, slip-slopping along, shuffle-shuffle, the ends of her old boa waggling behind her back. So the two worlds are encountering, meeting, together making the Festival of Christ in the Manger. . . .

Broad said to Titchett indignantly: "Now, look at this!" For there, curled up in a corner of one of the choir stalls, was a dirty shabby little girl fast asleep. "Well, I'm blowed!" Broad exclaimed, and stood there heaving with indignation, his hands on his hips, while young Timothy looked on, his eyes wide with interest. And Broad was blowed yet further when Titchett, twitching Broad's gown, whispered in his ear:

"Do you know 'oo it is? It's the little girl of that loose woman in Seatown, Fanny Clarke! That's 'oo it is."

"And how do *you* know?" Broad asked suspiciously.

"Everyone knows. She's always all over the town, stealing when she's got a chance——"

Broad leant forward and shook the child's arm. Dirty and dishevelled she was, her black stockings full of holes and her thin frock torn. She gazed at them with wild eyes, then slipped like a little eel under Broad's arm and was down the steps and along the Nave before a thing could be done.

"Well, I'm blowed!" said Broad again. "How the dickens did she get into the place?"

"Most mysterious," said Titchett. "Must have been in here all alone."

However, there was no time to waste. People were beginning to arrive although it was but a quarter-past seven. Mr. Doggett had gone up into the organ loft. Titchett stationed himself near the West Door. Broad moved through the Nave, seeing that the carol sheets were properly arranged on every chair.

Timothy, less afraid now of being alone, wandered away to the Black Bishop's Tomb and, as he loved to do, gazed at every detail of it. Someone had once told his father, he being by, a story about a visitor who was locked in by mistake one night and had to wait until morning alone in the Cathedral. This visitor had uncomfortably slept for a while, and then, waking, had seen the Choir blazing with candles and the Black Bishop officiating at the Altar. An old silly story about which Broad had been properly scornful. Not so Timothy, who had believed every word of it. He *knew* that, when all was quiet, they came out of their tombs and said their prayers. Why should they not? It seemed to him the most natural thing in the world, for he was an imaginative little boy and lived a life of dreams and fancies. So now he looked at the delicate lacework of the stone screen, the high pinnacles, the dark-blue stone of the tomb itself, and, most especially, at the black marble figure of the Bishop, the fine hands so quietly folded, the robes and mitre and crozier, the vizor and the gauntlet and the splendid ring of green stone on the right hand. The Bishop was a friend of his, the best friend he had in the world. . . .

It was half-past seven and people were pouring in. Doggett at the organ had begun a soft voluntary, an arrangement of "Gerontius." An air of happiness and even of gaiety began to spread through the church. Titchett, greeting his friends, showing people where to go, was so happy that he could have burst out singing, for this was one of the occasions when he *loved* to be a verger. He was a thin, pale young man who suffered from indigestion and a very tiresome bullying old mother.

At home he never had any fun at all, but now in a position of authority he was at his best, forgetting his indigestion and his mother and old Broad's pompous officialdom and feeling as though it were *he* who was welcoming everyone, as though he were giving a party and knew that it would be a great success. He smiled, he whispered Christmas greetings, and when Inspector Gurney, with his large wife and three children, stopped and insisted on shaking hands with him, wishing him a happy Christmas, his cup was really full.

The Marlowes had a reserved seat in the front of the Nave, and Broad, undoing the cord, tendered them Christmas greetings with great dignity. Penny knelt down and covered her face with her hands. Her thoughts would not be controlled. She tried to say the Lord's Prayer, but whether she said it or no she could not be sure. She was so very happy that prayers were meaningless. She had left the Donatello figure at Lampiron's house and now she wondered what he would do. She had never felt about anyone like this before.

It was a kind of worship, a longing to serve, to give, to surrender. She had no thought of any physical love. She did not see Lampiron as a man, but rather as a force, a power composed of all the elements that seemed to her most beautiful. She did not at all want that he should return any of her own feeling. She was not even sure that she wished to see him. All that she needed was that she should know that he was alive and not far away. And at the same time if she *did* see him her happiness would be almost more than she could bear.

She rose from her knees and sat demurely between her father and mother. Her father was very softly humming to himself, and this, Penny knew, distressed her mother. But she could think of nothing but that she might see Lampiron pass up the aisle. Because they were seated so far in front she could not get a sight of what Broad called the common people. The Cathedral aristocracy had their reserved seats, and here they were, with great dignity, wishing Broad a happy Christmas and then being wished it back again; Mrs. Carris in purple and with a marvellous little hat on the side of her head swept forward, followed by Mr. Carris and Mabel and Gladys. The girls smiled at Penny, which was very kind of them; Mrs. Carris, before she sat down, ever so slightly looked about her, as much as to say, "Is there anyone here I might ask to luncheon or dinner?"

Then Lady Mary Bassett arrived, scratching her nose and biting her lip. I wonder if she knows the faces she makes, Penny thought.

Then the two Miss Trenchards, a little old-fashioned in their black silk and a suspicion of puffed shoulders, but looking so kind and gentle, such grand ladies without thinking about it that Penny was lost in admiration at such unself-conscious dignity. Then there was Mrs. Braund with her son, who was, of course, a friend of Penny's and grinned at her. I'm sure he's thinking of the grand poet he's going to be, with the world at his feet. He thinks too much about himself.

She was then led to the speculation (as everyone was in Polchester at the moment)—how will Mrs. Braund look on a horse and in armour? *Will* she manage it? Probably she will, because of her Blood, thought Penny. That's almost the only use left for Blood nowadays—that it helps you to carry off difficult situations.

And now a sensation! for here were Lord and Lady St. Leath and their son Robert. Everyone was interested. How *sweet* Lady St. Leath looked, so wonderfully young! A pity Lord St. Leath was so fat and red in the face. But he looks so very good-tempered, Penny thought. And they say they are so *very* devoted. And although she had not the least little bit of snob in her, she could not help thinking (as everyone in Polchester was always thinking) that Lady St. Leath had been only an Archdeacon's daughter and that her brother had run away with a disreputable girl from a public house and her mother had run away with the Rector of St. James's. "What lives people have!" Penny thought.

After this, the Mayor with Mrs. Aldridge and all the little Aldridges. There were very many of them and they were a plain family and awkward. Two of the Aldridge small boys had squeaky boots and made a noise like mice in the wainscot all the way up the Nave.

Then the miracle occurred! Lampiron came stamping past! He was carrying a brown-paper parcel in his hand and seemed to have little idea as to his immediate destiny, for, on arriving in line with the Marlowes' pew, he realized that all the seats were cut off from him by thick red cords—nor did Broad, who was quite as good a judge of social distinctions as Mrs. Carris, make the slightest effort to assist him. So there he stood, extremely self-conscious, beginning to be angry, his body shaking a little, his head turning from side to side.

"Father," Penny whispered, "there's Mr. Lampiron. He doesn't know where to go. Do make room for him."

So her father obediently drew inwards (there was plenty of room).

"Mr. Lampiron!" Penny whispered.

He heard her voice, saw the space beside Marlowe and, frowning, sat down, stared in front of him, his hands on his knees.

At last, after a very long time, he looked, past Marlowe, at Penny. She smiled and he smiled. Then he turned and stared, frowning once again, into the Choir.

The service had, from time unremembered, been in this wise: first some prayers, then a carol, then after every successive carol the reading of a lesson. The first lesson was read by a choirboy, and so up the ecclesiastical scale until the last of all was read by the Bishop.

The quiet penetrating voice of the precentor floated through the Cathedral. Once Penny turned her head and saw that the Nave was completely filled. Beyond her own personal happiness she felt the happiness of that world within a world. Young though she was, she knew that the feeling of joy came from something besides the personal actual lives of this crowd of human beings.

What is it? she thought. I feel as though this would never end. I want it never to end. And I feel as though it had always been. They have been singing like this through all time.

For the first carol came to them from the candlelit Choir as though it had no earthly origin.

A boy (young Guy Klitch it was) sang the first verse alone:

> "*Awake, glad heart! get up, and sing!*
> *It is the Birthday of the King.*
> *Awake! Awake!*
> *The Sun doth shake*
> *Light from his locks, and, all the way*
> *Breathing perfumes, doth spice the day.*"

The choir sang the second verse:

> "*Awake, awake! hark how th' wood rings,*
> *Winds whisper, and the busy springs*
> *A concert make;*
> *Awake! Awake!*
> *Man is their high-priest, and should rise*
> *To offer up the sacrifice.*"

Then young Klitch, his voice rising and falling like a bird's cry:

> "*I would I were some Bird, or Star,*
> *Flutt'ring in woods, or lifted far*
> *Above this Inn*
> *And road of Sin!*
> *Then either Star or Bird should be*
> *Shining or singing still to Thee.*"

As the choir broke in again Penny bent her head. She heard no more, for it seemed to her that in literal truth the high roof had split its fastness, that a star shone, in almost intolerable brilliance, from a dark sky, and that the tune of the bird never ceased. . . .

Elizabeth Furze was sitting far back in one corner of the Nave. She had gone there because she did not wish to be seen—and then the most appalling event! Mr. Bird had come in late (she could see that he was flustered, his eyes gathered together under his brown eyebrows; yes, he was nervous, shy, self-conscious when he saw such a mass of people there!). Titchett had spoken to him, told him, perhaps, that there were seats in front. For he shook his head, smiled, turned his eyes nervously from side to side. Then he saw Elizabeth and that there was a chair empty beside her. He went at once and sat down in it. (Just at this time Lampiron seated himself beside Canon Marlowe.)

He knelt and prayed. The choir was coming in. Everyone stood, but he was still kneeling. When there was a pause before the first prayers he rose from his knees, and then, turning, smiling into her face, said in a low but happy voice, "Thank you very much for your present. You pleased me very much." And then added, "I often have chilblains, you know. I hadn't a pair of really warm gloves."

She said nothing. She stared in front of her, her hands lightly folded on her lap. She was aware that she wanted at once to leave the Cathedral, to go straight home and never to see Mr. Bird again. He had chosen deliberately before the whole world to come and sit beside her; there had been that happy look on his face, he was so close to her that his leg pressed against her dress, his hand, lying on his knee, seemed to say to her with a human whisper, "Touch it. Lay your hand for an instant upon it"—all these things, coming in a shock of active, positive revelation, struck her into a sudden consciousness of her position.

It was true. He was closer to her, to her heart and whole body, to her spirit and her soul, than she had, in her most excited imagination, supposed. She was a woman of facts. Life had been so bitter that it had fastened her to reality—and that reality, or *her* sense of it, told her that she must have nothing to do with

Mr. Bird. She was a woman apart, the daughter of a shameful man. This was no melodrama.

A sensible observer might certainly say to her: "Come, my dear, isn't this absurd? You are acting like someone in an old Victorian novel. Your father is a miser and usurer and is certainly unpopular. What has that to do with you? *You* are no usurer. Your life has been one of continuous self-abnegation and unselfishness." Yes, but the observer had not lived *inside* that life. The Inquisitor had, but not the observer. The observer had not experienced that constant day-by-day torture of slights, deprivations, humilities and (in watching her mother's tragedy) agony. The observer did not know how the life of that house, the Scarf, had become, for Elizabeth, the only real life. She did not see the house from the world, but the world from the house. Inside that house they were marked-off sanctified creatures, sanctified to a life of isolated contempt. She believed that everyone alive despised and condemned and avoided her—all save old things like Mrs. Dickens who did not know what the world said and thought. This outside contempt had grown into herself so that she sympathized with what the world felt. It was natural, inevitable. Only, for herself, like a plant that is nurtured and cared for in a dark room, she kept her own integrity and purity.

That integrity should not be contaminated by the weakness of drawing a good, unselfish, unwilling man into her spoilt life. Until this moment she had thought that an acquaintance (even an acquaintance strong enough to permit her Christmas present) could do no harm. Now she realized that for him it was more than an acquaintance.

She moved a little away. She wondered whether she would not leave the Cathedral. Then young Klitch's voice came to her as though it spoke to her directly:

"Awake, glad heart! get up, and sing!
It is the Birthday of the King.
Awake! Awake!
The Sun doth shake

BOANERGES

Light from his locks, and, all the way
Breathing perfumes, doth spice the day."

A moment later she was tested again, for the reader of the second lesson was Godfrey Burdon, the leading tenor of the choir. She knew him well, for he was an assistant in Bellamy's. But she knew him because, as all the town also knew, he was crazy about horse-racing and dog-racing, was always in debt and was deep in her father's debt. So now, when she saw his plump, rather babyish face and heard his familiar voice, her father came to her very side and whispered with his quiet gentleness, "You see, I'm everywhere. And you are with me. You will always be with me."

She did not know that, not far away from her, Uncle Mike was sitting. He was near the West Door. He was bewildered and he was exhausted. It was as though he had arrived at his destination after a long journey. He was so bone-aching weary that he might have walked a hundred miles. His confusion was partly because he had hoped to find rest here. What he had wanted was to sit down in the middle of all the people, listen to the singing, feel, as in other days he had felt, that this was the most comforting, most beautiful place in the world. But his body ached so sorely that he was prevented from realizing anything else. There were lights, colours, music. Someone was reading from the Bible, but the voice came, as it comes sometimes in dreams, as though from the end of a long corridor. He moved so restlessly on his little chair that his neighbours on either side looked at him. From where he sat, he could see, beyond the Brytte Monument, the little door that led up to King Harry's Tower, and this little door appeared to obsess him so that his mind would consider nothing else. The door, the dark stairs, the wall very cold to the touch, the thin slits of windows; then at a point complete darkness so that you must be careful lest you knocked your knees. Then the Whispering Gallery, then up again until you reached the little room with the gap against the wall that you must not tumble into. The door held him like a spell.

153

He felt that there was perspiration on his forehead, and he put up his hand, but there was no perspiration. His forehead was very cold. His thighs ached like toothache and his heart was beating as though he had been running in a race.

"Am I going to be ill?" he thought. "It's that stuff I drank in Seatown."

Then, with a great effort, he forced himself to be still and leaned forward, looking at the multitude of people in front of him, the patches of colour, faded blue and red in the old torn flags, the golden angel over the choir screen, the dim hazy fluttered light of the candles above the choir stalls.

"Now I must attend," he thought. "I am here to listen to the music. I have been looking forward to this for many weeks."

He looked at the carol sheet. A chorus of voices (that still seemed to be removed a great distance from him) rang out with startling suddenness. He, intently looking at the sheet, followed the words:

> *"All over were December's rains,*
> *And grass and herbs renew the plains;*
> *The shepherds quit the hills, and keep*
> *A watch around their feeding sheep.*

> *"Oh happy toil which Abel knew,*
> *And Moses loved, and David too!*
> *Oh, happy shepherds, favoured race!*
> *Who first shall see a Saviour's face."*

How beautifully they are singing, he thought, and a first sense of some distant happiness and tranquillity began to steal towards him. It was interrupted; it was prevented. It was exactly as though someone had touched him on the shoulder, someone antagonistic to everything that was being done here.

"Come away out of this nonsense. You are wanted. You have no time to be wasting here."

He had been a man all his life of weak decisions and he had

always covered his weakness with self-defending excuses. It was exactly the same now as so often before in the past. When in America or China someone had tapped him on the shoulder and said, "Come on. What are you hanging about for?" he had gone, often to some silly misfortune. Now he half turned his head as though he expected to see someone waiting for him. Everyone was listening to the singing. No one minded him.

Who wanted him? Where was he to go? Then he knew. It was this old impulse, that with every renewal seemed to be stronger, to drive him back again to the house that he hated. He had been in the Bull, drinking with his friends, or watching a football match, or talking to friends in the High Street, and this urge would come to him. But in these last weeks when he had no money to drink with his friends, this sudden insistence had been more powerful and more frequent. He had thought at first that it was the wish to hunt out his brother's secrets that drove him back, but when he was in the house he did nothing there—listened for steps and voices, skulked in his room, read an old newspaper, shivering because there was no fire.

Well, now he *would* not go! He sat back against the little chair as though he were clinging to it for safety. Canon Dale was reading a lesson.

Mike's eyes wandered from point to point. *That* was an old-fashioned hat! He noticed detail as though everything were enlarged in a magnifying glass—a purple vein in a cheek, a tie that had risen to the top of a collar, a thin and gnarled hand holding the back of a chair, a scarlet ribbon ornamenting a black hat.

"I'm not going," he muttered.

Then, very quietly, he got up and went.

It was towards the end of the service that, from very ancient tradition, they sang the carol that was the climax of their celebration. Old Ronder had read his lesson, had walked very slowly back to his stall. There was a pause and then, with a great joyful rush of sound, the whole world seemed to be singing triumphantly.

Unaccompanied, the choir, with a shout of magnificent greeting, saluted God:

> "*Hark! Hear you not a cheerful noise,*
> *That makes Heaven's vault ring shrill with joys?*
> *See! where, like Stars, bright Angels fly,*
> *And thousand heavenly Echoes cry.*
> *So loud they chaunt, that down to Earth*
> *Innocent Children hear their Mirth,*
> *And sing with them, what, none can say,*
> *For joy their Prince is born, this day:*
> *Their Prince, their God, like one of those,*
> *Is made a Child, and wrapt in clothes.*
> *All this is in Time's fullness done;*
> *We have a Saviour, God a son.*
> *Heaven, Earth; Babes, Shepherds, Angels sing:*
> *Oh! never was such Carolling.*
> *Hark! how they all sing at His Birth,*
> *Glory to God, and Peace on Earth.*
> *Up then, my Soul, thy part desire,*
> *And sing, though but a Babe, in this sweet choir.*"

At the words

> "*For joy their Prince is born, this day:*
> *Their Prince, their God . . .*"

the organ comes suddenly in with trumpets and shawms and all the artillery of salutation. Doggett, seated up there, solitary, isolated, not knowing what this life was for, save the divine procreation of music, seemed to himself to rise with this sound. For this one moment in the year at least he was one of a cloud of witnesses, and as he played, loving the Cathedral as he did, it was no sentimental nonsense that made him call his companions: "Come on, Arden and Wilfred and you, Henry Sainte who made the corbels, young Petre and old tow-bearded Holcroft. I'm a shy man, and I hate to say good-morning to my landlady, but here is a moment when I *do* understand what life is for. We are creators together before the Lord!"

Even Lady Mary, who thought the Christian religion a very absurd sentimental survival, threw for a moment her brains to limbo, and shared in the triumph. When, in London, Carslake, who wrote so brilliantly about the Versailles Conference and hates religion for the harm that it has done to the world, would say to her: "This sentimental flummery," she would say: "Yes, but, Carslake, you will think me too absurd for anything, but the Carol Service in Polchester brings out all the schoolgirl in me." It was a secret hidden from her, but the schoolgirl in her was her best part.

There were, in fact, tears in her eyes. Tears in Mrs. Braund's too. She was so very happy. Her dear boy was safe at home and delighting everyone with his cleverness, and the Archdeacon had been ever so much easier since he had finished his pamphlet on *Modernism and the Nicene Creed*. Moreover, she was to enact Lady Emily at the Pageant. She had not sought for this. They had offered it to her quite spontaneously and now the desire of her life was fulfilled. She had loved to act as a girl. In her young day, it had been of course impossible for anyone in her rank of life to think of being an actress. Nevertheless, she had had her dreams. And now they were to come true. Very fortunate, too, that she knew Percy Dalton, who was to come down and rehearse and produce the Pageant. Already she was reading everything that she could find about Emily de Brytte. It was almost as though they had become friends, and even now there were times when Agnes Braund, middle-aged wife of an Archdeacon and mother of a grown-up son, found herself lost in a strange world of cannon-smoke and coarse oaths and flying banners. Someone, at the last Pageant Committee Meeting, Mr. Romney perhaps, had said something about Lady Emily being no better than she should be, and she, Mrs. Braund, had felt quite personally insulted!

She was sorry that Mrs. Carris took the whole affair to heart. She had really been quite rude to her at the last meeting—but what poor Polly Carris lacked, had *always* lacked, was *breeding*. That everyone knew. . . .

> *"Glory to God, and Peace on Earth,*
> *Up, then, my Soul!"*

Up, up, up went Agnes Braund's soul and with her all the others. For an instant the one great purpose of human life was achieved; self was lost in worship.

But old Mordaunt alone (and he was crazy) saw and heard the true assembly, the knights in armour of gold and silver, the monks bearing the candles, Arden—his vestments stiff with gold—holding the great cross high in his hands, the snuff of the incense, the snarl of the silver trumpets. "Glory to God in the Highest and on Earth Peace. . . ."

Did this man, Michael Furze, ever in the course of the strange events that yet remained for him, reflect that this flight from the Cathedral to the Scarf was the true turning-point in his history? It may be. Once, on a later occasion, he said to his niece: "It was then—that time I allowed him to summon me— when I ran at his bidding—I can see now that that was the fatal blunder." To Elizabeth it was meaningless. Nevertheless it was true. All the later events in the town may be said to date from that. His flight from the place that, because of its beauty, had brought him here in the first place was the betrayal, in a way, of the finest part of him—a small part, something so weak that a short period of poverty, insufficient food, and terrorism had destroyed it. But the terrorism was not something of these few months only. It began when, a child of two or three, he had been ordered by his elder brother to "sit still. Don't move till I come back." And, weighted with fear, he had sat still. When he had had his fifty pounds he had made an attempt to fight. He had even, as has been said, played tricks with money, taunted his brother, pretended to spy on him. But at *that* game he had no chance at all.

Now he hurried through the town across the dark Green,

down the High Street, through the Market-place and so to the gate of the Scarf. He remembered nothing afterwards of the details of that short journey, spiritually so important to him.

Then at the gate he paused. It was as though someone offered him one last opportunity of escape. He looked up and saw how brilliantly the sky was lit with stars. In the next house he could hear a piano being played. They were dancing perhaps. A Christmas Eve party. The Scarf itself was the more silent by contrast. There was not a light anywhere. Only the branches of a tree creaked as though protesting against the life next door.

He was too tired to think; it was part of the inevitability of his circumstances that his brain, such as it was, had at that moment no chance to act. He had his key and he let himself in.

The house was in complete darkness. Stephen Furze might be working in his own room, but there was no expensive light burning in the passages or on the stairs. Mike struck a match, stumbled up the stairs and was on the way to his bedroom. Then Stephen opened his door and, looking out, said: "Is that you, Mike? Come in for a moment."

Mike followed him in. He stood by the door and when Stephen motioned him to a chair he shook his head.

"I'm tired," he muttered.

"Service over already? It's early surely."

Stephen's white nose with its big hollow nostrils was one of the unpleasant things about him, because it had, it seemed, a life and personality of its own. Now it was friendly and even kindly. A room, however, is not so easy a deceiver; it was bare, hard and very cold.

"I'm going to bed," Mike said. He noticed that, by a trick of light, his brother's body threw an elongated shadow on the wall. He appeared to see two men. Possibly there were more. Or, possibly, they were none of them there at all. He sometimes felt that his brother's body had no substance and that your hand, if you tried to grasp him, would paw the air. But that was absurd. He knew the cold hard touch of Stephen's hand.

"Well, good-night," Stephen said.

But Mike didn't move.

159

"What did you want me for?" he asked.

"Oh, nothing—simply whether you had enjoyed yourself."

"I? I never enjoy myself. You know that."

"Why do you stay here, then?" Stephen asked gently.

"Because you've sucked my courage out of me, my manhood —everything. How you've done it I don't know. I'm not clever enough to know."

"You've always been free to leave us."

Then Mike, looking clearly into himself, spoke a truth. "I've always done what others told me, all my life. You had that power over me when we were boys. I was a fool to come back here. My God, what a fool!"

Stephen shook his head, smiling, looking considerately at his brother.

"You exaggerate. That was always a fault of yours."

"Let me go," Mike said. "I'm dead sleepy."

"Why did you come away before the service was ended? You had been looking forward to it."

"Never mind that."

"No. Of course not. It's none of my business." He paused. Then, turning abruptly, he said: "One moment. There's something I want to show you. A Christmas present I've given myself."

He went to the table behind the roll-top desk and Mike saw, for the first time, that something wrapped in brown paper was standing there. Stephen quickly removed the paper and stepped aside. "There! Here's something that you will be able to look at whenever you like."

It was the crucifix. In its beautiful and lonely dignity, solitary against that bare ugliness, it was revealed. Mike drew a deep breath. He stepped forward, then stopped, his face working with convulsive anger.

"My God——"

"Yes. It's mine now. I saw it in Klitch's shop and liked it. I had to pay a pretty good price for it, too!"

"It's mine," Mike said. "The finest thing I've ever had. The thing I care for more than anything else in the world."

"Well—here it is. You can come and look at it when you please. It will always be here."

"You dirty swine! You got it to madden me with it——"

"No, no. To please you. You couldn't afford to buy it back and I liked it. I like it very much. Exceedingly handsome. It's not my custom to buy such things. But still——"

There was a long silence in the room. Stephen turned his back and sat down again at his desk. The shadow on the wall, having witnessed the scene that it had anticipated, disappeared.

Mike said only one thing more:

"You've gone too far. At last you've gone too far. . . . Now —look out—you!"

He stared at the crucifix for a long moment, then went out.

END OF PART I

PART II

Performance

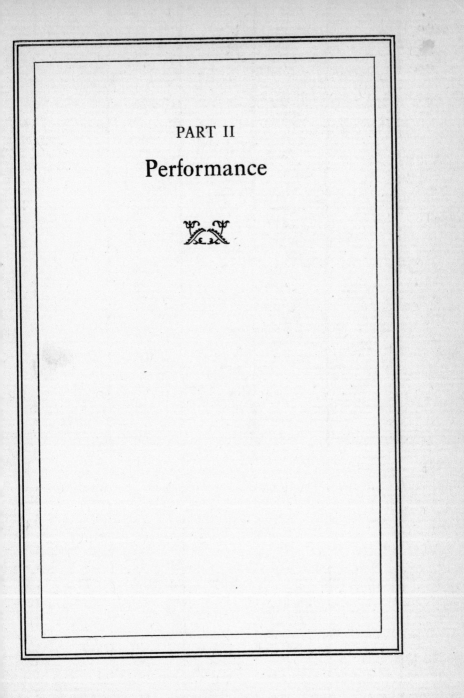

CHAPTER I

Penny's Day—Fine Weather and Mrs. Braund to Luncheon—the Bishop—Mr. Lampiron Talks about Old Age

On a certain spring day late in March, Mrs. Braund came to take luncheon with the Marlowes.

It must be, over many years, an absurd thing to speak of a spring day in March, but this year, 1933, will be remembered so long as they live by all, who received its lovely favours. The summer that year began somewhere about the 10th of March and then continued without let or fall until November. This also not only over the happy pastures of the South; the ribs and jagged edges of the North were tickled with a cloud-defying sun.

It may be—for weather can be responsible for so many things—that the prolonged heat of this year was in part to blame for the strange fancies and wonders that overtook Polchester that summer. That most happy of story-tellers, Giacomo Taquisara, has in one of his volumes an amusing fable that tells how Pan, having nothing better to do, came on a visit to a small Italian cathedral town. What he did to the canons, to the fat overfed Bishop, and to the Bishop's bad-tempered mistress, the story tells. The only similarity perhaps that this charming tale has with what occurred this summer of '33 in Polchester is in the description that Taquisara gives of the peculiar light and air that the little Italian cathedral town enjoyed while Pan was staying there. True, the disturber of Polchester was someone very different from that light-hearted human-loving Pan; nevertheless, there *was* that mesh of sunlight, that glow as of a faint apricot in the lighter washes of the sky, a stillness, a suggestion of warmth rather than the full perception of it.

Polchester had something of the quality of a dream during these months. The golden mist, faintest honey, that permeated everything yet did not prevent a sharpness of colour in detail. This was commented on by many persons. It was as though you saw with double vision, through a magnifying glass, maybe, as Mike Furze saw for a moment on that evening in the Cathedral.

Gaselee, who was a sharp observer, said afterwards, looking back: "I wonder whether I am imagining it, but it was as though for a time I was given the faculty of seeing *through* things, as though houses, trees, persons even, were made of glass. Of course it wasn't so really, but I think that the absurd stories that got about that summer and autumn would never have been believed in ordinary years. And yet how absurd were they? I know that I'm a great deal less confident about reality than I was a year ago."

It is certainly true that, in the March and April spring, it was as though everything were new painted. Polchester is, in any case, a very beautiful place in the spring. The woods on the farther banks of the Pol and below St. Leath and on the heights above Orange Street have a sharpness of green that almost hurts the eye when the sun is shining—a green of the most brilliant jade. Violets and primroses are thick in the hedges, their blue and yellow more intense in colour, it seems, than elsewhere. The town itself, in these spring days, when the pavements are warm with the sun, when the coloured jars shine in the chemist's window, and the sugar on the crystallized ginger in Bellamy's glitters, and some of the wealthier small dogs have new red leather collars, and the garden walls are pink like sunset —the town on such days has a gentleness of ringing bells, clergymen's black hats, the business of innumerable maiden ladies, the walls of whose drawing rooms are covered with bright water colours, their silver shining with old age. "Fine day," someone says in the High Street, and the shopman touches his hat to the gaiters of the Dean, and the tourist staring at the great battlements of the Cathedral sees every colour in that old stone—rose and silver, the green of Chinese lotus leaves and the grey smoky cloud of all past history.

It is queer, too, that these modern times have done so little to ruffle this ancient tranquillity. The Cathedral bells are stronger in spirit than the motor horns, and a flying aëroplane throws benison, when it catches the light, of a strong bird's silver wing. Under its brief shadow the barge moves slowly down the Pol, in the Cathedral Doggett practises for Sunday's service, and old Mrs. Dickens has gone to the Pol woods to pick primroses. . . .

On one of these fine days Mrs. Braund came to luncheon with the Marlowes. Marlowe himself was one of her very best friends. She was very happy in the Marlowes' house and lost any pomposities that she might have elsewhere. She talked a great deal. She was one of those women who, when happy, have not time enough for all that they have to say. Her rosy cheeks flush with pleasure and excitement. She loses words and properties, her grammar, her bag, her handkerchief, her caution.

The Marlowes were of the world of people she liked, her own kind towards whom she need not demonstrate the necessity for the right people to keep together. She understood them and they understood her.

From the first moment of Marlowe's coming to Polchester she had taken him especially under her wing, and that meant that there was nothing that she would not do for him, and also that she thought Mrs. Marlowe a little of a pity. No problem is a harder one for loving wives than this, but Mrs. Marlowe's spirit was equable, and she was so sure of dear Richard that she achieved what Jane Welsh and other eager souls failed over— she only wanted everyone to be happy, and when Dick was asked to the Braund festivities without her, as sometimes happened, she was content with a little irony on his return. So Mrs. Braund found her "a very good creature" and never really knew what Mrs. Marlowe thought of her.

Today, Mrs. Braund was so happy that no one could find fault with her. There were times when she looked very fine indeed, her height and her bulk all regal and surging—like the figurehead of a ship, Lampiron said she was, on good occasions. Now she strode into the Marlowe drawing room, her head up, her bosom taking the wind, so strong, vigorous and purposeful that you expected her to sail straight through the window.

"There's no one else coming. I hope you don't mind," Mrs. Marlowe said.

"Mind! I'm delighted! . . . There, darling, put that little parcel somewhere. It's a new kind of soap, for the Archdeacon. . . . How are you all? What weather! Doris, when she called me this morning said, 'It's fine enough for the Archdeacon to start his cold baths,' and he did, which always makes me a little nervous the first week or two because of his rheumatism. How are you, you darlings? Come here, Penny, and let me look at you. Why, you're blooming! Lovelier than I've ever seen you! And you, Richard? A little tired round the eyes? Too much chess?"

"Well, no—not exactly—although I did have a game at the Club last night which was a little irritating. We exchanged Queens in the middle of the game, and of course——"

"Don't talk to me about the silly affair. You know I don't understand it and don't want to understand it. . . . Listen, Penny dear, it's all settled. You're to be one of my handmaidens, and I'll see that you have the quietest kind of horse. You only have to sit still for about a quarter of an hour. When I raise my sword and shout you'll have to hold him in because of the trumpets."

"How's it all getting on?"

"Oh, marvellously. Except—what do you think? That Bolshevik lawyer, Symon—you know him, lanky-faced, wears glasses—has actually sent a letter to the Dean saying that there is a strong feeling in the Town about expenses and that the Town thinks that it ought to have more of the direction of affairs. The Town indeed—Bellamy and Crispangle and Carris, of course. And *what* do you think I heard about Polly yesterday? She went to call on Mrs. Bellamy and took that beastly little dog of hers with her. You know, the one that's a cross between a hair rug and a pen-wiper. Well, the horrid little thing had been in a puddle or something and was all wet. As soon as it was in the drawing room it jumped onto the best cushions and settled down there.

"'Your dog seems very wet,' says Mrs. Bellamy.

"'Oh, that's all right,' says Polly. 'She'll soon dry on your nice cushions!'"

"I hear," said Marlowe, "that the Committee Meetings are enlivened with many a duel between two famous ladies——"

"Oh, of course none of the Carris family will *ever* forgive me for being chosen. But *I* had nothing to do with it! If they think I'm the right person, it's my duty to do my best. I'll stand down tomorrow if anyone thinks I'm not suitable."

They went into luncheon, and Mrs. Braund resigned herself to the food, which would be home-cooking, very English, very lukewarm and ending with quite dreadful coffee.

"The great battle," she went on, "has been as to locale. At first everyone took it for granted that it would be on the St. Leath field. But Mr. Withers stuck to it that it *must* be in the Precincts in front of the Cathedral. Luckily the Green is twice as large as most Cathedral greens, and there's plenty of room for the stands in front of the Gate and Norman Row. And they'll have four performances instead of three. Then the Meadows behind the Cathedral give plenty of space for the performers when they're not performing. Percy Dalton came down for a night last week and says it's quite feasible, and *he* ought to know!"

"What's he like?" Penny asked.

"Oh, *so* distinguished. Pale and thin with a long nose, and he wears a stock with a pearl pin, and talks about Royalty all the time. 'But I *told* the Queen——' he says. All the same he *does* know his job and seems most enthusiastic."

"And Mr. Lampiron is to be the Black Bishop," Mrs. Marlowe said.

"Oh, he'll be magnificent, I'm sure. The scene of his murder ought to be superb. He stands at the West Door with the monks, defending them, then he has a magnificent speech, and when the knights rush at him he fights like anything. Then he is overborne and carried into the Cathedral. After that, complete silence. Then you hear a great cry. Then silence again. The knights rush out and away. Then the monks come, bearing his body, the bells ring, but the people creep away and his body is left with only one monk tending it, or something like that. Terribly moving and not history, because of course he was murdered on the altar steps. . . ." She broke off. "There, as usual, I'm talking too much. Do forgive me. Penny darling, I've never seen you so lovely. What *have* you been doing? Are you in love or something?"

"Of course she isn't," said Mrs. Marlowe indignantly. "Why, she's only just left school! Have a little more mutton, dear. Dick, give Mrs. Braund another piece——"

"No, thank you, dear," Mrs. Braund said hastily. "I never eat much in the middle of the day."

She was forced to return to the Pageant. "Romney's being too wonderful," she said. "His sense of colour—*just* like a woman's! Elizabeth's visit to the Cathedral—last episode but one—Mary Bassett is to be Elizabeth, by the way——"

"Isn't it a pity," Marlowe broke in, "that some of the townspeople haven't leading parts? It really would be more tactful——"

"Well, now I ask you! What parts *could* the leading townspeople play? Aldridge, Bellamy, Browning, Crispangle—they *or* their ladies?"

"Yes, I know, but——"

"Nonsense, Richard. This fuss the townspeople are making is quite absurd. And I'll tell you something: Crispangle and Symon are responsible for the whole of it, and I hear that they are busy stirring up any amount of trouble in Seatown. Romney knows. He's always going down to Seatown——"

"What on earth for?" asked Mrs. Marlowe. "Apple tart or junket or both?"

"Junket, please. What does he go there for? Oh, well, he likes all sorts. He's a most democratic man. He says that that horrible Mr. Furze is behind a lot of it—you know, the money-lender. But what was I saying? Oh yes, about Romney's sense of colour. He's worked out the loveliest scheme for Elizabeth's court—and *her* dress! Simply lovely! Dull gold, amber, a ruff stiff with pearls, garnets, and Mary's got to paint her face yellow. Her court will be violent crimson and topaz. One young man in the brightest green carrying a popinjay or something. All against the grey walls of the Cathedral." She flung her head up, her eyes sparkled, her bosom heaved, and Penny had suddenly an odd impression as though Emily de Brytte herself were there, sitting with them at the table. So that it gave her a queer shock to hear Mrs. Braund say a moment later:

"One funny thing. I sometimes feel as though Lady Emily were alive, watching me, waiting to see what I'll do——"

"I didn't know that you believed in ghosts," Mrs. Marlowe said placidly.

"*Of course* I don't! I'm not the kind of person ghosts appear to! No—it isn't as though she were a ghost, but a real living person. And more than that, it's as though she doesn't like me."

"Doesn't like you!" Penny cried.

"Yes. Of course it's all imagination, but the other afternoon when I was talking to Canon Dale about the clothes I was going to wear, it was exactly as though someone took me by the scruff of the neck and shook me!"

"Now that's very funny," said Marlowe, "because old Mordaunt has written the maddest letter to the Bishop imploring him to stop the whole thing on the ground that all the Cathedral saints and heroes, Arden and Brytte and Lady Emily and the others, are furious. They take it as an insult! Did you ever hear anything so crazy? He says that it's desecrating the Cathedral and that there will be some awful consequences. Poor old man——" Marlowe sighed, for he hated that anyone should be sick or poor or neglected—"I'm afraid he's going altogether queer in the head. He lives in that room in Pontippy Square with no one to look after him—the very house where an old woman was murdered once; do you remember? He doesn't have enough to eat, I'm afraid. It's a shame more people don't buy his drawings, because they're really very good—very good indeed."

"But his drawings are so queer," Mrs. Braund said, feeling guilty because she had never bought one. "He's always putting in such strange figures that aren't really there."

"He says they *are* there!" Penny broke in. "He's a friend of Mr. Lampiron's, and Mr. Lampiron told me that Mr. Mordaunt says that he sees someone standing there in the West Door. He says——"

But Mrs. Braund clapped her hands.

"Now I won't have any more of this nonsense, Penny dear. What *are* you thinking of? Believing in ghosts? Aren't you a modern girl, full of science and that sort of thing? Who is it? Freud or Einstein—and there's that dreadful man Lawrence who died the other day——"

"Lawrence was one of the greatest men who ever lived," Penny said, her cheeks flushing. "He told the truth and people persecuted him for it, and——"

"What did he write, dear?" Mrs. Marlowe asked, signalling to the maid to hand the cream cheese round. "Novels or what?"

"Novels and poetry and essays." But Penny, her little outburst over, dropped her voice.

"You must let me read some, darling. *Do* have a little cream cheese, Agnes. We get it from the Ervine dairies."

"No, thank you, dear. I couldn't possibly. Such a delightful lunch."

Now that the meal was over, Mrs. Braund was wondering what the Archdeacon was doing. Had Doris seen to *his* lunch properly? Did he remember the meeting of the Friends of the Cathedral? Was that touch of rheumatism in his right knee that had been tiresome at breakfast better by now? She had a thousand things to do, a thousand things to think of. Nevertheless, she had been observant. Two points: One that her friend Marlowe was not happy; something was worrying him. She knew him so well. He was a child and, like a child, could not hide things from her. About the people she loved she was tender

and kind and considerate. She must discover his trouble and
help him.

The other was the radiant happiness of Penny. It was as
though the lovely weather had clothed the child with some of
its golden, shining glow. Could she be in love? Was *that* what it
was?

Then her attention was distracted, for the maid entered and
said:

"The Bishop, ma'am. I've put him in the drawing room."

"The Bishop!" Mrs. Marlowe cried, starting up.

"Yes. He said he wouldn't be more than a minute. Something
he wants to say to the master."

In the drawing room the Bishop was waiting. He appeared
very tall in that overcrowded room, and he bore about him,
as he always did, an aristocracy of spirit that set him apart from
other men. And yet he was not apart. Bishop Purcell before
him had been a saint, but a saint removed. There was nothing
that happened in Polchester alien to Kendon. He had reached
a sympathy that led him to understand all human frailty. No
one in his company ever felt the aloofness of one who, in discovering the other world, had learnt not to despise this one. But the
quality of holiness when so rarely it is visible among men seems
an answer to all the questions that mankind so restlessly, so
fruitlessly ask. It is so clearly the only solution, but *how* is the
mystery to be discovered? Kendon could tell you nothing except
that he believed in God. He knew himself to be a sinner like
the rest of his fellow men. He believed that sin was a definite
loss of vitality—so much life missed—and that it must, one day,
be recovered; be recovered with pain and struggle. Nevertheless
he was no gloomy sinner—his happiness triumphed over his
own failures, his bad health, his bachelorhood (for he had loved
passionately in his earlier life), his distrust of so much that the
modern world about him was doing and thinking.

Dick Marlowe was a very old friend of his, for he had been
at St. Albans when Marlowe was a curate there. He put his
hand on Marlowe's shoulder now and said:

"I came in only for a moment. You must forgive the awkward time, Hester. I want to speak to Dick for a moment. No, I won't have any coffee, thank you."

Mrs. Braund, who worshipped the Bishop, said: "I can drive you anywhere. I've got my car outside."

"Thank you, no. I'd rather walk. It's such a lovely day. As long as I don't go up steep hills it's all right. I have to go in and see Ronder. Myers will have the car there."

He pinched Penny's cheek, smiled on them all and went with Marlowe into his study.

They made a rather humorous contrast; Marlowe with his rough, thick white hair, stout body, bewildered blue eyes, the look that he had of a child who had never matured; Kendon bone-thin, sharp-faced, black-haired, something of the soldier in his straightness and rodlike carriage. But they loved one another, and Marlowe knew Kendon better, perhaps, than anyone else in the world knew him.

"I won't keep you more than a moment, Dick. There's something I want to ask you."

"I wish you'd stay all the afternoon—and *then* all the evening. I don't see half enough of you."

Kendon laughed. "I'm quite a busy man. You mightn't believe it."

"Henry, what's this I hear about poor old Mordaunt writing to you?"

"Oh yes—a crazy letter. At least half of it was—about all the saints in the Cathedral rising and stoning us for daring to have a pageant. But the rest of the letter was rather true abuse."

"Abuse?"

"Yes; he said that we—Christians in general, and clergy in particular—had neglected, and were neglecting, our job. That we did nothing in the war, made no protests against the horror of it, never lifted a finger to stop it."

"That's an old charge. And some of us love our country. Did he want us to sit down and let the Germans do what they pleased?"

"Oh, I know. It's the old, old argument. All the same we

failed in the war. However fine some of them were individually, the Church counted for nothing, at the beginning, in the middle, at the end. It dealt itself a blow that it's never recovered from. And then since—as he says—what have we done? About unemployment, disarmament, housing, *anything?* Is there a churchman in the whole of England at this moment who counts for anything as Mussolini, Roosevelt, Hitler—even Baldwin and MacDonald—count? Oh, I don't mean in that *kind* of a way, not politically or financially. But in *God's* way. We've been too cowardly, too muddled, too playing for safety. The old man in his letter says that the Cathedral is sick of us, despises us. He writes—crazily if you like—of a figure that has been inspecting us, trying us all out, investigating us, one by one; a kind of spiritual Inquisitor. I'm going to see him. I believe he's half starved and neglected. I reproach myself for not having been to see him before." Then he shook his head and laughed. "Who's mad and who isn't, Dick? It's a hard question to answer. I expect God's test of sanity is quite different from ours."

Then he came closer to Marlowe and put his hand on his shoulder.

"Look here, I've got to ask a rather difficult question. Someone has told me—never mind who—that you're in trouble, financial trouble. Is that true?"

"Yes—it is."

"Can I help? We're very old friends, you know. You're the oldest and best friend I have. I haven't a long life in front of me, and I've more riches than I need."

"I know," Marlowe said. "You give away every penny you possess."

"Nonsense. I live a life of the wildest luxury. I get a letter every week from someone or other telling me so. What's the trouble?"

Marlowe shook his head. "I'm—in a muddle, Henry—in a fearful muddle. That's nothing new, of course. I'm always in a muddle about something. But I seem to be in the hands of a man here. I don't quite know why. I've borrowed from him in the past; more fool me—but I was never any good about money, and this living is shockingly small and I will buy books when I shouldn't. Then I like Hester and Penny to have what they want."

"Have you told Hester about it?"

"No, I haven't. I'm ashamed to. She sees that something is worrying me. I don't sleep properly."

"Poor old Dick! But why haven't you come and told *me* about it?"

"I haven't told anyone. It seems so shocking that a clergy-man should be in the hands of a man like——"

"Who is it?"

"His name's Furze. Stephen Furze. He lives a few doors from here."

"Oh yes, I know. Half the town's in debt to him one way or another. Everyone seems afraid of him. Well, look here—will a hundred help?"

"Yes—it will make all the difference."

"Right. I'll write a cheque now." He sat down and wrote it. "There—not another word—I must be off."

Marlowe gripped his hand.

Kendon said: "That's the least I can do—the friend you've been to me all these years."

He went to the door. Marlowe stopped him.

"You know, Henry, I'm dreadfully ashamed. Sometimes I think I don't know *what* I'm doing. God's hidden from me so often, and there are days when I think He's left me altogether—given me up because I'm no good. Let me see you more often. I'm lonelier than you know—a stupid muddled old man who buys books and plays chess when he ought to be serving God."

"Oh, there are plenty of ways of serving God. Chess is one, because it teaches you to watch your step." Then putting his arm round Marlowe again he said: "We will. We'll see one another more often. God bless you and keep you now and always."

At a quarter to four on that same afternoon Penny, unknown to her parents, went to have tea with Mr. Lampiron in his studio. She wore a dress of apple green with white cuffs and a

white collar. She had on one wrist a thin gold bracelet, her only
ornament, and a bunch of primroses at her breast, and a small
green hat.

The bracelet had been given her by Lampiron on her eight-
eenth birthday, March 3rd.

But now she had been to tea with him on a number of occasions and unknown to everyone save his old servant. Today
was, however, to be different from all the others, because she
was going to tell him that she loved him, that she would always
love him until she died and probably after that, that all she
wanted was to be with him, to defy the world, to go away with
him if he wished, to serve him forever and ever. . . .

Night after night, lying on her bed watching the circular
glow, like an illuminated spider web, reflected on her ceiling
from the light of the street lamp, she had thought of this moment, had said over to herself the words that she would use,
had imagined to herself all the possible consequences. Among
these consequences the physical played the least part. He had
never kissed her; when she had had tea with him they had
shared a delightful intercourse, playful, sometimes serious in
discussion, sometimes reminiscent when he would tell her a
little of his life. But he had never kissed her, had never put his
arm around her, had never stroked her hair. She did not know
whether he was aware that she loved him. When she thought of
the consequences of her confession she knew that he would kiss
her (the thought of this filled her with rapture), and she took
it for granted that they would sleep together. Also she would
look after his clothes, help with the cooking, shop for him and so
on. They would probably have to leave the town because of the
scandal, but, at this period, although she adored her mother
and father, she considered very little the catastrophe that this
would be to them. In all the novels that she had read recently—
novels by Lawrence and Aldous Huxley and Richard Aldington
—also many by ladies—the parents submitted with what grace
they might; they being old muddlers responsible for the war and
all the other horrors of modern civilization.

But here was a strange thing—that, although Penny assumed

177

it as certain and inevitable that she would sleep with Lampiron —all the heroines in all the novels did that kind of thing only too readily—and although she knew, from *Lady Chatterley's Lover* and other works lent her by her friends, all the details of the affair, she yet did not visualize its actuality at all. She had a soul as pure and virginal as the soul of the heroine of *The Daisy Chain*.

Her love for Lampiron was idealistic utterly; her conception of the actuality of sexual relationship as unreal as a fairy story. It did not seem strange to her that she should love a man who was between sixty and seventy, because he was not a man—he was the Holy Grail, the Happy Warrior, the Genius, the Perfect Friend.

The great longing of her heart was to defend him, to protect him. She saw herself standing in front of him, her arms outstretched, scornfully taunting the mob who wished to destroy him. She had often heard the now almost legendary story of the Swede, Harmer John, of how he had tried to bring beauty to Polchester and so they had murdered him down by the Pol— just as in her own time they had murdered D. H. Lawrence!

How, thus, *she* would defend her lover! She was on fire with the injustice in the world, man's disregard of beauty, the sufferings of the unemployed, the filthy conditions of the slums. Lampiron would show her how she could help in all these things. . . .

But, with all this, it must be owned her own life was extremely happy. She was compelled to admit that she enjoyed every minute of it. She had the capacity of obtaining great pleasure out of small things. The spring weather, the thought of the coming Pageant, her own radiant health, even Mrs. Braund telling her that she was beautiful—these, in spite of the unemployed and the slums, made her heart dance with joy. For—how could she help it?—she was in love and was ready to give everything that she had and was to another. . . .

Old Bridget let her in and took her straight through to the studio where Lampiron in a white overall was working.

"Tea, Bridget," he said.

She went without a word.

Penny took off her hat, shook her dark cropped head and sat down on the arm of the chair with a hole in it.

Lampiron went on working. He was chipping away at a small block of marble, black with white streaks and whorls. He muttered to himself as he worked, his big body controlled as though by a hair's-breadth, balancing on the very edge of restraint. She said nothing, looked at him and at the vast huge-breasted torso that, headless though it was, seemed to stare back at her. The warm spring sun floated in on thick dusty lines of light.

At last he stopped; stood back, surveying his work, then said: "There! I think that'll do for today. Very expensive this marble. I haven't paid for it and I don't know that I ever shall."

"What's it going to be?" she asked.

"A woman's head."

"Don't you want a model?"

"Not this time. It's an ideal head—something more than human."

She nodded. She meant to understand everything that he did but, at present, she must confess to herself that she didn't understand. She would never let him know. She had read the Van Gogh letters. She had ordered from Crispangle a book of Epstein's conversations with a friend and read it from cover to cover. In time she would learn, and meanwhile she would study every word that fell from his lips. With great pleasure she noticed, at every visit, the little Donatello David which stood on the dusty mantelpiece all by itself. She could understand the beauty of *that*.

The old woman brought in the tea.

"There!" Lampiron said. "Enough for today. The light's going."

He came and sat down, she poured out the tea; he lay stretching out his legs, wriggling his broad back into a comfortable position, thrusting his hand through his thick hair.

"Now—tell me all you've been doing."

"Mrs. Braund came to lunch and talked about nothing but

the Pageant. It's all settled—I'm to be her handmaiden and ride a white horse."

"Humph! There's a lot of row going on about this pageant."

"She says *you'll* be magnificent."

"How on earth does she know? But I've got one fine speech that I'm going to yell at the top of my voice." He turned and looked at her, then turned away again. She was, beyond any description, lovely. He closed his eyes for a moment. Then he went on:

"What do you think *I've* been doing this morning?"

"Can't think. More tea?"

"No, thanks."

"Bridget won't be coming back, will she?"

"No."

She moved over and sat on the edge of his chair, her hand on his knee.

"Tell me what you've been doing."

"A very odd thing. Bodley, the London architect, is down here. Hattaway asked me this morning to go up with himself and Bodley to look at the Harry Tower."

"Why?" asked Penny, wishing that he would make some little movement towards her. "What's the matter with it?"

"Oh, there's nothing the matter actually with the Tower as far as its foundations go, but some of the inside has dry rot. There's a lot of wood. They've closed it to the public twice already. They'll probably have to do it again. There'd be a fine scandal if twenty tourists tumbled through the Whispering Gallery into the Nave."

She laughed.

"Why did they ask you to go?"

"I've no idea. Hattaway's rather a friend of mine. Nice people the Hattaways. Bodley's a decent chap too. Now tell me some more that you've been doing."

"Oh, well . . ." She puckered her brow, thinking. "They've started tennis at the Club—three weeks earlier than usual. Lady Mary asked me to tea."

"Oh, and what did *she* talk about?"

"Mr. Romney was there. They talked about poetry and the right colour for bedroom curtains and bath salts. Don't you think Mr. Romney a *very* funny man?"

"In what way funny?"

She took his hand, as though unconsciously, and laid it on hers.

"Oh, he calls everyone 'darling,' and he brought his tapestry with him—he does *beautiful* tapestry—and he said that turbines are to the poet today what the lily was to Oscar Wilde."

"I daresay he's right—not that he knows much about turbines, I should fancy."

She put up her hand and touched his cheek. "You didn't shave very well this morning."

He stayed motionless. She felt that his hand trembled on hers. Then he got up abruptly. He walked away.

"Penny—I've got to talk to you. You must listen to me. I've been meaning to for a long time."

She was frightened. She stared at him through apprehensive eyes.

"What is it?" she asked.

"Well, it's this. . . . I'm sixty-eight. I could be your grandfather."

She burst out laughing. "How terribly silly!"

"No—it isn't silly. It's true."

She was gathering her courage back again. She got up and faced him.

"But I don't think of you as *any* age."

"Exactly. But *I'm forced* to! You don't get to sixty-eight without constant reminders. However . . . what I really want to say is that you mustn't come here like this any more."

"Oh!" She gave a little cry. Then she went to him, put her arms round his neck, drew his head down and kissed him on the mouth. For a brief instant he tightened his clasp round her slender body, holding her close to him, kissing her fiercely. Then he detached her hands and walked over to the mantelpiece. For a moment neither of them spoke. At last he did huskily.

"That's the first time I've ever kissed you, Penny. And it will be the last. It's not the way grandfathers kiss their granddaughters. In future they will not kiss them at all."

Penny looked at him. That kiss and the pressure of his body against hers had been something quite different from any expectation. With that instant of emotion had come an entirely fresh experience. She would never think of men in the same detached way again. She would never again be quite so virginal as she had been five minutes ago. He was not only Sir Galahad now; he was a man of flesh and blood as well. She was in love with him more than she had been, but loved him a little differently; that is, her love for him now was a degree closer to earth.

She remembered, however, that she was a modern girl.

"Why shouldn't you kiss me? I love you and have done ever since I spoke to you at our party. I'll go away with you or stay here and work for you or do anything else you want me to do. I shall love you as long as I live and never love anyone else."

"Now you're using words you don't understand," he said. "Sit down in that chair, Penny, and listen to me."

She sat down, her hands folded in her lap, looking at him almost ironically.

"I'm sixty-eight," he said. "But I haven't lost all human feeling—in fact I haven't lost nearly as much as I should have done. You're fifty years younger. Fifty! Just think of it! I'm a friend of your father's and mother's. They don't actually know you're here at this moment, perhaps, but all the same they trust me. I've done a lot of dirty things in my time—I shall do some more before I die—but I've never yet willingly hurt anybody—except an enemy or two, of course. I *have* hurt people who have trusted me, because one is always doing it, but not *intentionally*, you understand.

"Another thing—I've had a life with women that you don't even begin to conceive the details of. What I mean is that you *think*, as all modern girls do, that you know *all* about it. Well, you know nothing. I'm not a nice old man in any way at all, but I love what seems to me beauty passionately, and I believe, although I've not had much experience of it, that there is a spiritual beauty somewhere that beats all the other kinds. Look at the Bishop, for example. Now I'm not preaching, Penny dear, but it seems to me that our friendship hitherto has had some of that spiritual beauty in it. I daresay *that* beauty has its origin in physical things. I won't pretend or be a humbug. But I just know enough to be certain that the moment our friendship goes beyond a certain mark I'm a ruined old man. It's for my sake, Penny, more than yours, that you must do what I say. I'm in all sorts of other messes, financial mostly, but *this* mess, if I got into it, would simply finish me. I'm violent sometimes—do crazy things. There's one man in this town now that I can't trust myself over. But over *you* I've got to trust myself and you must help me. If you *don't* help me, then—well, then, I'll never willingly see you again. I'm at a kind of crisis just now. I feel as though the last tussle of my pretty useless life is about to be fought. What kind of tussle it's going to be I don't know. My life is of no value or importance to anyone but myself. But to me it is of value. *You* might make it valueless. I implore you not to."

She had listened to this long harangue with deep absorbed attention. It had been quite different from her expectations of it. She had thought that he would speak of the risks that *she* was running, of her own future, of spoiling her life. Not at all. It was *his* life that she mustn't spoil.

"If," she said, her voice a little broken, "I don't kiss you or anything—can I come here just the same?"

It was at that moment that he realized how deeply, deeply he loved her—passionately, paternally, selflessly and with the greediest egotism. It was the hardest task of all his life not to go to her and take her in his arms.

But, without moving, he said:

"Yes. Try it and see."

She looked him straight in the face as though she were making a vow.

"Very well. I will," she said.

She asked him no questions. She got up. Then, her hands

trembling a little, she put on her hat. She went to the door, looked back at him, smiling.

"We'll meet soon again, won't we?"

"Yes, we will," he said.

"Thank you for the tea."

Then he went back to his work.

CHAPTER II

Some Houses Are Always Cold

M AKE ME SEE IT, Elizabeth! Make me see it!"

"Well, the stands are all up now. They look very white and naked—new wood and bare, as though they'd be bare like that forever. And what's so strange is to see them staring at the Cathedral and the Cathedral staring back at them. In sunlight the Cathedral stone looks like silver and as though it had been there a thousand years. The stands look so *very* impertinent!"

"Yes, yes! I can understand that!"

Mrs. Furze was in bed, a shawl about her shoulders. It was the last day of June and a week before the opening of the Pageant. Mrs. Furze's bedroom was overcrowded with furniture. These were the things that her own father and mother had had. They were very large and very ugly, the wardrobe, the chest of drawers, and a safe, belonging to Stephen, that stood in the farthest corner of the room. The sun had but recently set and outside the house the world was bathed in an early summer twilight, the sky very faintly green with one sharp blazing star, and over the streets, the orchards, the gardens, the tightly packed town a haze of gold-dust.

But in Mrs. Furze's room it was cold. Elizabeth had lit the gas, although she knew that if her father discovered it burning so early in the evening he would be quietly furious. But she had a book on her knee from which she was going to read to her mother and she must have sufficient light. The book was a novel by Mrs. Henry Wood—*The Shadow of Ashlydyat*—Mrs. Furze had never forsaken the reading that she had liked as a girl. One of her favourite books was *Madcap Violet*, by William Black, and another, *Donovan*, by a lady called Edna Lyall. Elizabeth was telling her how the preparations for the Pageant were looking. Mrs. Furze sat up, her lined anxious face insignificant beside the intensity of her sightless lidded eyes.

"Yes, yes. Go on. So that's where all the people will sit. Will there be plenty of room for everybody?"

"Not as much, of course, as if they had it on the St. Leath field. But now it will be four days instead of three. They say the tickets have sold wonderfully."

"I'm so glad. Tell me again what the scenes will be."

"Are you sure you are warm enough, Mother?" Elizabeth leant over the bed and drew the shawl closer about the skinny neck. How cold the room was, although the sun had been beating on the house all day! Some houses are always cold.

"Yes, dear. I'm quite warm enough. Now tell me. First there are the Gascons——"

"Yes, first there is the scene of the building of the first church —St. Leofranc cures a child of fever and they all become Christians. Then there's the mission from Pope Gregory—when St. Augustine was in England and founded a church at Canterbury. The third episode is the coming of the Pilgrims from London and the town fair—dancing and all sorts of play. The fourth is the murder of the Black Bishop—that's Mr. Lampiron, you know. Then there's the chief episode of all, when Lady Emily drives the enemy back from the Cathedral walls. That's the one there's been so much quarrelling about, because Mrs. Carris wanted to be Lady Emily. The sixth is the Miracle Play in the time of Henry VII, when Abbot Bury died in the middle of the play. Canon Ronder is to be the Abbot. The seventh is the closing of the monastery by the officials from Henry VIII. The eighth is the visit of Queen Elizabeth— that's Lady Mary Bassett, you know—and the last is a sort of picture of all the history together when the spirits of the Black Bishop and all the others bless the modern world. There are nearly six hundred actors altogether, they say."

"Oh dear!" Mrs. Furze clasped her thin hands together. "It must be splendid. I do hope the weather will be fine."

"Yes. Everything depends on it. People are coming from all parts—special trains from London. Are you ready for me to read now?"

Mrs. Furze lay down, her head with its scattered grey hair resting on the pillow. Then, suddenly, she said:

"Elizabeth—I'm sure Michael came into this room last night."

"Uncle Michael! . . . Oh no, dear. You imagined it."

"No. Someone came in and bent over the bed. I pretended to be asleep, but I hear the slightest sound—more than ordinary people. I know it was Michael. He breathes through his nose. He was carrying a candle. I smelt it burning."

"I am sure that you dreamt it, darling."

"Oh no, I did not. I often *think* I'm dreaming in the daytime. Such strange things happen. Michael and Stephen hate one another, don't they?"

"Hate's a strong word." Elizabeth was surprised at her mother's calm. She lay there and her brain seemed to be working directly behind her lidded eyes as though, because of her blindness, the whole force of her energy, mental, spiritual, physical, had concentrated where her sight ought to have been.

"No. Hatred isn't too strong," she remarked calmly. "Your father has a great capacity for it, and after all, Michael is his brother. You know, Elizabeth, something very dreadful is going to happen shortly." Then she added in a kind of whisper: "Nothing can happen to *me* any more that I can mind."

Elizabeth had never heard her mother talk thus. She had often wondered what her mother had in her mind—pretty bitter things, she did not doubt. But nothing was ever said. Her mother kept always the same mild, rather dry, unemotional contact with daily life, except for Elizabeth herself, whom she loved.

"Yes," Mrs. Furze continued very tranquilly. "Things have been getting closer and closer to one another for a long while and when they do that they meet at last. Your father's a very bad man and deserves all that is coming to him."

This, to Elizabeth, was so amazing that she held her breath. She had lived so long in this house, so intimately and closely with her mother who, she had supposed, loved her father, was, indeed, the only living soul in the whole world to do so.

"You see, dear," Mrs. Furze continued, "—you don't mind not reading for a moment, do you?—I was really glad when Michael came to stay, because I knew that he would bring things to a crisis." Mrs. Furze nodded her head. "I shouldn't be blind now if it hadn't been for your father's meanness. There's never a minute of the day that I don't think of it, and especially when there's a fine thing like this pageant they're doing that it seems such a pity to miss. Such a *great* pity, because when I was a girl I always liked shows of every kind. I've got your father to thank for that, as I have for many other things."

Elizabeth said, taking her hand and stroking it: "Mother, let's go away. Just the two of us. Somewhere—anywhere. I've wanted to suggest it to you often, but I thought you cared for Father. I never dreamt that you felt all this——"

"Felt it!" Mrs. Furze nodded her head vigorously. "Oh yes, I've felt it all right. Go away? Dear me, no. I mean to stay here and see what happens." Then holding Elizabeth's hand lightly she went on: "But *you* should go, Elizabeth. I'm quite all right. I can manage very well—very well indeed. Why don't you find a good man who'll marry you and look after you? You'd make a man such a very good wife. And you ought to have children. Where would I be now if I hadn't had a good daughter?"

"I marry? I'm plain, Mother, a dry old maid. That's what I am."

"I'm sure you're not plain, dear. No one as good as you are could be plain. I'm sure there's a man who likes you. I know there is. I've noticed a hundred little things lately. And you're fond of him too, I'll be bound."

Elizabeth said nothing.

"There is, isn't there, dear?"

"Someone has been kind to me," Elizabeth said. "But I've told him that we mustn't meet any more."

"Oh, why? What a foolish thing to do!"

"How could I bear that anyone who likes me should see what this house is and what Father is——"

"Ah, there you're being sentimental, dear—talking like they do in those old stories you read to me. If a man cares for you he doesn't mind what your father is. He won't have to live here. He'll take you away."

"What will you do then?"

"I tell you I can manage very well. Besides it won't be for very long. Something is going to happen here and then everything will be all right." Then she added, sucking her finger, which was a little trick that she had: "Your father made one great mistake. He hasn't given Michael enough to eat." She patted the bedclothes. "Michael is stout. When I take his arm I can feel how stout he is, and a man like that needs food. Your father could have managed him quite well if he'd fed him; but that's like your father has always been. He grudges every penny." She moved her head placidly on the pillow. "And now, dear, I'm ready. I like Mrs. Wood's books very much. They are so absurd and they remind me of when I was a girl, when I was gay and had a lot of young men round me— before I met your father."

In another room Major Leggett was thinking, as he often did, how intensely he disliked talking to Stephen Furze's back. There the back was, bent like a hoop. The gas was not yet lit, and Leggett wondered how it was possible for Furze to see his rows of small figures in that mean pallid glow. The evening sun did not come into this room which, although dry and arid in spirit, was cold in body.

This house is never warm, Leggett thought. His private tastes were sadistic; perhaps the French literature that he read —he was quite an authority on Racine and could never mention the theatre without murmuring "Bernhardt"—assisted to make that sadism more intellectually coloured. In any case, he thought, as Michael and Lampiron had thought before him, that he would like to break that thin back with a snap of the fingers. He excused his own morals and unpleasant private habits on the ground that his brain was a superior one and, above all, that he had no use for sentiment and gush. He was a vain egoist almost to madness, so vain that he considered his bald head, his short fat figure, his raw-beef complexion, his jockey-like garments, all very fascinating phenomena. But he was, alas, a coward. He was afraid of death, of physical pain, of social slights, of the Jews, of the police and, most of all, of Stephen Furze.

"Were you not in the world," he might have addressed that stooping figure, "I might make a brave show. I'd get hold of Symon, and he and I would have a fine splash. You old devil."

But in actual fact he was saying:

"I wrote to Marlowe and reminded him that the hundred pounds that he paid you early in the year did not clear his debt. This I have informed him twice already. The old fool hasn't the slightest idea of what he does owe." Leggett coughed. "I suppose Symon has arranged it all right in case Marlowe *should* get someone to look into the affair."

"He won't get anyone," came a quiet voice from the table. "He's shy of anyone knowing. Besides, he *has* borrowed again. March last. Thirty-five pounds."

"Yes," said Leggett. "Then there's Stephen Burdon. I suggest we close down on him very shortly. His racing has gone very badly this spring. He's been drinking too, and they say he may be turned out of the Cathedral choir. There's old M'Canlis of Bridge Street. What about him?"

"Well—*what* about him?"

"We could sell him up and take over his shop if you like. We could put it onto Aldridge. Young M'Canlis is making trouble enough in Seatown as it is. This would about set him alight, I should fancy——"

"I don't mind. M'Canlis wants his pride taken down."

"What about Lampiron?"

"*What* about Lampiron?"

Furze suddenly turned round. His long pale face with the protruding nose had something the air of a considering philosopher—not at all unpleasant until you looked at the eyes. But Leggett's reflection, as it had often been, was that, in certain lights—dim like this one—you could almost see *through* the head to the furniture and wall space behind it.

"*What* about Lampiron?"

"Well, what are you going to do? You've been having him at the end of a rod and line now for over a year. *I* think he's getting dangerous."

"How do you mean—dangerous?"

"Well—violent. You remember that night last autumn when he was in here and caught hold of you? He's a rough old man and you've teased him pretty thoroughly."

"Yes, I have." Furze smiled. "It's amusing when I'm so frail and he's so strong. Are *you* strong, Leggett?"

"Why—how do you mean?"

"Of course you're thickly built, broad in the shoulder and all that. But you drink too much, don't you?"

"Oh, I don't know."

"Yes. You drink too much. One day, if you were drunk enough, you might screw up your courage to do *me* an ill turn——"

"Look here, Furze——"

"Oh yes, I know all about it. I know all about everything. I can be in two places at once, you know. Three sometimes. You were talking pretty violently down at Locke's the other night."

"I swear to you, Furze——"

"Oh, I don't mind in the least. I think I understand you very well. It must be humiliating often for a man of your training and culture to serve me as you do. You ought to be in *quite* a different position. However, you're nearly as fond of money as I am. I've never forgotten what you were like that day I took the box with the gold pieces out of the safe and showed them to you. I let you handle them, do you remember? Have you forgotten how cool and hard and round they were and the colour they had? No one ever sees a gold piece now. You were as excited as though you were beating one of your lady friends."

"Look here, Furze——"

"All right. Don't be annoyed. I don't mind how you amuse yourself. Only remember. If you were to do me in one dark night, you wouldn't be finished with me. I listened to a rationalist on the wireless up at Symon's the other night. 'We go entirely by our reason,' he said. 'What we can't prove we don't believe in. Heaven and Hell and all that nonsense—science has proved the God idea a silly superstition.' I couldn't help laughing. Symon asked me what I was laughing at. But I didn't tell him—it wasn't worth while. Symon could never see a joke."

"If you've finished with me," Leggett said, "I think I'll be going. I don't think there's anything more tonight."

"Oh yes, there's a lot more. Tell me, Leggett, what do you think of my brother?"

"Your brother? Not much. We're not very friendly, you know."

"Here, sit down. What are you standing for?" He pointed to a severe-looking chair whose back had the disapproving austerity of his own friend, Symon the lawyer.

"All the same, Furze, I have an engagement——"

"Yes, with me. What do you think I pay you for? Not that I pay you much. And I'll tell you why—because, as I very well know, you make your own pickings——"

"What about lighting the gas?" Leggett asked, sitting down again. "The day's about done."

Indeed, having all the nervousness of a man who drank too much, slept too little, and had moments of belief in God and the Devil, he disliked all the rooms in this house after dusk. He was cold and the place was more full of shadows than was natural. The crucifix on the table behind Furze's desk he could dimly see, and the bone-whiteness of the figure disturbed him. He disliked to be reminded of anything to do with religion. And, after all, why couldn't Furze forget for a moment his meanness and indulge in electric light? He would find it cheaper in the end, no doubt. There was something sordidly old-fashioned about gas—a kind of Charles Peace atmosphere, with its gurglings and pale glimmers and suggestion of mean streets.

He said, uneasily resting one stout knee on the other:

"Why not try electric light, Furze? You'd find it cheaper in the end. This must be the only house in Polchester with gas, I should think."

"Oh, would you?" Furze was now a shadow against the green-lit windowpane. "I like gas—it's a nice, friendly, companionable thing. Want some light, do you? Afraid to be alone with me in the dark? What about these?" He pulled towards him two candlesticks painted a shabby green, struck a match and lit the candles. "Now to return to my brother. What's your idea of him?"

"I don't like him and he doesn't like me."

"Oh, well, I know that. But that isn't what I mean. Have you noticed anything about him lately?"

"He's a miserable sort of brute—he's been very quiet."

"Quiet?" Furze sat between the candles, his head and shoulders like a cobweb on the wall behind him, a cobweb with a gigantic nose. "Yes. You're right. And you remember how noisy he was when he first came?"

"Yes. Always shouting at the top of his voice."

Leggett now was interested. His little sharp eyes were examining Furze with curiosity and it seemed to him that the man was apprehensive. This was *really* of importance, because he had never seen the man uneasy before. People who surrender themselves, soul and body, to some consuming passion become like men who walk in their sleep; moving in this world bodily but dreaming of another. So he had always felt that Furze was. But now he was *not* dreaming. He needed to be reassured, and it gave Leggett great pleasure to think that reassurance should be the last thing that he would offer.

"Well, I soon quieted him. Once his money was spent he went down like a child's balloon. There was never anything inside him. He was like that as a child. Wind and water, that's all my brother was made of."

"I can't think what he stayed here for," Leggett said.

"He hadn't the pluck to go. He's not so young as he was. He knew he'd never find a job in these hard times and he'd sold the only thing he had that was of any value."

Furze motioned with his hand towards the crucifix.

"Oh, was that his?"

"Yes, he sold it to Klitch the day of his arrival here. He got fifty pounds for it. Then he couldn't buy it back, so I got it."

"Ah, I see. . . ." Leggett drew a little whistling breath. "Just to exasperate him."

"It's valuable, you know," Furze said sharply. "It's worth a lot more than I gave for it. Anyway, my having it did irritate him. He came in and saw it on Christmas Eve after being at the Carol Service and I thought he would murder me. I did indeed." Furze giggled. (There was something feminine in many of his actions and movements.) "I enjoyed that five minutes," he added.

"I've often wondered what it was doing here," Leggett said, eyeing him intently.

"It's since then he's been so queer," Furze went on. "Before that he was always ready to explode if he had anything to explode with. He hated me so much that I was never sure he wouldn't attack me one day. But *since* that evening he's been as still as though he were dead."

"Dead!" Leggett exclaimed.

"No, not really dead, because I'm sure he's been plotting something. More than that—I don't think he's quite right in the head."

"What does he do?" Leggett asked.

"He walks about the house at night. He talks to himself and he watches me in a way that, quite frankly, I don't like at all."

"Why don't you turn him out, then?"

Furze rubbed his hands together. Then he turned and snuffed out one of the candles. "We've light enough with one," he said.

194

"He's useful. He saves money. He does plenty of little jobs for me. Then I like to see him. These fat men run all to seed when they're not well. You've run to seed yourself, Leggett. There's not a spare piece of flesh on *my* bones."

"No, I'm sure there isn't," Leggett agreed.

"I want you to talk to him a bit. Make up to him. See what he's got on his mind. I've told him I won't have him walking about the house at night. He just nods his head and says he's been sleeping badly. He stands in here staring at that crucifix as though he'd never seen it before."

"What I don't understand," Leggett said, "is how a man can change so quickly. Then he was drinking and joking with half the town—now he never goes out unless it's up to the Cathedral, and he speaks to no one."

"He was always moody," Furze said, "always moody. Gay one minute, crying the next." Then, suddenly, he snuffed the other candle. The room was in darkness and yet Leggett seemed to see the man, his thin legs stretched out, his white bony nose like an independent and most unpleasant creature.

Leggett found his way to the door.

"Good-night," he said, but there was no answer.

Mrs. Furze dropped off to sleep, and Elizabeth, seeing it, closed *The Shadow of Ashlydyat*, got up very quietly and went to her own room. It was early. She thought that she would read. She lit two candles, partly because she preferred them to gas, partly because her father might poke his head through the door and ask her why she was sitting in such a blaze of light. That would anger her and she did not want to be angry tonight. She did not attempt to read, but sat, a plain calm figure in that severe room, marvelling at the things that her mother had said to her. What a woman her mother was! How self-contained and secret and strong! It was true, of course, that blindness drove you in upon yourself so that in your world of darkness you created a world of light, yourself the only observer. Her mother had done that and now she was safe inside that world. But how could Elizabeth have been so blind as not to have

seen long ago that her mother hated her father? There must
have been many signs. And yet, perhaps not. Her mother had
a self-command that had been built up through years of disappointment, frustration and rebellion. That was what frustration and disappointment were for.

What a queer lot they were—she, her father, mother, Uncle
Michael! She looked at the book on her lap. She had almost
finished it. It was a novel that told about a day in the life of
many different people—a grand lady's house with herself and
her family, her servants, the charwoman and *her* world. It
was clever, amusing, and by a woman. It was a book of tiny
detail. The fashionable lady wakes up, has her tea, her bath.
There were many details about bath salts, powder, scent, silk
underclothes and so on. But the interesting thing to Elizabeth
was that the book never for a moment deserted its detailed
realism. It was like a picture that she had seen when Bellamy
had a little art gallery in his store, of a table with fruit on a dish
and a lobster and a loaf of bread. Every grape was real in this
picture and the loaf of bread almost too real. So in this novel!
But what interested Elizabeth was that, in their house, the
Scarf, life began just where the novel left off. Her father, her
mother, Michael, even herself would appear simply untrue in
this novel that she had been reading. Elizabeth put on her
clothes in the morning and took them off at night, but what did
her underclothes, her washing, her brushing her hair, matter
beside facts like her mother's blindness, her father's mad
cupidity, Uncle Michael's unhappiness? Lady Mary Bassett,
Mrs. Carris—women of that kind were occupied in all probability with just the little things that were important in this
novel, and Elizabeth felt a kind of resentment that they should
be—not because she was jealous or wanted the things that
they had, but because actual problems of life and death, of
love and hatred, were present now in this house. She would read
in the paper that Mr. Smith of Manchester had embezzled,
made love to a servant girl, murdered his wife and run away.
In the very next paragraph she would read that little hats like
penwipers were now the fashion and that Lady Shirforth gave

her last party in a swimming bath. Both worlds were real, then?
Where did they join?

She would, she thought, before she went to bed, go down and
see whether there were any letters. There was a late post at
nine. She had done this now for many weeks, and, being an
honest woman, she acknowledged to herself the reason.

"There are lots of women as silly as me, I don't doubt," she
said. She took a candle and went down into the chilly hall.
There was not a sound and the candlelight jumped on the wall.
There were three letters, two for her father and one for herself.
The envelope addressed for her was in Mr. Bird's handwriting.

She climbed the stairs to her room again, placed the candle
on the dressing table and, after a shy look round the room as
though she expected to find someone there, read it.

32 Orange Street.

*Dear Miss Furze—I hope you won't think it impertinent of
me but I have two tickets for the first day of the Pageant and I
should be very pleased indeed if you would come to it with me.
We haven't seen very much of one another of late and I have been
wondering whether I have in any way offended you. If I have I
do hope you will tell me what it is that I have done. I am often
clumsy and maladroit I am afraid. I do hope that this beautiful
weather will last through the Pageant week.—Yours very sincerely,*
James Bird.

She sat, with the letter on her lap, looking in front of her.
How wonderful of him! After the way that she had behaved
(for his sake—yes, yes, only for his sake), to offer this, to sit
with her in the face of the whole of Polchester, to choose her,
out of the whole of Polchester, for this pleasure! It was, perhaps,
the happiest moment of her life, and had anyone been present
at that moment to see her he must have thought her almost
beautiful; the thin lines of her pale face were softened by the
tenderness of her smile, and the attitude of her body as she
leaned forward, staring into the shadows of the half-lit room,
gave her grace and dignity. All lonely women are beautiful

when their terror of loneliness is removed from them. Elizabeth's plainness came chiefly from the long years of self-restraint and austerity that life had forced upon her.

Of course she must refuse. How could she sit there with him so publicly? She could hear the whispers, and jokes and comments: "What's Bird doing with the miser's daughter?" Then she remembered what her mother had said, that this sensitiveness was sentimentality, cowardice even. Colour came into her cheeks, her eyes softened and were gentle, her hand trembled against the letter. How good he was! How wonderful of him to think of her! She repeated it to herself over and over; her eyes filled with tears so that the room blurred with misty candlelight.

With a shock she heard a tap on the door.

"Come in!" she said, putting the letter on her dressing table. The door opened and Uncle Michael entered.

He was dressed only in shirt and trousers and he carried a lighted candle. He blew it out and closed the door very carefully behind him. He looked completely exhausted, as though he had been running, his forehead shining with sweat; his chest, showing through his open shirt, glistened. He looked at her, sheepishly smiling. Then he drew his shirt together and held it with one hand.

"What is it?" she asked. "What's the matter?"

"May I sit down for a moment, Elizabeth? I was sleeping in a chair in the dining room and I had a horrible dream——"

"Yes, of course. Here." She showed him a small shabby easy-chair. "I was just going to bed."

He sat down; she could see that his fat knees were trembling and, herself in a mood of tenderness, she was filled with kindness, remembering the loud buoyant man he had been only six months ago.

He became quieter. He wiped his forehead with his hand.

"I dreamt I'd done for him," he said huskily. "He was climbing the stairs, his neck all on one side. I caught him just where the little room is; he turned just too late and his neck cracked——"

She remembered her thoughts of half an hour before—the novel with the grand lady, the bath salts, the silk underclothing —and now here in this house there was something so real and so dangerous that she laid her hand on the dressing table, afraid that he would see that she was trembling. Then she was filled with pity for him.

"Uncle Michael," she said, "*what* is it? You've been ill for months now. *Why* don't you go away? I've asked you again and again. Tell me what it is. You can trust me."

He seemed to be recovering. His face was white here, streaky there, and his big loose body overfilled the little chair.

"Phew! I'm better," he said. "That was a bad turn."

"Why do you walk about at night?" she asked him. "Did you go into Mother's room last night?"

"I don't know. I don't know where I go."

"But you mustn't. You frighten us."

Then he smiled, like a child suddenly amused.

"So your father says. It's something for *him* to say he's frightened." Then he went on quietly. "It's your father ought to go away, Elizabeth. It's *he* that's in danger here, not me."

"Father! But of course he won't go away."

"Well—he'd better look out. He bought my crucifix just to torment me. He's gone too far. There are several in this town want to do him an injury." Then he went on, quite conversationally: "I've a kind of idea he'd be difficult to finish off. Plenty have thought it over, but it isn't so easy. You wouldn't be sorry to see the end of him yourself—would you, Elizabeth?"

"Now, enough of this," she said sharply. "You're saying monstrous things."

She looked at him with a sudden disgust—his long nose, the way that his forehead was white above his red face like a labourer's, his open shirt, his awkward ugly knees. Then, because she knew that he was unhappy, she softened again. "Please, Uncle Michael, don't stay in this house. It would be better for all of us if you went. I'm not unkind. It's yourself I'm thinking of. I want you to be happy again as you were when you first came here."

"I shall never be happy again," he said. His voice grew louder. "Never, never, never!" He struck his knee with his hand. "Remember that. I've gone the wrong way. *He's* driven me, and until—until——" His voice broke off. "Well, never mind that." He yawned, covering his mouth politely with his hand.

"Excuse me," he said. "I think I shall go to sleep now." He got up, hitching his trousers. He stood, his legs spread, stretching his arms and yawning.

"You're certainly right," he said, speaking now gravely as though he were considering a philosophical case, "in saying that it would have been better if I'd never come here. It would have been—*much* better. But once I did come here, once I spoke to your mother in the hall, the rest followed inevitably—inevitably, I being what *I* am, your father being what *he* is. You didn't know us as boys together, did you, Elizabeth? No, of course you didn't. But we hated one another, we did—from the very beginning.

"And now we've come to the end. And it's been a long journey."

"Well, you go to sleep now." She put her hand on his arm and felt his flesh damp beneath the shirt. "You'll feel better in the morning."

He shook his head. "Oh no, I shan't. I shall never feel better so long as he's about. But it's his own fault. He shouldn't have teased me, and taunted me, and made me work for him and taken my crucifix from me. A man can stand a good deal, but there *are* limits."

To her surprise he put his hands on her shoulders. Then he kissed her very solemnly on the forehead.

"Good-night, my darling," he said.

CHAPTER III

Who Passes?

THE DAY BEFORE the Pageant was close and sultry. The sky was darkly blue, and behind the blue you felt a pressure, as though a giant were pushing with his fist to burst through the papery sky. The heat in the High Street was terrible, and Bellamy sat in his shirt sleeves in one of the rooms above his shop looking down on a struggling, perspiring world. At his side was a large mug of shandy. Up and down the hilly street the crowds moved. Many had come in from the country who would not see the Pageant but *would* see and enjoy other things. For example, there was the Fair down in Seatown filling the whole of the space behind the river. There was even a booth with two real lions.

"What is it, Burdon?" Bellamy asked, eyeing his assistant distrustfully. Burdon might have a splendid tenor voice, but he would have to go if he didn't stop his drinking and horse-racing. Bellamy was wanted, down in the shop. A kindly impulse (he was very kindly when not thwarted) made him stop as he was going out and put his hand on the man's shoulder.

"You look rotten, Burdon," he said. "What's the matter?"

"It's this heat," Burdon said, wiping his forehead with the back of his hand. He added desperately: "It's more than the heat. It's Furze. He's driving me terribly, Mr. Bellamy. I'm almost off my head with it. I'd have lost my choir job by now

201

if Canon Ronder hadn't put in a word for me. I can't attend to anything."

"Furze?" Bellamy said. "Has *he* got his clutch on you?"

"I don't know where I am with him. I don't seem to be able to get clear."

"It would be a charity to the town if someone put a bullet through that man's brains," Bellamy said. "Come and talk to me about it sometime. You're too good a man to go to pieces."

After he had gone Burdon looked down on to the crowd. The sun blazed down on them. Through the other window a murmuring of voices and a steady shuffle of feet came up. Motorcars pressed slowly up the hill, hooting as they went, an old man was selling balloons and they floated, red and green and blue, above the people's heads. The Cathedral bells were jangling, and from the bottom of the street could be heard the lowing of cows and the bleating of sheep, for it was also market day. The voices of the crowd were very cheerful, laughter, men calling to one another, and a woman's voice suddenly raised: "Come here, Mary Jane, do. You'll be being run over."

"They all seem happy enough," Burdon thought bitterly. "And here am I in this mess. By God, the heat's awful."

Klitch was standing at the door of his shop, watching everything with a delighted, almost childish interest. He looked very smart and dapper with his rosy cheeks, his high wing collar and the gold pin in his tie. His short legs moved restlessly as though to a tune, and his bright eyes darted everywhere.

Norman Row had a strange appearance, for the backs of the stands walled it in. They ran with their clean, naked surface the whole length of the little street. For a fortnight Miss Bennett of the Cathedral Shop, Mrs. Fowler of the Glebeshire Tea Shop, old Humphries of the Woollen Shop, Broad and his family, Mr. Doggett the organist, Mrs. Coole and her old ladies, the Klitch family, would be shut in by this strange barrier. But they none of them minded. It wasn't for long and it gave them all a sense that they had their part in the general excitement. Moreover, it did not in any way stop custom—quite the contrary, for the crowds passed up and down, staring at the stands and the shops, getting peeps into the Precincts, enjoying everything.

During the four days of the Pageant, Evensong was to be at five-thirty instead of three-fifteen, and it was hoped that many of those who attended the Pageant would afterwards attend Evensong. Until the Pageant began, however, the public was allowed to pass through Arden Gate, along the path into the Cathedral. Many were now doing so, and Broad had a busy and profitable time conducting parties here, there and everywhere. Very popular were the Choir, the Black Bishop's Tomb, the King's Chapel, the Chapel of All Angels, the Harry Tower. About the last he was emphatic.

"Last time you'll have a chance for many a day," he said. "It'll be closed from tonight on, and no one knows when it will be open to the public again."

"Why, what's the matter with it?" the tourists asked.

"Wood rotten. That Whispering Gallery may give any time."

So the tourists paid their sixpences and tipped Broad lavishly.

On many a later occasion Klitch was to recall every detail of that afternoon. He remembered, for example, that after looking at his watch he called back to Mrs. Klitch: "Four o'clock. They'll be just coming out of Evensong. I'll be going down to the Gate for a minute, my dear, if you'll watch the shop." So he strolled down to the Gate just as the Cathedral gave the hour.

In front of the Gate a small crowd of sightseers watched the Precincts. There was nothing at that moment to be seen. The grass, green and smooth, shining in the sun, was deserted. The great pile of the Cathedral looked benignly onto the stretch of empty stands. He saw that near to him was standing old Mrs. Dickens.

"It will be different tomorrow, Mrs. Dickens," he said genially.

"Yes, Mr. Klitch," she said, smiling, pleased at being spoken to. "And I'm going to be there to see it," she added triumphantly.

"Why, that's fine!"

"Yes. Mr. Hattaway has given all the ladies lodging with Mrs. Coole tickets. A kind thought, and God will reward him."

"Very decent of him," said Klitch. "Let's hope it will be fine. There's thunder about."

It was then that both he and Mrs. Dickens saw Michael Furze. He walked rapidly past them towards the Cathedral, then turned as though he were bewildered and did not know where he was going. He saw Klitch.

"Hullo, Mr. Furze!" Klitch said. "Taking a look at things?"

"Yes," Michael muttered. Once spoken to, it seemed that he could not move again but stood there, staring at Klitch as though he had never seen him before.

"What a shabby-looking man!" Mrs. Dickens thought. "He *does* seem as though he wanted caring for." She had a maternal interest in all men, having no one to mother save a ginger cat which Mrs. Coole was forever molesting. This was one of the preoccupations and grievances of Mrs. Dickens's life.

But Klitch was touched. He had never forgotten that day when Furze had first come into his shop, his boisterous heartiness and self-confidence. "And now look at him," Klitch thought. "All down-at-heel and bewildered, poor devil."

On an impulse he said: "Come along and have a cup of tea, Mr. Furze. You'll be welcome."

"Oh no, no, thank you. I must be getting along."

"Come, now. I haven't seen you for weeks."

"No. Thank you. I have some business." He turned and disappeared. Klitch walked slowly back to the shop. Strange that a man could alter so completely in so short a time! He told Mrs. Klitch about it, drank some tea and then stood in his doorway again observing all that passed.

At a quarter-past four Lampiron left his house, and a little earlier Stephen Furze had shut the Scarf gate behind him in the company of Leggett. Furze was paying a visit to the Cathedral. This astonished Leggett very much.

"I didn't know you ever went near the place."

"No? Well, you don't know much," Furze said. He was wearing his old bowler with the soup-plate brim, and his coat, shabby with age, that reached nearly to his heels. He carried his umbrella.

"What he wants to wear a coat for on a day as hot as this beats me," Leggett thought. "I bet he's always as cold as ice."

They walked together as far as the Market and there separated. Tom Caul, who was moving with the crowd for curiosity's sake, saw them, and Crispangle, on his way home to tea, saw them.

Furze started slowly up the High Street. His intention was to catch Godfrey Burdon as he came away from Evensong. He knew that Burdon served in Bellamy's all the morning and in the afternoons when he was not on Cathedral duty—so that if he missed him at the Cathedral he would visit him at Bellamy's. He had a word to say to him.

Nothing gave him pleasure like the little personal conversations with those who had reason to fear him. This passion for power, whether over money or men, was his driving motive and, like all other passions, it thrived with what it fed on. He saw himself as a king among men. One day, when the right time came, he would gather together the money that he had made and use it for some grand purpose. He would become, no doubt, one of the great men of the kingdom. The trouble was that, to show his power, he must spend the money that he had collected. At the thought of letting that wealth pass from his own command to that of others he shivered with apprehension. And then he would comfort himself with the thought that he had power enough as it was. He would leave things as they were.

Now, as he started up the High Street, from somewhere or other an unpleasant discomfort struck him. Why? He liked to mingle with the crowd, to think that, in this case or that, by a little manipulation, he could use his power and acquire more money and more authority. As he walked in a crowd such as this he seemed to himself to exert an influence over everyone near him, as in that silly dream of his brother's when the figure had emerged and everyone had vanished.

But this afternoon he was uneasy. He even looked behind him as though someone were following him. He had half a mind to turn home again, but curiosity drove him forward. He would see the preparations that they had made for this ridiculous pageant, spending money like water. Even the Cathedral, which he visited more often than Leggett knew, would be interesting on a day like this. He sometimes went up to the Whispering Gallery and, looking down, wondered how much all the brass and stone and carving was worth. . . .

Then he saw Lampiron.

Furze was halfway up the High Street, between Bellamy's and Crispangle's and exactly opposite Bennett's, when he came upon Lampiron. It happened that, at the same moment, Canon Ronder and Gaselee came out of Bennett's and stood, for a minute or two, in the doorway, watching the happy crowd. Ronder had been wishing to acquire a certain novel, and old Bennett had been advertising for it and secured a copy. Ronder had it under his arm now and was looking greatly pleased. The novel was called *The Nebuly Coat*, by Meade Faulkner. "It is absolutely the best novel in English about Cathedral life after *Barchester Towers*," Ronder was saying. "I haven't read it for years, but suddenly the other night I couldn't sleep and, standing at my window, saw a caterpillar crawling in the moonlight across the ledge. I can't tell you how beastly the caterpillar looked. And it reminded me of *The Nebuly Coat*."

"The caterpillar did?"

"Yes; it's all about a caterpillar—a caterpillar, a picture, and the tune the Cathedral bells play. The caterpillar reminded me also of that terror of the neighbourhood, Furze." Then he caught Gaselee's arm. "Why, there he is! What a strange coincidence! And he's talking to Lampiron."

"Lampiron appears upset," said Gaselee.

Furze, on seeing Lampiron, had felt an unwonted amiability.

PERFORMANCE

The fact was that it was not at all of Lampiron's physical violence that he was afraid but of something much more elusive. So he greeted Lampiron almost as a friend. The sense of insecurity that had been with him for the last half hour vanished as he touched Lampiron's arm.

"What a lovely afternoon, Mr. Lampiron," he said in his gentle, dreaming voice.

Lampiron turned and a kind of physical disgust seized him that he should be touched by Furze. He had been walking slowly, through the crowds, up the hill, his mind intent on the part that he was to play on the morrow. These weeks of rehearsal had been a queer experience for him in that he had encountered, during them, the beauty of the past more actually than ever before. He himself had been engaged for a long time now on the most modern aspect of art. He had seen beauty in terms of lines, angles, cubes, squares, as bare, naked, strong and undecorated as he could make it. But now this pageant had thrown him back into the very citadel of decorated splendour, tapestries, jewels, armour of gold and silver, rich candlesticks, heavy purple vestments, stained glass, missals, caparisoned chargers, Romney's flaming servant carrying the brilliant bird. . . .

More than that. He had been in contact with a personality so strong that it seemed to him as though he stood at his side, advising him, showing him his thoughts, his movements. He knew Henry Arden now better than he knew himself. During rehearsal, once or twice, he had *been* actually, for the moment, Henry Arden. As, in front of the Cathedral door, he withstood the charge of the knights, giving his great cry of defiance, he thought: "This is the end. All my life, my hopes, my great ambitions have come to this. To be murdered by this scrabble of cowardly knaves," and he had to hold himself (his temper being what it was) not to give them back blow for blow. Percy Dalton, the Pageant Master, had come up to him after rehearsal and said to him: "That was magnificent, Mr. Lampiron. Never seen anything better. You *were* the Bishop himself."

He was thinking of all this when he felt the touch on his arm to find, to his disgust, that it was the loathsome Furze. His temper was up in a moment as Henry Arden's would have been had he been accosted by some villainous usurer.

So when he heard, "What a lovely afternoon, Mr. Lampiron," he nodded his head and would have moved on. But his progress was interrupted by people and Furze said:

"I wonder if you could find it convenient, Mr. Lampiron, to come in one evening and talk over a little bit of business."

"See here, Furze," he said. "Keep your hands off me. You can sell me up or do anything else you bloody well please, but in the street at least I'm free."

As usual when he was angry he spoke louder than he knew, and several people turned and looked at the two men.

Furze smiled. "Very well, Mr. Lampiron," he said. "Have it your own way. You're a rash man."

"It's you that are rash," he answered. "Do your damnedest but keep out of my way if you don't want something to happen to you."

He realized then that it was a crowded street and that people were passing, so he broke away and, furious with anger, crossed the street, strode away on the other side, not observing Canon Ronder and Gaselee whom he almost touched.

"My word!" Gaselee said. "*He's* in a temper!"

At a quarter to five Klitch was trying to sell a pair of paste earrings to an elderly lady who had come, as she informed him, all the way from Winchester to attend the Pageant.

Afterwards when trying to recall her he could remember nothing of her appearance but that she had a slight moustache and wore a skirt remarkably short for current fashion, and white stockings. The short skirt was three years out of date, the white stockings thirty. She adored pageants, she told him, and had seen more than forty. Just then the thunderstorm that had been threatening all day broke. There was one great crack of sound directly over the Cathedral. The boards of the stand opposite the window leapt into white brilliance. Then the rain came down in sheets.

PERFORMANCE

"These are very beautiful, madam," Klitch said, caressing the earrings, "and a hundred years old at least."

"I don't really want jewelry." She moved about, flicking a light-green parasol dangerously at this article and that. "That's pretty, that mirror, and what a darling chair! Now what *does* *that* cost?"

Klitch brought forward the chair, which *was* a good one, its seat worked in old tapestry.

"That's very good tapestry, madam. You can't go wrong with a chair like that. It would find itself at home anywhere— good in any company."

"Oh, but I don't know that it's a chair that I really want. *How* the rain is coming down! And I have only my parasol. Do listen to that thunder! It seems to be directly overhead."

"Let's hope it won't be like this tomorrow," Klitch said. "Now this chair is really cheap considering the tapestry, but if it's too expensive here is a pair . . ."

But the lady was still wandering.

"Oh, what a darling set of chessmen!" she exclaimed. "My husband *adores* chess! I wonder . . ."

It was then that Klitch, turning towards the centre of the shop, saw Stephen Furze. He was standing looking in, and over his head his big green umbrella. His face peered forward out of the umbrella as a tortoise protrudes its little tongue-licking head from its shell. The rain dripped from the umbrella. There was a fierce thunderclap and an intense savage blare of lightning. Klitch saw in that illumination the bowler hat, the thin line of eyebrow, the eyes, piercing and yet veiled, the large white nose, the long tight mouth with the sharp chin. The flash was gone and there was only the sombre rain-sodden light from the thunderous sky. A moment later Furze also was gone and the lady knocked over a blue vase with the point of her parasol. . . .

By Arden Gate, Ronder, who had felt even that short climb, said, "Service is over. I am going into the Cathedral for a moment."

Gaselee said, "I'll come with you."

He had been thinking while they were in Bennett's that Ronder was ageing very fast. Of course we must all die sometime, but it seems a pity when the brain is still so sharp and active that the rest of the body should not support it.

Ronder took Gaselee's arm across the grass and made the same remark that Klitch had made a little earlier: "It will all look very different this time tomorrow."

"Yes. I hope it's fine. There's thunder threatening now. Look at that black cloud over Harry Tower."

"Yes." The Cathedral bells rang the half hour. "Half-past four. Will you come and have a cup of tea after I've had a word with Broad in the Cathedral?"

"Thanks very much."

"I'm not young any more." He paused, leaning on Gaselee's arm. "I'm too fat, of course—always have been. I remember years ago, soon after I first came here, chaffing Brandon about our size, his and mine. He didn't like it at all. He had never any sense of humour about himself, poor fellow."

They passed into the Cathedral by a small side door that led directly to the Choir. Now, in a choir stall, Ronder sat suddenly down. From where they were they could see the Choir, the Black Bishop's Tomb, the High Altar. From the rest of the Cathedral they were shut off. There seemed to be no one about. There was absolute stillness.

"We'll wait here a moment before I hunt out Broad." He sighed, patted his stomach, passed his hand over his thinning hair. Gaselee, as often before, wondered at his shining, meticulous neatness. An old immensely stout man, but spotless, almost dapper. His eyes shot sharply out behind his large round spectacles. "People would nickname me Pickwick if I didn't sometimes look devilish," Ronder said about himself.

"Funny how people haven't forgotten Brandon," Gaselee said. "After all, he didn't *do* anything very special—not in the end, I mean."

"In the end he died at a Chapter Meeting," Ronder said. "He always thought that I was his enemy, that I was respon-

sible for all his misfortunes, that it was because of me that his
wife and son ran away. All quite false. But I won't deny that
I thought, at that time, that I was the New Order come, by
Divine ordinance, to supersede the Old. Now, when I look back,
there doesn't seem to be any difference between the two. In fact,
my dear Gaselee," here he laid his plump hand on the younger
man's shoulder, "you said just now that Brandon hadn't done
anything. Well, I haven't done anything either."

"Oh, come!" Gaselee said. "That's absurd. I don't want to
flatter you, but you have been the soul of this place for nearly
forty years."

"No," Ronder said, taking off his glasses and wiping them.
"Not the soul. Anything you like, but not the soul."

Gaselee raised his head.

"There. Did you hear that?"

"No—what?"

"Thunder."

A faint rumbling, as of heavy feet moving, came from the
organ loft and the Whispering Gallery. The Cathedral was
suspiciously still, as though holding its breath.

"We'd better wait for the thundershower to pass," Ronder
said. Then he sighed. "When you get to my age, Gaselee, and
are out of condition as I am, some part or other of your body
responds evilly to every kind of weather. If it's a lovely day and
the sun's shining, your eyes ache; if it's cold, your prostate
gives you trouble; if it's close, your head shuts down on you;
if it rains, you have rheumatism. Ah, well, my time's nearly
up—and most of it's been wasted time."

"What do you mean—wasted?" Gaselee asked.

Ronder looked at him with an affectionate but also cynical
smile. "I talk to you, Gaselee, more intimately perhaps than
to anyone else here. I'll tell you why, if it doesn't offend you."

"Of course it doesn't offend me," Gaselee replied, but a little
apprehensive all the same.

"You're young and ambitious. You have come here just as
I came here, thirty-six years ago, resolved to run things. And
you will, no doubt. There's no one to stop you. You'll stay here,

perhaps, over thirty years, as I have done. And then, as I do now, you'll discover that you've missed it."

"Missed what?" Gaselee asked.

"The essential thing—the thing that the Bishop and Purcell before him and Wistons discovered—that I have not. I went wrong, I think now, over a Pybus appointment. Oh, it's years ago and stale history. It was a question of appointing some young ass whom Brandon fancied or Wistons. Of course I was right to insist on Wistons, and I did insist, and it was that that broke Brandon up finally. But I insisted for the wrong reasons. I was proud of my intellectual superiority over the others, and the victory that my intellect won then confirmed me in my course. I wasn't malleable after all."

"Don't you believe in a good brain, then?" Gaselee asked.

"Yes, of course. The problem of Christianity now is just that—how to be intellectual enough to deal with modern science, higher criticism and the rest, but not to put the brain so high that you lose the essential thing. Because religion is faith. Religion is also intelligence. They can combine—they must combine—but the proper balance is the problem. There's a mystery, you see. The same mystery there has always been. If you miss understanding *that* you miss everything, however clever you are. I didn't see that then. I can see it now. I've missed it."

Gaselee felt uncomfortable. The Cathedral was cold and as empty as the tomb. A great clap of thunder like an explosion in the church's very heart startled them both.

"You're as spooky," Gaselee said, "as old Mordaunt himself with his watching figure and live knights and the rest."

"I don't know," Ronder said, "whether there isn't something in his idea. Do you realize what Arden and Leofranc and the others had that we haven't got? They had intensity. They may have been wrong, but they *believed* they were right and fought and sweated and prayed. Don't you see? Either this whole thing, the spiritual life, is nonsense or it's real. It must be one or the other. If it's nonsense, what rot this all is and has been for centuries! But if it's real, what are we doing about it? Have you attended ordinary Matins or Evensong at a country or town church lately? What do you find, nine times out of ten? A droning mechanical office without thought or meaning, an unreal sermon with a lot of dead symbolic phrases taken for granted. What's the daily Evensong in this cathedral or any other? A mumbled repetition with a lazy choir and a scrap of a congregation. *If* it's real, don't you suppose that someone is angry somewhere? Mordaunt's Inquisitor or another. He examines, perhaps, one after another and throws them away. 'No life here. Nothing worth preserving.' So in a little time it may be with me. When you're near the end, Gaselee, your values alter, and it's too late to do anything about it. . . ."

"You're not feeling too well," Gaselee said. "That's what it is."

"I daresay. The body has a lot to do with it. Physical things are fine while they last, but they don't last forever."

A great rumble of thunder came like cannon balls rolling down the Nave. Then there was an intense silence. The two men did not speak.

Ronder said suddenly:

"Did you hear anything?"

"No—what?"

"I thought—a cry."

Both men listened.

Ronder got up and walked to the end of the Choir, looking into the Nave. There was no one to be seen.

He went back.

"Well, I must find Broad—and then we will have some tea."

After ten minutes or so they discovered Broad coming in by a side door from the cloisters, wiping his mouth with a large red handkerchief. He was frightened of Ronder, who had been sharp with him more than once, so he began to excuse himself. He had but run away home to snatch a cup of tea. He had had a busy afternoon, for the tourists had been incessant.

Ronder talked to him about some affair and then Broad asked him to excuse him. He must hurry to lock the Harry

Tower door. "And it will be a while, gentlemen, before it's open again. I doubt that I did right having it open for visitors today, but the Dean allowed it. The wood of the Gallery floor is as weak as matchwood, they say."

With apologies he left them. But someone stopped him, and he left the locking of the door until later.

The thunderstorm had rumbled itself into the distance, and Klitch, Mrs. Klitch and young Guy strolled down to the Gate to see what the crowd was doing.

Over the Precincts a lovely sky of the palest blue, without a shred of cloud, lay like a summer sea. The grass was shining and fragrant after the rain.

Young Guy caught his father's sleeve. "There's Mr. Furze," he said. "The old miserly one."

"Where?" said his father, who had lit his pipe and was about to suggest a pleasant stroll down the High Street.

"There—crossing the Green."

But his father saw no one.

"You're seeing things, my boy. There's no one there. Come on. We'll go down to the Market and see how the Town's behaving itself."

CHAPTER IV

Pageant: During the Performance Enter Rumour

THE SUN was pouring down. It was a perfect day.

On the greensward behind the Cathedral the two great tents placed for the robing and disrobing of the general performers shone like snow. The grass was covered with the eager members of the Boy Scouts, the Girl Guides, the Young Men's Christian Association, the Town Guild, the Polchester Athletic Association, the Women's Institutes, all waiting, breathlessly and perspiringly, to perform their parts. It was extremely hot.

With a sudden magnificence there burst upon them the strains of "God Save the King." The Pageant had begun!

Mrs. Cronin and Canon Cronin were fortunate in possessing a house with a large garden that stretched from the Precincts to the edge of the lawns behind the Cathedral, overlooking the Pol. They had eagerly offered their house for the comfort and convenience of the special performers. This pageant in fact provided Mrs. Cronin with her ideal opportunity. She was a lady who had, all her life, suffered from an inferiority complex. She longed to be loved by everyone and at the same time saw only too clearly why it must be impossible for anyone to love her. The Cronins were not wealthy or clever or easy companions. He busied himself eagerly in Church matters but always failed to create an impression. No one in Polchester meant better—no one achieved less. And she, loving not only

215

her husband but all the world, insisted on kindnesses that were not needed, on anxieties for her friends that they felt to be tiresome, chattered when she should have been silent, was enthusiastic when a little sarcasm was the proper thing, defended friends who never suspected they needed defence, was intimate too quickly and bitterly disappointed too publicly.

Now, however, for once in a way, she possessed something that everyone wanted, and oh, how eagerly she gave it! The house had many bedrooms, bathrooms, large dining room and drawing room. There was the garden, there were summer-houses, food and drink for everyone! All so splendidly at hand that Mrs. Braund in her armour, Lady Mary in her ruff and pearls, Lampiron in his cope and mitre, these and the others had but to take a step and there they were! So Mrs. Cronin—a small woman with large wet blue eyes, a snub nose and a shrill high-pitched voice—moving here, there, everywhere, saying: "Oh, darling, are you sure you have all that you want?" "There are *lovely* cool drinks in the dining room!" "Oh, but it's *no* trouble, it's a joy!"—was happier than she had ever been since Canon Cronin proposed to her on the steps of the Acropolis, years ago, in a dust storm.

Mrs. Braund, Lady Mary, Lampiron had bedrooms to themselves; others, the Carris girls and Penny for example, shared and chattered and shared again. The whole house echoed with voices, laughter, cries, calls to servants. In every bedroom was a card with the time-table of the succeeding episodes. Every performer must be ready for his or her entrance ten minutes before public appearance. Through the open windows could be heard the high voices of the performers in the First Episode: Withers—the author of the book—was himself playing the part of St. Leofranc, and his rather shrill, piping voice came into the room where Mrs. Braund was:

"*Bring me the child.*

"*A fever, say you? At point of death? An it be God's will, sickness is nought. . . .*"

Mrs. Braund, a crimson wrapper concealing the first layer of her transformation, stretched on a chaise-longue, looked at her watch, out of window, back at her watch again. Her episode was the fifth and she had still an hour of this intolerable waiting. Her brain was a messy confusion. She repeated some of her lines to herself:

"*What, men, Englishmen, and afraid?*

"*With this cathedral here for your support, this fair town that trusts to you?*

"*Know you how I have loved you and built on you my faith? I, who . . . I, who . . .*"

What if the words would not come? Then she would invent them. She had had, at the dress rehearsal, an odd experience when it seemed to her that she had poured out a torrent of angry, abusive rhetoric that had, most certainly, never come from Mr. Withers. But no one had noticed anything. She had been greatly applauded and praised although she fancied that there had been an angry whisper in her ear: "Get off your horse, you fool! Do you fancy *that's* the way to ride?"

Oh, well, it was a queer business altogether and she would not be sorry when it was over. But how was it that she had known that there were stores of gunpowder laid down in the Cathedral vaults and that new wheels had been fitted on the guns brought from Drymouth, that her anxiety was about *these* things, the gunpowder, the wheels, and not about her words and the discomfort of her armour and her longing for a cup of tea?

She moved restlessly. Yes, and that trouble with the Carris girls! What perverse fate had arranged that they should be at hand when she had said some light mocking thing about their mother? Why was it that she seemed now to be surrounded with hostility? Jealousy, of course; her photograph—she magnificent on her horse with her attendants around her—in the London papers!

She had looked forward to this tremendously, and now something, someone, was spoiling it. The whole town was split into parties and factions. It was this heat, this unbroken succession of fine days. English people weren't accustomed to it. . . .

There was a knock on the door and Romney came in. He was in a state of almost hysterical excitement.

"Oh, darling, are you all right? May I come in? Quite respectable? There, the First Episode's over. The place is packed. Not a seat anywhere, and it's so hot in the stands that everyone is sitting in pools of perspiration. Feeling nervous, darling? You shouldn't be. You were superb at rehearsal yesterday. Simply marvellous. You and Lampiron—I thought Mary was a *little* Bloomsbury, didn't you? And she hasn't got nose enough. The real Elizabeth was *all* ruff and nose. And oh, darling, the Carris girls are *so* angry. They've just been pouring it all out! What *did* you say to them?"

"I didn't say anything. They're always eavesdropping."

Romney saw that tears were not far away. He understood *all* about tears, how to produce them, how to prevent them. He consoled her now as though he were her mother.

In the paddocks behind the Cathedral the crowd from the First Episode was streaming into the tents while the crowd for the Second Episode arranged itself under Mr. Percy Dalton's Napoleonic command.

"Now-now. Quiet. Quiet. What did I tell you? Group A to the left, Group C half-right. . . . Now. Remember. Group D—you follow the Pope. The Monks—all ready? Watch for Mr. Doggett's beat—in front of the orchestra. I'll give you the beat until you get where you can see him. . . ."

Many of the crowd who had figured in the First Episode were also in this, for costume had not changed so greatly from Leofranc to Gregory. It was afterwards said that it was by means of this confusion that some of the town roughs—Tom Caul, young M'Canlis, Fred Ottley (Ottley's good-for-nothing brother)—managed to push their way in. They had no right to be there at all, and afterwards there was much discussion as to where they found their costumes. Little Timothy Broad could have told a tale if he dared. He was one of the smallest and youngest of all the Boy Scouts and he was in Episode Two. He even had a line to speak when, running forward with a crowd of children, he shades his eyes with his hand and cries: "There is dust on the road. I hear the tramp of horses!" How wonderful it had all been, all through rehearsal, suddenly to take the centre of the stage, to cry his sentence, and it seemed to him that he was not looking into the stands, the roofs and chimneys of Norman Row, but that he in reality saw a long straight road, poplars bordering it, the dust spiralling up into a hot blue sky, and a group of horsemen against the horizon. Some of them were in armour. He could catch the sparkle of silver and brass. . . .

At the dress rehearsal he had stayed there gazing after his part was over, and Mr. Dalton, whose temper was very uncertain, had scolded him. Now, on the actual day, he had felt very safe. He would make no mistake. He was dressed in a bright blue smock, with a gold belt, bare legs and sandals. He wanted his handkerchief and he ran back to the tent. It was filled with Boy Scouts and men from the Athletic Association. He himself could have dressed at home, but it felt more important to be with all the others. He knew where his clothes were at the far end of the tent. When he got there he saw a very terrifying sight. Young Aldridge, the Mayor's eldest son, a young man of twenty or so, was standing in his underclothes looking very sheepish and even terrified. Over him, in a threatening attitude, stood what seemed to little Timothy a gigantic man, naked save for a pair of very shabby socks and tattered sock suspenders. He appeared to Timothy the largest man he had ever seen, with a red unshaven scowling face, a chest covered with black hair, and very unclean hands whose dirt stood out clearly against the bright whiteness of his thighs. This strange giant was speaking to young Aldridge in no uncertain words. "I'll break your blasted neck if you say a word——"

Then, to Timothy's astonishment, he proceeded to cover his nakedness with young Aldridge's costume, which was sack-like in shape, dark red in colour. The fierce face, the bare hairy legs, the great breadth of shoulder, all helped to make of Tom Caul a far finer native Briton than Aldridge would have made. His costume adjusted, he laughed, gave Aldridge a push that sent him reeling to the side of the tent. Then he saw Timothy.

"What the hell are you staring at?" Then his good-nature (for he was often good-natured) had the better of him and he caught Timothy Broad up, lifted him onto his shoulder and strode out, shouting as he went.

The fact was that he was pretty drunk during the whole of that week, which made it afterwards difficult for him to give an accurate account of his own behaviour. But, like many men who are drunk more often than sober, he was well able to look after himself in either state. But he was reckless. He didn't care a damn what happened. He'd set fire to the Cathedral for tuppence. When the crowd rushed into the arena to welcome the Pope he still carried young Timothy on his shoulder. He was shouting and waving his free arm.

"You'll have to let me go," Timothy whispered in his ear. "I have to speak."

Caul released him, but only just in time. Timothy ran forward with the other children, said his line, stood staring down the road, under his hand. How clearly he saw it! It ran straight between poplars, then there was a small wooden bridge beneath which ran a stream; then a small hill began and it was on the rise of this hill that he saw the horsemen, their armour glinting in the sun. . . . But he did not forget this time to move back with the other children. Now he lost the road but instead saw the mass of the audience, dark, scattered with pieces of colour —red, green, blue, and then to the left the solid block of the choir, more than three hundred of them, all in white.

It was at that moment that the first real trouble occurred. Pope Gregory (Mr. Bennett of the bookshop) was advancing, followed by the chanting monks, when, to everyone's consternation, Tom Caul ran out from the crowd, waving his arms, shouting, crying out some strange words that no one understood. Then, when he was in the very middle of the arena, he seemed to realize where he was, for he looked sheepish suddenly, scowled about him, and, shaking his fist (apparently at poor Bennett, down whose face sweat was already pouring because the sun was so hot and his clothes were so heavy), moved back into the crowd and disappeared.

PERFORMANCE

Yes, the audience was finding it extremely warm; the cheaper seats were not under cover and the upper covered seats felt the roof "heavy like thunder" on their heads. But there were, at present, no complaints. Everyone was in excellent temper. The Duchess of Drymouth herself was present—that large lady like a beetroot in grey silk and a purple toque, the kind the Queen wears. There was the Bishop, the Archdeacon, Aldridge and Mrs. Aldridge (Aldridge said, during the Second Episode, to his wife: "I don't see Bob anywhere, my dear. I've looked through the glasses at everyone." "Oh dear," said Mrs. Aldridge, "I do hope it isn't his stomach," because Bob inherited his faulty digestion from his father), Lord and Lady St. Leath with a party of friends, all these grand people sat in fine prominent seats bordered with red cloth. In front of the Duchess, who was so hot that perspiration dimmed her eyes and she saw everything through a haze, there was a large bouquet of carnations. Mrs. Dickens, who was on one of the uncovered stands to the right of the swells, with three others of Mrs. Coole's old ladies, saw the carnations and passionately longed that they should be put into water. There they lay, poor things, sizzling on the hot boards, gasping. Oh yes, gasping like fish out of water. Her red, hard-worked perspiring little hands clenched and unclenched. She heard the chanting of the monks and thought how lovely it was, but old Mrs. Anthony said, wiping her forehead, "My, but it's hot! What's the matter with you, Alice? You're as restless as I don't know——" "It's those carnations. There in front of the Duchess. Poor things, they're dying for water."

Canon Dale and Gaselee were sitting two rows above the dignitaries. "Good," said Dale, "that bit of colour. Do you see it? That crimson book Gregory is carrying against the white, and the soldier in the crowd with that apple-green banneret."

"Yes. Romney's doing," Gaselee said. "He's got genius. I've seen dozens of pageants before, but this is different from any other. I can tell that already, although these first two episodes are bound to be drab. Did you notice the stone of sacrifice in the First Episode? Romney had had an extraordinary devil

painted on it in red and gold. I happened to notice it in the
paddocks yesterday with some of the other properties. Well,
no one will know that devil is there except Romney himself
and a few connected with the immediate scenes. Yet, although
nobody sees it, it will help the general atmosphere. It makes a
difference. Then in the episode just finished did you notice that
rough-looking fellow rush forward with a boy on his shoulder?
Did you realize that he shouted gibberish, not English at all?
What a touch! I bet that was Romney's doing—Old Dalton
would never have thought of it."

"Didn't you recognize him?" Dale asked. "The ruffian, I
mean? He's one of the town villains—a fellow named Caul. He's
a Hyde Park orator, a communist, a spouter of revolt. I cannot
think what he's doing in the Pageant at all. And the child he
had on his shoulder was Broad's little boy—Broad the verger,
the most conventional, snobbish old time-server. A funny con-
junction!"

But now they were silent, for the Third Episode was beginning. In the stand nearest Arden Gate, well to the front on one
of the unprotected seats, was Klitch, and with him his wife and
children. The Cathedral choir was to take part in only one episode—the visit of Queen Elizabeth—so young Klitch had still
plenty of time before he need robe. He was to sing one verse of
the welcoming song as solo, but that did not perturb nor excite
him. He was a very self-composed unemotional boy, sure of
what he wanted. But the Third Episode—the visit of the Pilgrims and the Town Fair—excited and pleased him. He leant
forward, his eyes shining. This was the first opportunity for
both Dalton and Romney. Dalton, whatever his eccentricities
and snobberies may have been, had a genius for crowds. The
Pilgrims had not been, like those of Canterbury or Winchester,
ever greatly noble or distinguished, but Polchester had been
the Cathedral for seamen, fishermen, merchants owning cargoes
—and now Dalton had given his crowd a special seafaring
appearance. An appeal had been made (very rashly it was
afterwards thought) for men in Seatown who had something to
do with the sea.

PERFORMANCE

They had responded in considerable numbers, for they were
for the most part unemployed, and now a very lively rough
crowd they had made. They came pouring into the arena, the
respectable members singing the Pilgrims' Hymn, but the good
Seatown citizens, many of them happily in liquor, laughed and
shouted and tumbled onto one another like animals. The Pilgrims were met by the incoming at the other end of the arena
of the Town Fair. Here Romney had excelled himself. His whole
passion for fantastic, abnormal, and morbid creation had been
allowed its escape. On the surface (and with the majority of
the audience it was only the surface that was perceived) you
were aware that this was a scene of gay colour and clever movements, but not on the whole dramatic as the scenes with Lady
Emily and the Black Bishop were to be. Yet for one or two—for
Ronder, for Michael Furze, for Mordaunt, for little Tim Broad,
for a few more—it was the most significant moment of the
afternoon.

In all it lasted only ten minutes. The booths were placed.
There were two clowns in cherry-coloured tights, there was a
quack doctor with bottles of coloured liquid and a girl who
carried a snake on her arm, there were sellers of trinkets and
laces, there were performers of tragedy, there was a wrestling
match, there was a gilt coach with a grand lady, there was a
man dragged, by the Justices' order, to the whipping post,
there were children following a piper. . . .

Romney's sense of colour here was allied to Percy Dalton's
production. His sharp reds and sudden greens, his gold cloth
and silver tissue, brilliantly stabbed the dun background of
jerkin and woollen hose. But his spirit was no more in these than
you would suspect. It was about the things that you *didn't* see
that his queer abnormal nature took the greatest pleasure.
Gaselee and a few others suspected this. For Gaselee—who was
not, as it happened, on that day feeling very well—everything
had slightly the air of phantasmagoria. He suspected (in this
scene especially) that behind every figure that he saw there
was another figure. As the Fair people danced to the sharp acid
note of the pipe and drum, it seemed to him that other more

shadowy figures danced also, and as the Pilgrims moved in solemn file, singing, through the great doors of the Cathedral, he thought that at the very time there emerged a procession, a long man in black, his head a little on one side, followed by a kind of trestle carried by four men. As the little group approached, the Fair died away, the singing and laughter and music faded. The episode ended.

"That's clever of Romney," Gaselee said to Dale.

"What is?" Dale asked.

"Why, you know the tale that's been round the town this summer of a man who comes out of the West Door, followed by a corpse on a trestle. A ridiculous tale—heaven knows how it originated—but several people say they have seen him——"

"No. I hadn't heard it," said Dale. "This town seems to be full of stories just now."

"Well, Romney had. He used it in this scene."

"I wondered what that group coming from the Cathedral at the end meant. I wasn't sure in fact whether I *did* see it. The crowd of Pilgrims obscured it. A clever scene that, altogether."

Gaselee moved restlessly. His stomach was very unsettled and like all optimistic egoists he felt, when his bodily organs functioned a little uneasily, that it was an affront to his dignity and a menace to his security.

"I agree with you. We are a little far away. It's hard to tell what one's seeing and what one's not."

Klitch and Mrs. Klitch, in their seats high up, had no doubts about what they saw and did not see. But then they never did. They had, both of them, excellently clear sight, physical, moral, and æsthetic.

Klitch, as bright as a painted figure, with his high white collar, his gleaming tie pin, his round, ruddy and smiling countenance, was enjoying himself hugely. He was greatly proud of the whole affair as though he had himself created it. For weeks he had been pleased with the world-wide advertisement that Polchester was obtaining, the photographs, the paragraphs in the London papers. And now all was well. The sun was shining and the Pageant was proving itself an excellent pageant. There

could not surely be a better anywhere. This last episode, now
—the life, the colour, the movement! As it ended and the noise
died, the figures vanished, leaving only, once more, the great
wall of the Cathedral and the bright glittering greensward, he
turned to Mrs. Klitch, beaming.

"I call that first rate. You might be right back in the Middle
Ages, my dear. That dancing, and the music and the quack
doctor and the fellow ranting the play on the floor of that cart—
the Middle Ages, my dear! You could *smell* them."

And it was just then that little Mr. Crockett (whose second-
hand bookshop was poor Marlowe's temptation) leaned forward
and, speaking low in Klitch's ear, said:

"I say, Klitch, have you heard about Furze?"

"No," said Klitch. "Which Furze?"

"Stephen Furze."

"No. What about him? Broken his neck? I wish to God he
had."

"Not so far as I know. But he's disappeared."

"Disappeared?"

"Yes. Since yesterday afternoon. No one's set eyes on him."

Klitch was greatly interested.

"You don't say?"

"Yes. He never came home last night. They've been making
enquiries this morning. Nobody's seen him. Nobody——"

But the next episode was beginning. They must pay attention.

Bird was not far from them. He had a good seat but he was,
as yet, sadly unable to concentrate. For two reasons. One was
that Mr. and Miss Porteous were, by a fatal chance, in seats just
behind him. The other reason was that the place next to his was
empty. Elizabeth had not come.

He had counted on her absolutely. The note that she had
written to him had been simple and brief, but there had been
sincerity in every word of it. He knew now that he loved her.
He had never been in love before, but this had come to him with
complete certainty. He was clear-headed and clear-eyed about

it in every way. He knew that she was not beautiful (although at times she seemed to him to have in her gaze, her figure, her stature something more beautiful than physical beauty). He made no pretence to himself that he loved her only for her character, which was, he thought, finer than that of anyone he had ever known. He loved her in every way, physical, mental, and spiritual. He did not suppose that she, as yet, loved him. He believed himself to be entirely unattractive to women, in spite of Miss Camilla, who was sitting, as though dressed for golf, so close behind him. He recognized very well the type that he was—the little, gentle, mouse-like, uncared-for man whom he encountered so frequently in novels and the pictures. Figuring in such romances the little man was always passed over by the proud beauty, although his heart of gold won something worth while before the end. Yes, that was his *external* figure, a sentimental and moving type. But *inside* he was entirely different. He was not sentimental nor touching nor appealing. He had often the rudest and most violent wishes and desires. He frequently disliked people very much and wished to tell them so. He had not, as such little men in books often had, complete trust in every human—he did in fact discover that many people were greedy, cruel, selfish and lustful. Were it not for his trust in God he would have poor hopes for many of his fellow-creatures.

He had always thought himself a coward, but, since his defiance of Porteous over the Carol Service, he had found his courage grow. He did not know that Porteous had, only this last week, said to his daughter: "I cannot *think* what is happening to Bird. He seems to have no real sense of playing the game." If he had heard, he would have been pleased. His love for Elizabeth and his friendship with Lampiron were bringing out of him qualities that had always been there but had received little encouragement.

Now, when Porteous boomed in his ear: "Splendid! Quite splendid! The team work is magnificent!" he nodded his head but made no other reply. What would they say, Porteous and his daughter, when they saw Elizabeth come in and sit beside him?

Well, they could say what they liked ... it would do them good.

But why didn't she come? The Fourth Episode was beginning, the episode of the Black Bishop. It was to this that he had
chiefly been looking forward because his friend was to be glorified in it. He had heard from many sides that Lampiron was
most remarkable, that it was as though Henry Arden himself
had come to life. A group of knights came in, a lonely little
group on the empty sward. They dismounted from their horses
and waited. A crowd of people passed into the Cathedral, the
bells pealing. Then a procession of monks singing. Then the
Black Bishop, followed by two monks. The knights started
forward; the Bishop turned and looked at them. The bells
ceased and there was a great silence.

Lampiron looked superb in glittering vestments. But there
was much more in it than clothes and vestments. As he stood
there he seemed the embodiment of law, order, strength. There
was defiance, there was saintliness and, in some curious way,
there was also the foreboding of doom. Then he passed into the
church.

Crowds gathered, idly looking on. Then the knights, pushing
their way through the crowd, also passed in. There was silence—
and Bird, who for a moment forgot Elizabeth and everything
in the world but the reality of this scene, held his breath. So
with all that crowd. Dale said afterwards that it was all he
could do not to rush forward and help to defend, or at least to
warn, the victim. It was too late for warning. Through the open
door there came a great cry and then the clash of swords. The
crowd moved, calling and shouting.

Then, from the West Door, there came a mêlée of struggling
and fighting men—knights, monks and the Bishop himself. One
knight had him by the shoulder, his sword uplifted, but Arden
tore himself away, stood, his feet planted, his head up, and
called in a voice that rang through the arena:

"God's servant! Beware of God's servant!"

A divine rage seemed to seize him and, raising his crozier,
he shouted his defiance, not because of their attack on himself
but for their insult to his church. For an instant he was alone,

his strength and power seemed to dominate not only that scene, but the town, the country, the world. Then the knights fell upon him. For a moment he was above them; he had caught two knights by the shoulders and was beating them off as though they were dolls. Then he fell.

The knights, their work done, ran to their horses. No one in the crowd stayed them. They rode off furiously. Two monks were slain. The others gathered about their master and, at last, bore him up into the Cathedral again. The crowd knelt, the bell began to toll. At length there was no one there—only a torn cloak on the sward.

Bird drew a deep breath. For a brief moment of time—or had it been an experience out of time, without beginning or end?—he had watched (and powerless to help) the death of his friend. It was as though, with abrupt hands, a rough segment had been torn from a heavy all-embracing curtain. He had looked through and had seen more, far more, than that one scene. He had realized fragments of building—crocketed pinnacles, arch-moulds delicately patterned, an openwork gable flanked by turrets, windows of burning glowing glass deep-set in thick walls, a strange rank smell of horse dung and tar after smoke of incense, and Arden himself in some small room with black panelling, turning to him with a gentle smile. . . .

He pressed his hand against his forehead and, as though he awoke from a dream, was aware of the murmur of voices and the sun striking the Cathedral windows; he heard the trumpet blow to announce the next episode.

Then he saw also that Elizabeth Furze was coming in.

How glad he was! As he watched her, moving so quietly and with such dignity towards him, he felt as though he had known her forever and ever. He knew her shyness and diffidence. He saw that people were noticing her and saying, doubtless, as she always heard them saying: "There goes old Furze's daughter." Perhaps the cruel ones were adding: "I wonder she has the impertinence."

But he thought to himself: She need never have any fear any more because I shall always be with her.

PERFORMANCE

As she sat down beside him she said in a low voice:
"I'm sorry I'm late."

"It doesn't matter a bit now that you've come!"

How he enjoyed that moment when she took her place beside him! What old Porteous and the others would be thinking! And, maybe, afterwards Porteous would be saying to him: "I don't think, my dear fellow . . . What I mean is that in a town like this one has to be careful——" And wouldn't he enjoy replying: "Well, Rector, if you don't like my friends . . ."

Then she said an extraordinary thing:

"I am late because we are in great trouble. My father went out yesterday afternoon and has not come back. We——"

But the episode was beginning. He saw that she turned with a great effort of will and faced the scene, her lips set, her hands clasped tightly on her lap.

He was afterwards greatly to regret that, because of his preoccupation with Elizabeth's trouble, much of the scene that now took place was to remain dim to him. For it was now that the sense of disturbance that had, in an undefined way, been growing throughout the afternoon, was for a moment to become visible to everybody.

Here at least Dalton's famous talent for the mastery of crowds was seen at its finest. Every actor in the Pageant, great and small, figured in this scene. A tumultuous mob rushed in, to the discordance of guns, trumpets, and all the riot of warfare, as though to protect the Cathedral. A confused mass of soldiers ran back from Arden Gate. The whole multitude of people was driven huddling and crying against the very walls of the Cathedral.

Then Emily de Brytte appeared on her white horse, her women behind her, clad in armour, waving her sword, rallying her soldiers.

The crowd turned, sweeping around her, the soldiers again advancing. Dalton here gave a marvellous sense of peril and threatening catastrophe. You must feel that the high climbing street of the town was crowded with the enemy—you could smell the smoke and feel the hot tongue of the flame. Before

Arden Gate there was mêlée and confusion. The crowd hurled itself into the business of shouting, yelling, screaming with all the joy in the world. The issue hung in the balance. . . .

It was at this principal moment of the scene that Bird could not clear his impression. But he was not alone in that. A hundred different versions were afterwards given of it. The common account was that some rough fellow laid hands on poor Mrs. Braund's white horse and even on Mrs. Braund herself. It was said that there was a good deal of general fighting in the crowd and that the fighting was not imitation Pageant business either. However that might be, there came unquestionably a moment when Mrs. Braund seemed in danger of being dragged from her horse and trampled on the ground. And more than that—there was, behind her actual personal danger, for a brief time, a consciousness everywhere that a general riot might break out. Many people rose in their seats. Someone cried shrilly: it was as though, in that second of time, everyone were warned of the actual reality of the peril that lies always beneath the thin crust of conventional conduct.

Then it passed. Order was restored. Mrs. Braund, her helmet a little askew, rode to the Gate, was cheered by her now victorious soldiers, and then proceeded forward slowly to behind the scene, her people following her.

And the audience sat in a vaguely astonished silence, settling back to conventional safety again.

He turned then to Elizabeth.

"What do you mean? Tell me. Your father hasn't returned?"

"No. He was seen last yesterday afternoon. A number of people saw him going up the High Street. Last night I waited for him. He's sometimes out late on business. And then, about one o'clock, I went to bed. But I woke about four. I don't know why. I don't know what disturbed me. It was a hot night with a full moon. I couldn't rest, and at last I went downstairs and there in the hall I found my uncle."

"Your uncle?"

"Yes. He's been very restless lately and has taken to walking about the house at night. The hall was lit with the moon. He asked me what I was doing there, and I said that I had left the door unlocked because Father hadn't come in when I went to bed. I said that I came down to lock it. Then my uncle said that Father was still not in. He had been to his room and he was not there." She drew a deep breath and lowered her voice as though she were afraid that people might hear.

"I didn't wonder then what Uncle Michael was doing in Father's room, although now, when I think of it, it seems odd. Father always hates any of us coming near his room. I said nothing. I went upstairs again. Then I slept. But when I came down in the morning my uncle was waiting for me and he told me that Father had not returned." She looked at him as though to reassure herself. "You know what everyone thinks of us— how they hate us. What I've wanted for years is that we— Mother and I—should do nothing that anyone would notice. And now my first thought was that Father *must* come back or everyone would begin to talk. I went upstairs to tell my mother —she's blind, you know, and hasn't been very well. When I told her she seemed to know it already. When I asked her what we had better do she said we'd better wait. He might return at any moment. He might be in the house now."

She stopped.

"But he wasn't?" Bird said.

"No, he wasn't. There's no sign of him. At first I thought that I wouldn't come this afternoon. And then I thought— yes, I would, just to show them all that there's nothing the matter."

He interrupted her. "Listen. Don't you be frightened."

"I'm not frightened. There's nothing to be frightened of. Father must have taken a night train to Drymouth or some- where without telling us. That's the only possible thing. I expect he's back at the house now or he will come tonight."

"Listen," he said again. "Whatever happens you've got me to depend on. All these months I haven't forced myself on you, have I, or hurt your feelings?"

"No. You've been very kind."

"Well, now, I'm not going to wait any more. It may be as you say—quite all right, nothing wrong at all—but if anything *is* wrong I'm beside you, do you see? I'm your friend, the best you have. There's nothing I won't do for you. There's——"

"Hush," she said. "People will hear."

"I don't care whether they hear or no. I love you, Elizabeth—I——"

"Oh no, no!" she whispered. "Not now. Not here. And not myself. Nobody can—nobody must——"

"Somebody does. Wait. You'll see——"

The Pageant had begun again.

They neither of them realized what was happening. Ronder as the Abbot in the Closing of the Monastery, Lady Mary as Queen Elizabeth, the great assembly of all the actors at the close. . . .

They spoke no more. Only he realized, at the last, that his hand touched her glove, that she did not move but suffered the contact.

The sun was low and Mrs. Cronin's garden was wrapped in a green shade. Inside the house everyone was preparing to depart.

Mrs. Cronin ran from place to place. She was exquisitely happy. "It has been splendid, hasn't it? Pins, darling? Why, yes—thousands, of course. Oh, of course. They say it got very rough once or twice, but how delighted everyone was. And the weather! . . . Yes, my pet, there's cup and iced coffee. . . . No, wait, I'll arrange it for you. . . ."

She tapped on the door. "May I come in?"

She entered and found her maid arranging Mrs. Braund's armour. "So that you'll find it exactly in the same place to-morrow, madam—all ready to put on."

Mrs. Braund, in a little purple hat that suited her none so well, was sitting in a round armchair staring into the long looking glass. She must have seen Mrs. Cronin's reflection in the looking glass but she said no word, made no movement.

"Well, darling—you were splendid. You were wonderful.

You were simply magnificent. Everyone is admiring you quite
wonderfully!"

Mrs. Braund said nothing. She sat there, staring. The maid
gave her mistress a quick intimate glance. Mrs. Braund got up,
pulling her big heavy body together. On her left cheek there
was a faint, a very faint dark bruise the size of a penny.

"Oh, darling, were you hurt? I heard that they were a little
rough."

Mrs. Braund pulled herself together.

"They can't frighten me," she said. "I shall go on with it."

"But of course, darling. . . . Do come and have a drink before
you go. Some cup, or there's iced coffee. . . ."

Mrs. Braund touched her cheek, then picked up her rather
ugly tortoise-shell bag from the bed.

"They can't stop me with threats," she said. "See you tomorrow," and went.

Lampiron, lastly, in the darkling garden (soon to be
drenched with the pale ivory shadow of the moon) met Penny
Marlowe with the two Carris girls.

"Wasn't it topping?" Mabel Carris cried. "And isn't it
lovely to think that there are three more days of it?"

"And you *were* good, Mr. Lampiron," Gladys cried. "Better
than anybody."

"Will you *ever* forget," cried Mabel, "old Mother Braund
with her helmet all on one side clinging to her horse's mane?
The old cat! Serve her right. She'll get it worse before the week's
over."

A figure passed.

"Oh, Lord! I believe that *was* Mother Braund!"

"Never mind! I'll tell her to her face——"

But Penny had not spoken a word. At the gate that opened
onto the Cathedral Green the Carris girls went ahead.

He turned back.

"Well, Penny, did you enjoy it?"

"Yes, in a way. Our episode suddenly got unpleasant somehow. Some of the crowd were rough and I was afraid that I
wouldn't be able to hold my horse in." She added: "Everyone

says you were wonderful. And I can't see you because our scene comes just after. Isn't it a shame?"

She wore a thin summer frock, white with pink flowers and green leaves. In that green dusk she was like a Botticelli child. Such a child and of such lovely unreality that he put his arm round her and kissed her. With a sharp indrawing of breath as though a miracle had occurred she lay for a moment against him, her heart beating against his. She put up her hand and laid the back of it against his cheek.

"Because—in this light," he whispered, "you are unreal——"

Then, his head down, he walked across the Green. She did not move from where he had left her.

Just as he neared his house someone stepped out from the shadow. It was Leggett.

"Hullo, Lampiron!"

"Good-evening." He loathed the man and did not intend to stop, but the thickset body wavering a little on the short quivering legs was in his path.

"Fine show," Leggett said. "I was there. And nothing better than your Bishop. A grand bit of acting. Everyone said so."

"Thanks."

Leggett put out his hand and touched Lampiron's shoulder. Lampiron moved back.

"I say—heard the news?"

"No—what news?"

"Stephen Furze has disappeared."

"Disappeared? How do you mean?"

"I mean what I say. No one has seen him since yesterday afternoon."

"My God!"

"Rather! I agree with you."

"But you—you knew more about him than anyone else. What do you think has happened to him?"

Leggett sniggered

"I don't know—no idea. May have gone off for a jaunt somewhere. Or he may have been murdered."

"Murdered?"

"Yes; plenty of people disliked him—you for one."

"I did—and do."

"Quite so." Leggett moved close to Lampiron, as though examining his face, then turned away.

"I told you about it because I knew you'd be interested. You were one of the last people to see him. So long. Good-night."

CHAPTER V

Elizabeth's Journal: I

I INTEND TO WRITE a brief narrative of the events connected with my father's disappearance. I know that this is a very old-fashioned thing to do. All the heroines of Victorian novels did it, including the dreadful Esther Summerson. But I am going to write with no other ambition than to tell the truth so far as I can. It is now two days since my father's disappearance and I know from the things that are already being said how useful it may be later on if I can have something to show, can tell some of the things that have been going on in this house, give evidence in fact that everyone will *have* to admit is true.

I think also that for a long time I have been terribly repressed and have done myself much harm. When I considered yesterday doing such a thing as this I thought that I would keep myself—my feelings, troubles—entirely outside it. It was to be the plainest, coldest narrative of events. But I see already that that is impossible. This is to be (I hope very shortly) the story of my mother, my father and myself—and afterwards, of my uncle. But more than any of us it must be the comments from one point of view on the life of this town. It is the *town*—our town, Polchester—that is really the chief person in the story.

I have lived in this town a great many years and have loved it and hated it. How I have hated it! How I hate it now when it is already beginning to talk about us and spy on us and laugh at us because of Father! But then I cannot criticize it for that.

236

PERFORMANCE

Father has been the most important and the most hated person in the town. And then, also, how I love it! How I have envied men like Mr. Bellamy, women like Mrs. Carris, because of the opportunities they have had of serving the town, of making it more beautiful, of keeping its old spirit alive!

The last person to see my father, it seems, was Mr. Klitch, the curiosity-shop man. At a quarter to five on Tuesday afternoon there was a thunderstorm and Mr. Klitch saw my father, standing in the rain, staring in at the window. He says that when, later, he was with his wife and child near Arden Gate his son says that he saw him, but Mr. Klitch is sure that that was the boy's imagination. I myself saw my father last at about ten past four. He came downstairs with Major Leggett and, seeing me through the open door in the dining room, said: "You and your mother can have a good time now, Elizabeth, because I shall be out of the house for an hour or two." He often—in fact generally—spoke to me in that sarcastic way as though he hated me. He has hated me for a long time, I know. He has always, since I was a little girl, grudged because he has had to support me.

Yesterday was the opening day of our pageant and I went to it because I wished to show everybody that there was nothing the matter with us. Mr. Bird gave me a ticket. It was a magnificent pageant.

In the evening my uncle Michael came home about seven-thirty a little drunk. At least I *think* he was drunk. He had recovered all his old noisy shouting ways that he had when he first came to us. He was another human being from the miserable, silent, frightened creature he has been during these last months. We had suffered alone, he and I. He was quite frank about his happiness. "Do you not feel, Elizabeth," he said, "that a weight is lifted from our heads? Be honest now. You know that you do. Let's enjoy ourselves for the little time there is before my dear brother returns."

"You think he has gone on a journey somewhere?" I asked him.

"Of course. What else?" Then he added, stuffing his mouth

237

with food: "They're saying in the town that he's been murdered."

And then I was horrified at myself. I didn't care if someone
had killed him. My instantaneous thought was: "Oh, if that's
what's happened, then I shall never see him again!" I want to
make this clear so that there can be no mistake. Until my uncle
said that, I had had no thought but that for some reason of his
own my father had gone secretly to some place and that very
soon, at any moment, he would return.

As soon as my uncle spoke it was as though I entered into
some kind of conspiracy with him.

I lowered my voice, although there was no one in the room
but ourselves.

"Of course that can't be."

"Why not?" my uncle said. "Hundreds of people hated him."

They did. That is undoubted. And yet I am sure, in my own
mind, that he is alive. I have even the fantastically ridiculous
notion that he may be hiding somewhere in this house. And my
uncle said: "Don't you *know* that he is not? Can't you *feel* that
he is out of the house? The house is different. Everything is."

Yes. Everything is. Only now I have realized what it meant—
that uncertainty of his appearance, the consciousness of his
being everywhere at once, and then the sneering hateful manner
when he spoke. The house was starved. Which reminds me that
we shall have to do something about money. My uncle is going
to see Mr. Symon, Father's lawyer, about it today. Symon
(whom I cannot abide) and Major Leggett were Father's two
confidants—the only two who knew anything about his affairs.
Of course if Father returns in the next day or two and discovers
that we have been spending his money freely he will devote a
week at least to punishing us (and myself especially) in all kinds
of subtle ways. But we must live, especially as my uncle has
returned to his old large appetite and noisy extravagance.

. . . . .

This morning I had a long talk with Mother about everything. It is now five days since Father's disappearance. We

have decided to apply to the police for help. The talk in the town is growing fantastically and everything is helped by the strange mood in which everyone is—the extremely hot weather, the disturbances yesterday on the last day of the Pageant. I hear that there are three opinions as to my father's disappearance— that he has been murdered, that he has gone away on some private business and will reappear at any moment, that he is in the town, that he has been seen by various persons in the last twenty-four hours. This last seems to me very likely although to any outside person it must be absurd. My father was a most mysterious person not only by intention but by temperament. I remember when I was quite a little girl staring at myself in a looking glass and seeing, quite unexpectedly, my father reflected in it. But, when I turned round, he was not in the room. Of course that is easily explained. He slipped away, probably, when he saw me start at seeing him, but the little incident is an example of his unexpectedness, elusiveness, pleasure in giving unpleasant surprises.

Mother and I have talked over very frankly all these theories of the people in the town. I should like here to explain a little of my relationship with my mother.

I have led, in many ways, so lonely a life that I have read a great deal and thought a great deal too in a silly, confused, unsatisfied way. I am a virgin—I have never experienced physical love—and I know therefore that more than half of real life has been shut off from me. Even the life that I have experienced has, because of this, been bathed in unreality like a room that is tinged with green because its door has green glass. I have had desires and they have been continually repressed. I have not been in the least ashamed of these desires because they are perfectly right and natural. I have even thought more than once of going out and offering myself to the first man who would take me so that I might know exactly what life is. I have not done so because I have known that what I should gain in experience of life I should lose in my experience of love. That experience of love my mother has given me—not physical, not intellectual, not even spiritual or maternal (although it has perhaps all these elements), but love in its purest, most perfect essence. If—and when—I love a man who draws out of my nature love from this same world as my mother's (and I am beginning, very slowly, now, to believe that perhaps that may be one day my experience), then I will yield to it completely. When it comes it will have all the elements—sensual as well as spiritual—but sensual alone, or spiritual alone, is not enough, is too weak, too worthless and, if I yielded to it, it would sully that clear knowledge of love that my mother has given me. I know that this sounds confused, illogical, perhaps silly. But I am trying, above everything else, to be honest.

My life has taught me that one lives two lives, that they must be experienced together and valued together. One is real in the photographic tangible sense as chairs and tables and human bodies and cancers and foods and drinks and money are real. The other is *more* real but it is intangible. This second life lies inside the first one. One knows it is there although one cannot see it. Perhaps it is even not there, but the thought, belief that it is there is enough. I know that *full* experience embraces both these lives and that neither must be denied. If I had relations with a man whom I did not love I should be denying the more important life although extending the less important.

Neither my mother's love for me nor my father's hate have been so important to me in their *physical* results (although they have been important) as in the inner life experiences they have given me. Once, when I was a little girl, my mother was away staying with friends. I was very hungry. My father knew that and ate in front of me, refusing me food. He said he was training me, but he really did it because it pleased him. But he *was* training me. In order to maintain my pride and self-reliance and keep myself to myself he forced me into another world where food had no value. Although he has been so hated here and has made so many people unhappy, he is perhaps doing the town a great benefit because he is making it so uneasy, so *nervous* that it is compelled to examine itself, to see where it stands, to be an inquisitor of itself. He prevents it from thinking only of the one world, the less important world.

PERFORMANCE

In the same way, after Mother became permanently blind, I read very often the Gospels to her, and we both have seen very clearly how the less important *actual* world has covered the teaching of Christ with a great fog so that what He was and taught is hidden away. So the life of the Cathedral here has become altogether false and perhaps the Cathedral itself has come to resent this. I have lived with it so long that it does not seem to me absurd that it should have a spirit and impulse of its own, but most people would think that unreal. I imagine though that reality may be quite opposite from what we think it is and that the lives and thoughts of most people today are quite unreal, so unreal as to be almost nonexistent. I have come to feel this perhaps because so much of my life has been lived *inside* the blindness of my mother. Loving one another as we do, I have shared her physical blindness and have shared her sense of values. Nearly everything that is important to her now belongs to the important inside life and not the less important outside life. Physical discomfort, food, clothes, money—and yet with her disregard of these things she still has a childlike love of little things, pleasures, physical beauty, and it is because my father took these things from her that she resents him. But not fiercely. Passively. He is only real to her in what he *is*, not in what he *does*.

I had not intended to write down these naïve ideas, but I find that I have done so because they are behind all the external events that I must describe. One belongs to another. I will try now to be practical and definite.

My mother and I love one another as friends, as sisters, as mother and child, and then—beyond these relationships—we belong to one another in a deep, fathomless region where love has no terms, is indefinable and is eternal. As I know from my own long, tested experience that such a love is possible, and as my mother and I are in no way exceptional persons but quite ordinary, therefore it is evident that thousands of other human beings must know such love, and it follows from that, it seems to me, that the truest, most real life is spiritual, not physical, I am afraid that this all sounds as though my mother and I are very dull nonhumorous people, but that also is not true. We enjoy all kinds of things. Life seems to both of us a very comic affair. But then you must remember that for years we have been living under a heavy weight of ostracism and disapproval. Mother has lived for so long an interior life of her own that people matter to her very little, but I *could* have enjoyed everything. I should have loved to be liked, to wear pretty clothes, to have money and to travel. I enjoy small things so much. A very little would have contented me. Mother knows this and I think that is partly why she loves me. But now about Father.

This morning, Mr. Gurney the police inspector came to see us. It is his visit that has made me decide to write this. He is a large stout man with a round rosy face, a kind expression which he tries to make stern and official. We have all known him for years. When he sat in our bare, ugly sitting room he looked so kind and friendly that it was difficult not to smile. When he talks there is a dimple in his left cheek and there is a large fat curl that lies benevolently across his forehead. He is a finely built man and has been a good footballer. He adores his wife and children. If he had his way there would be no crime, no wickedness. He would prefer a world of milk and honey. On the other hand, he takes his official position very seriously. In a year or two he will be retiring, and he is very anxious that the higher authorities shall have no chance to cut down his pension before his time is up.

He interviewed my uncle and myself, his notebook on his knee, sucking his pencil. I saw very quickly that he was disturbed and unhappy, more nervous and even frightened than the head policeman in our town ought to be. He told us frankly at once that he didn't like the way things were going. I asked him what had really been the trouble in the Pageant yesterday, and he said that they hadn't as yet got to the root of the matter, but that undoubtedly a lot of roughs from Seatown had been largely responsible. It was true that Mrs. Braund had had her ankle broken and two people were in hospital with concussion and bruises. He said that trouble had been brewing for several months, that the unemployed had objected to the Pageant and the part that the head people in the town had played in it, that there was a lot of bad feeling between the townspeople and the Cathedral clergy, and that he thought that the exceptional unbroken hot weather was getting on everyone's nerves. I mention all this because I think—and he seemed to think—that my father's disappearance is mixed up with the general feeling of uneasiness. He said that the most ridiculous stories were already current in the town, and that he thought that we ought to know that many people were saying that my father had been murdered. So—rather like a distressed child—he begged us to tell him everything that we could. Had my father said anything about going away? No, I said. He had not. But Major Leggett and Mr. Symon, the lawyer, knew much more about his affairs than he did. Had my father seemed restless and uneasy of late? Had we noticed anything peculiar or different about him? No, I said, he had been the same as usual. He asked us whether we thought it might be true that he was somewhere in the town and whether there could be any reason for his doing such an extraordinary thing? I said that he was a very unusual man and had many mysterious affairs of which he spoke to no one. Mr. Gurney said that he knew that that was so. I remember that he took out his handkerchief at this point. It was a very hot morning and our house, which is usually so cold, was exceedingly warm. I opened the window but there was no breeze. He asked us if we knew of any friends that my father had anywhere —in Drymouth or St. Mary's, or Trelearne or Bodsworth. I said that he had acquaintances in certain places but that he was not a man who made friends.

Then Mr. Gurney said that we must consider seriously the possibility that he had been done away with. He intended to make very strict enquiries of everyone who had seen him on that last afternoon. It was clear that he had gone up the High Street towards the Cathedral. But after that? If anyone had done him a hurt, where could they have found him so that they would be unobserved? There were so many people about on that afternoon. . . . The town was packed with strangers. Besides, Mr. Gurney added, my father was not the kind of man who would be likely to be lured away to some quiet spot. It was not as though he were a child. Mr. Gurney got up there, looking very large in our shabby little room. My uncle had said not a word all this time. Mr. Gurney looked at him and I noticed at once that he saw what I did—my uncle's air of well-being, of self-satisfaction. He was sitting back in his chair with his legs stretched in front of him as though he owned the room and indeed the whole house.

It flashed through my mind that Mr. Gurney had known my uncle ever since he had come to this town, must remember how gay and noisy he had been at first and then how deeply depressed, and that he, Mr. Gurney, must think it very odd that my uncle should be so cheerful again—as though he were relieved of a great burden.

He must see, I thought, that everyone in this house was light-hearted. I realized for the first time how undistressed and free of anxiety I myself had been in this interview, and a cold shiver caught me. I found my hand was trembling. Mr. Gurney, always so amiable and good-natured, appeared sinister and menacing. Suppose that he thought that we, all three of us . . . ?

Soon after that he left—very kind, good-natured, genial. But was it only my imagination that made me think that he looked at both my uncle and myself with a sharp inquisitiveness? All he said was: "You can be quite sure, Miss Furze, that we will do everything possible to solve the mystery."

"What do you think yourself, Mr. Gurney?" I asked him.

He looked at me with his mild, childlike blue eyes.

"I, Miss Furze? I'm altogether at a loss. I should imagine, though, that he has slipped off somewhere. He'll turn up again at any moment. That's *my* idea. Mind you let us know at once if he does."

After he was gone, my uncle, who was now walking about the room smiling, turned round to me and said:

"Elizabeth. Come to my room a moment. I want to show you something."

As we went upstairs he caught my arm, stopping me, and said:

"Isn't this house different? It's warm for the first time. Do you hear that bird? Look at the sun streaming across the stair——"

I moved away from him.

"Suppose, think——" I began.

"Think what?" he asked.

"Why, that you and I and Mother——"

But I stopped. The words were absurd, monstrous. As I remember, I said something about my father returning—at any moment—and I recollect that we both turned and looked down into the hall as though we expected to see the door open and his entry. . . .

I went with my uncle into his room and was ashamed, as I had been many times before, at its bareness, the shabby iron bed, the poor wardrobe, the holes in the carpet. But now my uncle was triumphant.

"Look!" he said.

His stout, rather shapeless body (I always think of my uncle as of someone who was left uncompleted by his Maker. Many people are thus. You say to yourself: "Another hour spent on them . . .") was really shaking with pleasure. On the little stained table beside his bed was standing the crucifix of black marble that has been in my father's room for so long.

"That's Father's," I said.

"No," he answered, laughing. "It's mine. He paid for it but it was mine all the time. He only got it to taunt me with it." Then he added something that I didn't understand at all. "That was the biggest mistake I made—coming back that day from the Carol Service. Everything afterwards followed from that."

Then he patted my arm. "I'm all right again, Elizabeth. Can't you see that I am? And I'll treat you generously, you and your mother. You see if I don't. I'll be generous to everyone. I haven't been myself for months. Well, you could see that I wasn't. I was half starved for one thing. But now——"

But I interrupted him. There was something dreadful to me in his exultation, and then shame of myself also.

"When he comes back——" I began.

"But he'll never come back. You know that he won't."

"How can you be so sure?" I asked him, and I looked him full in the face. We stood looking at one another, and the beautiful crucifix on the table looking at both of us.

"I can't be sure," he said. "I don't know any more than anyone else. But is it reasonable? He's been away for days and without a word to anyone. Even Leggett and Symon haven't heard anything from him—not a word! Has he ever done anything of this kind before? Has he? Tell me."

"No," I said. "He hasn't."

"Has he ever been away even for a night without letting you know where he was?"

"No."

"Well, then——"

"He may be," I said, "staying somewhere in the town. It may suit his plans to watch privately how some scheme of his is working."

"If he were wouldn't someone have come forward by this time and said so? If he's staying somewhere it must be at a hotel or a lodging."

"He was always unlike anyone else," I answered. "You know how mysterious he's always been."

"Mysterious! Mysterious!" he muttered, looking away from me, looking, I remember, at the crucifix. "Perhaps he has been mysterious just once too often."

I cannot be certain that these were the exact words of our conversation, but here was the gist of it. He himself was a mixture of bravado, excitement, uneasiness, jauntiness and, finally, a sort of childlike kindness and eagerness to give pleasure. I am not good at analysing my fellow creatures. Although I have watched so much and have, I think, observed many things and people with accuracy according to my own point of view, I have never before analysed anyone on paper. But what I want to emphasize is that there is something very likeable and also very contemptible about my uncle. He has no character: he is weak and unstable. He is often oddly hysterical for a man. He is in no way admirable. Only you often want to protect and defend him, and any woman must feel kindly towards a man whom she wishes to protect even though she despises him.

I went in then to see my mother. She had been in bed now for some weeks. There was nothing very wrong except for a weakness, a weariness of her limbs.

She was tired so very easily. But it was curious to me, nevertheless, that of her own wish she had gone to bed and stayed there, for, in spite of her blindness, she had been a very energetic person always, and was restless and uneasy if compelled to be inactive. It had seemed to me, during these last days, as though she had retired to bed in order to allow something to take place without her presence. She said once: "You know, dear, it's nice lying in bed just now. If I were up and about I should want to see that Pageant and I couldn't."

And again: "I used to want to meddle in things. Now you can tell me instead."

Indeed, I told her everything that would, I thought, amuse her, and we had, for so long, lived so closely together that our imagination was one imagination and our sense of the ridiculous one experience. But now, when I went in, she called me at once to the bed, put out her hand and drew me to her, kissed, very gently, my eyes, my cheeks, my mouth, then rested her head on my breast.

I find it very difficult to give any true sense of her quietness, her repose. It was as though she had attained such complete control of her emotions, her desires, her disappointments, that she was able to live tranquilly in a world of security. She had the quality that belongs to so few human beings, especially in these restless days—she knew that she was safe, that nothing could disturb her. Nevertheless, there *was* an additional intensity this morning in her embrace.

"Well?" she asked, stroking my hand as blind people do with a kind of tenacity because physical contact with those they love means so much to them.

I told her about Mr. Gurney, and then, my arms around her,

her head on my breast, I made my confession—that the thought of *his* never returning again had created a kind of exultation in me, that I was *glad*—whether it were sinful or no could make no difference. I was glad. She kissed my cheek. She said:

"Of course you are glad. It will be better for everyone if he is dead. He should have died long ago." Then she added, after a pause in which some kind of inner sight seemed to flood her eyes:

"But he isn't so easily got rid of. He is very obstinate."

I told her then of my fear that Mr. Gurney might suspect us of knowing more than we said. He had looked at my uncle strangely.

"Ah, yes, Michael," she said. "*He* knows more. And one day he will tell everybody all that he knows. He has never been able to keep anything to himself."

She pressed my hand, then sat up in bed. "Tomorrow I'll get up. I've been lazy long enough. And there will be things to see to. For one we must have something to live on."

I told her of my own conviction that he was staying somewhere in the town, that many people thought so.

My mother nodded. "Yes, he might be. It wouldn't be at all unlike him."

"They say he is in Seatown."

"Maybe." She patted my cheek. "But don't you worry about it, darling. He can't concern us now. Perhaps we are the two whom he concerns less than anyone else in the town. And now let us have a little of that silly but delightful Mrs. Henry Wood."

Only one thing more I would add at present. This seems to me to belong to myself and I would write nothing of it here except that one moment of it has, I feel, a wider significance.

On the afternoon of this same day a friend of mine called very unexpectedly to see me. I was greatly surprised. I did not wish him to come into the house for my own private (and possibly absurdly sensitive) reasons, but I consented to go out with him for a short walk. It was a summer evening of exquisite beauty. I have no gift for natural description, but as we sat on the brow of the hill above Orange Street the town lay below us in a grey mist, and the gentle sky, very quiet and, I felt, beneficent, changed from rose to a very pale orange—then to white, faint, almost vanishing white, with silver stars. Before dusk came the Cathedral was subdued by the mist but, just before the sun set, for a minute or so it shook off the mist and stood like a rock against the sky. I have tried to describe this just as I saw it because it was at this moment of sunset that I realized how deeply I loved this town. I felt that I would die for it, endure any insult for it. I felt too—perhaps because I was so preoccupied with the fate of my father—that it was being threatened with some danger. That peace and beauty were a blind. My fancy carried me beyond this and I seemed to see my father coming out, now that dusk was falling, from some hiding place and moving, as I have so often seen him, like a shadow, on his business.

I don't know why it was but I began to cry. I was unnerved by the difficulties, the loneliness, the longing for things that I ought not to have. And—very wrong perhaps—I let my friend comfort me.

CHAPTER VI

Penny and the Last Tournament

To grow up is sometimes a matter of years, sometimes of moments. Often the brave deed is never accomplished.

Penny Marlowe grew up on the final and most eventful day of the Polchester Pageant.

The early morning of that day was, unlike its predecessors, cloudy and overcast. This did not oppress Penny because her happiness was such that the sun was there however clouds might choose to behave.

After Lampiron had kissed her in Mrs. Cronin's garden her fate was fixed. She simply waited for him to take the next step. She had not spoken with him since that evening, although she had seen him. She remained in a state of perfect and tranquil bliss. This would be the last moment of that kind of tranquillity. It belongs only to immaturity; those who remain in it too long lose, alas! reality, as their wives, husbands, relations and friends discover so unhappily.

Her mother had gone, the night before, to Drymouth to visit a close friend who had suffered an unexpected and severe operation.

Penny was singing as she came downstairs. Then she saw her father. She stopped singing.

He stared at her as though he scarcely recognized her. He had been becoming lately, as she knew, more and more distressed. He spent hours alone in his church. He had not played

chess for many a night. Now, standing by the dining-room fireplace looking at the breakfast table in bewilderment, he was like
a dog who had lost his home. She kissed him, and he caught
her to him and held her as though he were shielding himself from
some danger. "I've had a bad night," he said. "I always miss
your mother when she's away. Do you ever have bad dreams?"

"Not often," she said. She put up her hand and stroked his
white hair because it was stiff and strong. She stroked his cheek,
which was soft and warm. "Have some breakfast. You'll feel
better."

"Yes, I will." He smiled. "I'm still half-asleep. I dropped
off about six o'clock. I only had about two hours all night. It
isn't enough."

"No, it certainly isn't." Then, when she had given him his
coffee, she said: "What's the matter?"

"The matter is, my dear, as I ought to have told you long
ago, that I am badly in debt to someone. The Bishop helped me
and I thought I was clear, but I'm not, it seems. You won't tell
your mother about this, will you?"

"Of course not. Is it a lot of money?"

"I don't know. It oughtn't to be, but I'm in such a state of
confusion about it."

"Why haven't you been to a proper lawyer about it?"

"Well, that's just the thing," he said. He was cheering up.
His blue eyes were shining more clearly. "I've been so ashamed
about it. It seemed to me so disgraceful—a clergyman, someone
whom everyone knows——"

"That's all right," she said cheerfully. "No one shall know
but you and me. I'll put it all right."

"Yes, but that's just it," he said. "The man I owe it to has
disappeared."

"Disappeared?"

"Yes. It's that horrible old usurer, Stephen Furze. He disappeared four days ago."

"Poor Mr. Furze—I've always been sorry for him," she said.
"Anyway, if he goes on disappearing you won't have to pay
the money."

"Of course I shall have to pay. And now all sorts of people will know. Anyone who has anything to do with his affairs."

"How do you mean?" she asked slowly. "How could he disappear? People *don't* disappear."

"Well, *he* has. Everyone's talking about it. Many people think he's been murdered. Others think he's hiding in the town somewhere. He's a horrible old man—capable of anything! I daresay they'll be saying *I* murdered him!"

"Darling, what nonsense!" She went over to him, got his cup and refilled it. Then she sat on the edge of his chair, her arm round him.

"Do you know what you are? You're a baby, an infant. You've been keeping all this to yourself until it's grown into an absolute nightmare. There's nothing disgraceful about owing money—everyone does. No one would think the worse of you even if they *did* know."

He caught her hand.

"How sweet you are! I really don't deserve a child like you. You're right about the nightmare. That old man made it so. He would come and visit me and I'd be upset for hours after. Last night I dreamt of him. I saw him coming out of the Cathedral door, his head on one side. I couldn't move out of his way. He caught my hand with his. His hand was all bones like a skeleton, and he said to me, 'My home's in there now,' twisting his head towards the Cathedral. 'But I do my business just the same.' It was during one of the few bits of sleep I had. I woke up and I could have sworn I saw him just going out of the door." He drank his coffee and spread his toast with marmalade. "I've got him on my nerves, I expect. And I miss your mother. We've been together so long. I don't like sleeping alone. I'm a silly old fool, and that's the truth. And you're right—I've kept all this to myself too long."

It was then that she felt more strongly than ever before her responsibility. And this sudden consciousness was accompanied by a recollection of a word that Lady St. Leath had had with her only the day before. It had been but a moment. Penny, dressed after her share in the Pageant, had been coming out of the Cronins' gate onto the Cathedral Green. They were in the middle of Evensong, which was later on these Pageant days, and the sonorous undertone of the organ coming from the Cathedral seemed to tremble from under her very feet. A lovely hazy mesh of light, like a net of minute sparks of gold, had caught the ivory Cathedral walls, the long stretch of green, the empty stands. The only sounds where but an hour before the shouts and music of the Pageant had triumphed were the cooing of the doves from the Cronins' garden, and the organ undertone. Lady St. Leath had been saying good-bye to some friends and was at the door of her car. She saw Penny, whom she knew very slightly, and stopped. They shook hands, Penny blushing, greatly pleased, because she admired Lady St. Leath so tremendously. Lady St. Leath had something very young, naïve almost, still about her. People sometimes laughed at her for that.

"Isn't it a beautiful evening?" she said. "I'm so glad the Pageant has had such lovely weather. Have you been enjoying it?"

Penny said she had.

"Just now," Lady St. Leath went on, "I was thinking of evenings like this in the old days. I grew up here, you know." She looked at Penny with a charming, shy, friendly smile, and Penny remembered all the tragedy of her youth, so that it did not seem incongruous that Lady St. Leath should then say, "How is your father?"

"He hasn't been so well lately," Penny said.

"Oh, I'm sorry. I must call on your mother one day soon. I should like so much to see her again. And you must come out to us." She held Penny's hand. "Look after your father. You'll never be sorry for any trouble you take now. But I know how good you are to them both." Then she smiled her sudden, shy, lovely smile. "They are so *very* proud of you." Penny thought that Lady St. Leath looked at her almost longingly, as though she would like to kiss her. But she did not. She got into her car and drove away.

Penny remembered this now. It was as though Lady St. Leath had said to her: "I can see, now that I am old, that nothing in all my life, not my love for my husband nor my love for my child, has mattered so much as my love for my father. Because he was old and in trouble and I was all that he had."

At that moment, sitting in the pleasant room with the sun pouring in upon the china and silver and the crimson roses in the crystal bowl, she assumed her responsibility.

"I am realizing something," she said; "that I haven't been close enough to you lately. You haven't had anyone to talk to. You don't want to worry Mother. That's all right. But you *ought* to worry *me*. I'm grown-up now."

He stroked her hair. "Are you grown-up, darling?" He looked at her with his blue eyes, considering it. "Yes, I suppose you are. I hadn't taken it in. Time moves so fast."

"And therefore," she went on, "you must share everything with me. I wouldn't be shocked at anything you do, especially with regard to money, where I'm not so very strong myself as a matter of fact."

"It goes deeper than money, my dear, I'm afraid—I've been a traitor at my post. I've been tested and found wanting."

She patted his head cheerfully. She knew his liking for rather childlike nursery similes.

He munched his toast and marmalade. He was now very much more cheerful.

"The soul. . . . Everyone today thinks that a tiresome unnecessary topic. But it is the root, the origin, the essence. From that seed everything springs, the lovely lilies, the young musk roses, the cabbages and carrots, the nettles and—what is that weed that smells so unpleasant . . . ? Never mind," he went on, shaking his head. "At intervals the Examiner comes and looks at the soul—at yours, at mine, at everyone's. He has examined mine. It has withered away—a dried, musty, decayed nut of a soul. I am no good any more—no good, no good, no good."

He began to walk about the room, his hands clasped behind his broad back.

"And people think this of no importance any more! No importance—then the spirit is withered for lack of nourishment.

No lilies—not even nettles. Nettles, nettles—they would be better than nothing. Have I not reason to be unhappy?"

He is enjoying it, she thought, and yet he means it too. He is deeply unhappy. I can't be near enough to him because I am so happy, because I am in love, because the sun is shining and these roses burn with an ecstasy of life.

Meanwhile he, with that funny sense of incongruities that he had, looked at her, laughed almost like a wicked child and went quickly out of the room.

She remained in the sunlight, for the thunderclouds had passed, changing some of the roses in the crystal bowl and thinking—about his incongruities. She did not know him. He was her father and she loved him dearly, but she did not know him at all. He was unhappy and she could not help him. A sudden shame of her inexperience, her inability to help anyone, whether her father, Mrs. Braund (who was, she knew, badly in need of help) or Lampiron, attacked her. Standing there, holding in her hand a rose so red that the secret of its colour was cynical in its scorn of human knowledge, she learnt in one swift moment of experience a great lesson—that to help others one must have a long training in self-forgetfulness. She could not forget herself: she was too happy, too deeply in love; the scents and burning sharpness of that wonderful summer seemed too acutely to be provided for her personal joy.

In a dress of faint rose and a small hat of white straw she went out to enjoy the world. And then, outside, on that burning summer morning, she discovered (many people in Polchester just then were making such a discovery) that she did not seem to be altogether a free agent. What was it? The hot air quivered above the little street and the sky was a sheet of intense light. There was the apprehension, as one has in hot countries but so rarely in England, that to cross the sun-blazed road from shadow to shadow was dangerous.

She walked to the point beyond the church where the street descends to Seatown, and to her own surprise found herself descending instead of going, as she had intended, to the Market.

She had thought that the shaded alcoves of the Market would be cool, that she would buy some flowers for Mrs. Braund, who, with every day of the Pageant, had become more unhappy and remote.

These streets at the top of the hill were in her father's parish, but as she dropped downwards and the houses became meaner and older she was in almost unknown territory.

It was up here, she thought, that the armed men struggled. There was no road then. They clung to the rock, fighting from ledge to ledge, and below, on the river that was wilder and stronger then, their boats waited. The shining slabs of rock flashed in the sun, or perhaps the rain poured down or fog crept up from the river—a man lost his foothold, gave a desperate clutch for safety, then lost his hold, his arms flung wide and he fell, fell . . .

She stopped, looking about her, almost as though she were in a dream, so vivid was it, so dramatically part of it was she.

It is almost as though I had stood here, screaming for battle, and I looked up and up and the Cathedral was there, but not the twin northern towers, only Harry soaring into the sky. And I ran . . .

She shaded her eyes against the sun. That, she thought, smiling, is what a week of pageants can do for you.

She had walked a long way down and soon would be level with the river. She read some of the names above the shops— M'Canlis, Tobacconist; Sandy Lugge, Old Clothes Purchased —and a sweet shop with the name "Mary Murphy," its little window decorated with evil-looking sweets of black and pink and yellow over which flies were crawling.

Under the blazing sun the houses, crooked, misshapen windows tightly closed, wore a look of shamefaced sullen obstinacy. No one stirred. It was a dead street lit with the hard brilliancy of a sun on a dead world.

A little girl passed her. This child was shabby to forlorn pity. She wore a grown woman's torn skirt that caught about her feet, and an ancient black straw hat, its brim twisted. The heel of one shoe clop-clopped against the road as she moved.

Then she fell. She lay, a small tangled confusion of thick matted hair, a woman's torn skirt, a broken shoe—and she did not stir.

Penny ran to her and picked her up. She was as light to hold as the crystal bowl with the crimson roses, but from her there came an acrid smell, stale, bitter. On her forehead two flies were crawling. She had struck her cheek against the curb and it was bleeding, but she regarded Penny with an outraged fierceness; her black eyes glared like an affronted and fearless cat's.

She struggled.

"Tell me where you live," Penny said.

Then the child fainted. Her head fell forward, and her body with a shiver as of her very spirit seemed to surrender itself to Penny's care.

Then out of a dark house a woman, a dirty red blouse open at the neck to the breasts' cleft, came.

"Give her to me," she said.

"She has fainted—and her cheek is cut——"

The woman gave Penny a long look. She took the child.

"She's soiled your dress," she said. She tossed her head, but, moving back to the house, she held the child tenderly.

Penny followed. That little sighing gasp that the child had given, that surrender against her breast, had touched her with a poignancy that forbade her to let her go.

So she followed—out of the sun, into the dark house. The room where she was seemed to be kitchen and bedroom combined, but there was no fire in the range, and on the bed a man in shirt and trousers lay, his hands behind his tousled head, and on his lap, sleeping, a large tortoise-shell cat. Penny saw also a gilt cage with two canaries, a pot in the window with a brilliantly red geranium, a table with some tumbled bottles and dirty glasses. The room was close, infested with heat, airless, stinking of stale drink, geranium, and the soot that fell, once and again, with gentle patters down the grate.

Penny stood at the door. The woman, who had a broken young beauty and even grandeur, laid the child on a small broken sofa in the window, stretching over a patchwork quilt of sharp fragmentary red, green, orange squares. She leaned over her, went to the shelf and poured a glass of water, bathed the child's head. There was absolute silence in the room save for the twittering of the canaries and the falling soot. The man had not stirred. Only the tortoise-shell cat rose, stretched itself, dropped with miraculous lightness to the floor, raised first one leg then another in sleepy indolence, walked over to the sofa to investigate.

The woman bathed the cut, murmuring, "Chrissy . . . Chrissy . . . you'll be better now. You'll be better now."

The child suddenly sat up and, pushing back her hair from her eyes, stared in front of her.

"She fell—cut her head on the curb. How did you fall, Chrissy?"

"I don't know."

"Does your head hurt?"

"No. . . ." Then she as suddenly lay down again. "Yes, it aches."

Penny came forward.

"Can I do something? I could bring a doctor very quickly."

"A doctor?" The woman laughed scornfully. Her blouse had slipped, leaving one breast, white and very firm, exposed. She did not attempt to cover it. "No, thank you. We don't want no doctors here." Then, straightening herself, raising her head, she said politely but with a real and native dignity, "It was good of you, miss, to trouble. She's my daughter and she won't stay still any place. She's always hiding down by the river, in the Market, in the Cathedral. It's so she shan't have to go to school, we reckon."

Penny went over to the child. She had persistently the feeling that the child belonged to her. She laid her hand on the soiled forehead.

"Don't you think really that I should get a doctor?"

"No, miss. She hasn't done herself any real hurt. It will teach her not to go running off."

The child opened her eyes and stared at Penny. They were

large, lustrous, and filled with a kind of fierce and audacious wonder. Penny and the child looked at one another.

"Well, if I can do nothing——" Penny said. She turned and saw that the man was sitting up. He was young, large in build with massive shoulders, and where his shirt was open there was a pelt of black hair.

He said: "Puss, puss—come here, puss." The cat came to him. Then, as though he were speaking to himself: "M'Canlis says he saw Furze last night—down bottom of Daffodil Street. But he didn't. They've choked Furze all right." He stretched his arms, yawning. "They say that Lampiron done it."

"Fetch a bit of that rag, Tom, from the dresser, will you?" the woman said. "It'll keep the place on her head clean."

The man got up, crossed the room, searched for the rag, found it. Then, whistling, he came over to the sofa and, kneeling, bound the cloth, after damping it, very gently, holding the child against his chest.

"There, my lass, lie quiet. It's a scratch."

What had he said? He had mentioned Lampiron's name. . . . She held out her hand.

"I am Miss Marlowe. I am the daughter of the Rector of St. James's. If I can do anything, now or at any time——"

The woman touched her hand for an instant.

"My name's Clarke, Fanny Clarke."

They have both, Penny thought, the woman and the girl, the same eyes. She went and, bending down, kissed the child, who did not stir.

"It was kind of you, I'm sure," the woman said. The man was looking up speaking to the canaries, the tortoise-shell cat was rubbing against his leg. Abruptly he turned.

"My name's Caul. Tom Caul. I don't think your father's ever paid us a visit."

"His parish doesn't include these streets," Penny said, smiling.

"No. Well, parsons aren't much use in these parts and that's the truth." His eyes rested on her. "You're in this pageant. I've seen you."

"Yes, I am."

"I've got it. You ride a horse. I'll be seeing you this afternoon."

"Why?" asked Penny. "Are you in it too?"

"Am I?" He grinned at the woman. "You look out for me this afternoon. There'll be thunder, I reckon."

"Yes." She wanted to question him but she was afraid, afraid of the room, the cat, the geranium plant, the whispering soot.

She said good-bye to them and went out.

A large greedy cloud like a white billowing apron swallowed up the sun just as the First Episode concluded. Mrs. Cronin, who was so sorry that it was all coming to an end—it *had* been a good time! How charming everyone had been, appreciating her poor little efforts, because really she had done nothing—"Oh yes, Clara, you have." . . . No, no, it had been no trouble at all, putting her house at her friends' disposal. What, after all, was one's house *for?* And such a lovely Pageant. Would anyone *ever* forget it?

(No, Agnes Braund said, no one ever would.)

Mrs. Cronin, who was so sorry that it was all coming to an end . . . . Then she realized that something must be done about Agnes.

"What *is* it, Agnes? We are all so concerned about you. I'm afraid you've *hated* the Pageant."

Mrs. Braund was in a dressing gown of dark blue silk peppered with little silver moons. There was still an hour before her episode.

She looked gloomily at Clara Cronin whom she had never liked and now altogether loathed.

"If Penny Marlowe is in her room, I wish you'd ask her to look in and speak to me."

"Of course, darling. She's certain to have arrived. I'll go and tell her."

The applause of the audience came like a breaking sea into the room. . . .

"Oh dear, isn't it oppressive! I'm sure there's going to be a thunderstorm!" She hurried away.

Penny came in. She kissed Mrs. Braund, of whom in these last weeks she had become very fond.

"Listen, dear." Mrs. Braund took her hand. "I'm sure something *awful* is going to happen this afternoon."

"Oh!" said Penny. "What *could* happen?"

"I don't know." Mrs. Braund's large bosom heaved convulsively. "I'm sure I don't know. I'm altogether bewildered." She held Penny's hand tightly. "Quite honestly, dear, I can't stand it any more. Frankly I wanted to be Lady Emily in the Pageant—I won't disguise it from anybody. You remember one day when I lunched at your house, when the Bishop called?"

"Yes?"

"That was the last happy moment I knew, positively the last. Ernest" (Ernest was the Archdeacon) "is nearly distracted. He has never seen me like this and I can't explain to him. That's the awful thing—I can't explain to him——" Her eyes were filled with tears.

Penny, full of concern, held the soft moist hand more tightly.

"Mrs. Braund, dear. *What* can't you explain?"

"Why I am like this. I'm more terrified every day. I thought I'd *never* get through yesterday's performance. For one thing everyone hates me."

"Oh no. Of course they don't. No one hates you."

"Oh yes, they do. It isn't that I mind the Carris girls or Mrs. Aldridge being rude, or Mr. Crispangle being odious. After all, I've done no harm. They are simply jealous. But it's more than that. Every time we do our scene it gets worse. Didn't you see those horrid men in the crowd yesterday? I was sure they were going to pull me off my horse. All those roughs from Seatown. I'm sure they're all communists and they *hate* anyone to do with the Cathedral. But it's worse than that even. It's Lady Emily herself. I feel as though she were there all the while wishing me ill. And I haven't been well—I haven't been sleeping. I've never known the town in such a state, with the unemployed and the shop people so rude—and now there's this murder——"

All this had come pouring out. It was an appeal for help as real and moving as any that Penny had ever known.

"Murder? What murder?"

(Although she knew well enough and had been thinking of nothing else all day. For what was it that man had said . . . ?)

"Oh, you must have heard about it. That horrible old man Furze disappeared four days ago—the afternoon before the Pageant opened. Nothing has been heard of him since. Some people say they saw him at the Pageant yesterday. Romney, who always knows everything, says that some are saying it's only the first of these disappearances, that there'll be others ——" She stopped. She put up a stout bare arm and drew Penny's face to hers and kissed her. "Darling, you're so sweet, so kind. Mind you're very close to me this afternoon. Don't let them do anything to me."

"Do anything? But of course not. What could they do?" Then Penny added slowly: "Who do they think did this murder —if he *has* been murdered?"

"Oh, my dear, they say all sorts of things. Romney says the police are investigating everybody's record. I mean everybody who had anything to do with the man. They say people all over the town owed him money."

(Yes, thought Penny. Father—Lampiron——)

"There were plenty of people who hated him, it seems," Mrs. Braund went on. "And threatened him too. Lampiron for one."

"Oh no!" Penny cried.

"Oh, but he did. On that very afternoon Mr. Gaselee saw Mr. Lampiron quarrelling with Furze in the High Street. He was with Ronder—Gaselee was, I mean. Oh dear! Listen to that!"

There was a rumble of thunder. Beyond the window a black thick cloud with a grey furry edge gave the trees in front of it a metallic brilliance.

Towards the close of the Third Episode there was a fierce thundershower. Twice there was a clap as of gigantic hands that

262

seemed to come from the very heart of the Cathedral. Then the rain poured down, soaking the Town Fair, which was hurriedly concluded. But, before the opening of the Fourth Episode, the Death of the Black Bishop, the sun had come again, a fierce hot sun that beat down upon the grass, sparkling and shining after the rain. Many people afterwards said that the hour that followed was the hottest and most oppressive ever known in Polchester. Against the sun the Cathedral was jet, as though encased in black armour, and beyond the trees little spongy clouds could be seen stealthily, maliciously moving forward upon the pale stretch of nervous blue.

Yes, the sky was nervous and the people in the stands were nervous too. Those in the uncovered stands, wet with the shower, watched the clouds beyond the Cathedral anxiously. Everyone felt the exhausting oppressive heat. There was something foreign to the English sense of decency and order in its fierceness.

Some of the people in the uncovered stands got up and went, and this added to the general disturbance, because until today the attention had been breathless; no one had conceived of leaving before the end.

Then, too, it had generally been noticed that from the very beginning of the performance the actors had been restless and uneasy. The crowds in the first two episodes were noisy and disorderly. Everyone had commented during the previous days on the easy naturalness of the crowds, the remarkable way in which the right atmosphere had been caught, but now the crowds were *too* natural, noisy, and even, once and again, some of the men would advance close to the stands and make very audible and rude remarks about some of the spectators.

After the first day's performance it had been widely admitted that it was a mistake to allow so many of the roughs from Seatown to take part in the Town Fair. People blamed Romney for this, and a good many malicious things were said in whispers about the friends he had in Seatown, friends very rough and strange for so æsthetic and cultured a gentleman as Romney. It was now, in fact, that people first began to gossip about the mischief that Romney was making, encouraging men like Tom Caul and young M'Canlis to do and say what they liked.

"We might as well be in Russia," Camilla Porteous, who hated Romney, said loudly everywhere. "If we are all murdered in our beds I know where the blame will lie."

It was a fortunate thing, perhaps, that the first shower came when it did, for there is no doubt but that that scene would have ended in a general riot.

It was at this point that Gurney sent for all the available police in the town, and, as it turned out, this was a fortunate thing.

However, with Lampiron's scene, absolute order was restored. Everyone listened breathlessly. Throughout the episode the thunder rumbled in the distance and the light from the sun was thin, opaque, as though seen through gauze. Lampiron himself was superb. Everyone agreed that he excelled himself. At the moment when, in his magnificent robes, he made his first appearance, turned and looked in silence at the group of knights, it was as though the whole audience drew a deep breath of wonder and admiration. Afterwards, when he cried out: "God's servant! Beware of God's servant!" it was as though he were warning the whole world. People said afterwards that the Cathedral itself with all its thousands of inhabitants was listening—and, when he fell, a hush of awe, voiced by the rumbling of the thunder, held the world. "This is what will come to you all if you forget my Law." "A God of mercy—yes, and a God of thunder also," Dale said to Cronin. Therefore, by the beginning of the Lady Emily episode, the proper atmosphere had been restored. No one thought any longer of leaving, although the small clouds had now banded together and the sun had vanished.

Penny's steed, of which at first she had been much afraid, was by now her very good friend. It was a small white horse, not very much bigger than a pony. Penny had taken riding lessons during the last month and had made up her mind to buy the horse when the Pageant was over.

The first thing that she saw when she rode onto the scene,

close behind Mrs. Braund, was the man whom she had met in Seatown that morning. As the crowd surged forward he touched her horse's flank, looked up at her grinning, and said: "Hullo, miss! I said I'd look out for you." She smiled back at him, for his eyes were friendly and he was a fine rough figure; he was broader and stronger than the men around him and seemed to be their leader.

After that first entry, however, she had little time to think of him, for now everything went wrong. She was never able to give a very coherent account of what occurred. It seemed to be all over very quickly. When Mrs. Braund began to speak, confusion was everywhere. The crowd surged hither and thither. Nothing was in its right order. Everyone shouted at once. Towards Arden Gate free fights were taking place. The sky now was black, and the flashes of lightning, the rolling of thunder, the first drops of heavy rain added to the disturbance. Penny, remembering Mrs. Braund's appeal, held closely to her, but there was a quick rush of the crowd; poor Mrs. Braund was tumbled off her horse, which started off, plunging amongst the crowd. Penny could see people standing up, many leaving, others calling out incoherently. Police were advancing over the sward. Then the rain came down in a deluge, fiercely delighted, as though it wanted to drown the world. . . .

And that was the end of the Polchester Pageant.

Later, unexpectedly, miraculously, followed the most lovely moment of her life. As to that, who knows? For Penny has still so much of her life in front of her. But will there be, *can* there be any interval of time packed, like a treasure box, with so many sweets, so many fragrances? A glory of the moon, of the peace after storm, of perfect trust and understanding, of love given and returned?

For peace did follow the storm. Poor Mrs. Braund had broken her ankle; also on her forehead there was a dark bruise. She had been carried to her home and now, in the dark room scented with the roses beyond the window, the Archdeacon sat beside the bed holding her hand. He felt the hand shake and heard her whisper: "Ernest, everyone hates me. They tried to kill me."

But at Mrs. Cronin's it had been like the chattering of birds. "My dear, *what* happened? Oh, but *do* tell us? You were there? Was Mrs. Braund dragged from her horse? Did someone hit her? What was everyone else doing? There was a sort of free fight, wasn't there? Do you think they'll do something tonight, come up and burn people's houses or something? Anyway, what's it all about? Why is everyone so angry? Is it the unemployed? Someone said they're going out to Carpledon to burn the Bishop's palace down."

"*That* they won't do, anyway. Everyone loves the Bishop."

"They don't down in Seatown. They don't love anyone. They say the money ought to have been spent on the unemployed instead of having a pageant."

Out of all this Penny escaped to find a fair evening sky, the air scented with flowers and the freshness of the rain, swallows, the symbols of English tranquillity, flying high. She had intended to hurry home because she was afraid lest her father, who meant something new to her since this morning, had heard exaggerated tales of the afternoon.

But she did not hurry home, because, at the gate of the Cronins' garden, Lampiron was waiting for her.

"I had to wait—to make sure that you were all right." When he saw her happy face he added: "Come—we'll walk to the end of the Cathedral and then I'll see you home."

She put her arm through his and slowly they crossed the Green.

"You're all right?" he asked.

"Of course I'm all right."

"I was changing when it all happened. I knew nothing about it until I heard the rain, looked out of the window and saw everyone running. What *did* happen?"

"Oh, very little, I think." Her hand tightened on his arm. "I really don't know. Suddenly everyone seemed to get excited, people rushed about shouting, Mrs. Braund was thrown off her horse."

"Is she hurt?"

"I'm afraid she is. They say she's broken her ankle." Penny looked up into his face and loved him so much that for a moment she could not speak. He did not look old at all. Other people felt that about him. She had heard someone say that he was ageless. She did not know how grand he had been that afternoon because she had not been there, but, nevertheless, there was still upon him the effect of that performance and she realized it.

"Tell me what's the matter," she said.

"What's the matter?" he repeated. "With us?"

"Oh no, not with us. We are perfect. With everything else. With the world. I seem to have grown up today, to realize things I never knew before. What is the matter in the town? Why is everyone so angry with everyone else? It's never been so before."

They had reached the great West Door and stood there, looking out across the darkening Green to the stands.

"Oh yes, it has been so before," he said. "Over and over again. It recurs. All the shapes have to be broken up. They become so set that people stop thinking, miss the important thing about life. As though they were asleep. They have to be broken up."

"Who wakes them?"

"I don't know. The life force. Whatever you like to call it."

"You don't think it's God, then?"

"That word———" he said. "Who knows what it means?"

The world was now so deeply hushed that they both stopped to listen.

"Isn't it still? Lovely. Beautiful."

They walked on.

"I suppose this is one of the dozen most interesting crises in the world's history that we're living in just now. We've had nearly twenty years of it already, but that's nothing in time. There's plenty more to come. And what's happening all the world over is happening in miniature in this town. Men are uneasy, suspicious, and when they're suspicious they're dangerous."

She pressed closer to him as though to protect him.

"They are all talking about that man who they say has been murdered."

"What man? Oh, Furze! Well, if he has been murdered, it's a good riddance."

She could have cried out with relief. Of course she had known that he had nothing to do with it, but now, in the way that he had spoken, she was reassured forever.

"You know, don't you," she said, "that whatever happens, whatever anyone said, I would always be with you—nothing could make any difference——"

"Yes, we love one another, don't we?" he said quietly. "And it will be like this—always——" Then as they turned away towards Arden Gate: "Don't you see now how much better it is like this? You're giving me the one thing I've never had—a better thing than I've ever had. You must watch over it, you know. See that nothing spoils it. Make me better than I really am."

"I can't do that," she answered. "But it shall be always as you want it to be."

She realized, as they turned into the town, that this was the best and happiest moment of her life so far.

CHAPTER VII

It Is Queer, the Things that Can Happen to Towns—Michael as Spy—He Is Also Spied Upon

IT IS QUEER, the things that can happen to towns. Or is it, perhaps, not so queer? Are towns only the camping places for human beings on duty, or do they by means of the battles fought on their territory acquire independent life because the ground is soaked in blood and the air thick with the after-smoke of the cannon? When one man, falling with a bird's scream from the Rock to the stream below, saw in his last plunging moment that town, slanting roofs, walls, and all in mockery of him, was that man's small bursting heart an addition to the town's personal spirit?

Is the Cathedral, as Crispangle selling Bibles and prayer books in his bookshop calls it, "the dead palace of a forgotten king," or are the palace passages thronged with servants, suppliants, warriors, members of the Royal Family? At least we can say that we know nothing about either Death or Time, whether, even, they have any existence or no. . . .

September was as lovely a month as its predecessors had been in this extraordinary year, but there was mingled with its summer glories the gold leaf and the still sunshine of autumn. The heat was now less intense, but it had lasted just too long. The disturbances on the last day of the Pageant had killed the sense of security in the town. Citizens went to bed at night wondering whether there would be riot before morning.

There were ghosts in the Cathedral. Someone had seen the Black Bishop leaning against a pillar and yawning. People said that there was something disturbing in the Cathedral. Lady Mary said that sometimes during service there was a distinct *odour*.

"Do you mean a smell, darling?" Mr. Romney asked her.

"Not a smell exactly. You know. Damp. Decay. As though someone had been reopening a grave."

Broad's boy said that he had seen lights behind the Cathedral windows one morning about three when he had woken up and looked out.

People said that it was quite true that a strange figure emerged from the West Door. Others, more credulous, said that he was followed by four men bearing a coffin!

"And this," said Crispangle, "is the twentieth century!" and sold with a kind of pleased vindictiveness to an old lady who asked for a nice novel a pocket edition of Aldous Huxley's *Antic Hay*.

"But then," Crispangle went on to Hattaway, who had been talking about one of his favourite works—Morris's *Sigurd*— "we haven't moved on one little bit since Sigurd and his Volsungs. Look at France and Germany, America and England over the Debt, look at our own town. Haven't they been behaving to poor Mrs. Braund exactly as they would have behaved to the village witch two hundred years ago? And they don't like you down in Seatown either, Hattaway. You'd better look out one of these dark nights. They say you want to pull the whole place down."

"And so I do," said Hattaway, whose rosy face, bright blue eyes and broad shoulders were among the pleasantest sights in Polchester.

"All very well," said Crispangle, studying two poetry shelves. "Miss Wilkens, where is that new consignment of Noyes? And someone was asking for the Masefield *Collected Poems* on

Saturday and we hadn't got one. Yes, you'd better order two. It's always in demand even if it *is* tripe."

"How severe you are, Crispangle," Hattaway said, smiling. "What kind of poetry *do* you read?"

"Can't read poetry. Only poetry I've ever enjoyed was *The Ingoldsby Legends*. Well, as I was saying, Hattaway, it's no use your trying to pull down Seatown. People have done that again and again, given them baths, water closets, every kind of luxury—always comes back to the same in the end. Remember Harmer John? Anyway they're out for trouble down there."

He gave his nervous (and to some of his friends extremely irritating) little cough, and drew his big friend into the corner where the Children's Books were.

"You know what the real trouble is, Hattaway?"

"Yes, of course. The usual. Stupidity. Hatred of beauty. Meanness to one's fellow creatures."

"Pshaw! No, I don't mean that kind of virtuous claptrap. The real trouble is Furze. Stephen Furze."

"Why?" asked Hattaway. "He's gone. It's a good riddance. What about it?"

"Well, he isn't gone. That's exactly it. Either his ghost or himself haunts this town."

"Why," cried Hattaway, laughing, "you're not going to tell me that a modern atheist and cynic like yourself, Crispangle, believes in ghosts?"

"Believe! Believe!" said Crispangle impatiently. "I hate that word. How can you believe or disbelieve in anything? No. Furze was murdered that afternoon before the Pageant all right. Most people know it. But most people are childish too. Furze was a great influence in this town and, in their hearts, most people think he's still around. Anyway, they want to make sure that he was murdered. Where's the body? Who committed the murder? Gurney's baffled, although that says nothing because the man's a fool anyway. But what I mean is—" and here he took the lapel of Hattaway's coat between his finger and thumb— "is that everyone's apprehensive. They imagine the most ridiculous things. They see Furze coming out of the Cathedral, slipping about down in Seatown, looking out of the window of his house. That brother of his knows something, and his girl too, I shouldn't wonder. Leggett too. And Lampiron."

Here Hattaway broke in excitedly. He was often excited.

"That's enough about Lampiron. He's a friend of mine. One of the finest men ever born."

"Oh, *I'm* saying nothing against him. But the town's crawling with rumours. Why, I've even heard poor old Marlowe mentioned. All I mean is that Polchester isn't the nice quiet place it used to be."

"The world," Hattaway said, "isn't the nice quiet place it used to be." He sighed. "What we want is Morris's Volsungs back again. They'd soon put it straight."

"I don't know," said Crispangle. "You've got Morris's Volsungs in Italy and Germany and a lot of good they've done."

"What you want," said Hattaway, "is a triumphant Christ with an army of angels behind Him."

"Yes," said Crispangle drily. "That's just what the Nazis think they are, with Hitler for the Christus. Lord, it's getting dark. I must be shutting up shop. Look after yourself, Hattaway. Don't let anyone give you a knock on the head one of these evenings."

"I'll look after myself," Hattaway said.

Meanwhile Michael Furze was looking after *himself*, and very well indeed he was doing it. Yes, everything was all right, everything was splendid. He must say it again. Everything is *splendid*. Who is that? Did anyone knock? I must open the door and see. Is that someone disappearing round the corner of the passage? The whisk of a long overcoat? No. No one. Silence. But the house is warm. Even in this September weather. It has cherished the summer heats. The house has been cold for so long.

Two strange events have occurred. One most unexpected and unpleasant? You never can tell. There are so many people listening and watching.

The first is the opening of the safe—the green-and-white

safe that stands against the farther wall in Stephen's room.

That is the room that Michael has never greatly liked to enter. He has suffered there so much. It was in that room that Stephen first showed him the stolen crucifix. Stolen? Of course it was stolen, even though Stephen had paid money for it. It had always belonged to Michael.

It was in this room, too, that Stephen had shown him one day the combination that opened the safe. A very remarkable thing for Stephen to have done—but then, whether you liked him or no, Stephen *was* a remarkable man.

And Michael knew well why Stephen had done this. Michael was no fool. Stephen on that warm sunny afternoon had turned, grinning, to his brother and had said:

"See here, my dear brother. Would you care to know the combination for this little safe? A secret between the two of us. It brings us closer together, doesn't it?" He told him the combination. He opened the safe.

Then he showed him the box with the gold sovereigns. He poured them out in a glittering stream before him.

"You don't see them often, these days, do you? Aren't they lovely? Aren't they beautiful?"

Then he closed the safe. Michael remembered the combination.

Yes, he knew why Stephen had told him—because, when he was being starved, when he hadn't a penny in his pocket, the temptation to open that safe and take something out of it would be tremendous in its power. So it had been. It had been one of the things that had broken Michael down, made him the wretched thing that he became. He was haunted by that safe, morning and night, worst of all in the evenings when Stephen was in the town and the house was so still and the safe was waiting there in that silent empty room. Michael was hungry, almost starving. . . . He had almost yielded. Almost but not quite. He had resisted with all the poor force remaining to him only because this was the one thing that Stephen wanted him to do, to take something from that safe. Once he, Michael, had yielded he was in Stephen's power forever.

But now—Stephen was gone. The door locked, Michael had opened the safe, and what treasures he had found there! Not only one box of sovereigns, but two! And a box with jewelry, rings, necklaces, bracelets. And papers with names and addresses, giving Michael, if he wished, and after a certain time had elapsed, power over the whole town.

Michael had proceeded very cautiously. Real gold sovereigns were not often seen in these days. People would wonder. He had made an arrangement with Lanky Moon of the Dog and Pilchard, who himself had more money than anyone knew, who asked no questions, who gave Michael, with a reasonable discount, notes for the coins. It was to Lanky's interest to keep this business to himself.

The only person in this matter of whom Michael was not sure was Leggett. No one else seemed to take any interest in the safe. Even Symon the lawyer, who was now making Mrs. Furze and Elizabeth a weekly allowance, asked no questions. But did Leggett know the combination? He alluded to the safe on several occasions. He was altogether too familiar, Michael thought, too often in and about the house. He adopted now to Michael a laughing, friendly and confidential manner, as though they were conspirators together in some secret. Michael did not like that at all, and was very stiff and dignified with the beef-faced vulgar little brute, but the more dignified Michael was the more Leggett laughed. He would clap Michael on the back. He would appear in Michael's bedroom. He even lay on Michael's bed one night, his legs stretched out, his hands behind his head, watching Michael undress. "I like you, old boy," he would say. "We're pals."

And then one day quite suddenly he asked:

"You know who did your brother in, don't you?"

"Of course I don't. He'll turn up one day and surprise us all."

"Oh no, he won't. Never again. Lampiron's the culprit."

"Lampiron?"

"Of course. All the town knows it, or soon will."

In fact Michael hated Leggett, detested him. Leggett had better look out.

PERFORMANCE

The other disturbing person in the house was Elizabeth. What did that woman know? What was she thinking? No one could tell. She was so very silent, going about her business without a word. She and her mother. Better out of the house, both of them. In connection with Elizabeth there had been this surprising incident: Michael had come into the house one afternoon and, of all things in the world, had found a little clergyman in the hall—a neat, tidy, insignificant little clergyman. Michael knew who he was. His name was Bird, and he was Porteous' curate up Orange Street.

"Well," Michael said. "Is there anything I can do for you?" The house was his now and he didn't want clerical nobodies spying about there.

But Bird had stood his ground. "I am calling on Miss Furze," he said.

"I'm afraid Miss Furze is out," Michael had said.

"I think not," Bird had said. "I have just spoken to her." One for Bird!

At that same moment Elizabeth appeared on the staircase, her hat on, ready to go out.

"You are Mr. Michael Furze?" Bird had said.

"I am."

"Then I think you ought to know that Miss Furze and I are engaged to be married."

Well, there was a thing! But before Michael could reply, Elizabeth herself, coming down to him, had cried:

"No, no! It isn't true!"

"Of course it's true," Bird had answered firmly. Then he had taken Elizabeth's arm. "Good-day, Mr. Furze," he had said, and walked Elizabeth out of the house.

Yes, *there* was a thing! Michael sat in his room considering it. Amazing! That someone should want to marry Elizabeth! Amazing that Elizabeth should deny it! She should be thankful enough to find somebody, at her age and with her looks! He sat and considered it, breathing hard, his hands on his fat knees. What did this mean? It meant for one thing that Bird would take her away. But would he? Would he not rather be coming to the house when he pleased, be looking into everything, asking questions, telling others what he found there? That must be stopped. I'll stop him. I'll not have rotten little clergymen spying around, telling tales. . . .

He found that his forehead was damp with sweat, that he was trembling. They would be plotting together, those two. Who knows whether it wasn't a clever plot of that damned fool Gurney—Gurney who was always poking around, asking questions. Gurney, Bird, Leggett, Elizabeth. He got up, stripped to the waist, washed in cold water, drank from a bottle of brandy that he kept in a cupboard. Then he felt better. He passed into a mood of elation. Let them do what they pleased, Leggett, Elizabeth and her little clergyman. He had the power, he had the wealth. And with his power and wealth he would do good. He would not use these things, as his brother had done, for men's destruction, but for their good. He would cure the distress in this town, be a great benefactor, make everyone happy. For he wanted everyone to be happy, he had always wanted it. His heart was generous and good and kind. Oh yes, that was what he was if he was only allowed his own way. Any wrong he had done in his life had been because he was *not* allowed his own way. What was the matter with the world, why was there so much distress and misery and hatred? Simply because there were not enough *good* men with power. *He* was good, and now he was powerful. Give him a little time and he would show them what he would do. . . .

"Who's there?" he cried. He went to the door and opened it, but there was nobody there.

He went increasingly into Seatown to discover what they were saying. Leggett was in part responsible for this, because his favourite phrase, gaily, lightly delivered, was:

"They know all about it in Seatown."

"About what?"

"Oh—about everything."

But Michael could never discover what exactly it was that they were saying down there. He knew that Caul and M'Canlis and Moon and several more were stirring up all the general trouble that they could. But that did not interest him. A trivial business, working up unemployed boys to break shop windows or throw stones at old women. No, what interested Michael was the gossip, the chatter about his dear disappeared brother. For they persisted in saying that Stephen had been seen down there, down there and around the Cathedral. The story that he was hiding in Seatown for his own purposes was still prevalent. How absurd! How very absurd! But supposing—just supposing —that Michael *did* come upon his brother in his old bowler hat with his long white nose protruding. . . . What would he . . . ? *How* would he . . . ?

On this particular evening he had an especial purpose, for there was to be a meeting at Charlie's Hall, a room for dances, meetings, general gatherings, dilapidated now and shabby, at the bottom of Primrose Street. The meeting was for the extension of the Communist Fund—that and other things. Tom Caul would be the principal speaker. Michael would look in there, pay a visit to Lanky, and perhaps have a drink or two.

One thing he would *not* do, and that was end up his evening with the round turn up Primrose Street, through the Market and so to the Cathedral, so to the great West Door, so to that absurd listening with his head pressed against the stone, listening for what? A ridiculous fancy that of late had been almost a habit.

He could not leave that Cathedral alone. Or was it that the Cathedral . . . ? So tonight he started out, rather smartly dressed in a blue reefer suit that looked well on his broad chest, a dark blue tie with white spots, a bowler cocked a little on one side of his head. He had unfortunately yielded during the last few weeks to some of his old drinking habits, and his round face with the long nose was again in danger of some of that old purple blotchy colour that was, he knew, unbecoming. But his little eyes looked mildly, almost beseechingly, on to the world, as though they would say: "Be friends with me. I've done nothing wrong. I am all for charity. I want to give my fellow man a helping hand. Believe me, that is my honest desire."

And so he set out, but he was not five steps away from the house before Leggett joined him. Michael jumped almost out of his handsome blue suit. His eyes that had been so amiable narrowed to fear and anger.

"Don't do that."

"Do what?"

"Jump out on me from nowhere."

"I'm sorry, Mike. Indeed I am. Do you mind my coming a few steps of the way with you? I'm due for the meeting at Charlie's. You're going there too, aren't you? Don't be hard on me, Mike" (he was laughing all the time, his hand through the big man's arm); "after all, we're pals, aren't we? Or we ought to be after all that's happened."

"What do you mean—all that's happened?"

"Oh, I don't know. . . . Stephen leaving us all in the lurch like that. By the way, isn't it awkward about money now? Stephen's been gone more than a month. What are you doing about it?"

"Oh, I'm all right."

"Yes, I can see you are. You've got a new suit—very nice one too. But where's the cash coming from? You don't mind my asking, do you, because after all I had a good deal to do with your brother's affairs. I know that Symon is allowing Elizabeth and her mother something a week, but that isn't enough to allow you a new suit. And you hadn't a bean up to the moment of Stephen's disappearance. You don't mind my asking, do you?" He gave Michael's arm a squeeze. "After all, we're pals."

Michael stopped. He took his arm away from Leggett's hand. He faced him. They were standing in the light of a street lamp, close together.

"No, we're not pals," Michael said slowly. "Never were and never will be. I'll tell you something more, Leggett. It was you who murdered my brother."

Leggett laughed.

"Come on," he said, touching Michael's arm. "Don't be a fool. I didn't murder your brother, and we'll be late for the meeting. Anyway, who cares?"

Michael felt his anger rising and at once he guarded it. For he was learning. He no longer allowed himself to be boisterous, noisy, ill-controlled. . . .

All the same, he shook off Leggett's arm.

"Who cares?" he muttered. "You'll find out who cares——"

They walked on down the street again. Leggett talked.

"What a thing to say casually in the middle of the street! And I repeat—who cares? Look at the Nazis in Germany. Do you think they bother about a life or two? What about gangsters in America? But I repeat—I did *not* take Stephen for a ride. Lampiron's your man."

He took Michael's arm again and kept him close to his side. "Listen to me. Don't fool with me, you big bum. Don't you like my American expressions? We are partners—for the present at any rate. *You* know who killed Stephen. So do I. Lampiron is our man. I'll tell you why one day. You leave me alone. I leave you alone. By the way, now you have money, why don't you hire a maid? It's hard on Elizabeth and her mother. They've been working like slaves for years. Why don't you give them a holiday?"

"I haven't got money."

"Sez you."

"I tell you I haven't."

"All right. You haven't. By the way, I should keep off the Cathedral."

"What do you mean?"

"People will begin to think it a bit funny, won't they, your going up there so often. After all you are scarcely a religious man."

"I *am* a religious man."

"All right. Have it your own way."

"I only came to this town because of the Cathedral."

"Is that so? Very interesting. But why make people talk unnecessarily? Look here, Mike, don't be such a bloody fool. Ever read Marcel Proust? No, I suppose not. Ever see Bernhardt act? No, I suppose not. Well, there are two perfect things. You and I properly united are a third. You're not a fool—or

279

are you? Anyway, you can take it from me that whether you like it or no we are Siamese twins. Get that?"

Michael stopped again. His chest was heaving with emotion. His eyes had tears in them.

"Do you know what you are, Leggett? You're bad. Through and through. You're treacherous, false. What I mean to say is that you'd give your best friend dud cheques in spite of your fine French and passion for the theatre. You'd whip your own child and enjoy it. We're not together—we never could be—because I want to do good, I want to help people. I've never been given the chance before. There's always been someone bothering me. But now there isn't going to be. And I warn you. Look out! You killed Stephen, and everyone shall know it if you don't let me alone."

His voice rose hysterically.

"You know that I didn't," Leggett said quietly. "But never mind that. The thing will die down. They'll think Lampiron did it, but they'll never be able to prove it. The only thing I *do* want to know—it puzzles me, I confess—is—whoever *did* do it— where did he tuck the body away? Damned clever he was. Have *you* any idea, Michael?"

"It's for *you* to tell *me*," Michael answered almost in a whisper.

Leggett laughed again.

"Well, have it your own way," he said. "But that's a poor game you're playing, Michael. You can't possibly keep it up. I'm much too clever for you. You'll come to me in the end and my terms may be harder then than they are now. You and I, and Symon to advise us. When the scare's passed off——"

"What scare?"

"Can't you see how scared the town is? Haven't you heard? Why, Stephen's more alive than he was before he was killed! But the thing for us to do is to give the boys down here a little encouragement. A riot or two. Some of the canons tarred and feathered. Some of these swollen-headed gentry robbed of their pants and a window or two broken."

They were down by the river now. There was no sound anywhere, save the faint whispering sound of the water. "Let them believe in their ghosts and some Cathedral inspector with a broken neck. And perhaps there is. Did you ever hear of Rimbaud? No, you never did, but one night he and Verlaine were drinking in some dirty inn or other when some stranger came and sat down beside them. He explained that he had been making an inspection and that nine out of ten of the people he had been examining were due for Hell.

"'I greatly prefer Hell to Heaven,' Rimbaud said.

"'You won't when you get there,' the stranger said. He was just a poor drunk, of course. But there may be something in it. We'll ask Stephen, if we meet him. He's been there by now and can tell us what it's like."

Michael turned on him once again.

"You're taunting me. You're threatening me. But I tell you, you can do nothing to me. I'm my own master."

"Your own master!" Leggett answered contemptuously. "You never were. You never will be."

They had arrived at the bottom of Primrose Street where Charlie's Hall was. A crowd of men and youths surged about the mean and shabby door. Michael, moving forward, found to his relief that Leggett was no longer with him. He felt that his whole body was trembling, and he wished that he could have a drop of something before he went in. He wished, too, as he had often wished of late, that he could make himself invisible. They were staring at him, whispering about him, he wouldn't wonder. How had Stephen managed that, to go about so secretly, to flit from place to place without anyone noticing him?

Even at that moment he had a shock, for, as he showed his ticket at the door, he fancied that he saw that large bowler hat and old shabby overcoat just in front of him. It was not Stephen, of course, but the clothes reminded him. . . . And there was the girl, Fanny Clarke. Desire stirred in him, and with a self-pity, as though he were a little neglected child, he reflected how badly he needed that some woman should be kind to him, take him and stroke his hair, his cheeks, fold him in her arms. . . .

"Fanny, sit beside me," he said, and she nodded her head.

He saw that she was a little drunk. That didn't matter. He wished that he were a little drunk as well. They sat down in about the eighth row, on the left near the wall. The hall was not very large and would soon be full; young boys and girls for the most part. There was already much whistling, shouting, cat-calling . . . it would be a lively meeting.

"Comfortable, Fanny?" Michael asked. He felt an incredible relief at being away from Leggett—incredible because until to-night he would never have believed that he could have taken Leggett so seriously. He was worried not so much by Leggett's threats as by his erudition. To look at him you'd think him a racing tout with nothing but racing notes for his literature. He should be standing, his legs straddled, sucking a straw. Instead of which he had read all this French and criticized actresses.

"I wish," Michael said suddenly to Fanny, "I'd had a better education. Don't you, Fanny?"

"Not me," said Fanny, whose head continued to turn from left to right as she greeted her friends. "Hullo, Charlie! Where's Mac tonight? Not coming? Why, there's Tom's blind brother, the one who has the stall in the Market-place. They're leading him in. Why, do you know he can tell who anybody is just by the touch of the hand! My little girl's educated," she said, turning towards Michael and considering him. "You'd be surprised at what she knows. And I'll tell you another thing she knows" (here Fanny dropped her voice): "she knows who did your bleeding brother in."

"She—what?"

"Oh yes, she does. She won't say *what* she knows though. The men were trying to make her the other night, twisting her arm and all that until I stopped them. She wouldn't say. But she *knows* all right."

"*What* does she know?"

"I'm telling you. She's always creeping around—skipping school. She was somewhere around *that* afternoon and *she* knows all right."

"Have the police questioned her?"

"Oh, Gurney's been after her—but she just says she don't

know nothing. Hullo, Eels! That's Eels Braddock what did his aunt in and stole the cash under the bed. He's quite open about it, but they can't bring it home to him nor never will. Why, look —there's Mr. Romney."

Michael looked and there Romney was, very elegant in a dark blue suit, very quiet, leaning against the wall, surveying the room. His arm was on the shoulder of a stocky thick-built young man.

"He's with Eddie Grant. I like him," she continued reflectively. "He's no use for women, but what's that to me? He's always kind and thoughtful, never rude. Gave me a pearl necklace once—not real pearls, you know, but pretty."

"What did he do that for?" Michael asked.

"Oh, I don't know. Someone pinched the pearls. Some stranger when I was sleeping. Damned shame. I generally keep an eye on them, but that night I was all in and when I woke he'd pinched everything—even my silk garters. And I've never had a pair since."

"I'll give you a pair," Michael said. He put his hand on Fanny's knee. "I want someone to be kind to me, Fanny, I do really."

"Do you really?" She gave him what seemed to him a strange look.

"What are you looking at me like that for?"

"Oh, nothing. You've got some cash again now, haven't you?"

"Cash? No. What do you mean?"

"That's a nice suit you're wearing." She pinched his arm. "Nice material. You hadn't a penny to bless yourself with when your blasted brother was around. What I say is, whoever done him in has done the world a good turn. That's what I say." She patted his arm. "I've been kind to you before and I'll be kind to you again. We'll make a night of it."

But the meeting was beginning. An old man with a grey beard was on the platform—Sam Keating, well known in the district for a fiery reckless agitator. Of course they said that he got money from Russia. But he didn't. Twenty years ago his wife had been killed by a policeman accidentally in a raid after coiners in Drymouth. That was all. He brooded on his wife's death night and day. He would burn the world down to avenge her. . . .

He spoke, however, very quietly with a soft penetrating voice. He said the usual things—that there would be no peace for man until the capitalists were destroyed, that Russia had done it, Germany was going to do it. When Germany and Russia were a united communist power, then we would see what would happen to the world. America was going the same way. China was going the same way. England would not be far behind. And so on. And so on.

Old Father Sam was listened to with attention and respect. They knew just what he had to say. They'd heard it many times before. But they knew too that he meant what he said, and that when the time came, then he would be in the front of the battle. He was followed by a woman whom none of them had seen before. She did not look like a communist; rather, with her pince-nez, her short thick grey hair, her plain dark costume, like a respectable school-teacher.

She too spoke very quietly, but she knew her job. She told them that she was always travelling, moving from place to place, studying conditions. And conditions were fearful. She then, in a gentle reposeful way, gave them figures—housing figures, unemployment figures, the sufferings of children, the tyranny of workhouses. Then, without raising her voice at all, she described some of the luxuries of the capitalists—gay scenes in London, Paris, New York. She read from a newspaper the description of a party at a hotel in London when Lady So-and-so had worn a rope of pearls that cost . . . and someone else possessed a mink coat that cost . . . and so on and so on . . . Very quiet she was and very effective.

Then Tom Caul jumped onto the platform. Michael noticed that at this same moment Romney rose from his seat and advanced to the front of the hall and stood, leaning against the wall, looking at Caul. The consciousness of that intense gaze gave Michael, to whom men physically were precisely one as another, a vicarious sense of Tom Caul's power. He saw, as it were, for a moment, with Romney's eyes; and Caul, who was dressed decently for the occasion in a rough dark suit, appeared to Michael suddenly the most powerful man in Polchester. The strength of his body—of his voice, his hair, his shoulders, his chest, his legs—was only a symbol of his iron, savage, even joyful determination to upset everything, to burn, ruin, destroy, not for personal vengeance like Old Sam, nor for socialistic theory like the grey-haired schoolmistress, but for the releasing of his own energy, the pure, shining violence of the old mediæval knight. Here, if Hattaway had realized it, was his Morris's Sigurd returned to earth—Sigurd with the baleful blood of Regan in his veins. Hattaway, had he been present, might also have recognized what Michael was too stupid and uneducated to perceive—that in Sam, the grey-haired woman and Tom Caul he had the three-headed dragon that at present was disturbing the world.

Romney, however, gave Michael also another idea—that the Town was now, in all its different social strata, one and indivisible, just as Europe was so rapidly becoming. What happened here tonight in Charlie's Hall would affect, most intimately, the lives of Ronder, of Lady Mary Bassett, the Crispangles, Mrs. Braund and the rest.

There was Romney, intimate companion of many in that hall, who yet could call Mrs. Braund "darling," offer Lady Mary a liqueur in his white dining room, examine Ronder's first editions of the poets. Michael knew nothing in actual detail of the white dining room or the first editions, but he was right nevertheless in this idea—that we are now all bound together as the man, the ape, the serpent, the dog were enclosed in the bag in the old Roman torture.

But soon he was carried away in the storm of Tom Caul's eloquence. Caul's power came partly from the force of his amoral recklessness. Nothing bound him, nothing held him. He had indeed nothing to lose, and there was all the thirsting sincerity of the destroyer in his soul as he saw, through his own words, the grand panorama of towns burning, women raped and screaming, himself in a position of lordly power ordering men to execution. *He* was not hungry nor ill-clothed nor suffering because of his starving children. He was gaily, gladly, with the happy superabundance of a healthy schoolboy, the ruthless Destroyer.

Such eloquence caught the room like a fire, for there were many there who *were* hungry and ill-clothed, many also like himself longing to destroy.

"Listen, friends—have you not been cheated long enough? I'll bet you have. I'll bet you've thought for twenty, thirty, forty years there's a better time coming soon. We can stick this out because it isn't going to last. Last! My God, it will bloody well last forever if you don't up and do something about it. What about this town you live in? What did they do only the other day, those blasted priests and their women, but take the town's money that should have gone to the starving poor and spend it on a bleeding pageant. Pageant! I tell you we'll give them a pageant! It's our money they've taken, money that should have given us clothes and food, and with it they dressed themselves in gold and purple for all the world to see! Do you remember that old woman on the white horse? We pulled her off that all right, and so we'll do with the rest of them!" He paused, then he went on, laughing. "There's Mr. Romney there! You can all see him. Well, he helped to dress them up, he did, but all the same he's a friend of mine, he's a friend of all of ours. And why? Because he knows our poverty and that we haven't enough bread to eat nor clothes to our back. *He* comes down and visits us, but what do the others do? They look on us as dirt and spit on us. But they won't be spitting forever! It's they who'll be starving and crying out to us to pity them. That will be some bloody pageant, friends, when that day comes, and may you all be there to see it!"

Much more of the same thing—poor, turgid stuff in words but fired by his energy, his abandon, his physical gaiety and brutality. He was gay. He was brutal. He was as ruthless as he was ignorant, and behind his eyes there was the fire of a superb, a magnificent bonfire.

PERFORMANCE

The room rose to him. Men sprang to their feet and shouted. Women, in shrill voices, cried: "Bravo! Bravo!" He could have led them there and then, had he wished it, to the breaking of windows, the breaking of heads. But he did not wish it. The time was not yet. With a coarse joke or two he quieted them, and Old Sam appealed for funds and the meeting was over. Michael saw that Romney had vanished. What would his grand friends say, Michael wondered, to Caul's praise of him? What would *he* say to his Lady Mary and the rest? But the meeting was over. Michael had Lanky Moon to see. He said good-night to Fanny and went. The soft gentle air by the river cooled him and he smelt the strong scent of some summer flowers—sweet Williams, carnations, roses. He watched for a moment the slow progress of the waters under the moon—the still strong drive and the sudden unexpected check with the contorted eddy, spinning now in trembling lines of silver. So he was staring at the river when he thought he saw his brother. Against the moon, shadowing it, rose an umbrella and from below the umbrella a long hanging overcoat. This rose straight from the river, hung for a moment swaying, then sprayed out, as a fountain touched by the wind sprays, and passed into moon mist.

Michael shook his shoulders like a dog just out of the water. I'm beginning to see him everywhere. That umbrella and bowler hat . . . Nerves. And all this talk about him. Oh well, it will die down soon. I'll get a drink out of Lanky.

He did—but nothing was right this evening. Lanky's little room, up the stairs and along a passage, then down some stairs, was anything but a cheerful place. It was in this very room, they always said, that just two hundred years ago, when the Dog and Pilchard had been an inn with the worst reputation in all southern England, two highwaymen had tortured an old rich shopkeeper. They had stripped him naked, held flame to his toes, and pulled his teeth out, finally his tongue. He had been found there raving mad next morning. They said you could hear him cry at nights. He was reputed to scream: "Oh, Nellie, Nellie! They'll have my tongue!" Who Nellie was no one knew. Anyway, on this warm moonlit scented night the place was weird enough. The window was open and the smell of the river, the flowers, the neglected offal, came floating in. When the Cathedral bells chimed they were as clear as though they were in the very room. The moonlight lay on the floor scattered like quivering silver fish scales. There were pictures of naked women on the walls—photographs cut from Art Publications, Twelve Studies in the Nude. There were boxing gloves hanging on the wall and an enlarged photograph of a French bulldog that Lanky had possessed and adored. There was a stink, as always, of stale drink and tobacco.

They came, at once, to business. Michael produced a small packet and in the packet were gold sovereigns. Lanky took them, counted them, went to a drawer, found some five-pound notes and gave them to Michael. Some drunken singing came up to them from the bar.

"What was the meeting like?" Lanky asked.

"All right."

"Yes? I'm glad. There'll be something doing one of these days."

He leaned on his thin arms and looked at Michael.

"I don't want anyone to know about these coins of yours."

"No," said Michael. "Nor do I."

"Can anyone else open that safe?"

"Leggett maybe. I don't know."

"What does Leggett say to you?"

"Oh, nothing."

"Doesn't he though?" Lanky spat out of the window. "Yes, he does, though. Doesn't he say that Lampiron did your brother in?"

"He pretends to think that."

"Oh—pretends or not pretends. What the hell! . . . But that's what *you've* got to say, Mike. Understand me? We can get the whole town to believe it."

"What's the idea?"

"What's the——?" Lanky's face curdled with contempt. This bloody soft-witted fool! Why, look, all his body all soft fat, trembling and shaking. And yet he had brains somewhere, sometimes. He must have courage, determination somewhere too. . . .

"Look here, Mike," Lanky said, putting his hand on Michael's arm. "Don't let this get you down. You look a bit scared tonight——"

"Everybody's talking. Everybody——"

"Oh, Christ! Let them talk! Everybody my foot! Let them get Lampiron into their heads and they won't ask any more questions. And for all I know," Lanky added, laughing, "perhaps he *did* do it. What do you say, Mike?"

"Maybe he did," said Michael, clearing his throat. He wanted to get out of here; in spite of the open windows the room was stuffy. There was a smell of dead geraniums and stinking fish. Tonight everyone had behaved queerly. He wanted to get somewhere by himself, away from eyes, from voices, from sound. . . .

"I think I'll be getting along," he said, rising.

"Wait a minute," said Lanky, looking up at him from his strange narrow Chinese-like eyes. "There are things we've got to talk about. Not tonight perhaps. And we'll have Leggett here."

"Leggett!" Mike cried, with that shrill feminine note that was sometimes in his voice. "What's Leggett got to do with it?"

"Everything," said Lanky slowly. "Everything. Why, we're like your Siamese twins, Mike, Leggett and me. You didn't think you'd be going on alone, Mike, did you?"

That horrible simile! Leggett had also used it.

"By God!" Michael cried, his fat body shaking. "I did believe it and I do. What have you got to do with me—or Leggett either?"

Lanky filled his long thin pipe with the stinking coarse tobacco that he favoured.

"You are no more free from us," he said slowly, "than my stomach is free from my lungs and my liver."

Michael looked over Lanky's head to the window.

"I'll show you whether I am," he said. "I am free the first moment I want to be," and he went out and stumbled down the dark twisted stairs, pushed through the bar, and found his way into the open air again.

He had had only one drink with Lanky and not a one with anyone else, and yet there he was, confused in the head. He stood, uncertain, while the moon, like an orange-faced clown with a straw in his mouth, swung just to the right of the Harry Tower and grinned at himself.

His feet mechanically took him a step or two up Primrose Street. There he was—on his old round again! His head was just befuddled enough to slacken his determination. He seemed, as he so often was, only a step away from a grand state of self-command and world authority. In bitter fact he was governed by others as all his life he had been. As he climbed the street he thought of the splendid man he'd be if it were not for that little grain of weakness. Always letting others get the better of you—and you finer, nobler in purpose than any of them. How you care, Mike Furze, for beautiful things, how you long to be generous, to give everything to the poor, to make everyone happy. . . .

He stumbled against someone. The town trailed a thin summer mist, and through it the Polchester moon, like Shelley's once, leaned crazily. Mike looked to see who it was that he was holding by the hand. It was Caul, the blind stallkeeper, Tom's brother. His girl had him by the arm. Caul stroked Mike's hand in the way that was so very unpleasant—"like spiders crawling."

"Ah—Mr. Michael Furze. Good-evening. My daughter is seeing me home."

Mike murmured something. The unagreeable thing was that he could not take his hand away although it was but lightly held. But Caul was very friendly. It was wonderful, they said, how pluckily he took his misfortune, what cheery spirits he had!

"I saw you at the meeting. Tom spoke well."

"Aye. His usual nonsense. He never cares what he says so long as he hears his own voice. I haven't spoken with you, Mr. Furze, since that day—let me see—the afternoon before the Pageant—up by the Cathedral—you and your brother."

Mike sharply withdrew his hand.

"It wasn't my brother. I was alone."

Caul sighed. His gentle philosophic smile lit his face with real beauty. "Maybe. I fancied I touched his hand first, then yours, Mr. Furze. But I'm often wrong."

"It's important though," Mike said, "because my brother's never been seen again since that afternoon, as I daresay you've heard. You had better tell the police about it. But if my brother was there I never saw him."

"Yes," said Caul, with the dreamy self-absorption that blind people acquire. "Mr. Gurney did ask me. I told him what I thought: I daresay I was mistaken. Good-night to you, Mr. Furze."

A moment later, so it seemed to Mike (and such things can be when the town is queer, when the river runs swiftly to its destiny, when the orange moon sucks a straw and the Cathedral bells ring for your ears alone), he was by the great West Door and, as had been the case now so many times, his cheek was pressed against the cold stone as though he were listening to all the busy life within those walls.

But if he was listening he did not know it. He was terribly, terribly unhappy, as he often was when he had taken a drink or two. A strange sight for anyone passing, this fat flabby man, on his knees now in the thin mouse-coloured moonlight, the Cathedral towering above him, tears coursing down his cheeks.

A peculiar sight for a passer-by! Klitch, for example, who would sometimes walk out to admire the moonlight sleeping on the grass. This drunken penitent, lover of the beautiful, idealist! But tonight not so drunken, only bewildered, pursued, spied upon. . . .

The bells rang midnight, and all about him, from under the ground, from above at the moon's very heart, from the stern Inquisitor himself, the bells shook and quivered and, obedient to law, pursued their eternal ceaseless course. He was plain drunk by now or so unhappy that his common sense betrayed him. For the Great Door opened and, without sound, the little procession passed out: the Inquisitor continues his investigation.

THE INQUISITOR

Poor Mike! There is nothing and no one there—only Klitch sees, in the moonlight, a heavy man on his knees, his cheek pressed against the stone, sobbing.

Klitch will not interfere. He is too cautious a man. Smoking his last pipe of the day, he returns to his house.

CHAPTER VIII

Three Visitors for Lampiron

On the afternoon of September 3rd, Gurney, the police inspector, paid a call on Lampiron at his house. This astonished Lampiron very much indeed, just as Lampiron's sculpture astonished Gurney. This was the first intimation that Lampiron received that he had any connection with Stephen Furze's disappearance.

Gurney was pleasant and friendly, wiping his forehead with a large yellow-and-black handkerchief, for it was a warm afternoon—and, between his remarks, he shot surreptitious glances of wonder at the fearful bosoms of the gigantic female torsos. But he liked the little statue of the naked young man on the mantelpiece. He asked Lampiron whether he had made that.

"No," said Lampiron, smiling. "That's a copy of a statue by Donatello, one of the greatest sculptors who ever lived. It's David who killed Goliath."

Gurney nodded his head. He had begun by saying that he hoped Mr. Lampiron wouldn't think his visit an impertinence. It was all in the way of his duty. He only wanted to ask a question or two. What he *did* want to know was exactly what Lampiron was doing on the afternoon that preceded the Pageant. Could he throw his mind back?

"Why, good God!" Lampiron burst out. "You don't mean to say you think *I* murdered Furze?"

"He's a fine-looking old man when he's angry," Gurney thought. "But he's got a temper all right."

Why, no, Gurney explained, laughing, that *was* silly! Of course not. Only this was a baffling case. They were making very little progress with it. And they *did* understand that Mr. Lampiron had had a few words with Stephen Furze that same afternoon in the High Street. Several people had noticed it.

Lampiron, to whom this was all a thundering insult, understood, however, that he must be calm. So, quietly, he threw his mind back. Yes, he'd left his house about a quarter-past four. It was quite true that, going up the High Street, he had encountered Furze; the man had been impertinent and he told him to go to the devil! He had always hated the man, had been in debt to him for a long time, as everyone knew.

"And after that?" asked Gurney.

Well, after that he had walked on up the High Street, looked at the preparations for the Pageant, gone into the Cathedral, where he had expected to meet Mr. Hattaway. They were to meet in order to discuss the danger to the Whispering Gallery from wood rot. The Whispering Gallery, as a matter of fact, was closed later that same evening. Hattaway had not turned up. He, Lampiron, had stayed quietly near the West Door for a while. There had been no one there. Once he thought he heard steps in the Choir, but he had not stayed for long. Five minutes after he left the Cathedral a thunderstorm had broken out, he remembered, and he had taken shelter in the Cloisters. About a quarter-past five he had gone home.

"So no one saw you between about four-twenty-five and five-fifteen?"

"No. I suppose not," Lampiron said.

"The last person who saw Furze alive, so far as we know," said Gurney, "was Klitch, the curiosity-shop man, at about a quarter to five. He saw him, standing in the rain, staring through the window at the shop."

Lampiron nodded his head.

"Well, Inspector," he said, "as I seem to be drawn into this

I may as well tell you what I expect others have already told you. The man you want is Furze's brother."

Gurney agreed.

"Well, he *is* acting a bit funny, Mr. Lampiron. And there *are* one or two things." He looked mysterious and also child-like. Like a baby who has suddenly thought of a new way to steal jam without being observed.

"I must be off," he said, rising. "I'm most grateful to you for your courtesy, Mr. Lampiron. That certainly *is* a pretty statue," he added, throwing one last glance at the David.

Afterwards Lampiron was both annoyed and puzzled. They surely couldn't seriously think that he would be such an ass? Of course he had declared many times that there was nothing that would please him better than to wring Furze's neck. . . . Had he not, on one or two occasions, been perilously near the act? There had been that visit to Furze's room. Why could he not command his temper better? Why, after all these years, had he learnt just nothing at all?

Then for the first time it occurred to him that there might be people in this town who really believed that he had murdered Furze. He burst out laughing—and then was suddenly serious.

On the evening of September 8th he received three visitors. The first visitor was the Reverend James Bird.

Marcel Proust says somewhere in his beautiful tangle of reminiscent regrets that when society feels itself to be attacked it draws, for self-confidence, closer together and admits into its ranks those who had always hitherto been excluded.

Mr. Porteous was experiencing something of that kind at the present. Ever since the disastrous close to the Pageant, the accident to Mrs. Braund and the disappearance of Stephen Furze, men of common sense and obvious good-will had been very welcome—men like Canon Cronin, Hattaway, and most especially Porteous. Everyone said that it was a real comfort to be with Porteous in these days, that one knew that *he* didn't believe in ghosts or care whether old Furze had been murdered or no—and that if Seatown *were* to make a little trouble Porteous would be the first man to send them skulking back to their kennels. Mrs. Cronin said that he might well turn out to be our Mussolini, and this name stuck both appreciatively and also, it is to be feared, derisively. Romney made the most of it and always spoke of Porteous as "Il Duce." He made many people laugh, in the drawing rooms of Polchester, with his imitation of Porteous acknowledging the Fascist salute from his choir boys. Porteous heard of this; he and Romney were now declared enemies and cut one another when they met. This delighted Romney, who had all the feminine love for dramatic situations.

The immediate result of Mr. Porteous' new popularity was the rather unfortunate change that overcame that gentleman. For, as with all men who are noisy and dictatorial because of their inferiority complex, popularity turned his head altogether. It was said afterwards that he really did at this time begin to fancy himself Mussolini. His voice had always been loud: it reverberated now like thunder, and when, first thing in the morning, he rebuked the maid for not dusting the top of the banisters, he could be heard on the bridge at the bottom of Orange Street. His intimate acquaintance with God, always remarkable, was now greatly strengthened.

"Is that what God really wishes of us, Bird? I think not. I can assure you that God's plan is quite otherwise—so if you don't mind, eleven-thirty at the Broad Street school. Eleven-thirty sharp."

Poor Mrs. Porteous, a colourless lady with a harassed eye and short legs that gave her an odd resemblance to a dachshund, admired him now so tremendously that he became to her St. Paul and Mussolini rolled into one. Miss Porteous, Camilla, reserved her opinion. She confessed in a letter to a friend that she was getting rather tired of papa, and in that same letter added: "Once again, dear Agnes, the curate is disappointing. An insignificant little man, often impertinent and always evading his duties." She did not, in fact, call him "Birdie" any more but "Mr. Bird," and for this relief he offered thanks.

It is to be feared that by this time James Bird had grown to detest Porteous very thoroughly—and this was a pity, for Porteous had many most excellent qualities which Bird, in other circumstances, would certainly have recognized. However, much as he disliked Porteous he disliked Camilla more. Mrs. Porteous was the only member of the family whom he could endure.

He knew that a climax was approaching, and on this afternoon of September 8th it advanced a step nearer.

Bird had just left Porteous' study and was about to pay a visit to a cheerful old lady who was dying uncomplainingly of cancer when he met Camilla in the hall. She was passing him in silence, and with a kind of spiritual toss of the head, when she thought better of it. She smiled and his heart sank, for he had hoped that she would never smile at him again. She dropped her voice, which meant that she was about to say something unpleasant.

"Pardon me, Mr. Bird," she said, "but you are a friend of Mr. Lampiron's, are you not?"

"I am."

"Well—oh, you know what gossip is, especially in a little town like this."

"I do."

"Perhaps you have heard—what everyone is saying."

"No, I have not."

"Well—it sounds absurd—but after all you never know. Everyone says that it's Mr. Lampiron who murdered Stephen Furze."

"Lampiron!" He turned upon her so fiercely that, as she said afterwards, she thought that he would strike her.

"Yes, isn't it dreadful? But after all, he's a very strange man. And they say his house is full of naked statues. And it's shocking the open way he goes about with Penny Marlowe who's young enough to be his granddaughter. Anyway that's what everyone is saying."

"It's a lie, Miss Porteous—a monstrous lie."

"I daresay it is—people chatter. I'm sure he knows something though. And that daughter of Furze—she guesses something too."

Bird's voice trembled. "You had better be careful, Miss Porteous. There are libel laws, you know." Then he added quietly, "And in any case you mustn't say such things to me. Miss Furze and myself are engaged to be married."

He walked out of the house. At the same time he knew that he had done it! Within half an hour it would be common talk in Polchester, and he had promised Elizabeth that no one should know. That promise was given after his outbreak to Michael Furze. She had denied that she *was* engaged to him, had refused to engage herself to anybody until this mystery concerning her father was cleared.

"Elizabeth," he had said, "that's what they do in novels. The heroine *always* cries 'Clear our family name and I'll marry you.'"

But that did not amuse her. She saw nothing funny in novels, because she had had to read so many bad ones to her mother. Moreover her life had been too hard for her to take serious things lightly—and Mr. James Bird's love for her was certainly serious. It had ended in Bird's saying that they were engaged and in Elizabeth's saying that they were not engaged but that if they were no one was to know about it. And now he had told Camilla! Well—what did he care? He threw up his head defiantly as he walked down Orange Street. Nothing could separate him from Elizabeth and he could do his duty to God in any place. *He* didn't mind nor did Elizabeth. He would not be sorry to leave Polchester, which now possessed for him a strange corrupt odour as though Furze's buried body was on the move somewhere, circulating hither and thither in the town drainage system. Thinking of Furze made him think of Lampiron. He would pay him a brief visit before looking in to read the Bible to the old lady with cancer.

Friendship as understood by the Englishman is both more emotional and more enduring than with any other peoples in the world. It is also more silent and less sentimental. The American is too restless, the Slav too excitedly preoccupied with women, the Scandinavian too hygienic, the Frenchman too materialistic, the Italian too egoistic, the Spaniard too completely male. . . . These nationalities do not trouble to educate the principle of fidelity sufficiently. It simply is not worth their bother. But the principal reason why men are more important than women in England is that men can in that country do without women in every element of life except the least important, the physical. Of no other country in the world can this be said.

Friendship among men in England is never expressed, but once the pact is made it can withstand every attempt to break it—geography, history, sex, finance, erudition, even sport—none of these can affect it.

So Bird felt for Lampiron. After Elizabeth, that old lion-headed man meant more to him than anyone else in the world. But when he stood with Lampiron in his studio it was difficult. What he wanted to say was that if Lampiron was in any kind of trouble anywhere at any time—murder, adultery or robbing an old blind man of his pennies—he, James Bird, was there at his side.

But all that he actually said was: "Thought I'd look in for a moment."

"Stay and have some supper with me," Lampiron said.

"No, thanks. I have to read to an old woman."

Lampiron looked at him with great affection and put a hand on the little man's shoulder.

"Don't get too religious-minded, Jimmie," he said.

"Why—what do you mean?"

"Religion drives out friendship and, as a matter of fact, I need a friend just at the moment. I had the shock of my life once. I had a friend for five years—the best I ever had, kind, humorous, intelligent, understanding, unselfish. Then this good man met God and became such friends with Him that he was always talking to Him. God is Love, he said morning, noon and night. We must love everybody all the time. But the result was that he soon came to love nobody. He was so snobbish about his new splendid divine friendship. When I told him this one day he was deeply hurt and he never spoke to me again. I've missed him ever since *and* thought ill of religion."

"I expect," Bird said, "that it wasn't God he met but his own glorified idea of himself."

"Maybe," Lampiron answered. He sat down wearily, leaning his head on his arms. He looked up. "Jimmie, tell me—have you heard any gossip about me?"

"I never hear gossip."

"Oh yes, you do. Have you heard, for instance, that I have been busy seducing Miss Marlowe?"

Bird hesitated. Then he said, "I've heard that you're very friendly with her."

"Disgusting, isn't it? A man old enough to be her grand-father." Lampiron looked steadily across into Bird's face. "What a filthy town this is! Or no—not filthy. Just like any other town." He paused. "Have you heard something else— that it was I who killed Furze?"

Bird answered at once.

"I heard it just now—half an hour ago—for the first time."

"From whom?"

"Camilla Porteous."

"Ah! So it *is* going around. I'll tell you something else, Jimmie. Five days ago Gurney, the policeman, came to see me. He wanted to ask me what my movements were on the fatal day—the day before the Pageant. I told him."

Bird said quietly, "Look here, don't take this too seriously. They're asking everybody."

"Have they asked you?"

"No. But——"

"There you are. Of course they're not asking everybody. Gurney was very kind, very friendly. All the same, his large soft eye was heavy with suspicion. Now, Jimmie, two more questions. First, do *you* believe that I have seduced Miss Marlowe?"

"No. Of course not."

"Good. Second, do you believe that I murdered Furze?"

"No." Bird laughed.

"Good. Would you believe either or both of those things if I myself told you I was guilty?"

"Never. I should think you were shielding someone."

"Right. I haven't done either and I'm not shielding anyone."

Bird forgot all his own affairs. He was caught into Lamp-iron's crisis. For he knew at once, by the innate sympathy that friendship brings, that there was beginning now the crisis of Lampiron's whole life. The man looked old and Bird had never seen him look old before, but he had also a touch of the super-human, that expression in the eyes, that line in the mouth that men catch when they have known great suffering or great tri-umph. Lampiron's massive shoulders carried some burden but carried it defiantly. This was a picture of an old man fighting— old in experience, in ambition, in passion, not in years.

"I'll tell you," Lampiron said, "first about Miss Marlowe. You ought to know. I like you better than any other man any-where."

"Do you really?" Bird said, delighted.

"Yes. Now, listen. Miss Marlowe and I love one another. We have kissed and we shall kiss again—and that is all. Messrs. Crispangle, Bellamy, and the lads of Seatown would split their sides laughing if they heard that. Nevertheless it's true. This, Jimmie, is the finest thing I've ever had, finer than I thought any relationship between the cats and monkeys could ever be. It will remain so. Do you believe me?"

"I do," said Bird. "But people——"

"Oh, people! To hell with people! . . ."

"Yes, but for her sake . . ."

"I tell you, Jimmie, that the finest thing I can do for her is to give her a grand idea of life—a design for living, full of colour, humour, irony, beauty, and love when love's worth it. That's the best thing, just about the only thing that the old can do for the young. And how often do they? Almost never. And how often do the young listen? Also almost never. But she loves me and, God forgive me, thinks me wonderful. So *that* I can do for her—strengthen everything in her that will help her to accept life and find it worth while to be alive. What does she care about people talking? Aren't we cowards if we care? We know what we are. No one can say worse or better than we must say of ourselves. . . . So that is that. Do you trust me, Jimmie?"

"I trust you."

"Good. But now listen. The other is much worse. Because—don't jump—I warned you—I'm not sure that I didn't kill Furze."

"What!" Bird half rose from his chair.

"No, no. Don't be so agitated, Jimmie. Of course I didn't actually kill him. I think you won't have to look further than his brother for that. But I *wanted* to kill him. I suppose I've wanted nothing so much physically for years as to give him one annihilating blow on his horrible shining nose. Twice at least I was very near to throttling him. On that very last afternoon, as I expect you've heard, I met him in the High Street and quarrelled with him publicly. That's what my cursed temper does!"

"Wanting to kill him," said Bird, "isn't killing him. If I were bigger and stronger I *might* hit Porteous one day and that *might* kill him. I've always thought murder one of the lesser crimes—in certain cases of course."

"Now I'll try to explain what I mean, Jimmie. I've been haunted by Furze. I was haunted by Furze before he died—if he *is* dead—but it's been worse since. To me, during the last weeks, it has been as though some thin paper wall (like the Japanese room walls) has been torn down in this place. Two worlds are mingling, and it's nasty because it's wrong, because it's against Nature. I told you that when I was acting in that silly Pageant I felt as though Arden were alive—as though *I* were the shadow and *he* the reality! Others felt the same. Perhaps this has become a haunted town. After all, what do we know about death? Why shouldn't the two worlds mingle? And I tell you, Jimmie, we've got to lay these ghosts. They are more powerful than we are, for they have had experience of both worlds, *we* only of one. Maybe Furze has joined them. *He* knows now more than he did and he's a nasty malicious spirit. It's as though he whispered to me that I killed him and he'll have his own back. . . . Is this altogether nonsense, Jimmie? How can I say so now that the living are beginning to whisper as well as the dead? The very children are saying that Furze walks out of the Cathedral West Door with a broken neck. Powerful now he will be. The Inquisitor, as old Mordaunt says, of this town. Nice for us, isn't it?"

Bird looked at him anxiously. "Have you been getting your sleep all right?"

"No, I haven't. I've not slept properly for weeks. I know you think I'm crazy, Jimmie—but in the Pageant they did something to me. I ought never to have acted in the damned thing!"

Bird got up to go.

"I've something to tell *you*," he said. "I'm engaged to be married to Elizabeth Furze."

Lampiron looked at him as though he were his son. "I'm proud of you, Jimmie. This is just the time you *would* announce it."

"As a matter of honest truth," said Bird, "she refuses to consider herself engaged until all this business is cleared up. I promised her that I would keep it dark, but I lost my temper just now with Camilla and told her—so it will be all over Polchester tomorrow."

"The plot moves," Lampiron said, smiling. "That's a strange house to marry into, Jimmie."

"I'm not marrying a house," Jimmie said, "but one of the bravest, truest, warmest-hearted women ever born. She's been starved, mentally, spiritually, physically. She thinks the hand of the whole world is against her. She shall find that it is not."

Lampiron straightened his shoulders and threw back his head.

"Damn the ghosts!" he cried, as though challenging his own fears and driving them like mist vapours into sunlight. "You're real, Jimmie. I've been living for five days in a fog."

But when Bird had gone the fog closed in again. Lampiron sat in his chair, his legs stretched out in front of him, brooding. For five days he had been able to do no work. That was bad. He felt old and he felt frightened. That was worse. This was the first time in his life that he had been afraid and he didn't like the unaccustomed feel of it. He got up and switched on the electric light. Then he lit a fire, for the room was cold. He looked at every corner of the room, now clear and defined in the light. There was no one there—only his work which seemed to him now without life or savour. Then ashamed of his nervousness he switched out the light again—only the thin vaporous flames threw little shadows on the wall.

Of what was he afraid? Not of the gossip. When had he ever bothered about gossip? Of something intangible. He did not believe in ghosts in any crude fashion. He did not believe, for example, that dead men with broken necks walked the town. No. . . . Not that. But he was not at all sure that this physical world was the only one, nor that it might not be interpenetrated with others.

There are times, he thought, when a man feels hemmed in. I'm not young any more. I haven't the strength I had. Even with Penny it is easier to be virtuous than it would have been only a few years ago. As my body grows weaker I realize more actively the reality of non-bodily power. For it *is* real. It can be active. Have I enraged someone, disturbed some settled order with which I had no right to interfere? Have I for years treated with contemptuous indifference powers of tremendous importance? Perhaps that happens to all of us and then we blame our ill-luck. . . . I have been blaming mine. . . . In any case I'm uneasy, apprehensive. . . . (He shook his head at the fire-light.) I'm damned if I will be. What does it matter? Let them say I murdered Furze if they like. What do I care *what* they think?

But it wasn't *they*—the simple citizens of Polchester—of whom he was apprehensive. He got up and began to pace the studio. This damned thing was interfering with his food, his sleep, his work.

He longed for Penny then, longed for her as he had never done before. Only to see her. Not to touch her but to sit near to her and worship her youth, her courage, her clear-sighted honesty—the things she had that seemed to be abandoning himself. As one grows old, he wondered, does this world begin to slip away, long before death comes; does one begin to realize how empty and false one's sense of value has been, ironically now when it is too late to do anything about it? I painted pictures once and into the painting I put all the ardour, the hope, the enthusiasm that I had. Then one day I saw that they were nothing, worse than nothing. How could I have been so blind? Have I been blind in the same way about life?

He had suddenly a dread sensation of disintegration, as though the flesh were peeling from his bones as he watched it, as though the stone and plaster of his walls were fading into air. Was this even possibly death? He placed his hand above his heart. It was beating steadily. He got up again and went to the female torso and felt on the flesh of his palm the cold strong stone of which it was made. He stood firmly on the ground. He opened his shirt, laying his hand on the crisp, curling hair of his breast.

These were real. His love for Penny was real. But there were shadows too. Half the room was in shadow and old Furze with his long nose might be standing there, watching, with cold satisfaction, his unworthy terrors. . . .

He stared fixedly at that side of the room where the shadows were thickest, and it was not strange that his disturbed gaze now should trace for him a shadow against the shadow, the thin outline of a thin mean old bastard whose throat someone somewhere had so rightly twisted.

Then the door was flung open and the light from the passage streamed in. The old woman stood there.

"Why, sir, you're all in the dark. There's Canon Ronder outside wonders if he might have a word with you."

Ronder! Nothing in the world could have surprised Lampiron more and, as he moved forward to greet him, he had, even more strongly, the sense that events were moving in upon him even as the walls of the room stole in upon the prisoner in the old story. Ronder! But he scarcely knew him! They were the merest acquaintances. What did *he* want here?

Ronder stood in the lighted doorway rather like a Chinese idol, immobile, stout-bellied, shining. He held his soft clerical hat in his hand.

"Canon Ronder! Come in! I was dreaming in front of the fire. I'm delighted to see you."

"Thank you so much." Ronder's soft rich voice had exactly the same cadence as thirty-six years ago, was as resonant and as beautifully rhythmic. "A pleasure to listen to Ronder," Crispangle always remarked, "even if all he says is, 'Pass the butter please.'"

"No. I'll keep my hat. I have looked in for the briefest moment. Thanks. I will sit down. My heart isn't too good and I'm much too fat."

He sat back in the easy chair, his black shining head, his round plump face with the gleaming spectacles, his protruding stomach, his round thick thighs, his immaculate glittering black shoes, all like something carved; his body, or rather the personality within his body, had the rounded finish of a completed artistic work. "This," God might say, opening His new art show, "is one of the finest works in the exhibition. There is not a flaw—allowing of course for what it is meant to be."

Nevertheless, Lampiron perceived that Ronder was in pain. A faint bluish tinge coloured his cheeks. His white plump hand pressed above his heart.

"Have you a glass of water?" he asked. "My walk has been a little too much for me."

Lampiron fetched him a glass of water. He took two pills from a little bottle.

"There's nothing radically the matter," he said, quickly recovering. "I'm too fat, and that gives me wind about the heart. How have you managed to keep so fit, Mr. Lampiron? You look as though you were made of steel."

"Yes, my health's all right," Lampiron said, smiling. "Won't you stay and have some supper with me, Canon?"

"Oh, no, thanks. The fact is I looked in only for a minute. I want to make an apology."

"An apology?"

"Yes—although I haven't, I think, done anything wrong. Not in your case at least—although in plenty of others," he added, smiling.

An old man, Lampiron thought, wearing a mask. Has worn one for years and years and it has bitten in and in until now—is it all mask? or is he a real suffering lonely human being like the rest of us?

Lampiron had never greatly liked him because he had felt a certain shyness at Ronder's social accomplishments. He had accounted for this within himself by saying that Ronder was a snob. But he knew well that if he, Lampiron, had been able to enter a room and greet its occupants with the grace that Ronder so naturally had, he would not have called him a snob but would rather have commented on his kindliness of heart.

The other thing about Ronder (and this was felt in greater or lesser degree by everyone in Polchester) was that the Canon was a trifle out of date, like last week's newspaper. Had he not been so powerful twenty years ago he would not now be a little faded. But the battles that he fought successfully *then* seemed so unlike the battles that everyone was engaged in *now*. (As a matter of fact they were the same. Neither the battlefield nor the combatants ever change—only the fashion in armour is different.)

Ronder folded his hands across his stomach and said:

"I'm feeling better now. I'm an old man, you know. I forget that sometimes."

"I'm no chicken myself," Lampiron said, smiling.

"No. But how strong you are! You should have known that Swede—or Dane, was it?—who was here years ago. He used to massage me out of existence. . . . But come. I ramble on, living in the past. A shocking habit. What I came here to say was this—I'm afraid I may have done you an injury."

"In what way?"

"The police inspector, Gurney, called on me. He wanted me to tell him all that I knew of a little scene I witnessed one afternoon in the High Street between yourself and Furze."

"Yes. I know. He's been to see me about it."

"Oh, has he? Well, as a matter of fact I discovered that he had already spoke to Gaselee—you know, Gaselee of St. James's —who was with me that afternoon—so that, so to speak, it was of no use my keeping my mouth shut."

"There was no reason why you *should* keep your mouth shut," Lampiron said genially.

"No. Quite. I told him all I knew, which was very little—

that you *did* have a row with Furze. And I'm sure I don't wonder! If ever there was an unpleasant human being he was one. . . . By the way, many people seem to think that he's not dead at all but is still hiding in the town."

"Yes," Lampiron answered, looking at Ronder and wondering what he was really thinking behind those large shining spectacles. (Did he, perhaps, suspect . . . ?) "I've heard that theory. And also that he comes out of the Cathedral every night at twelve with his neck broken."

Both men laughed.

"Well," said Ronder very pleasantly, "it was only that after I told Gurney this—what a *very* stupid man to have for our leading policeman by the way—I wasn't at all comfortable. What right had I to be interfering in your private affairs?"

"Every right in the world," said Lampiron heartily. "If they *were* my private affairs. But they seem to be very public ones!" he went on, laughing. "I understand that it's very generally supposed in the town that *I* did the ruffian in!"

"No! is it really?" said Ronder. "How absurd!"

"Not altogether absurd. I hated the man. I was in debt to him. And he hated *me!* More than anyone else in the town, I think. If he *is* walking about with a broken neck it's he who is pointing me out with his long skeleton finger."

Ronder rose.

"It's very good of you to take it like this. You can be sure that I resented being questioned. As a matter of fact," he went on slowly, "there was one thing I *didn't* tell Gurney. I was in the Cathedral with Gaselee that afternoon. We were in the Choir and, as far as I know, quite alone. A thunderstorm broke out and so we stayed. Then, somewhere about five o'clock, I fancied I heard a cry."

"From where?" Lampiron asked.

"I don't know. I'm not even sure that I heard one. I didn't give it another thought until all this disturbance began. And *what* a disturbance!" He raised his hands. "I don't think I ever remember in all these years here the town to have been so upset. Why, I hear that young men are going out at night with clubs lest they should be attacked. And poor Mrs. Braund. They say she is not at all herself. In quite an hysterical state. That wretched pageant——"

"Yes, the Pageant," Lampiron said. "An unfortunate ending."

"Unfortunate everything!" Ronder cried. "Upon my soul I begin to wonder whether old Mordaunt wasn't right when he said that the Cathedral resented it. It well might! How we dared risk comparison with those old people . . . Well—I must be getting along."

"You're sure you won't stay and have some supper with me?"

"No, no. I only sit with my feet on the fender and my eyes half closed and grumble. It's all that life has left to me. Old age!" He shook his head. "A horrifying affair! You'll find it so when you get to it, Lampiron."

After he had gone Lampiron reflected. Lord, he intended that as a compliment. Why, I'm nearly as old as he! He also thought: He never said a word about my sculpture. That also was a compliment. And his last thought was: What did he come here for? To look at me? To see whether I *seemed* a murderer?

His supper that night was a melancholy meal. He was in poor spirits. He suffered from that loneliness, well known to all of us, when we return to almost nursery terrors of wind echoes, wall shadows, and the threat of impending darkness. He longed for Penny now as though some relentless piston rod impelled him forward. For twopence—oh yes, for nothing at all!—he would hurry from the house, hasten up the dark street, make some excuse to see her. But that way lay destruction. . . . He put down his bread and cheese, stared in front of him. Why, now that the town thought these things of him what would *she* be thinking? She would stand by him whatever they might do, but, secretly alone with herself, where there could be no treachery, what did she think?

He jumped up. This was like madness in his brain. He must *know* what she thought. If she suspected him might he not begin to suspect himself? Already he was wondering what it was he *had* done! If Arden was more real, more alive than he, then Furze was alive—alive to all eternity! A nasty thought that the little quiet streets of this country town would never again be free of that mean figure, the hat, the coat, the mushroom-fungus-stained umbrella. . . .

And now it's time, Lampiron thought, for a drink. I'm going dotty in here tonight. Getting drunk is safer than other things. Ten minutes later he was saying aloud: "They can go to hell, the lot of them!" Neat brandy was what he preferred, and he drank plenty of it. He waved his glass at the marble-breasted female. He went to her, laid his head on those breasts, then—his arm around her—defied all the worlds—the first which is physical, the second which is mist and vapour, the third where the Sacred River runs, the fourth . . .

The bell rang. What! *Another* visitor! I haven't been so popular for months. He switched off the lights. There was a large fire burning now, a golden molten cavern out of which little tongues of flames eagerly licked the air.

Lampiron stood in the firelight sobering himself. He had a mad, frantic hope that it might be Penny.

But the old woman said: "It's a gentleman, wouldn't give his name—says he must see you."

Then Lampiron saw that Leggett was standing there. Leggett came down the steps into the studio.

"I didn't send my name in because I thought that you wouldn't see me."

"What do you want?"

Leggett came forward into the firelight.

"I want to talk to you."

Lampiron turned to the fire.

"Not tonight, I'm afraid. I'm busy."

Leggett came further into the room.

"See here, Lampiron. I know you hate the sight of me. But you shouldn't. I'm not your enemy."

"What the hell do I care," Lampiron said, "whether you're my enemy or not? It doesn't matter to me *what* you are!"

"Well, it might," Leggett said. "There've been funnier things."

Then he sat down, took a cigarette case out of his pocket, lit a cigarette.

Lampiron looked at him as though he would pick him up out of the chair and throw him into the hall. But he did not. What did the little swine want? The evening had been already significant. It should end significantly.

He stood, the firelight throwing gigantic shadows of him on the wall, and lowering his head, rather like an old bull, said:

"What is it?"

Leggett looked at him with admiration. What strength the old man had!

"It's very simple," he said. "I know a thing or two and I want you to know what I know."

"I don't care what you know."

"But listen," said Leggett very amiably. "It's important. Mind you—don't think I take any views in the matter. I dare-say you did quite right. Anyway I've been often tempted my-self. And he was one of the nastiest bits of work in existence."

"What are you talking about?"

Leggett crossed one knee over the other.

"You killed Furze, didn't you? Oh, don't worry. I'm not go-ing to tell anyone. People are guessing, of course. But I *know*."

"Go on," Lampiron said.

"Well—isn't this the way it happened? You quarrelled with him in the High Street. Then you went into the Cathedral and waited for Hattaway. Furze meanwhile was wandering about—I myself had left him only a little while before. Then a thunder-storm came on and Furze looked in at Klitch's window. As Hattaway didn't turn up you came out of the Cathedral and wandered along, beyond the West Door, to Prior's Garden. There to your surprise you found Furze. You quarrelled again. You gave him a sock in the jaw and pushed him, over the wall, into Prior's Well. An excellent spot, I must say, because no one knows how deep the Well is. It's supposed to go to the river bed. You hadn't planned it or intended it. It was simply that you were there, lost your temper and hit him. But you couldn't have found a better or safer place. The odd thing is that no one has thought of the Well. But then, Gurney's a fool. . . ." He looked at his cigarette which had gone out. "Got a match?"

Lampiron came over and gave him a light.

"Thanks."

Lampiron turned on his heel, wandered meditatively across to the female torso and slowly stroked the cool substance with his hand.

"You know that I didn't kill Furze," he said at last. "But what's your point in coming here? That puzzles me. Is it black-mail? Because if so, you know, you're on a hopeless game with a man like me. *That's* not the kind of thing I'm afraid of. . . . No," shaking his head, "something far different."

Leggett said: "Do you mind if I smoke a pipe? Better than cigarettes."

"No. Of course not."

"You're pretty insulting," said Leggett. "I'm not a black-mailer. I told you I came here with no other purpose than to tell you I know what *you* know."

"Well, all right. You've told me. What now?"

"I'll be philosophical about it if you like," Leggett said cheer-fully. "What I want, I suppose, is power. Here am I, stuck in this twopenny-halfpenny place for years, ordered about by Furze, despised by men like yourself when in reality I'm cleverer, better read, have better taste than all the rest of the town put together. I'm being quite frank with you. It's true what I say. I have my vulgar side of course—who hasn't?—but my sexual life's my own. It wouldn't do if everyone knew everything about *everybody* in this town, would it?

"Well, with Furze's disappearance I seem to have a kind of opportunity. I can acquire the sort of power that a man of my brains ought to have. After all it's power that everyone wants. That was what made Stephen Furze a miser—it's what makes his silly brother now strut about in a new blue suit. It's every-thing to men like Ronder and Crispangle and Carris and Arch-deacon Braund.

"They would all like to be Mussolinis and Hitlers if they could. What's going on in Polchester at this moment is exactly what is going on in the world. You can't tell me that Mussolini or Roosevelt, when they lie down in their beds at night, don't feel a kind of personal elation and pat their stomachs a bit—and I don't blame them!

"It's time *I* patted *my* stomach a bit! Some of you people who have been looking down your noses . . . Oh, well—what am I boasting for? I only want to say that I know your guilty secret and that it's safe enough with me—that is, as long as we're friends, you know."

Lampiron had listened to his long harangue with great patience. He had not spoken. He had not moved.

But now he came forward and stood quite close to Leggett, facing him.

"I'll tell you what I did," he said. "I waited in the Cathedral for Hattaway as you say. Then, as he didn't arrive, five minutes before the thunderstorm broke I came out. Afterwards I took shelter in the Cloisters. Then about five-fifteen I went home."

"I understand," said Leggett. "Did anyone see you in the Cloisters?"

"No one—so far as I know."

"That's a pity."

"Did anyone see me at Prior's Well?" Lampiron asked.

"It won't be difficult," Leggett said slowly, "to find witnesses."

Lampiron came close to Leggett's chair.

"Now get out. I wanted to see what your dirty lie consisted of. If you ever dare to come here again, to speak to me anywhere, to hamper or annoy me in any way, I'll have you arrested instantly."

"Why," said Leggett, laughing, "do you think *I* murdered Furze?"

"No. You will be arrested for indecent behaviour in Seatown. For tying naked boys to a bedpost and beating them, for being concerned in company with Caul and Lanky Moon in procuring girls under age, for conspiring with Symon and the late Stephen

313

Furze to rob many people in this town of their savings—there are other things also."

Leggett got up. He went across to the fire and knocked the ashes out of his pipe against the fender.

"You know a lot, don't you?" he said quietly. "And you're a fine fellow to talk anyway—you hoary old seducer of pretty young girls."

Lampiron hit him between the eyes. He fell, missing very narrowly the edge of the armchair. He lay there, huddled; a thick trickle of blood slowly streaked his nose, his cheek, and began to drip from his chin.

"Now I really have killed someone," Lampiron thought. But was conscious of no regret. This would be something definite in a world of shadows. However, Leggett stirred. He opened his eyes, felt the blood on his cheek.

Lampiron watched him. He would fetch him no water, carry him to no chair. Only—if the man died—the police should be informed.

The man did not die. He raised his head, took a handkerchief and wiped his cheek. He sat up, felt his head, looked about him, scrambled to his feet. Lampiron never moved.

Holding his handkerchief to his face, he found his hat. Then, a little uncertainly, he walked to the door. He said no word and Lampiron said no word.

Then he went away.

There was no blood on the floor; no sign of any disturbance. Lampiron felt a strong relief, even elation.

He had begun to fight. Things were moving. They could do their damnedest if they would but come into the open enough to be hit.

END OF PART II

INTERLUDE

The Bishop Writes a Letter

Carpledon, Sept. 10, 1933.

MY DEAR ANNA—It is two years or more, I think, since I last
wrote to you and it is more than that since I last heard from
you. I am not at all sure that this old Heidelberg address will
find you. I only am certain that you are alive because, according
to our pact, I was to hear if you were ill. In any case I would, I
think, know if anything serious had happened to you.

Something serious has happened to me—or rather something
that people call serious—although I can't pretend that, at the
age of seventy-three, it can seem very terrible. That is why I
am now writing to you—once again according to our pact. If
this is a lengthy letter you must forgive me. It is so long since I
have written—that is one thing. And I am commanded to spend
one day of every week in bed. That is another. So here I am
propped up with pillows, a beautiful board covered with green
leather that the ladies of St. Monica's Guild gave me last
Christmas, my blue-and-white dressing gown and (if you promise not to tell anyone) a pipe in my mouth. (I have been told
that I must smoke very little!)

From all this you will gather that I am ill. Well, I suppose
that I am. In any case I went up to London last week and was
seen by a specialist. The verdict was that I have some six
months more to live. For a moment it was a shock. He was in
two minds whether to tell me—a fine keen face he had with

315

rather whimsical ironic eyes—young enough to be my grandson. But he saw that I would prefer to know, that, after all, I was seventy-three; he realized that I must have many things to settle before I went. So he told me. Yes, for a moment it was a shock. We were in one of those rooms in Harley Street that look onto nothing but walls and chimneys. But I remember that the sun was striking the wall with a blaze of light, and I remember thinking, In six months from now I shall not be able to see that! Something in me—the life force or whatever it is—shrunk, trembled, went cold. Then, as I have so often noticed before, at a crisis you are given *extra* force. It is perhaps rather that you see values differently. At any rate, in a minute or so I was myself again—and I'm a coward, you know, Anna. Yet I assure you I minded this less than a headache. I asked him some questions. He said that the trouble was internal; that I could have an operation but that with my heart and at my age it would mean certain death. He was sure of that. I asked him whether I should have much pain. He said—probably none at all, but that in any case I would be looked after. It would be seen that I didn't suffer. He was charming to me—rather like a mother to her boy who is going off to boarding school for the first time.

I am telling you all this, Anna, because you are the one person in the world who will want to know, whom I want to tell.

Had things been otherwise you would now be my wife, would be sitting here, we would be hand in hand and I would be saying this to you instead of writing it. But God's will be done!

No one here knows nor will know until near the end. The one who will feel it most—perhaps the only one here who will *really* feel it, is Coniston. I have written about him in other letters. He has been with me so long now that, apart from any personal affection, his life will, I am afraid, be aimless and purposeless without me. His feeling for me is one of those strange, dumb devotions that you sometimes see. Quite honestly I have done nothing to deserve it. Often he has irritated and exasperated me and I have shown, I'm afraid, all my exasperation! But time, propinquity, and the maternal strain that there is in every man who is worth anything—what wonders they work!

INTERLUDE

One of my gravest doubts, since my return here, is whether I have not done Coniston grievous wrong. When he first came to me he was young and vigorous. Had he not given up his life to me he would have married, had children; my death would have been only a passing regret to him. And yet I don't know. There is something very fine in such unselfish and grand-hearted service.

After yourself, Anna, he is, I think, the noblest human being I know. How shy, confused, almost affronted it would make him if he knew that I was writing such words!

As it is, he is of course disturbed. He knows that something is wrong, that I went to London for a consultation, and it is sufficiently startling to him that I should stay in bed one whole day every week!

Then I fancy that he perceives a change in me since my return from London. For I *am* changed. It is subtle, underground, only to be perceived by someone very close, very intimate. Of course I am changed! So many things have already almost vanished from one's sight. One begins to go so long before one's actual departure!

I think, in fact, that I knew my sentence nearly a year ago.

At an evening party in Polchester one of my canons died quite suddenly, sitting in his chair. A dear old man for whom I had a great affection—one of the true saints of God.

His death that night seemed to put a period to things. Another of my canons, Canon Ronder (I have written of him several times in letters), has also, I am sure, received his sentence. When Moffit and Ronder and I are all gone there will be a new clerical world here. Men like Gaselee and Dale and others are coming along. A period that began with old Purcell's death thirty years ago will be closed with mine. So in the bigger world also.

All this will not interest you except that I would like to explain to you how I feel now about this matter of change. To hear people talk you would think that there had never been change before, that times were never disturbed before, that safety and security are so terribly important, and that once upon a time—before 1914 perhaps—everyone was safe.

You will say that it is very well for me to talk about safety, I who have always led a sheltered and comfortable life! It is true that I have never known what it is to starve, to be without a livelihood, not to have enough clothes. I thank God for those blessings. But I have lived in the midst of the direst poverty— you remember those slums in Liverpool when—ah, how long ago?—we first met. Afterwards in Lambeth. There was that year in Africa, in the Leper Settlement, too.

Yes, I have seen misery and degradation and suffering, God knows. But I still say, Anna, and indeed I know it more clearly now than ever before, that physical suffering, material happiness, are not the last word in a man's history.

I will never forget (nor I think will you) those weeks in the Bergstrasse when we used to talk about such things the whole night through. Do you remember (as of course you do) how we would start off in the little train—you, I, Franz Bürger, Stassen, Marion—for Frankfurt, and there the seats, near the roof, for *The Ring?* Do you remember the tenor, Forchhammer the Dane? —and then at midnight back in the train again? Such happiness until you told me that morning in the wood behind the hotel that you were going to marry Stassen. You have said since then that it was the mistake of your life, but I have been sometimes comforted a little to think that you would not have been happy here, the German wife of a London rector, through the war. However dearly you loved me you would have been irritated by my patriotism—and I would have suffered with you and been able to help so little. I remember that at that time you and Goethe and my beloved Schubert were all three in my heart together—as though I were sheltering you until the storm should blow over!

And now, dear Anna, so soon to leave it all? Or shall I? When you reach my age you seem to walk through Time as through a door. I am at this moment eating the ham and eggs, drinking the beer with you in the restaurant on the hill above Heidelberg, or walking on a Sunday afternoon down one of those clean grey

German streets, all so silent, so empty, so metallic, looking at the house numbers for your address.

Coniston has come in with my luncheon. He says that these days in bed are meant for *rest*. Have I been resting? Obviously no . . . writing all the morning. . . . "I have been writing to a very dear friend, Coniston," I say, and, at once, I perceive that I have roused in him that uncomfortable suspicion again. Why should I be writing to a friend so long a letter? *Is* something the matter? I can see that he has almost made up his mind to speak, then decides against it. But he is watching me and behind his eyes I see a real *maternal* love. If the offer were made to him here and now to change places with me, acquiring my six months' death sentence, he would accept it without a moment's hesitation. . . .

I have eaten my luncheon. I have even had half an hour's nap. That last word about Time accompanied me in my sleep. The Past—if you call it so—is everywhere about us in this corner of England. Within an afternoon you can find a Saxon battlefield, a cave in a sand dune near Portreath where only last year they found the bones of prehistoric man, a silver mine worked by the Romans, the field two miles from Polchester where, in a skirmish, Charles I's forces were defeated, and in the Cathedral the mark in the stone that was the stain of Henry Arden's blood.

Even as I write, Anna, an aëroplane is passing; its silver wings flash for a moment in the sun beyond my window.

"A thousand years in Thy sight are but as yesterday"—the truest word man ever spoke.

I believe most surely that one clue to our riddle is this disregard of Time. Brush it aside! Forget it! And with Time go the physical bonds. Forget those too except that they are the conditions binding this term's schooling. How well I remember at Rugby my dread as I moved up into a certain form. I had been told of all the restrictions, enforcements, that the master of this form imposed on his class. And at first I found them almost unbearable, then submitted to them, finally had a kind of pride in them!

And so with every hour in my new conditions I feel an increasing lightness and freedom. I belong to no place any more. It is Love only—love of people, of place, of God—that is a link—Time, possessions, pride of position, bodily lust or pain, financial greed or anxiety, all these are gone or are fleeing like clouds before the sun!

> My home
> The shimmery-bounded glare,
> The blazing fire-hung dome
> Of scorching air.
>
> My rest
> To wander trembling-weak
> On vague hunger-quest,
> New hope to seek.
>
> For friend
> The dazzling breathing dream,
> The strength at last to find
> Of Glory Supreme.

"The dazzling breathing dream." . . . Truly, Anna, I am not making (as you used once to accuse me) the best of a bad business. I don't wish to pass on. I love my life, my work, my friends, this town and Cathedral, this lovely tree-shady sea-windy country—I don't *want* to go, but, with every new day, I am taken a little further into new country.

One thing, lying thus on my bed and confronting as honestly as I can my soul (honesty is *so very* difficult!), surprises me greatly, and that is that I am not *sure* of my personal survival after Death. Is not that terrible when I have been preaching it all my life? What I mean is that I have no conviction as to the *form* of my survival after my physical death. I really do, in actual positive fact, leave that to Jesus Christ, and by *that* I mean that He has become so real to me through my life, I have grown to love Him so dearly, that it does not seem more unreal to leave my next step to Him than to leave on going to bed my clothes to Coniston to brush! The *peace* that comes to me now as I think of Him is truly past understanding. This is not because all my life long I have "practised" religion. There *was* a time—a long time—when he was to me little more than a historical figure—a wretched time, Anna, before I knew you, when I thought seriously of leaving Orders and becoming a doctor. Those years were strange and sinister indeed. I lived in a kind of fog, something like the sea-river mist that is creeping over the fields this afternoon. Indeed this very town that I love so has been in something of that same state these last months. I won't tire you with it, but an old usurer was, it seems, murdered here some eight weeks back; also there was a pageant that has roused the disorderly elements in the poorer parts of the town. Absurd stories are abroad everywhere —ghosts and assassins and Bolsheviks and contemners of idle canons and good-for-nothing bishops!

Any silly story is believed. People are afraid to go out o' nights. They say that Mass is celebrated at midnight in the Cathedral and that an Inquisitor with a broken neck walks about the town condemning folks to instant execution! Seriously, Anna, you would not believe the things that can happen to a place when this sort of uneasiness starts. I remember it in my childhood in the Jack the Ripper time—and again in Portsmouth when I had a curacy soon after the old Queen died. Some sailors were robbed and killed, I fancy.

These crises come to persons, to towns, to countries when a little stirring-up is needed! And anyway the forces of evil are real enough. Some fighting has to be done. If life isn't a battle, a perpetual warfare of good against evil, I don't know what it is!—and it's like enough the Inquisitor goes on his rounds once and again to see how the combatants are faring!

I love this town so dearly, Anna, that I would like to see it healthy and happy again before I go. Let them lay the ghost of the old usurer before I pass on! You were never here. You have never seen it on a market day when the farmers slap the rumps of the cattle, and boys finger the volumes on the twopenny bookstall and in the shadows of the arcades buy toffee balls for their girls! When, in the spring, you can see through a break in the old grey houses the daffodils blowing on the high banks of the sloping fields, and in the summer roses scent the very provision shops and in the deep shadows of the High Street the Cathedral bells linger like birds skimming a mountain tarn. And days when from the hills above Orange Street you can see the thin silver line of the sea, smell the hay, look down on the huddle of roofs resting under the evening chimney smoke and watch the Cathedral towers catch the last triumphant gestures of the setting sun!

And the Cathedral itself! Every window, every tomb, every brass, every wooden carving has become dear and personal to me through these years. Once again it is making itself felt through all the town. People enter it expecting they know not what, and sometimes remain to pray.

At least I know that a great tide of life eddies between its walls. As there is no time, so there is no death—Gloria in Excelsis! And one day on earth there will be Peace.

So, dear Anna, farewell for this little hour. I have loved so many things, from scents and running water and unexpected music and food and drink and sleep and rain and the first snow and autumn leaves to the great things—my love of you, my friends, my consciousness of God and this preparation for departure.

I touch your hand and wish you God-speed and look to our next meeting.

Always
Your loving
HENRY.

PART III

Michael Furze

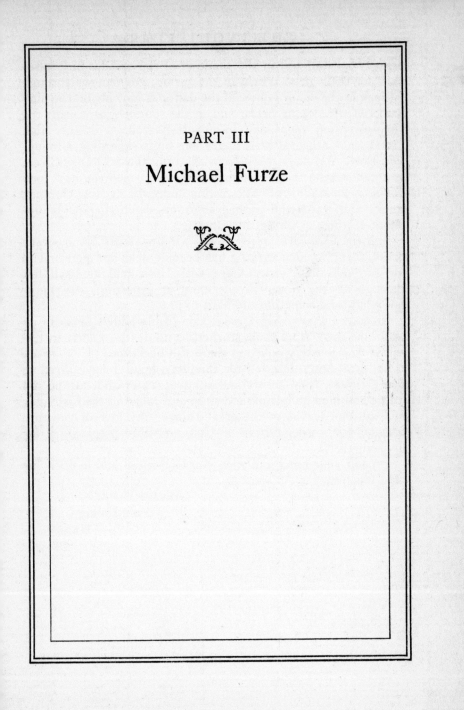

CHAPTER I

Of the Famous Party Mrs. Braund Gave

ON THE EVENING of September 18th poor old Mrs. Dickens, so long a boarder at Mrs. Coole's, was found dead in Green Lane not far from Canon's Yard. For twenty-four hours afterwards it was asserted everywhere that she had been foully done to death. It was said that her throat was cut from ear to ear, that she was stabbed to the heart, that she had been strangled, that her face had been knocked in with a hammer.

The plain truth was that she died of heart failure, poor old lady, hurrying home (if Mrs. Coole's could be called home) to avoid an oncoming shower.

The case of Caul the stallkeeper was rather more mysterious. Early on the morning of September 5th, Police Sergeant Camberlege, one of Gurney's best men, found the body of poor Caul in the hollow known as Tam's Cave. This is a small space halfway down the Rock. There is a path here, and for generation after generation Polchester lovers have used it for their closest intimacies. This path, known as Tam's Path (called after a legendary sea rover Tam Penrool who was said to have terrorized Polchester with his robber bands and pirate ship in the thirteenth century), is bounded at one end by Bridge Street, and at the other runs finally below the Cathedral and finishes at the Well. It is a narrow path and the Rock falls from St. James's Church sheer to the railings that guard its dangerous narrowness. Just beyond St. James's there is a small square of ground that runs to the Rock's edge. There was a railing here, but the Town Council had been warned of its age and rottenness. After the discovery of Caul's body it was found that the railing was broken in several places. Caul's daughter admitted that on the evening previous to the discovery of her father's body she had not gone to fetch him from the Market. He did sometimes find his way home alone. It was supposed that on this occasion he had gone the longer way round. In fact, Fanny Clarke's little girl acknowledged that she had, at his request, taken him to St. James's and then left him. He had told her that he wanted to *see* Furze's house. (He often spoke of *"seeing"* places. Other senses—sound, touch, taste—took the place of his blindness.) When there he had said to her, "Put my hand on Furze's gate, dear," and she had done so. It had been an afternoon of drifting sea fog. She ought not to have left him, but his home was so near and he was so clever at finding his way that she had done what he told her. She was a strange little girl, wild, uncouth, sullen. Miss Penny Marlowe who, it seemed, took an interest in the child, accompanied her to the inquest, and it was only with Miss Marlowe's encouragement that the child could be got to answer questions.

There was no reasonable doubt but that, mistaking his way, Caul had caught the railing at the Rock edge, that it gave way and he fell sheer to Tam's Cave. His body was horribly broken. There could be no other possible explanation, for Caul was no man's enemy.

It had happened, however, that these two deaths—of old Mrs. Dickens and Caul the stallkeeper—occurred at the very time when there was much uneasiness, and that they certainly added to the general apprehension. People said that both Mrs. Dickens and the stallkeeper knew something about Furze's disappearance and that it was certainly to somebody's advantage that they should be out of the way. Poor Mrs. Dickens was a rambling, rather senile old woman with a passion for her cat and her hatred of Mrs. Coole as the two leading motives in her life, but after Furze's disappearance she was full of mysterious hints—as to how on that very afternoon she had been

watching the preparations for the Pageant, been talking to
Mr. Klitch who had gone in to his tea, but that she herself had
"mooned" about a bit, and that then—well, then? But at this
point she always became vague and what Klitch called "mut-
tery."

As to Caul, it was well known that he could tell, by touching
a hand, the identity of his companion. On that by now historic
afternoon or evening just before packing up his traps he had
had a brief conversation with somebody—and here he too
became reticent. Nothing was odder in this whole affair than
the reluctance that everyone showed to be dragged into the case.

Poor Gurney, now the laughing stock of the town, defended
himself by saying that nobody would tell him anything.
"You'd think," he said, "that that old bastard really *was* alive
and they were all afraid of his twisting *their* necks, instead of
someone having twisted *his*."

In connection with this it happened that towards the end
of this month, September, there were no less than three definite
accounts by people who said that they had seen Stephen Furze.

Sarah Constable, an old rag-and-bone woman who lived in
Daffodil Street, swore that on the evening of the 27th as she
was coming up from the river Furze passed her, looked her full
in the face. As old Sarah was always the worse for cheap liquor
this might be discounted. A more respectable witness was
Mr. Browning of the St. Leath Hotel, who said that, coming
out from the Arden Cinema, he had seen for an instant in the
light from the street lamp the bowler hat and ugly visage of
Furze. At first he thought he could swear to it. Then he was
less sure. Finally he laughingly discounted the whole story.

The third story came from Broad's boy, who said that he
saw Furze one afternoon in the Cathedral leaning against one
of the pillars of the Brytte Monument—but Broad's boy was
always seeing things. Not at all the common-sense practical
son you'd expect a man like Broad to have!

These were all idle tales enough but, quite naturally, they
added to the general discomfort.

Then, in the last week of September, someone broke Hattaway's front windows. This was the first act of violence to occur. Hattaway himself took the incident lightly with a laugh, but the Town could not do the same. The incident was considered extremely serious. Two men were arrested, one a gipsy called Harkness, the other a half-imbecile boy, Billy Roach, but there was no satisfactory evidence and they were released. It was known that Tom Caul said everywhere that he was behind the thing and that it was only a small foretaste of what was coming. He also said that Lampiron had thrown his brother over the Rock because the stallkeeper knew that Lampiron had killed Furze.

Altogether the town was in a disturbed state. As always happens when public events create alarm, private domestic events were also uneasy. People were nervous, hysterical, ready to pick a quarrel. Some said that wherever they went they felt that they were watched and spied upon. Privacy was invaded and, however securely you locked your door or drew down your blinds, you were not alone. Furze's disappearance had by this time quite definitely divided the town into three parts. The first was of the opinion that someone in his own household had finished him off—his blind wife, his proud, plain daughter, or his crazy brother. They had, perhaps, all three taken part in it. It was said loudly that Gurney ought to inspect with the utmost thoroughness the Furze house—under the kitchen flooring or in the cellar the bones of the old usurer would certainly be discovered.

The second party in the town accused Lampiron. Lampiron had thrown Furze into the Well behind the Cathedral. This was very widely believed. And the third party maintained that Furze was still in the town. It was of no use to argue with these people that he could not possibly remain hidden for so long a period. He was, by now, capable of absolutely anything!

It is quite certain that by the end of September people were everywhere behaving as though they were guilty of great crimes. If it is true that everyone alive possesses a closet and that in each closet there dangles a skeleton, then it would be true to say that, at this time in Polchester, the autumn air was alive with rattling bones. Good and faithful wives found themselves hinting to their husbands at half-suspected infidelities; men resented a sudden uneasiness in themselves which made them ashamed of everyday trifles—an extra pound on a horse, a sudden smile and nod at a pretty woman in the street, a sharp word at home about a badly cooked meal. . . .

Crispangle, the least nervous and the most cynical of Polcastrians, said: "This town is becoming one large distorting mirror." Then, as usual, he blamed the snobbishness of the Cathedral lot, the monstrous superstition of religion, and misunderstanding of the proper working of the colon. Have an *auto-da-fé* for the social snobs, destroy all religions as the Russians had done, irrigate the colon and the world *might* be something of a place.

And it was at this time of *all* times that Mrs. Braund decided to give a big party!

One of the mysteries of the general situation had, for some time now, been Mrs. Braund's condition. The Carris party, which included most of the wealthier shop people, said that her illness (if that was the name for it) was nothing but an affected pose. Their view of her was that she must, in one way or another, be the central figure and, as her share in the Pageant had had so unfortunate a climax, she was trying now to see what "a state of nerves" could do.

Her friends asserted (and with a good deal of heat) that she had suffered a shock to her system from which she would probably never recover. What kind of a shock? Oh, fits of intense melancholia, general lack of energy and, worst of all, insomnia. She complained that she was no sooner asleep than something or somebody would waken her! She complained that she saw people in her room. And she was haunted by the ridiculous idea that old Lady Emily de Brytte was "after" her, haunting her, driving her into her grave.

The obvious cure for all this nonsense was that she should go away. The Archdeacon, it was understood ("poor man, what a time he must be having"), was anxious to take her for a cruise, to the West Indies or Ceylon or South Africa. . . . No.

She would rather stay here. She wanted to see what was going to happen. . . .

"What do you mean, dear?" Hester Marlowe asked. "What *could* happen in a quiet little place like this?"

"Quiet!" Mrs. Braund laughed bitterly. "It's stirring with malice and envy."

She had changed, in fact, from a stout, rosy-faced, jolly wife of an Archdeacon to a sallow, nervous, irritable and unhappy hypochondriac.

She expected, she told Mrs. Marlowe, to be murdered in her bed "any day; they all hate me. Why, I've never been able to discover."

And then, of all astonishing things, she decided to give a party. It was said that the Bishop (who was looking none too well, dear man—people whispered that they had told him in London . . .) had advised her to make a great effort, to throw off her nervous fears, to brave the world. She took his advice. It was to be a tremendous party and everyone was to be invited to it—Cathedral, gentry, trade—everyone from the Bishop to Crispangle, from Lady St. Leath to the town librarian, Miss Merivale.

And everyone accepted. It was rumoured that it would be a *very* interesting affair. It was hinted that the "sports" of Seatown might choose the occasion to break the Braund windows. There was a reaction too (it had been growing for some time) in favour of Mrs. Braund. After all, the poor lady had never done anyone any harm. If she had been a bit grand and a bit patronizing she had always meant well, and most people liked the centre of the stage if they could get it. Only in the Carris camp there was no relenting. Nevertheless, the whole of the Carris family attended the Braund party.

The Braund house was a heavy dark affair on the far side of the Cathedral, detached, with a high garden wall and guarded by trees. It was a very silent house, perhaps because its walls were so thick. The walls were often damp; the kitchen and offices "crawled with black-beetles." What the house wanted, Hattaway said, was central heating, but the Archdeacon pooh-poohed central heating as an American effeminacy.

The house was filled with heavy furniture inherited by the Archdeacon—vast chests, immense armchairs, oak bookcases like ancient monuments—everywhere, on the landings, in the bedrooms, the bathrooms, these massive pieces of oak. The dark wall-papers were covered with oil paintings also inherited by the Archdeacon from his father, who had collected paintings. Very large pictures they were and every picture told a story, as had been the Victorian fashion—Boadicea Defying the Romans, Robin Hood and Little John, Christians Refusing the Heathen Sacrifice, James II Throwing the Great Seal into the Thames.

Hattaway said that the oil paintings, the furniture, the silence, the manner in which the trees shadowed the windows and obscured the light—these things were quite enough for Mrs. Braund's disorder.

The only answer to that was the fact that she had lived in the house for a great many years and had been very well and very cheerful.

The night of the party was damp and foggy and the house was very cold. The drawing room where the guests were received had been cleared of the smaller articles of furniture, but no one could escape the menace of the vast oil over the fireplace—Early Christians in the Arena, a really harrowing picture, for one Christian lady was in the pitiful position of being devoured by two lions (who had, however, most amiable and complacent faces), and one gallant Christian boy (naked save for a wisp of cloth most happily blown by the wind in the right and decent direction) was in the process of having his face clawed by a rearing tiger. The Emperor Nero playing on his violin (and bearing a striking resemblance to Canon Ronder, it was maliciously observed) showed a sublime but cold-blooded indifference to the proceedings. This picture ("one of the very finest in my father's grand collection," the Archdeacon told his friends) is worthy of detailed mention because, from the very start, it seemed to dominate the party.

Many of the guests had never entered the house before, and standing now awkwardly on the sombre carpet, trying to appear at their ease, their gaze wandered again and again to the bloody bosom of the Christian maiden and the torn fibres of the Christian lad.

The townspeople were inclined to arrive among the earliest, partly because they didn't wish to miss anything and partly because they believed it good manners to be punctual.

The Aldridges were, in fact, the very first arrivals, and it was very fitting that the Mayor of the town should be able to supervise the entries of all his fellow townsmen—and supervise them he and Mrs. Aldridge did; after a time it seemed that it was *they* who were receiving the guests and not the Archdeacon and Mrs. Braund. Mr. and Mrs. Carris and their two girls also arrived in good time. Mrs. Carris, wearing a grey dress scattered with roses, her auburn hair very efficiently waved, came into the drawing room as though she were about to announce a divine party to which she intended to invite everybody. Mrs. Braund in dark red, two splendid strings of pearls round her neck and a diamond spray in her hair, greeted her enemy with a glittering militant smile.

"How are you, dear? I haven't seen you for quite a time. How are you, Mabel? How are you, Gladys?"

Mrs. Braund was not related to the Howards and the Herries' for nothing. Mrs. Carris realized it. It was as though she had heard Mrs. Braund say: "Poor little Polly Lucas! You have, with frantic efforts, managed to have a success or two, but you have still a long way to go—and time is passing." Mrs. Carris, in fact, as she moved on into the room, was suddenly ashamed of her husband and her girls, and the sense of this shame infuriated her—with herself, with them, with her hostess. She snapped quite fiercely at Mrs. Browning of the St. Leath Hotel, who in her turn was rather cold to Miss Merivale the librarian, who, remembering this next morning in the library, behaved like a demon to the little girl from the orphanage who came in to dust the books and arrange the new novels on the centre table.

People now were pouring in. Mrs. Braund and the Archdeacon had shaken hands with everyone. Miss Consetti, pianist, and her brother Alfred, violinist, had also arrived. The library had been cleared and there was to be dancing there. Bridge tables had been arranged in the little sitting room on the other side of the hall. The Archdeacon, who passionately loved bridge, led two sets of players to the tables—Canon Dale, Lady Mary Bassett, Miss Katherine Trenchard and Mr. Ferris the lawyer. These were among the dozen best bridge players in Polchester. But in arranging the second table he had made a fatal mistake. Wishing to "settle" Mrs. Carris as quickly as possible, knowing how dearly she loved bridge, he had insisted that she play. She was at first flattered until she discovered that she was set down at the second table with Mr. Porteous, Mrs. Hattaway and Aldridge. Both Porteous and Aldridge were of the vilest, most outcast "untouchables" in the bridge world—that is, they played an abominable game but were cheerfully unaware of the fact. Porteous was most especially irritating, for in his booming voice he told his partner of mistakes and loudly denied his own errors. When tempers were roused he would cry, "Now, now, friends, play the game! Play the game! And what is this after all *but* a game? . . ." And so on.

When therefore Mrs. Carris discovered her fate and watched the quiet determined professionalism at the next table, her anger, already awake, shook behind her eyes.

This was, on the part of the Braunds, a deliberate arranged insult. She would not forget it. . . .

By this time most of the clergy had arrived—Ronder, the Cronins, Gaselee, James Bird, the Marlowes. They were inclined at first to stand about in little black-coated groups. There were some twenty clergy in all.

Two of the guests especially performed that useful duty of helping to "break the ice." These were Mrs. Cronin and Mr. Romney. Mrs. Cronin had, ever since the fortunate chance came to her of lending her house during the Pageant, begun to believe that her luck had come at last. For years she had been working and working to achieve popularity and for some obscure mysterious reason she had not achieved it.

The plain fact was that Mrs. Cronin was a "whisperer." Wherever she might be she would find somebody, and then, in order to be liked (for no *malicious* reason at all), she would whisper something confidential about someone else. Her immediate success was magnificent. She aroused interest, secured intimacy and, apparently, friendship. But the Whisperers are very quickly suspected by the Whispered-to. Wherever Mrs. Cronin was, trouble sprang up, and this was the stranger because she never spoke of anyone with unkindness.

"Don't you think it a pity . . ." she would begin. "I'm telling you in real confidence . . . I like her so much but I do wish that someone would warn her . . ." And as she whispered her confidences a warm glow suffused her being. She radiated kindness and good-will. Her friend into whose ears she was whispering looked at her with so much interest, so strong and confidential a companionship. "I will do anything, tell you anything," little Mrs. Cronin's heart was urging, "if you will only like me."

Tonight she had not been in the room ten minutes before she was whispering to Camilla Porteous: "I've just had a peep at the bridge players and—what do you think?—Polly Carris has been put at the bad bridge table."

"I know," said Camilla sharply. "The one where my father is playing. . . ."

"Oh, I didn't mean that!" Mrs. Cronin was greatly distressed. "Your father is such a fine player. He——"

"He isn't," said Camilla, swinging a masculine leg. "He's awful." She looked at the door. "There's that dreadful little curate of ours. He's got himself engaged to the daughter of old Furze."

"I hear," whispered Mrs. Cronin, wishing to recover from her earlier mistake, "that they are saying the most terrible things about Lampiron. Not that I believe a word. He's a splendid man, although I do think it's a little careless of him to go about so much with dear little Penny. But they say . . ."

334

The other guest who put everyone at ease was Romney.

Romney often said of himself that he was the only true democrat in the whole of Polchester. It was certainly true that "class" meant absolutely nothing to him. If he saw a young farmer in corduroys driving some cows through the street to market, he would very likely speak to him and entirely charm the young man within two minutes. He was at ease with simply anyone in the world from one of the Royal Princesses in London to Tom Caul in Seatown. It was only if his charm did not work that he became unpleasant, and then he was very unpleasant indeed. No one could be more destructive of an enemy than he. Or rather a "supposed" enemy, because the very smallest imagined slight or neglect would irritate him. He would then say everything malicious he could think of, suddenly discover that there had been no slight at all, and at once become the warmest of friends again. During the hostile interval, however, he was apt to do a good deal of harm.

Like all real artists he was an egomaniac and altogether regardless of any harm that he might do with his tongue, and, again like all egomaniacs, he was infuriated when any other tongue did *himself* harm.

At this moment in the history of the Furze affair his vanity was undoubtedly stirred by the part that he was playing. He was the *only* authority on all sides of the question. He stated everywhere that he knew precisely who had murdered Furze and exactly when and where he had committed the crime. He knew everything about the intrigues in Seatown, and especially he knew every word that was said everywhere by Mrs. Braund, Mrs. Carris, the Carris girls, Crispangle. His attitude was that everything was "too screamingly funny." When he was attacked to his face because of the part he played in the Seatown disturbances, attending meetings there, openly greeted as a friend by Tom Caul and other violent agitators he did not for a moment deny it. Lady Mary was very bitter about it and worked herself into a kind of St. Vitus' dance of agitation.

"Darling," he was crying in Mrs. Braund's drawing room.

"But of *course!* Come with me to a meeting one day and see for yourself. They don't mean a thing."

"They've broken Hattaway's windows all the same."

"That's only a little playfulness. If *you* were unemployed you'd find you had to do something to fill up the time."

"Do you *really* know who killed that horrible old man?" Lady Mary asked, biting her nails.

"Yes, I do. And Gurney knows too. He's only biding his time."

"Well, I wish he'd hurry up. A few of us will be murdered while we're waiting."

"Oh well, darling, *you* needn't be afraid. You're perfectly safe! Did you notice Porteous and Mrs. Cronin? Isn't he just like a dinner-gong?—and she's one of those whispering everlastings that landladies in seaside towns have on their chimney-pieces."

Nevertheless, in spite of his fun and good-humour, there is no doubt that Romney made everyone uncomfortable. He implied beneath his chatter that something very serious might at any moment occur. He joked about danger in the streets at night, ghosts in the Cathedral, old Mordaunt's broken-necked Inquisitor.

Even about the deaths of Mrs. Dickens and poor old Caul he implied that there was something hidden, something known only to himself and one or two more. And he undoubtedly encouraged the feuds that were everywhere breaking out. On this very evening he gaily whispered in Mrs. Carris's ear: "Enjoying your bridge?" He spoke to Lampiron as though he shared some special secret with him and enraged Porteous by congratulating him on the score he had made for the Orange Street Boys' Club. He was very busy that evening indeed.

About nine o'clock Lady St. Leath arrived, and shortly afterwards the Bishop. Everyone realized then what a wonderful party this was. The whole of Polchester was represented save the denizens of Seatown, and even they might, for all that anyone knew, be gathering in the dark garden outside and pressing their noses against the windowpane.

Music had started and there was some dancing. But it could not be said that everything was going with a swing. This was partly due to Mrs. Braund herself, who moved among her guests with a very preoccupied air. She would begin sentences that she did not finish. She would stare at her guests as though she were wondering who they were. Her stout heavy figure, her dark gloomy preoccupied eyes—these were evidence enough that she was not herself.

Ronder, sitting with the Bishop in a corner, said:

"Our hostess doesn't look very well."

"No," said the Bishop. "She should go away for a rest and forget Polchester for a while."

"I hear that *you* have not been too well. I hope there's nothing seriously the matter?"

The Bishop smiled.

"Well, Ronder, my friend, between you and me this is likely to be one of my last parties."

Ronder nodded.

"Yes—and mine."

The two men, who had never been greatly intimate, felt a sudden bond of warm and protective affection.

"It's queer, isn't it," Ronder said, "when the actual realization comes? When you say to yourself, 'This is September 29, 1933. By September 29, 1934, I shall not be here.'"

"I don't know," the Bishop said. "There's not been a night of one's life that, on going to bed, one has been sure of waking in the morning. The only way to treat death is to give it no importance. We've done our work, Ronder—or tried to. Frankly I'm tired—or have felt so these last months. I shan't be sorry to go."

"It's like an approaching cloud," Ronder said. "Gradually one is swallowed up. First a thin mist, then a light darkness, then——"

The Bishop put his hand on Ronder's stout arm.

"Then the cloud passes and there is light again."

But in his secret self Ronder shivered. It was as though at that very moment a cold hand of inspection were exploring him and then slowly withdrawing life from his heart, his veins, his entrails. . . .

He looked at Penny Marlowe who, in a dress of rose-coloured tulle, was standing near him talking with a great deal of animation to Miss Dora Trenchard. She looked tonight as though the fire of life were burning in her at its clearest, brightest, most eternal. "This lovely thing cannot die, suffer corruption, be turned to ashes by the furious flame or crumble earth-deep to be eaten by worms. There is something immortal here!" But was there? Everything for Ronder tonight was tainted with corruption. This dark gloomy house was crowded with ghostly occupants. Beside every living guest the shadow stirred.

He lifted his body ponderously from the chair and walked almost as a man moves in a dream, waking to the soft happy voice of Mrs. Cronin.

"Ah, Canon. The very man. Can you tell me when we are going to have our Whispering Gallery back again?"

It had for so long been second nature to him that tactful courtesy should always come first that although he scarcely saw her he bent forward benevolently and said in his rich, considering, kindly voice, "Whispering Gallery, Mrs. Cronin?"

"Yes. You know—the Harry Tower. It has been closed for repairs ever since the day before the Pageant. But there have *been* no repairs! Someone was coming down from London or something, but no one has been past that door since it was closed. I know it isn't my business," she went on, looking into his impassive mask of a face and wondering whether he liked her, hoping that he did, contemplating some interesting thing that she could tell him and so win his regard. "It is only that I have some friends coming down from London next week and I should like so much to take them up the Tower."

"I'm afraid I know nothing about it," Ronder said, smiling. "Ah, there's Lampiron. Perhaps he can tell us. Lampiron, has Hattaway or anyone told you how long the Whispering Gallery and the Tower are going to be closed?"

Little Mrs. Cronin watched Lampiron with absorbed, excited attention. He always looked magnificent in evening clothes, the most socially testing garment in the world. She wondered how old he was—and what a head with that great forehead, the piercing eyes, jet-black hair! What shoulders, what muscular limbs! And so on, and so on. . . . She always romantically coloured everything up. It made the business of winning people over twice as exciting. And had he really committed a murder? He looked so noble, so kindly. And yet everyone said that he had a terrible temper, carved such indecent statues and had no personal morals whatever!

She could not withhold from her eyes that excited air with which we gaze at prisoners in the dock, Royalty in a carriage, or a film star making a personal appearance.

Lampiron recognized this at once. He had come to the party for two reasons: the first that everyone should understand that he did not care in the least what was said of him, the second that he should talk to Penny.

He was finding, to his own surprise, that he *did* care what was said of him. He realized that tonight people could not take their eyes from him. He felt that the whole room was staring and whispering. He caught again and again from the people who spoke to him that little, excited glitter of the eye. . . .

Only Ronder gave him no especial glance, but that, Lampiron reflected, was because Ronder was deeply preoccupied with himself.

"Why, Mrs. Cronin," he said, "I must say I don't know. On the afternoon before the Pageant I went to the Cathedral to meet Hattaway and an architect from London about it, but the London man never turned up and that same evening it was closed. I've heard nothing more."

Subconsciously he thought: There you are! Mrs. Cronin is saying to herself: Ah, *that's* when he did it, *that's* when he shoved him into the Well. And a strange longing came to him to shout at the top of his voice:

"Ladies and gentlemen, you wonder whether I murdered Furze or not. Well, you can inspect me. Take my clothes off if you like, feel my heart beat, ask me any question you please! I *didn't* kill Furze, but if it pleases you to think that I did . . . !"

That's what Henry Arden would have done—shouted at the lot of them, defied them, called God's curse on them! He felt as though Arden's armour clanked about his body. He, Arden, to murder a petty villainous little usurer when he had so many greater matters to consider!

All he said was:

"How is your garden, Mrs. Cronin? Are the chrysanthemums coming out yet?"

Penny Marlowe was watching him. While she was talking to Miss Trenchard she was watching, for the centre of her life was there. She had worn the rose-coloured tulle only twice before tonight. She had put it on for him. Before she had dressed, after her bath, clothed only in the gold-and-red Japanese kimono that her father's brother had brought her from Japan, standing at her window she had watched the mists creep about the garden and the small auburn heads of the first chrysanthemums burn dimly like little lanterns before the full dark came. She had learnt a great deal in the last year. She had been a child until that day when Lampiron had first kissed her, and after that so many experiences had succeeded—her father's bewildered unhappiness, Furze's disappearance, the Pageant, Mrs. Braund's illness, the discovery that in her own home everything depended on *her* now, the other discovery that people were talking about Lampiron, the further discovery that people again thought that she was Lampiron's mistress. . . . A great deal to be crowded into one year of a very young girl's life, but she took it all, eagerly, almost rapturously, because her spirit, fiery, ambitious, passionate for life, told her that it was through this experience that wisdom came.

But, she thought, as she turned and looked at the rose-coloured tulle on her bed, she had not expected that love would be so wonderful a thing! She had read of it, been told of it, heard scandalous things of it, but this inexhaustible desire for self-sacrifice, this constant joy and the love of every form of life that came from it—she had not known of these things. What had she had from Lampiron but some kisses, some hand-clasps, some talks, some silences? She did not want more.

As, looking into the glass, she raised her arms and brushed her hair, she smiled, eyes smiling at eyes, because she was so deeply satisfied with all that life was giving her. Perhaps, even now, she suspected that the character of this first meeting with love was exactly suited to her nature—a nature that would always be happier in giving than getting, in loving than in being loved, in service than in acceptance of love. She was no saint; she could be fiercely intolerant, she had a fiery temper, she could be arrogant, but as she was intolerant so she was proudly loyal, as she was hot-tempered so she was courageous, as she was arrogant so she had no vices of meanness, the fierce bitter jealousies, the hoarding of money or power.

She was free. Miss Trenchard was attacked by Mrs. Aldridge; Mrs. Cronin moved away from Lampiron. They advanced, without looking at one another but in absolute certainty, into the hall and then into a conservatory, filled with geraniums and dusty palms. Here were two little white-painted iron chairs and in a stuffy semi-dusk they sat down together.

"Penny," he said, "for a moment I'm going to speak as though I had never seen you before, as though you were twenty and I twenty, because perhaps it's one of the last times."

"What do you mean," she asked, "one of the last times?"

"Never mind that. I suppose I only mean that *my* situation can't go on like this much longer. The whole town thinks I murdered that wretched old man and I've got to clear myself of that. That's one thing. My love for you is going beyond the limit I set for myself. That's another. A third is that very soon there's going to be an explosion in this town and some of us perhaps will be blown up by it. This may be one of the last quiet times we have, that anyone here has."

"Why, what do you think is going to happen?" she asked, speaking, as she sometimes did, like a child.

"I don't know. Never mind. What does it matter to us? Listen. I love you so that the inside of my skull is burnt dry, my throat is dust and ashes. I want so desperately to have you in my arms and lie thus with you, all the night through, without moving, without stirring, that all my bodily movements are connected with that longing. When I walk through the street I am, in my actual life, curving myself about you, closing you in, my lips on your hair. . . ." She saw that he was shaking from head to foot, but he went on:

"All the same I know just as clearly as I knew that first time we talked at my house that, afterwards, I would be better dead. I would have broken the only rule worth keeping. Help me now, Penny, as you've never helped me before."

He moved his chair further away from hers.

"There's something cowardly, isn't there, in my telling you how I feel and then asking you to help me. But I have to depend on *your* strength. I must. I'm so weak myself. I——"

"Don't you think," Penny said, after a moment's pause, "that it might be better to do what you want? We could go away——" She broke off because she suddenly realized that she wasn't free as she had been. She could not just now leave her father and mother. . . . Only last night she had heard him pacing up and down the floor of his bedroom. After a while she had knocked on his door, but he had not answered—only the sound of the pacing had stopped. Going back to bed she had lain there seeming to hear all over the town this same pacing of floors, half the town pacing, the other half listening to the pacing. No, she could not go away just now—it would be like deserting a besieged city when all your fellow citizens were fighting for their lives. She knew that Lampiron also could not go.

Because she was entirely honest she said at once:

"No, I realize. We can't go away. I don't know what's happening here, but it would seem like desertion to leave the town, wouldn't it? Besides, Father and Mother aren't very well."

"I'll tell you one thing, Penny," he said quickly. "I know as certainly as I'm sitting here that I'm never going to leave this town. My story finishes exactly here. If there's a war there's a battle, and if there's a battle men are killed. . . ."

"*Is* there a war?" she asked.

"Yes. We are what you said, a beleaguered city. The whole

business of living quietly is to make terms with the other Powers. We've grown arrogant and not bothered to make terms, so they've up and attacked us. They're not really hostile. All they want is to remind us that they exist, and *that* they're doing. As soon as they've reminded us sufficiently and killed a few of us off, they'll leave us alone again." He leant forward and laid his hand on her knee. "Oh, Penny, I love you so! Darling, darling, darling. . . . *Morituri te salutant.* . . . And remember afterwards when perhaps life, in the middle years, seems dull, to have lost its fragrance, that you have been loved . . . loved . . . loved." He bent his head, looking down at the dusty conservatory floor. "Loved and worshipped."

She laid her hand on his. Hand gripped hand.

"So many lovers," she said, "have sworn that death can't part them, but I *know* that nothing can separate us." She looked at his face and put up her hand, laying it against his cheek. "I'll kiss you once," she said, "and then we'll go back." She kissed his cheek where her hand had been. "Don't think we'll ever part—I'm learning that death is nothing."

They came back into the room together and of course everyone noticed it. Old Marlowe did not. He was obsessed with his own troubles. He had got it into his head that all the town now knew about his debt. Someone was going round telling everybody. Then he had a particular headache, all his own, he had nearly broken down in his sermon last Sunday. He was wondering whether he couldn't escape from this town all by himself and walk and walk till he got to the sea, and then he would sit down, take the sand out of his shoes and rest.

It was about now—something after ten o'clock—that everyone began to get very gay.

Mrs. Cronin's account, frequently given to eager friends in the next few days, was a little confused: "At first, dear, it was *dreadfully* dull! And the house was so cold. I assure you that after half an hour in that drawing room—have you ever been to the Braunds'?—oh, it's a great big room with enormous pieces of furniture and the most dreadful painting of Christian Martyrs over the mantelpiece—a little while in that drawing room and one was simply frozen. I would have sent over to the house for my furs if it hadn't seemed rude! Well, for a long time nothing happened. There was certainly something the matter with our dear hostess. You know how bright and chatty she used to be? Now she just walked about looking at people as though she wished they'd go. Everyone was there! Oh well— you know what I mean. You never have known the Braunds very well, have you? What I mean was that it was the most incredible mix-up! You should have seen Mrs. Aldridge with a rope of sham pearls and Técla diamonds in her hair! Of course we *are* a democracy with Labour governments and everything, but all the same you *can't* get over a kind of social awkwardness. You know what I mean! Crispangle—the Smith Bookshop, you know—looking and listening, picking things up to talk ironically about. He's a *really* bitter man, and if there's anything spiteful to say you can be sure he'll say it. Then the Pageant seems to have left so much sore feeling! I certainly had a good time myself. Everyone was so nice to me, and then I was able to lend my house. Oh, it was *really* useful, I'm glad to say! All the same the Pageant would have been better another year —when there's not so much unemployment. And there was a good deal of jealousy over little things. I'm sure I don't know why. Many people said to me, for instance, that Queen Elizabeth or one of the other parts would have suited me beautifully, but do you think I felt even a *twinge* of jealousy? Of course not. All the same Lady Mary wasn't good, was she? Almost *anyone* would have been better. She did her very best and she's such an agreeable woman. I like her so very much. Well—where was I? Oh yes.

"After a time some people got rather rowdy. I didn't see much drink myself, and the Archdeacon is *supposed* to be a teetotaller. But drink there was. Some people said afterwards that people like the Carrises brought their own. I don't suppose it was true for a moment. Not a thing you would expect even the Carrises to do. But there was that Irish cousin of theirs— Mr. Ted O'Hara. Do you know him? He often stays here. Generally at the St. Leath Hotel. Oh, don't you know him?

Long thin man—always playing practical jokes. He wore a bathing suit and drove a pig up the High Street for a bet once. Did you never hear that? He *says* he's a cousin of Mrs. Carris, but I've heard that very much doubted. In any case, he soon became very much in evidence. Of course what I always say is —mix the classes if you like but you'll probably regret it. I'm the least snobbish of people, but do you know what happens? Just what happened at Mrs. Braund's. As the evening went on the *shop class*—I don't mean anything derogatory, I assure you—got noisier and noisier. The dancing became very wild indeed; and that Mr. O'Hara—a long thin man with a prominent nose—*not* a gentleman, and many people say that he's not a cousin of Mrs. Carris at all but something quite different—he became most obstreperous and Mr. Bellamy danced with Mrs. Aldridge in a way—well, really, although I've seen the strangest things in Paris and Vienna, I felt quite uncomfortable. And the Carris girls! You know how noisy and vulgar they are when they're a little bit excited.

"It was about now that the Bishop and Lady St. Leath and one or two others left. My husband and I—we'll be delighted to come on the thirteenth by the way—so charming of you to ask us—we also left. I'm sorry now that we did because, as it was, we missed . . . but you've heard, haven't you, of what occurred?"

What occurred was really rather terrible. One eyewitness was Jim Bird. His account of it to Elizabeth was as follows:

"I was thinking of going. I hadn't wanted to stay so long— I hadn't enjoyed myself a bit—but I was nervous about Lampiron. I think that, oddly enough, everyone was nervous about someone. I worried about Lampiron because he looked pretty desperate. You know, Elizabeth, he's the best friend I have, but he *has* got a fearful temper. He nearly killed Leggett about three weeks ago and I felt somehow that he might do something on this particular evening. People were looking at him as though they expected him to, but for the most part he was quiet, sitting like Landor or Garibaldi or Tennyson—he always makes me think of one of those massive old men. He *should* have achieved things as big as *their* achievements. He was *meant* to do something terrific, but all it has come to is that he sits in a small cathedral town suspected of murder and seduction. . . . Anyway he was quiet enough. And after the Bishop and the Marlowes went he went too, with just a nod to me. Then I noticed that things were becoming lively, in fact livelier than they ought to be in an Archdeacon's house. *My* belief is that someone or other had brought a lot of drink into the house. Dancing was going on and people you would never expect, like Mrs. Bellamy and Aldridge, were quite tipsy. The worst of all were the two Carris girls. I've always disliked them but I can't tell you, Elizabeth, how their commonness came out last evening.

"Their mother, I've heard since, was furious because she had been put down to play at some inferior bridge table. In any case, whatever it was that upset her, she was herself a little tipsy and went about the rooms with that Irish cousin of hers, O'Hara, making insulting remarks. Honestly, Elizabeth, I had never seen an evening in any decent house in Polchester like this one. All the better people had left—only Romney and Gaselee I saw, and the Cronins. They looked as though they were expecting any moment something to happen, and indeed you might, for you never saw anything queerer than Mrs. Braund, who walked from room to room and stared at some of the guests as though she wondered who they were.

"I don't want to give an impression that things were actually rowdy. I daresay, if you'd been a stranger and not known anyone, you'd have thought it a very decorous party. In the room where they were playing bridge there wasn't a sound and even the dancing wasn't riotous. It was only if you knew who people were and above all knew all that had been happening here during the last months, that you became apprehensive.

"Honestly, Elizabeth, I wouldn't have been surprised if Mrs. Braund, Archdeacon's wife or no Archdeacon's wife, had slapped Mrs. Carris's face at any moment. You say that English ladies don't do such things. No, not if they are normal. We are scarcely any of us here normal just now. . . . Then

346

—well, it must be all over the town today—so I may as well tell you exactly what I saw. I heard the clock in the drawing room strike a quarter to twelve and I thought it was high time for me to be going. I went into the hall to find Mrs. Braund to say good-night. There she was, saying good-night to the Cronins. On the left was the room where they had been dancing. Opposite was the small room where they were playing bridge, and out of that room, as I came into the hall, stepped Romney. I noticed that he looked up at the hall clock. I noticed it because I thought to myself, Oh, Romney's leaving. We can walk most of the way home together. But he stood there looking at the hall door, and that, on thinking back, makes me sure that he knew what was about to happen.

"Mrs. Cronin was going on—do you know her?—well, she's a sort of pussy-voiced gossip—'Oh, *dear* Agnes. We've had such a *lovely* evening. I don't know when I've ever enjoyed myself——' and so on. Mrs. Braund was standing there looking at her with a kind of nervous twitching smile, the Archdeacon at her side. The front-door bell rang. No one thought that it was more than the announcement of someone's car, I suppose. But we all turned and looked. The Braunds' butler—a stout, red-faced, pompous old man with white hair—came forward to open it. Jokes had been going on all evening about some of the Seatown population haunting the garden, looking in at the windows, preparing to throw stones. So when the door opened and a great rush of cold air blew in we all felt a little jumpy, I imagine.

"Someone was standing there, outlined vividly in the light of the hall lamp. It was your father, Elizabeth. But absolutely motionless—the green umbrella, the bowler hat, the long grey overcoat, the grey gloves. You could see his long white nose. He never moved. There was a piercing fearful shriek from Mrs. Braund, who fell with a crash to the floor. The figure vanished. I don't believe in ghosts, Elizabeth, but I tell you that I was terrified. The sense of the dark, the cold night air, the nervousness and expectation of something happening that there had been all the evening—all these things together helped. I know that for a moment I was altogether taken in. So there *are* ghosts! I remember thinking. Now I know! But a moment later there were other things to think of. Mrs. Braund was lying motionless on the floor, the Archdeacon bending over her. People who had been dancing came hurrying. I saw Mrs. Carris and her two girls. Mrs. Cronin was crying hysterically something like, 'I saw him! I saw him! With my own eyes!' Everyone was shouting and talking at once.

"It was Romney who compelled attention. He came forward and said, 'Don't be alarmed, anybody. It was O'Hara dressed up. I recognized him at once. It was a practical joke.'

"A pretty idea of a practical joke, with Mrs. Braund probably dead as the result of it. But everyone realized at once that Romney was right, and the next thing that happened was that the Archdeacon, out of all control, shouted to Mrs. Carris that *she* and her friends had arranged this, it was *their* doing— that they had murdered his wife whom they had been persecuting for months, must leave his house instantly, he would have them arrested for murderers and so on. . . . It was a dreadful scene. The poor Archdeacon didn't know what he was saying. Gaselee then took command of the proceedings. He led the Archdeacon into the other room, advised everyone to go as quickly as possible. Go we did, I assure you. Of course Mrs. Carris was eagerly protesting that she had known nothing about it, and Crispangle and Bellamy loudly supported her.

"Before I left I heard that Mrs. Braund wasn't dead but had suffered a stroke.

"I can tell you, Elizabeth, it was queer enough, after all that, walking home through the quiet little town. The breeze rustled through the trees, all the houses were dark, the Cathedral was so majestically at rest. Behind some window you could see someone sitting reading a book. It was a fresh, chilly evening. You could smell the breeze from the sea. . . .

"Yes, the whole town's talking of it today. Whether Mrs. Braund will recover no one knows. I hear that most people think that O'Hara and the Carrises arranged it. O'Hara himself says that it was intended as a mild little joke. Mild! He had meant, he says, to walk into the house, take off the bowler hat and reveal himself! In my opinion he was a coward, let alone anything else, to run away as he did! Anyway there's no end to the trouble his little joke will cause. They say that the Archdeacon may bring an action against O'Hara and that Mrs. Carris may bring an action against the Archdeacon for defamation of character. What's the matter with this town, Elizabeth? What's happening to us all?"

CHAPTER II

There Is No Private Life Here Now . . .

By VERY MANY CLEVER PERSONS September is considered the loveliest month of the year in Glebeshire—*but,* they quickly add, *not* October. In the north, where Things (birds, flowers, heather and coloured clouds) are later, yes, October is divine. But in Glebeshire, after October 1st—"you are never SURE."

That is very true, Miss Merivale, the queen of the library at the top right-hand corner of High Street thought, reading a novel by Miss E. B. C. Jones. Thin, alert, dressed always in soft grey with white collars and cuffs, contemptuous, intelligent, she salved her loneliness by allying herself with the lady novelists she loved. These ladies allowed Miss Merivale to despise everyone in Polchester save only Mr. Romney, who, if he had written novels, would have been made Colonel of the Regiment without delay.

Not only did these ladies write with brilliance, notice instantly the tiniest folly committed by a neighbour (male or female, it mattered not, but female for preference), but they reassured, most gallantly, all the clever non-writing ladies in England. Miss Merivale was one of these; having been brought up by an atheistic father (Professor, Manchester University) to believe in nothing that she couldn't see, her eyes were of the very sharpest.

Her tongue was sharp too, with the result that she was not

very popular in Polchester. None of this mattered. Seated on
her little platform in the Library (the same for the last fifty
years), she dealt with her clients and customers quite regally.
She felt as though Mrs. Virginia Woolf had given her her
benediction, as though *To the Lighthouse* had been especially
written for her—and, in honest fact, that lovely, tender and
understanding work had done something to ripen her thin
understanding and enrich her rather arid perception. She was
arid because no man had ever loved her. Because no man had
ever loved her she devoted all her energies to seeing life as it
really was.

Therefore now, in this first week of October, seated alone in
her library reading the novel of Miss E. B. C. Jones, she was
disturbed, greatly disturbed. Because she was frightened.

The town was filled with sea mist. She had turned on the
electric light and drawn down the blinds, but oh, how she
wished, how strangely, disturbingly she wished that someone
would come in!

Even Mrs. Cronin, who liked the stories of Mr. Frankau, Mr.
Deeping and Miss Berta Ruck, would be better than nobody.
Even Miss Dora Trenchard who returned a novel by Miss Mary
Butts with the comment, "I understood almost none of it, and
what I did understand was indecent," would be better than
nobody! Even it might be that these ladies, being stupid, without perception, without æsthetic taste, might be better than
Lady Mary Bassett, Mr. Romney, or Canon Ronder, more
comforting, more reassuring. What was the matter with her?
Why was she constantly looking over her shoulder as though
she expected the high rows of dusty bookshelves with their
long-forgotten Godwins, Bayes, Eugene Sues, G. P. R. Jameses
to open and from their depths to emerge—whom?

For some weeks now she had felt this discomfort. She regarded the Library as the very heart of the town. Here it lay,
the centre, and from it radiated the Cathedral, the canons'
houses, the shops, the market, the quiet streets with their old
sober houses, the Rock, Seatown, the river, the sloping hills.
And because it was the centre, here was hidden the secret of the

town's disturbance. But there *was* no disturbance! The spirit of Miss Merivale's father reproached her for her foolishness. "Believe, my dear Anthea, only in what you can see with your good eyes, touch with your cool firm fingers." Well, she could see the paralysed body of Mrs. Braund lying in that cold dark tree-embedded house by the Cathedral, she could touch hands that might, not so long ago, have been reddened with a fellow citizen's blood; that poor old woman from Mrs. Coole's had died, they said, from heart failure—but who could tell? That blind stallkeeper had fallen by accident from the Rock. . . .

She jumped up. She could endure it no longer. The dim eyes of those old books watched her; behind the drawn blinds the fog rolled up the street. The door opened. She stifled a little terrified scream. It was Lady St. Leath's chauffeur.

"Her Ladyship understands——"

"Yes, here are the books she asked for." Then, after a little pause, because she didn't believe in being familiar with servants, "It's foggy, isn't it?"

"Yes, it is. Got to go careful with the car." He went, closing the door behind him. She would have wished to keep him there, to have thought of some possible conversation. . . .

Miss Truscott and Mrs. Pender met Miss Merivale for a moment in the rolling manœuvres of that sea fog, for they also were frightened—frightened by the thought of poor old Mrs. Dickens and by the silly illusion Miss Truscott had that she saw poor Alice Dickens leaning over her shoulder and looking into her teacup. Miss Truscott and Mrs. Pender had been lodgers with Mrs. Coole for a longer time than Mrs. Dickens. They were the oldest lodgers there. Miss Truscott was a mild old lady who liked bright colours and was afflicted with a constant trembling of the head. This trembling irritated Mrs. Coole almost to a frenzy and she would cry, "*Can't* you keep your head still?" and Miss Truscott, brilliant in a magenta blouse, would answer, "No, I *can't!*" Mrs. Pender, on the other hand, was a very slim old party with a heavy black moustache and beetling eyebrows. She was the only one of the ladies at Mrs. Coole's who stood up to that tyrant; daily had been their battles for many years and all the other lodgers enjoyed them.

On this afternoon Miss Truscott was having tea in Mrs. Pender's bed-sitting-room and the thing that was really disturbing them was Alice Dickens's cat. On the night of Alice Dickens's death the cat disappeared. Mrs. Coole had always detested it and had hinted in no uncertain fashion of the things that she would do to the cat "once Mrs. Dickens was gone." So the cat was acting wisely in disappearing. The trouble was that it didn't *completely* disappear as it should have done. Every night its plaintive mew was heard and, although it was never seen, its paws pit-pattered on the oilcloth, and Miss Truscott declared that she felt it rub itself against her bare leg as she was stepping into her bed. Mrs. Coole's house was No. 10 in Norman Row and Mr. Klitch's shop No. 11. Mrs. Coole roundly accused Mr. Klitch, whom she had always detested (she approved of very few people), of harbouring the cat. He merely shrugged his shoulders and smiled. . . .

But Miss Truscott, having tea with Mrs. Pender, not only saw Alice Dickens looking into her teacup but heard the cat mew for milk in the way that it always used to do.

Both ladies stared at the fog that crept in wisps of lawn across the Cathedral Green, and "wished for company."

"Nonsense, Millie," said Mrs. Pender. "Poor Alice is dead and there's an end of it."

"Listen!" said Millie Truscott.

And both old ladies listened: the washstand also listened, and the bed and the three chairs and the photograph of the long-dead Mr. Pender on the mantelpiece. The Cathedral chimes rang the half hour but neither lady stirred. Miss Truscott held her teacup in her hand.

"Have another piece of that seed cake," said Mrs. Pender, "and don't be silly. It's only the trickling of that pipe in the attic."

But it wasn't. It was Mrs. Coole who opened the door without knocking and stood, a great mountain of flesh, her vast breasts heaving, her short thick grey hair, absurdly bobbed, emphasizing the white rolls of fat on the back of her neck.

She looked at her two lodgers, then—without a word—closed the door again and could be heard flip-flapping in her slippers down the stairs.

"One day," Mrs. Pender said slowly, "there'll be another murder in Polchester."

"There, Laura," Miss Truscott said. "Didn't you hear it? Most distinctly a cat's mew."

"There," said Michael Furze to Elizabeth. "Don't you wait for me. I don't know when I'll be back."

But he did not go out. He went into his bedroom and stood looking from behind a corner of the blind which now he kept always drawn. The room had assumed something of the air of a fortress. The only beautiful thing in it was the crucifix which stood on a bare table against the naked wall. For the rest the furniture, ugly and uncompromising, seemed to be on guard as though it were waiting to be pushed, in defence, against doors and windows. Now, as Michael stood there looking down to the shifting wall of sea fog that broke suddenly in front of him, throwing into his face walls and chimneys and an old man walking with a tapping stick down the road, he was wondering whether he could summon up courage to tell Elizabeth and her mother that they must go. His head had not, during the last fortnight, been as clear as it ought to be. And with reason. He was pestered now with so many persons who wished to interfere with his private life. Standing there, gazing down into the fog, he shook with anger as he thought of them. Gurney, Caul, Lanky, Klitch, Leggett, Lampiron—these were only a few. Everywhere now steps followed him, eyes peered into his, ears listened to the very beating of his heart. He shook the edge of the blind with his indignant hand. My God! Was there ever anyone more foully treated—he who wished only good to the town, who longed for chances to prove its benefactor?

Men, he now noticed, would not hold conversation with him, but spoke a word or two, then moved away—not disappearing, however, but rather staying, just out of sight, hiding, watching. And that lazy, fat policeman, Gurney, why must he be forever turning up and asking questions? He'd better look out, he had! And the foul and slimy Leggett (here Michael's whole body shook with anger), what right had he to put on these airs, to pretend to be Michael's friend? Friend indeed! Michael knew *his* game! It was the money he was after, but money was the last thing . . .

Michael turned. What was that? Was not someone turning the handle of the door? His face was chalky white, blotched with red, as he moved, looking at the door. Blast these foggy days! The damned stuff crept into the very room. There was no one there. But he wouldn't wonder if that blind woman wasn't listening on the other side of the door. That was why she and her daughter must go. He was master here now. And it would be better if he were alone in the house—no one to spy on him then. He could draw the blinds and bolt the doors and so stay, safe against the world.

No one could enter. No one? No privacy any more. . . . That brother of his was clever enough to push blinds aside and slip through bolted doors. . . . That damned, cursed, bloody brother of his. . . . And, peering from behind the blind, he thought that he saw, rising from the thin white mist, like a bound figure from the grave, the umbrella, the bowler hat, the long shapeless overcoat, the grey gloves. . . .

It was about the overcoat that they were speaking, knocking the billiard balls about, at the St. Leath Hotel—Browning the proprietor, Bellamy, Mr. Ironsides from London, and little Mr. Adamson from Drymouth. Under the electric light the green table shone with a warm and friendly glow. Browning, who prided himself on his billiards, bent forward, his white shirt-sleeves gleaming, then suddenly straightened his stout back and his large comfortable behind and said sharply:

"That's enough, Bellamy—running down the town to outsiders. What do you call that—business?"

"I'm not running it down," Bellamy said aggrievedly. He disliked rows, but what was the matter with Browning? What was the matter with everyone's temper just now, come to that? . . . "I was only saying that everyone's on edge. Why, in the High Street shop you wouldn't believe—their minds are never on their work, always looking out of window, and the younger men are all Town Guards, every man jack of them."

"What are Town Guards, if I may ask?" little Mr. Adamson enquired. He looked as though he should always be standing, legs astride and begaitered, sucking a straw, with his hat on the back of his head. As a matter of fact, although he travelled in woollens, that was the way he often was.

"The Town Guards," Bellamy said solemnly, "is an organization recently sprung up in this town for protecting the streets at night."

"Protecting the streets!" Adamson cried. "Why, what's threatening them?"

"Nothing at all if you ask me," Browning said angrily. "Damn! I've missed my shot! Left you an easy one, Mr. Ironsides. The fact is this town's gone balmy over nothing. People are afraid of their own shadows."

"Now that's a funny thing," said Mr. Ironsides, who was thin, blue-shaven, with a little bunch of black hair on the tip of his nose. "Something happened to me this morning. I've got a grey overcoat, loose, easy affair. I was going out in it this morning—Crispangle of Smith's had called for me. We were going down to the bank together. Crispangle says: 'Wouldn't wear that overcoat, Ironsides,' he says."

"'Wouldn't what?' I ask.

"'Wear that overcoat. Foggy day like this people might mistake you, you being thin and tall as well.'

"'Mistake me for what?' I ask. There you are, Mr. Browning, your turn. ''Tisn't *what*, it's *whom*,' Crispangle says. And all I could get out of him was that some old boy was done in here a month or two back wearing a grey overcoat, and the whole town's gone potty on the subject. . . ."

"That's a funny thing," little Adamson began solemnly. "Knew the same thing happen in Brightlington once—you know Brightlington?—smart little town Gloucester way. I had a business there once and an old woman was murdered—kept a tobacco shop—murdered for the money in the till. Well, do what they could, they couldn't find the murderer—hunted high *and* low—whole town went creepy. Women wouldn't go out at night. Everyone lost their nerve, couldn't sleep, took to drink. . . ."

"That's enough," Browning interrupted. "*That's* enough! What are we? A pack of old women? And what's going to happen to the trade of this place?" He rested his cue against the wall and went up to Bellamy. He was usually a mild amicable creature, with a fine presence for his guests, a good business head, and a blind adoration for his large, tranquil and plain-faced spouse. Now he was angry. "I wonder at you, Dick," he said. "Helping to spread these jackass stories."

"I'm not helping," Bellamy began indignantly. (He didn't want to quarrel with Browning, but he was damned if he was going to be insulted before two strangers. Almost as though he had murdered Furze himself!)

"Oh, aren't you? Well, I say you are, and others too——"

The door of the billiard room very slowly opened. All four men turned and stared. At first it seemed that there was only a wisp of fog there. Then they could discern a long thin figure, the head a little bent as though he were listening. Ironsides dropped his cue. "My God!" he cried. But it was all right. It was old Shepperson, the head waiter.

"Might I have a word with you a moment, Mr. Browning?"

Browning went over to him.

Then soon after four o'clock in the afternoon the sea fog cleared for a brief while. A little wind sailed through the town; the vapour mists swung high, and at their very heart there burnt a dim warm glow like the reflection of a heavenly fire. A ray of sun pierced straight to the copper weather vane above the Market roof, and then blue suddenly flooded the town, reflected in puddles left on the Market cobbles by the cattle, reflected in the windows of the Town Hall, Bellamy's shop, the old Georgian houses in Orange Street. All the sky was blue.

The lanes and the thick trees, the fields, the woods beyond the Pol, were powdered with gold under the new sun, and a scent of spice and sea freshness and the prophecy of autumn fires penetrated the town. All scents, all colours had the fresh joy of things all day imprisoned, unexpectedly released.

Lady Mary, who was entertaining Mr. Romney and Mrs. Cronin to tea, went to the window and looked across the huddle of roofs shining in the sun to the line of hill that hid the sea.

"Dear me! The sun's out!" Mrs. Cronin, who always took the weather as a personal compliment or insult, smiled at discovering the sun liked her after all. (She had not been invited by Lady Mary. She had had luncheon alone today and that had depressed her. She wanted to make sure before night that someone liked her, so she was paying a call or two.) Until Lady Mary had said that about the sun she had been really depressed. Lady Mary and Mr. Romney knew one another so very well and, although they apparently included Mrs. Cronin in their conversation, practically they excluded her. Mrs. Cronin felt herself an intrusion and this made her miserable. But when the sun streamed into the room she smiled at Mr. Romney like a very old friend. At the same time she was making a little collection of items that would amuse others in days to come—a new ring with a large green scarab that he was wearing, the shrill laugh that he gave at mention of his old friend Porteous, and the sharp glance of investigation that he had thrown at Lady Mary's young footman, who was new and had very bright blue eyes. All these things Mrs. Cronin noticed while engaged in what was (although she did not know it) the completely lost cause of winning Mr. Romney's affections.

Then Mrs. Cronin did a very silly thing. She said: "Oh Mr. Romney, do tell us—in confidence, of course. They all say that you know just who murdered old Furze—how, why, when, where, everything. . . ."

She looked up at him with what she had come to believe was her most endearing expression—confidential, intimate, rather young and simple, human and good. The change in Mr. Romney's expression simply terrified her.

358

"The less said about that, Mrs. Cronin, the better."

Even Lady Mary noticed the change in him, for, turning from the window, scratching her left thigh, she said:

"What are you cross about?"

"I didn't mean——" Mrs. Cronin began. She was frightened out of her wits. Romney was like an evil poison-planning spinster. His voice was shrill and feminine.

"Can't you understand," he cried, "that I'm sick to death of this silly business? Why should I be eternally pestered about the affair? You'd think I'd murdered the man myself!"

"I'm so dreadfully sorry——" Mrs. Cronin began. Neither of them helped her. There was silence. She rose. "I'm afraid I must be getting on now. I've several calls to pay. Thank you so much for a delightful . . ." She departed, knowing that the coming hours would now be bitter to her with the thought that both Lady Mary and Romney detested her.

After she had gone Mary Bassett said, "What on earth made you——?"

But Romney only shrugged his shoulders. At the door, before he went, he said: "There's no private life in this town any more. Everyone knows everything."

Inside rooms where walls can become surprisingly thin you may perhaps feel this; it is in the crowded street that the private life is always safest. So Michael Furze, lured by the unexpected sun from the cold house, walked slowly up the High Street which was now crowded with citizens. The sunshine made everyone gay. He was wearing his hat at a jaunty angle, his blue suit; he had taken a good brave toss of brandy before leaving the house. He had stroked the crucifix with his hand, even, clumsily kneeling, had kissed the cold marble mouth, saying: "You know that I am not evil—that I wish well to all men. That I do not deserve to be hunted. That they are following me now and trying to close me in. Master, protect me. Our Father which art in Heaven . . ."

For he said his prayers now, he was always saying them. He would kneel on the floor at his bed, as he had done as a little child, and say the Lord's Prayer over and over. Only the figure on the Cross understood how they had driven him, denied him freedom, hemmed him in. . . . "Our Father, Our Father . . ." he prayed over and over again, the sweat beading his brow.

And he prayed further that he might be given strength not to go to the Cathedral whither now his steps were always leading him. He had money now; there was work he could do—affairs he could attend to. But he seemed to be unable to work. He was drawn, as once years ago in Havana he had been drawn to a bad Cuban girl who drained the life out of him and the money too. So now—but oh! how differently!—he could not stay away from the Cathedral, but was there twice, even three times a day!

In the sunlight he felt safer, even gay. He jingled money in his pocket. The crowd passed by him and no one gave him that peculiar, penetrating stare as though soon they would stop and, crying, "There he is!" bar his way. So, because he had money in his pocket, he went into Bellamy's to buy some collars. The young woman who served him had red hair, for which he had always a partiality. She was plump, with firm breasts, and wore a white blouse and had crimson finger-nails. She smiled. "Can I help you?" He spoke about collars and his heart began to beat, just as it had done in the old healthy days when he saw a woman who pleased him. She brought out the boxes with the collars. Their hands touched. A delicious shiver of affection and desire and the anticipation of someone comforting him again (so that his head lay on those firm breasts and those long fingers with the blood-red nails caressed his hair) ran down his spine. Then, before he actually saw, he was aware that someone was staring. A male assistant in a black tail-coat. An elderly female assistant. He looked in front of him at the glass on the other side of the counter and there were eyes everywhere. Eyes. Eyes. Eyes.

He dropped the collar box that he was holding and, almost knocking down a woman with her child, stumbled into the street.

He turned up the hill towards the Cathedral.

The pale autumn sun, released from its thin provoking

bondage, turned the Nave floor into froth and spume of colour, for on these days of faint sunlight the colours of the window soaked the floor, filling with purple and dark cherry and oyster-white the hollows where feet had worn the stone away, the brasses, the pale honey-coloured shadows that a stiff memorial tomb could throw. Above these bloomy shades the great church hung airy, cold and empty.

Michael knew how empty it was today. He stood staring at the Virgin and Children window, his ears cocked as though he were an animal hiding in the brushwood from the hunters. The colours of this window, always more vividly alive on a day of mild sunshine than in a brilliant flood of light, caught Michael's heavy fleshy body and transmuted it. The bright green of the dress of the Virgin, a green of fresh leaves after rain, the purple of the clothes of the children chasing the white kid, a colour deeper than the darkest sun shadow on mountain heather, than the grape bloom of a sunset cloud, the snow white of the field of lilies where the Holy Child is playing—these stained his cheek, his clothes, his hair.

He stood there, looking up, and, almost unknown to himself, began to cry. He was utterly wretched. He was deserted by God and Man. He wiped the tears with the knuckles of his hand, but, through the misted gaze, it seemed to him that the Virgin raised Herself from watching the Child, that the Child stopped in His play and regarded him with serious eyes, and that, as Father, Mother and Child passed up the steps of the Temple, they paused, and turned and looked.

How cold the church was; how unstirring the air!

He turned and saw that Broad the verger was looking at him. Now *here* was a man that he hated! How he hated him! Of late this heavy, stupid creature tracked him from pillar to pillar. Wherever Michael might be in the church there was Broad watching him. There was something in that heavy figure draped in its black gown, with its complacent mouth, smooth rosy cheeks, supercilious brows, that infuriated Michael—so that now, forgetting all caution, his eyes still bright with his self-pitying tears, he stumbled over the uneven stones to him and said huskily: "Look here. You're always watching me. What's your game?"

They were alone in the church, and the silence was absolute. Old Broad, very calm, very friendly it seemed, raised his head and sniffed.

"Why, Mr. Furze, *I'm* not watching you! What put that into your head? But tell me—can you smell anything—a sort of odour, as you might say? My imagination maybe."

But Michael pursued his idea. "You *were* watching me. You have been for weeks. And I ask you not to. I do no harm here."

Mr. Broad was very dignified. "Funny, that smell." He gathered the folds of his verger's gown in his hands. "There! It comes and goes! Come now, Mr. Furze. You're imagining. It's my place to see that order's kept. No more *and* no less. . . . You're here pretty often. Seems the place kind of draws you."

"That's *my* business," Furze angrily answered.

"True enough, Mr. Furze. True enough," Broad said, moving away, swinging the tails of his gown. Then, with confidential friendliness: "They'll be opening the Tower again next week— long time they've been, not coming down. Must have their summer holidays, I suppose. But they'll be down next week for sure." He looked at the tight-shut wooden door. But Furze was gone. He had vanished into the shadowed depths of the King's Chapel.

Even as Broad looked for Furze the light went out of the Cathedral. The windows fell dun and dead; the bloomy colours of purple and green no longer stained the uneven stones. "The fog's come up again," Broad sniffed, pressing his hands against his buttocks. Maybe true what they say, he thought, you can almost *smell* the dead these damp days. Then, more wholesomely, he considered his tea and moved towards his home.

At that precise moment in *his* home Inspector Gurney was thinking of Broad.

"The fog's coming up again," Mrs. Gurney said, looking out of window. "I should wait a bit till it clears." Mrs. Gurney had the comfortable stoutness that comes from good temper and no imagination. In spite of loving Gurney with a real devotion and bearing him three children, she was never anxious about him.

Mists, fogs, murders and the Town Guard meant nothing to her. Even now when Gurney was more nervous and anxious about the future than she had ever, in their twenty years of married life, known him, she was quite unperturbed and fancied it was his liver.

Gurney said, his legs stretched out, his head back, his hands on his stomach: "Broad, the verger, knows a damned sight more than he'll say. What are they all keeping so silent for?" Then he told off on his fingers: "Klitch, Broad, Leggett, Tom Caul, Moon, Fanny's girl, the Furze mother and daughter, Mr. Romney. . . ."

"I wouldn't worry," Mrs. Gurney said placidly. They rented one of the little houses in Clark Street, one of the oldest and most retired quarters in all the town, up above Canon's Yard, running to the Barham Fields where the Town Wall used to run and there are still some old stones to be seen. Mrs. Gurney loved this little house. Here she had borne all three children, and the dahlia-scattered wall-paper was almost hidden with the framed photographs. Gurney, a young policeman of twenty-two, herself and Gurney on their wedding day, Mrs. Gurney's father and Mrs. Gurney's mother, the children at all stages from naked innocence rolling on a horsehair mat to self-conscious Sunday-school fine clothing.

Gurney loved the house too *and* his wife, children, photographs, wall-paper, medals presented him for life-saving and runaway-horse stopping, cups for swimming and running, and, best of all, the personally presented and personally signed photograph of Lord St. Leath. There St. Leath was, thick, beefy, kindly eyed, but, as Gurney loved to declare, "a haristo-crat every inch of him"—and, written on Lord St. Leath's stomach were the words "To Peter Gurney from his friend St. Leath." His friend! Well, it was true. There had been a friendship for many years now between them that Gurney valued more than anything else in his life—more than his wife, children or career. Many an evening Gurney had been at the Castle, smoking his pipe in St. Leath's library, neither man saying overmuch, both of them feeling, in an odd undefined way, a kind of brotherhood. . . .

And now the awful thing had happened! For only yesterday, passing through Canon's Yard on his way home to Clark Street, Gurney had met St. Leath. And St. Leath had said, quite sternly: "Well, Peter, when are you going to clear this mess up? Quite time you did."

And Gurney, his heart hammering in his big chest, as though he himself had been accused of the murder, answered, very soon, he hoped; in strict confidence he knew who'd done it; it was only a matter of putting two and two together.

"Isn't right, you know," St. Leath had said, "state this town's getting in. Just been visiting Mrs. Braund, poor lady. Shocking thing."

"Yes, it is," said Gurney.

"Well, why don't you arrest the fellow and have done with it?"

"Can't find the body for one thing," said Gurney. "For another, people won't speak. There's plenty in the town knows."

"It's your job to make them speak, isn't it?" said St. Leath quite angrily. "Town's getting into a regular upset, breaking Hattaway's windows and all. Don't know what the world's coming to—all this damned communism." And he had started off with that clumsy gait peculiar to him, but without one word, not even a "good-night" to Gurney. Oh, Gurney had felt it terribly! It was only a climax to all the troubles of the last weeks. He had come home late, sat there without a word to his wife, and then, in bed, tossed heavily from side to side. He was not good at expressing his feelings; he was by nature lazy, too amiable by half, apt to let things slide. But over this affair he had worked, worked hard. And now what? Reprimanded by St. Leath, mocked at by the town, haunted by the figure of that miser, Furze, who seemed, with every step that he took, to hang along at his side!

There was for him, too, the further ignominy of the Town
Guard, this indiscriminate, unauthorized body of young oafs
and idlers, who, simply to give themselves pleasure, threw
themselves with their cudgels and earnest sense of self-impor-
tance upon the innocent town. He was waiting for the first sign
of disorder and he would be down upon them, but he was compelled to admit that up to now they had been orderly enough.
Only let the Seatown communists emerge in their bands and
then there would be trouble!

"Well, Hannah, I'm off!" Without another word to her,
without looking at her or the children, he was gone.

After a visit to the police station and finding there was nothing new except a drunk and a pickpocket, he lumbered through
the sea mist down Daffodil Street. Lazy and comfort-loving
though he was, he was no coward. There had been a time when
his physical strength had been famous throughout Glebeshire.
He was too fat now, but yet he could hit a man hard and true
if the need came. All the same he felt soft tonight. That repri-
mand of St. Leath's had wounded his very heart. He did not
know why he cared for St. Leath so much, save that he was a
proper English gentleman, believed in the right things, did his
duty by his position and country. But there was more than that
to it. Gurney had always been a sentimentalist rather than a
sensualist—he liked babies and dogs and always remembered
the anniversary of his wedding day. After a drink or two Johnny
St. Leath seemed to stand for everything that he valued—old
England with her green pastures and the thin bright line of sea
beyond and this little town huddled in the hollow of the hill,
the low of the oxen and the still stream under the bridge, the
first colour of the dawn behind the Harry Tower, and the scent
of the roses and carnations in Mrs. Cronin's garden. . . . St.
Leath stood for these and for England, all now threatened by
forces that Gurney only dimly comprehended. But he felt that
St. Leath and himself, two big men, standing side by side, could
face all the dirty communists and murderers the world over. But
if St. Leath deserted him, was his friend no longer . . . He
stopped in his steps. He was by the river now and here the fog

was thick. He could not see his hand before his face. But he heard breathing. Quite close to him. Someone was standing there. And more than one.

An instant later three men had thrown themselves onto him. In that moment of contact he felt a wave of satisfaction surge at his heart. He had been moving for weeks in mists and shadows—now he had something tangible to deal with. One man's arms were about his neck, another was dragging at his knees, trying to pull him down. At once he had luck with the third, for he struck out and felt his fist crash into a face, heard a cry and a fall. But the man at his neck had arms like snakes. He must be a little man for he was hanging off the ground onto Gurney's broad back, his knees in Gurney's posterior.

In the elation of having, at last, something practical to do, much of his old strength had come back to him. He was out of condition, but he hadn't boxed and wrestled through years of his youth for nothing. He kicked back viciously with one foot and felt the man at his knees give. Then he swung his body round, the little man on his back swinging with him. Meanwhile he was wondering how many more there might be. Was this perhaps the beginning of that outbreak that had been threatening now ever since the Pageant? They would choose just such a night of fog as this. . . . The thin fingers were digging into his neck. His collar and tie were gone, his shirt torn, and he could feel the damp air blowing on his flesh. The other man had him now about the thighs, and his hands were digging into his groin.

He kicked again, then, as his right trouser leg tore, he swung forward and down and threw, with a great effort that seemed to burst his heart, the small ruffian over his head. The clutch at his neck was broken. The hold on his naked thigh was released. He knew that he was master of the field. He straightened himself, pulled up his torn trousers, wiped some blood from his face, and then through the mist was aware that the little fellow was lying at his feet motionless. No one else was there but they two. He blew his whistle. Then, bending down, he caught the little man by the collar and dragged the body along the ground to a distant lamp. He had killed him, perhaps, and no harm if he had. In the lamp's opaque light he saw that this was young M'Canlis, the tobacconist's son, one of the worst wasters in Seatown. He was not dead but stirred, raising his arms. His forehead was badly cut.

So Gurney stood there, blowing his whistle and waiting. He breathed deep with a very genuine satisfaction. Not only had he proved himself *to* himself, always a satisfactory thing to do, but now they would have young M'Canlis in jail and it would be their fault if they didn't get from him something worth having. He was a coward, a sneak, a tell-all when in trouble, and what he knew Gurney would know before many hours were over.

Out of the fog the long thin body of one of his men emerged.

"Good God, sir!" he remarked when he saw his inspector bleeding in the face and half naked.

"That's all right, Merry. Three of the bastards set on me. I've got one, young M'Canlis, and we'll keep him. Just what we've been wanting."

They set off up Daffodil Street, M'Canlis tenderly borne between them. And Gurney was happy. Lord St. Leath would approve of this. It was the kind of job that he'd like to have shared in. . . .

When the Cathedral chimed nine of the clock the sky was nearly clean. A film of mist like a spider's web revealed rather than hid a moon like a copper filing and a mesh of stars. The air was sharp and cold.

The town was very quiet. An occasional motorcar, rushing through, shook the silence which swiftly resettled as though, finger to lip, it gave an added warning. Old Mordaunt, in his room, empty save for two packing cases, a table and a chair, sat, a shawl about his shoulders, finishing a drawing by the light of a candle. On the walls the paper was peeling. Only one picture hung there—a copy of Dürer's Melancolia. He sneezed, shook his head, and continued, a smile of pleasure on his old dried lips, his drawing.

Klitch looked at the moon and turned to his spouse who was mending a hole in her son's shirt, seated at the table, threading a needle, humming through the thread. Klitch turned from the table. "Do you know one thing?" he said. "I'll make you a prophecy. Within a month from now that crucifix I sold Furze will be back in the shop." He jingled his money in his pocket. "I'll be glad to see it here again."

Aldridge switched off the lights of his extremely ugly sitting room. He called out: "Going for a bit of a walk, love. Help the digestion."

"Don't be long," she called back.

He went along to see Bellamy.

"Look here, Dick," he began. "We've got to do something about this situation. . . ."

Mrs. Braund tried to say something and the nurse bent down to hear. She could speak only with the left corner of the mouth.

"Want to see the moon?" the nurse said brightly. "Why, of course." She let the blind swing up. "There it is. Just above the Cathedral roof. Quite new. Pretty, isn't it?"

A tear rolled out of Mrs. Braund's eye and rested on her cheek. But the nurse was used to tears. She sat down and said briskly, "Now, where was I? Oh, here we are," and began to read from her novel.

"I feel as though all the houses were made of paper tonight," Elizabeth said to her mother. "There's a sweet little moon. The fog's nearly gone. It's as though I could see into every room in the town."

Her mother smiled. Then began, as she sometimes did, softly to move about the room. She moved with a wonderful assurance. She stopped beside Elizabeth and, putting her thin hands on her shoulders, kissed her forehead. "Everything will soon be settled, dear," she said. "In another week or two. Is that Michael?"

The two women stood there listening. There were stumbling steps on the stair. They waited to see whether he would come into their room, but he went on. They heard a door close.

"And now I think I'll go to bed," Mrs. Furze said.

MICHAEL FURZE

At nine-thirty the Town Guard assembled in the Market-place. They were all young men, wearing no uniform, carrying sticks and cudgels. They divided into bands of four; without a word spoken they marched off to their respective districts.

When they were gone a cat crept out from under the arcades and passed slowly through the square, sniffing for garbage. Once it stopped, its body stiffened, it raised its head and stared. But what it saw no one but itself could tell.

CHAPTER III

October: Bole Sands

The week of october 9th to October 16th, which will be undoubtedly remembered by everyone who lived in Polchester at that time, opened with a day of beautiful post-summer splendour. On that Monday a miracle was presented to Lampiron.

Like all miracles it was exceedingly simple. At 9.15 A.M. he walked into the Smith Bookshop to order a copy of *The Diary of a Nobody*. He told Crispangle that in future there must be always a copy in stock. Crispangle, who was in a bad temper, was short, and added that he understood that there had been a clash on the previous evening between a number of the Town Guard and a number of the Seatown lads. Lampiron grinned and came out into the sunlight. As the Cathedral chimed the half hour he met Penny Marlowe. He knew that he was moving now by destiny, that time was short, that he must take his chances, so he said at once: "Penny—you're coming with me for the day to Bole Sands," and she, as though she also recognized destiny, said, "Yes—wait while I telephone to the house."

She went into Smith's and telephoned. When she rejoined him he asked her, "What did you say?"

"I said that I was going to Bole Sands for the day and would be back for dinner. It was Father who answered. All he said

was: 'The sea will be beautiful today. Enjoy yourself, darling.'"
As they went down the hill she went on: "I've got to take him
away. Once he's out of this town he'll be all right. And I've got
a plan. Mother goes at the beginning of next week to Solton
Tracey, to some friends there for a fortnight. The moment she's
gone I shall smuggle Father into the train and carry him off to
the place he loves best in the world, Lyme Regis. *Why* he loves
Lyme Regis better than anywhere I don't know, but he does.
Mother hasn't been any use to him these last weeks. She's full of
common sense. She thinks ghosts are nonsense. But they aren't
nonsense so long as you believe in them. Father's going mad
because he thinks God has looked into his case and thinks him
despicable. So he told me last night. It began with the money
he owed that wretched old man, it went on with his death.
There was a horrible person came to see him yesterday—called
Leggett."

"Yes," said Lampiron.

"I don't know what he said to him, but Father's all broken
up. And it's all about nothing. Father is about the best man
who ever lived. So I'm going to rescue him. He likes Lyme Regis
so much, because of Jane Austen, I think," she added incongruously. Then she caught Lampiron's arm. "I think your asking
me like this is the best thing that ever happened."

They arrived at the little Bole Street station. Bole Street is
the oldest station in Polchester and has been practically left
alone since, somewhere about 1850, it seemed a bold and
glorious enterprise. Now it is a little dark place save for the
garden beyond it. Black, smoky, decrepit, it huddles down at
the edge of the stationmaster's blazing mob of flowers. All
through the summer the carnations, tulips, roses, sweet Williams
had flung their colours and scents into the bare waiting room,
the windy, melancholy platform. Now, as Lampiron and Penny
walked there, they could see the sun blazing down on the late
summer roses, pink as coral and deeply crimson and ivory
white.

The train came in, and there was no one with them in the
grimy hard-seated carriage with its sun-and-dust-worn red

backs, hot and hostile like iron, its dirty floor, its cold photographs of Rafiel and St. Mary Moor and Bole Sands. Penny's hand was curled in Lampiron's, but they did not talk. The train wandered out of Polchester almost, as it were, by accident. As they crossed the high bridge Lampiron looked out and down to the river and Seatown.

"There was some trouble, I hear, last night," he said, "between the Town Guard boys and the Seatown roughs."

But she did not make any answer. She had taken off her blue hat and leaned her head against his shoulder. Her eyes were closed. The train threw the last villas behind it and ran now between sloping fields drenched with sun and guarded by plum-dark woods.

The air was warm with the sun and fresh-salted by the sea. In pools of shadow under hedge and tree cows lay, their mouths lazily moving, their tails flicking the flies while the sun soaked and soaked the ground as though this were a divine preparation of the soil for some miraculous sowing. The light was so intense, the air, as winnowed by the train, so fresh and salt, that Lampiron thought: It is as though I were escaping from some doomed city. For weeks and weeks now I have not left Polchester. I have never even walked up the hill towards Carpledon where I used to go to get that view of the thin line of sea from the Four Trees. I have been thinking of it as a beleaguered city and I feel now a kind of surprise that Penny and I can escape from it so easily, that no one has challenged us, no guard at the gate. I should be moving now into the enemy's camp. But the town is beleaguered inside itself. It is there at its very heart that the enemy is hiding, that that old bad decaying corpse is somewhere lying. It may be that it is really down at the bottom of that well where they say I shoved it away, and if that's so it will never be found. Will that nasty old man haunt that town forever then? Will the Inquisitor with a broken neck come every night from the Cathedral door and disturb the people with his tiresome questions? (Lampiron was nearly asleep now. His arm was around Penny's slim child-like body. She was sleeping.) He has disturbed me too. And old Marlowe. And poor Mrs.

Braund. Mrs. Braund and I committed an impertinence when we called up spirits before a cheap public. Even the Witch of Endor selected her audience. But that's what it is. . . . You must keep the balance. If you neglect their world altogether they punish you. If you enter it too intimately, forgetting your manners, then they punish you too. Mrs. Braund and I forgot our manners. . . . How do I know so clearly that everything here is over, that I shall never see these sun-drenched fields again, never hear these slow country voices at these stations, never smell this salty tang?

There was one thing that he hadn't told Crispangle, that he hadn't told Penny—namely that the disturbances last evening between the Town Guard and the Seatown roughs had been caused by himself. He had been up to see Ronder, who wasn't so well. (His heart was tiresome, worn out with all that flesh that it must support.) Making a short cut above Canon's Yard to Orange Street, in a narrow lane with high walls, he had met Caul and two others. Caul barred his way and said something about Lampiron's murdering his brother. They were going, they said, to give him the hiding of his life. Meanwhile Caul insulted him as foully as might be, calling him double-dyed murderer, seducer of young girls, rotten maker of images or some other high-flown stuff. Then they were going for him. It showed what the town was coming to for this to follow so quickly on the assault on Gurney. Lampiron would have been in a bad way, but four young men turned up. Aldridge's son was one of them. It was dark; there was a kind of scrimmage. Someone went for Lampiron with a knife. One of the Seatown fellows had his eye closed up. Then the Seatown men ran. It might have been an ugly business. Lampiron himself was sure that it was Leggett's doing and that Leggett was now busy directing all the Seatown energies against himself, Lampiron. Children in the street now called after him. Lady Mary and Mrs. Cronin had both cut him dead. Mrs. Porteous had paid a visit to Mrs. Marlowe especially to tell her that if she did not forbid her daughter Penny to see Lampiron any more she would be considered a ruined girl. Yes, himself and Mrs. Braund had gone too far. He knew as surely as that he was now sitting, his back against the hard red dusty carriage, his arm around Penny, that his time was short.

Well . . . he would enjoy this day. So he bent and kissed her cheek and, a moment later, they jerked their way into Bole Sands Station.

"Wake up, darling. We're there."

She woke up, looked about her, stretched her arms, smiled. Then they were happy. Any care, any fear, any thought of the future, left them altogether. They had never, from the beginning of their friendship, known any awkwardness. That sympathy and ease sprang from a perfect unanalysed understanding, something very rare and quite independent of age, sex, nationality. So many lovers watch every step taken with fear, but Lampiron and Penny loved one another so instinctively that they could be no more afraid of their relationship, once they had made their rules, than they could of breathing or sleeping.

Bole Sands Station stands on the very edge of the sands that run, when the tide is out, to a great distance beyond Condall Rock. This morning the sea was far away, a glittering dazzling curtain of sun and light, swinging above the hot sparkling pale amber sand. To the left were the Torle Rocks and Hunter's Cave and Pollen Cave. The tide would turn about midday. First they bought some papers from the station bookstall. Lampiron bought the *Weekly Telegraph* and a detective story. Then they bought provisions—pork pies, pears and apples, apple pasties, toffee and bottles of ginger beer.

They walked slowly across the great floor of sand to the Torle Rocks. It was only twelve o'clock and they were alone, two tiny figures on that vast expanse. Penny had bought a bathing dress and Lampiron a pair of trunks. They walked slowly along and the sand, the sea, the horizon danced in a blinding haze in front of them, as though a great wall of glass had been splintered.

Hunter's Cave, when they reached it, was cool like velvet. Away from the sun a breeze caressed their faces as though with cold pale fingers. They sat with their backs to the rocks and, hand in hand, like spectators in a box, watched from their security the dancing blazing spectacle of sun on sand, sky on water. Faintly, like the rhythm in a dream of the advancing drums of an army, the sea thrummed.

They took off shoes and stockings, he opened his shirt and she lay with her head on the hollow between shoulder and breast. He talked to her, half sleepily, brokenly.

"When I've gone, Penny my darling, I want to have left you a belief in life. . . . I think you've got it now, but a time's sure to come when you're tempted to lose it. Bad things happen, you're frightened of the future, you've made some bad mistakes, you're lonely, ill. . . . Don't think then that yours is a unique experience. There's something terrible in life. Fear is at the back of every man's experience. He's meant to be afraid and then conquer it. But that isn't an insult to you personally. So many people have a kind of notion that life owes them something— that it's life's duty to be kind to them and look after them. Life doesn't give a damn. No one's going to protect you or pity you or be sorry for you. You meet your own dragons, ride your own tigers. . . . I'm telling you these things and they're platitudes, but you love me and perhaps you'll remember that this has been my kind of experience and I'm wanting you to have a fine life as I've never wanted anything. . . . I've tried everything and failed in everything, and now, at the last, in a place where I was very happy, they accuse me of murder, rape, everything short of sodomy. All the same these last months I've had new experience. I've been in touch with things I never knew existed. I see that death is unimportant and that every moment of beauty is eternal. I thought it was all copybook. There's a letter of Charles Lamb's I used to be very fond of. I can't quote it exactly but one sentence I remember because I had it written above the fireplace in the house I had at Mount Newcombe: 'The sun and moon yet reign in heaven, and the lesser lights keep up their pretty twinklings. Meat and drinks, sweet sights and sweet smells, a country walk, spring and autumn, follies and repentance, quarrels and reconciliations, have all a sweetness by turn.' Have all a sweetness! By God, they have.

375

"And there's one verse of Blake's over your Donatello in the studio:

> *Abstinence sows sand all over*
> *The ruddy limbs and flaming hair,*
> *But Desire gratified*
> *Plants fruits of life and beauty there.*

Desire gratified! I've never known it—never! But to have the desire, to love you, to see this light and glory—oh, God! I'm an old man by years but my heart is not tamed. . . . I love life and all the lives to come, and if, after this, there's only silence, I accept that too. . . . Don't laugh at life, Penny, or sneer at it, or take offence at it, or say it's a cheat. Rebel when you suffer and curse and kick. Don't be resigned or meek. But never patronize life or despise it. That's a small poor thing to do. . . . God, but I'm thirsty. Shall we have a bottle of ginger beer each or shall we wait till we've bathed? Shall we bathe now or wait till the sea's nearer in?"

Penny said: "You're talking as though you were leaving me a kind of last testament. That's nonsense. Our lives together are only just beginning."

He felt her fear, her heart beating wildly against his breast. This day at least should be perfect happiness. . . .

"Yes, Penny darling. Our lives will go on together forever and ever. Nothing can separate us. This isn't a last testament —it's because I'm happy, and when I'm happy I talk. I've no original matter in me. I can't say a thing that hasn't been said again and again before, but you won't mind that. You won't mind anything I say or do, because we love one another." (And this, he added to himself, is our last day together. And it's going to be perfect. She shall remember it as long as she lives. I see with a clarity I've never known before. It's as though the sand and sea and sky were transparent. I can almost see through— through into what?) "Penny dear, tell me what you're thinking. *You* talk now. I'm finished. And what you say will be ten thousand times wiser than anything I could say, because you're young and all life's in front of you. . . . Penny darling, tell me what you're thinking."

"I'll tell you what I'm thinking," Penny said. "While you were talking I was planning things out. I don't mean I wasn't listening to what you said, but you were talking like a book, darling, as you sometimes do. You do love to talk about Life with a capital L like the mottoes you tear off in calendars."

She put her hand above his heart. His skin was warm and dry. She could feel his heart pounding with a grand scornful indifferent steadiness.

She suddenly felt that he didn't belong to her—that in reality he was quite indifferent to her, and the fear that she had five minutes before returned, menacing. . . . So she went on talking.

"I've been planning it all. As I told you, I'm going to take Father to Lyme Regis and make him all right again. I'll read silly novels to him and pretend to enjoy chess, which I *never* can understand, and we'll go to the cinema in the evening where I *hope* there'll be a picture with Marie Dressler and Beery because he likes them better than anyone. *Then*—we'll come home. We won't come back till everything's right again, until they've discovered old Furze's skeleton or ceased to bother. Until they aren't afraid to go out at night and don't think ghosts walk out of the Cathedral. Then—" she paused—"we'll go away, you and I——"

"Go away—where?" he asked.

"Oh, the South Seas, or Australia, or China even."

She caught his hand and held it so tightly that he knew she was frightened. As the pulse of his hand hammered against hers the last remnant of any physical feeling that he had ever had for her vanished. His love moved, like a traveller, into the country where it truly belonged. She was a child and frightened and he was her protector forever and ever.

"Why the South Seas?" he asked. "They're greatly over-rated."

"China then."

"That's overrated too." Should he tell her yet once again,

how, in a few years, he would be an old man, physically weak, flabby, a nest of tiresome ailments, unable to go where she wished, insisting that he must have his nap, snoring with his mouth open? No. Why should he when there was to be no old age for him? No old age? He could have risen, stretched his arms and shouted—No old age! No old age!

"Wherever we are," he said, "we'll be happy." (My going will save us, he thought. There's no other possible solution to this.)

She sat up and looked out to sea. As he stared at her he thought that he had never seen her so lovely as now, so filled with the certainty of life, glowing with colour, energy, confidence. And so it should be. It would be best if he should never see her again after today, for now all physical desire for her was gone and soon she would be aware of that and disappointed, she knew not why. She was too young as yet to realize that because physical desire was gone, he loved her more dearly, more truly than ever before.

"I was only a child," she said, "until these last months. I grew up in a moment that first time you held me against you and kissed me.

"Now I feel I can do anything—look after Father and Mother and love you and tell the town what I think of it. When we go away together I must work—I can write a little, I think."

"There are far too many writers in the world already," he murmured. "*Far* too many."

"Yes, perhaps there are. Well, it doesn't matter. I can do something else. And anyway I'll have babies. They'll keep me busy."

"I'll be a *very* old father," he said, cupping her face in his hand, looking into her eyes. "The children will scream when they see me."

Was she frightened again? Her eyes stared into his. She said almost breathlessly:

"If I lost you—if anything happened to you——"

"Nothing shall happen to me," he said, kissing her. He thought—so it will be for six months after I'm gone. And then she will begin to forget. Then she'll begin to lead her life without me. Then I'll be a memory. Then in her middle age she'll tell her husband, at some art gallery perhaps, "I knew a sculptor once——"

"Now let's bathe," he said.

CHAPTER IV

October 10th: Elizabeth's Journal (II)

October 10th, 1933.

I AM WRITING in my bedroom 2 A.M., October 11th. I have
headed my paper the 10th because it is of the events of the 10th
that I am writing. I am putting down as quickly as I can the
happenings of the last twenty-four hours, partly because I want
them to be accurately recorded, partly because the writing is a
relief and a safeguard. I also believe that matters here, in this
town, are reaching a crisis and that in this house in any case
everything will shortly be changed. I am not a practised writer,
as I have discovered very often in this Journal, but I shall try
to state exactly what occurred and to remember things said and
done in this house since yesterday morning as accurately as
may be.

I am not, I think, as women go, a coward but at the same
time I don't despise myself for being afraid. Fear is part of
everyone's experience. I am as badly afraid at this moment as
I have ever been. I fancy that if I get this fear down on paper
I may dissipate some of it. I have been, I can see now clearly,
far too repressed, cautious, self-accusing in the past. I intend to
be so no longer.

At about half-past ten, yesterday morning, the 10th, Leggett honoured me with a visit.

I have hated Leggett as long as I can remember. I can see
nothing wrong in hating some people so long as you love some

others. My feelings have always been extremely strong with regard to people. When I read a modern novel it nearly always disappoints me because the characters are so colourless. Of course nobody is wholly good or wholly evil. I suppose I believe rather in the *powers* of good and evil than in good and evil people. My father and Leggett are examples of what I mean. If there is anything in words at all, then they have increased the evil in the world—lust, greed, cruelty, selfishness, arrogance —and if that is so, then I think that the modern indifference to their activities is all wrong. I'm not a prig and I *hate* prigs, but I think that men like my father and Leggett ought to be put away where they could do no more harm. The harm they have both done under my eyes in this town is incalculable.

Since my father's disappearance Leggett has been absorbing all that remains of his personality—and that is quite a lot! It has been very curious and mysterious to watch Leggett becoming more and more greedy of money and power in a cheap second-hand way. My father had a kind of power—everyone felt it—but the essence of him, so to speak, has reached Leggett a stage removed with the result that it is thinned, vulgarized, cheapened. My father really cared for nobody and was afraid of nobody. (I am not sure that he was not a little apprehensive of Uncle Mike after he had bullied him and tortured him and drained him.) But he had a kind of grand loneliness—he simply hated and despised us all.

Leggett is daring and terrified, a bully and a sycophant. He feels that he's got some grand chance here but doesn't know how to seize it. He's as frightened as is most of the town, although he's got, so to speak, inside knowledge. The horrible thing about Leggett has always been his cowardice. He's frightened of his friends because he's betrayed them, of his talents because he's prostituted them, of the moneylenders because he won't pay them, of his vices because they're against society (and he's *terrified* of the law). All the time he defies his friends, his enemies, his talents, his moneylenders, his vices, public opinion, *and* all the time he cringes to all of them. He's terrified of living, terrified of dying, greedy of fame and repute, but his character has destroyed his chance of being more than an ephemeral commentator. He's like a mangy dog skulking against the wall, baring his yellow teeth, slinking his head from side to side to avoid the stones, and nipping out at a trouser leg or fleshy bit of arm if he gets a chance. He's petty and despicable, dangerous and worthless, and yet I feel a kind of pity for him, almost a kind of tenderness because he's, finally, so miserable, so frightened, so bewildered.

There! That's enough about Leggett. I feel a lot better.

He arrived at ten-thirty and asked for a special interview on a matter of great importance. We shut ourselves into the dining room and as I looked at his streaky, cold-beef countenance, his reddening nose, his horrid bald head, his little paunch and his slightly bandy legs I wondered how I could ever have feared him. How these last six months have altered and, I think, strengthened me, taught me at least never to fear men like Leggett.

He realizes this difference in me. He knows that I've grown. What he wanted to propose to me was an alliance.

He told me at once that my father's murderer was now known. All they were waiting for was the discovery of the body, and this might happen at any moment. They had obtained some very important information from young M'Canlis, who had attacked Gurney in Seatown and been arrested. He said that the moment my father's murderer was taken up everything would change—the town would settle down and be as it used to be.

He said my father had left a good deal of money and, in the absence of a will (there was no sign of a will and Symon was sure that none had been made), everything would go to my mother. He proposed that we should make a triple alliance— my mother, myself and himself. What about Uncle Michael, I asked? Well—Uncle Michael would be elsewhere. He looked at me and I at him. I needn't worry about Uncle Michael. Why, I asked him, had he been making it his duty to put about everywhere that Mr. Lampiron was concerned in this business when, as he very well knew, Mr. Lampiron had had nothing whatever to do with it? He shrugged his shoulders and said that his quarrel with Lampiron was his own affair. He continued, very seriously, and plainly trying to be as attractive to me as he could, to explain that my mother and myself, under his direction, could do extremely well with our money and need never have an anxious moment again. He asked me whether it was true that I was engaged to marry Mr. Bird? I said it was. He said that, in his opinion, it was a pity but it was my affair and not his. I said that was so. He then came to the heart of the subject, which was that it would be very easy for him to make things unpleasant for my mother and myself by hinting that we had been concerned, one way and another, in my father's disappearance. He had not the least wish to be unfriendly, quite the opposite, but he thought I ought to know this.

I answered very simply and directly. I said that my mother's affairs were, as far as I could see, no affair of his—in any case, my mother and I had always detested him and now I detested him more than I ever had before. I told him I had once been frightened of him but was so no longer—he, in fact, was the more frightened of the two. I advised him to get out of Polchester as fast as he could, and I said that he knew I was right.

Something very queer happened then. We both became very nervous and our mutual nervousness drew us in some strange way together. The dining room where we were sitting has always been a very ugly room with hideous furniture. Like every other room in the house except my mother's, to which she gives something of her own vitality, it is dead and has always been dead.

When I told Leggett he had better leave Polchester I too felt that I must get away, and Jim and my mother and everyone for whom I cared. It was a sunny morning and while I was speaking a butcher boy rode on his bicycle down the road beyond the little dry garden and I could see that he was whistling cheerfully. I knew that all the morning bustle of the town was going on, people shopping with baskets on their arms in the

Arcade, motorcars drawing up near the Gate and tourists getting out of them to visit the Cathedral, ladies exercising their dogs, and a canon or so walking up the High Street, sunshine everywhere, chrysanthemums banked together in Anderson's window—all this normal daily life—and yet suddenly I pleaded with Leggett to leave the place almost as though he were the best friend I had in the world. I told him that it was not because either my mother or I cared in the slightest whether he went or stayed. Curiously enough I at once convinced him of that. He looked out of the window, at the door, half rose from his chair, sat down again, then asked me why I said that. What did I think was going to happen to him? I told him that he had enemies, the town was in a disturbed state, and I was sure he would do better for himself elsewhere.

Then, for the time, he got the better of his fears. He got up and strutted about the room. He said that he intended to be the most important man in the town, and already he was taking over the affairs of many of my father's debtors (did I know old Canon Marlowe, for instance? he was making that old boy wince!). He had a better business head than my father, and more talent than any other man in the place, and if my mother and I would not come in with him he would find ways to make us. He ended by standing over me, shaking his fist at me and, in a voice trembling with anger, telling me that at any moment now the whole thing would blow up and my mother and I would be blown up too. He was, he ended melodramatically, the only person in the world who could save us. And then he went, banging the door behind him.

After he had gone I found that the chief impression he had left with me was that he was right in one thing—namely, something was about to occur and the suspense of the last weeks would be ended. I went straight to my mother and told her everything Leggett had said.

It is difficult not to imagine that the blind see so much further than the rest of us do. Second sight in their case is often a reality, although there is nothing spooky about it. My mother had certainly through all the strange story of this year known more than the rest of us, more, I fancy, than anyone else in the town.

I think now that, from the very beginning, she has known exactly what has happened to my father. She would have nothing to do with Gurney, however, or anyone else. She would not take a step herself but has simply waited for events to evolve. When I went to her and told her what Leggett had said she sighed and murmured, "This week will see the end of it." She sat close to me, her thin dry hand on my lap, looking in front of her. Her pale drawn face had always a great beauty for me—such self-command, such concentration on an inner life, also such suffering, mental, physical, spiritual—all this growing over a very long period—gave her a power that no one else I have ever known possessed. I am no philosopher, but simply for myself the necessity for pain and struggle in this world has always seemed to me clear when I look at my mother. She had used it all for her own strength—no easy life could ever have given her the power or the tranquillity she now has. She might be called a mystic, I suppose, in that she has conquered all physical experience and subdued it. I now know that those early years with my father were for her a most terrible agony, but she took them and used them and even deceived me over many years about her attitude to my father.

She is no soft weak sentimentalist. She felt about my father, I think, what any saint felt about his or her own particular devil—nothing very sweet or edifying.

If she is a mystic she is of the militant kind—the kind I personally prefer. Leggett had never interested her very much, I fancy, being a pale, common reflection of an evil power that she had shared most of her life with.

The next event was that, at about three in the afternoon, I was preparing to go out when the bell rang. I myself opened the door. My mother was asleep in her room; Uncle Michael had left the house after breakfast and had not returned.

On the doorstep stood a lady to whom I had never spoken, whom I knew well by sight—Miss Camilla Porteous. She was wearing a severe sports costume of grey tweed and had on her

head a hard, ugly little hat with a green feather in it. She said:
"You're Miss Furze, I think?"

I said that I was. Very stiffly, trying, I could see, to be very
important and authoritative, she said that she would like to
have a word with me. I was quite as capable of authority and
stiffness as she was. Besides I had always greatly disliked her
because of Jim.

In she came and into the sitting room we went. The sitting
room is quite as repellent as the dining room. It is not, I think,
that I have no gift for making my surroundings pleasant. One
day I shall have, I hope, a house of my own, and it shall be as
bright and fresh and gaily coloured as this damnable house has
been dead and cold and inhuman. Miss Porteous did not add
to the splendour of the room. She sat on the edge of the faded
sofa, her thick legs widespread, looking, as Jim has so often
described her to me, about to enter for some athletic contest.
I did not sit down but stood, leaning against the mantelpiece,
looking at her.

"You may think," she said, "that this visit is an impertinence. I don't intend to be impertinent."

I said that I was sure she did not. The only thing was
that I was on the point of going out and had an appointment
in town to keep. (My appointment was with Jim, but I did not
need to tell her that.)

She said stiffly that she would not keep me for more than a
moment.

"It is simply this," she went on, rather as though she were
the captain of a hockey team and was giving me directions as to
the tactics of my play. "It is said in the town that you and Mr.
James Bird are engaged to be married. Is that correct?"

I said it was correct. My temper is not, I am afraid, all it
.hould be, although circumstances have taught me to control it.

She then explained that Mr. Bird had for a considerable time
been a curate of her father's, and therefore she and her
father took a friendly interest in his affairs. She hoped I
would forgive her saying that he was a man ignorant of the ways
of the world, liable to hasty and sentimental actions, and just

now his whole future was at stake. An injudicious marriage would certainly altogether ruin that future.

Then I knew, God forgive me, a rage beyond my common experience. It was an odd irony, and also shows, I suppose, the strain that the events of the last months have been on my nerves, that this ridiculous interfering female could upset me as not my father nor Leggett nor Gurney had been able to do. I discovered that I was trembling from head to foot, but I hope and believe I showed her no emotion. I would have died before I let her know that she could disturb me.

"Would you mind telling me," I asked her, "two things— first why Mr. Bird's marriage to me should disgrace him, and secondly why *you*, to whom I have never spoken in my life, should interfere in the matter?"

She answered my first question very readily. She repeated that she had no wish to appear impertinent, and she hoped I would not take it so. This was a very unpleasant thing to do, and she was only doing it because she thought it her duty. She was sure that I knew quite as well as she did why my marriage to Mr. Bird would be at the moment most unfortunate for him. Owing to no fault of my own I was closely involved in a very unpleasant case of murder that was greatly upsetting the town.

"Please," I broke in, "if you wish to accuse me, Miss Porteous, of murdering my own father, do so." (Childish on my part, I fear.)

She said that was absurd (but quite as though she did not think it altogether absurd). The point was that this would be a ruinous step for Mr. Bird to take. She was sure I could not realize fully *how* ruinous it would be and she implored me to release him.

I hope that in my reply I was brief and to the point. I told her that although she did not wish to be impertinent, she *had* been so. She was not, I understood, so close and personal a friend of Mr. Bird's that she could take his affairs on herself (I saw her wince at this). We had every intention of being married, and that she must try and bear it as best she might.

There was nothing for her then but to get up and go. At the

door of the sitting room she turned and told me what she thought of my action. She said that perhaps I didn't realize what public opinion felt about me. She was very sorry to say it, but this horrible affair of my father's disappearance would hang about me for the rest of my days, and therefore it was a shame to ask a good honest man to share my life.

I don't know then what I might not have done. I was, I'm afraid, not far from slapping her face, an action of which I should afterwards have been greatly ashamed. I was saved by the ringing of the bell. I went to the door, opened it, and saw Jim standing there.

Miss Porteous gave him one look, coloured, and murmuring, "I might have guessed as much," strode out through the door and vanished down the street.

In the cold and horrible sitting room I told Jim that he could marry me tomorrow if he wished. I cared nothing for anything that anybody said nor whether I ruined his career or no. I told him I loved him, heart, soul, body and mind. I said all this quite fiercely, standing by the fireplace and looking at him as I had looked at Camilla Porteous. But with a different expression. Oh yes, a very different expression indeed. And Jim laughed. He was so happy that it gave me great pleasure to look at him. Then to have him in my arms—I had been starved for a long time. We never troubled to discuss Miss Porteous. This was the happiest hour of my life so far.

Uncle Michael came in between half-past ten and eleven. I am very anxious to make my account of everything that follows as honest as possible. I shall write down nothing I did not see and hear with my own eyes and ears. When Uncle Mike came in I had said good-night to Mother after reading to her for half an hour. She was tired and thought she would drop off to sleep. I went to my own room and began my first love letter to Jim. I wanted him to realize what a strange and unexpected thing that hour in the afternoon had been to me. That anyone should care so much for *me*, plain, awkward, silent as I am! And that I, with so many years' inhibitions, fears, selfcontempts, pride, scorn of others, longing for the affection of others and never daring to ask for it, after the terrified years with my father and the suspicions and alarms that have followed my father's death, that such a one as I should be able to be suddenly liberated, should throw away fears and repressions! And yet all I could write was, "Dearest Jim, thank you, thank you, thank you. . . ." And I couldn't help thinking, so self-conscious have all these years made me, how sentimental and silly I would think it if a woman as unattractive as myself told me of writing sucha letter. I should think: Poor man! He can't be in love with her. He must be doing it out of pity—and yet Jim is in love with me—in love with me and loves me. If I serve him for the rest of my life I can never repay him for what he has done for me!

Well, I was sitting writing my letter and I heard Uncle Mike come in. I looked at the old brown marble clock on my mantelpiece and saw that it was ten forty-six. I listened, as I had grown into the habit of doing, to his stumbling uncertain walk past my door. Sometimes he is drunk; most times he is not, but he always stumbles as though he can't quite see his way. I stopped writing and strained my ears for every sound. I am always afraid that he may go into my mother's room. He is afraid of my mother and resents his own fear. You can never be sure what Uncle Mike will do. I got up and went to the door. I knew suddenly the alertness that comes often before danger. I knew that I was caught by more apprehension than usual. I did not hear Uncle Mike's door shut, and very soon I knew that he was walking back down the passage again. He stopped outside my door and there we were, the two of us, on either side of the door, listening. Then he knocked, a timid uncertain half knock. I opened the door.

"May I come in for a moment, Lizzie?" he asked. He has been calling me Lizzie lately.

He has grown fond of me, I think, and yet I knew quite well that nothing would please him better than that I should go away and he never see me again. I told him to come in. He really looked terrible. He had gone into his room to take off his tie and collar, and through his open shirt I could see that his breast was shining with sweat. He had not shaved for several days and under his eyes were heavy dark pouches of sleepless-ness. His long white nose also was covered with perspiration, and the backs of his freckled hands.

He sat down and, looking up at me, said:

"Lizzie, I can't stand much more of this. They're hunting me everywhere." Then he added: "This is the first cool place I've been. How nice your room is, how tidy. How cool and neat you are yourself." He touched my grey dress with his hand.

There was a white bowl with some chrysanthemums in it on my dressing table. He went up and fingered them as though he had not thought they were real.

I asked him who were hunting him.

"Look here, Uncle Michael," I said. "If there's something you ought to tell them, something on your conscience, go and tell them. It's much better."

"There's nothing on my conscience," he said fiercely. Then he went on: "If they'd left everything alone it would have been much better. Only, of course, they couldn't," he added. "They weren't allowed to."

I said that what he needed was sleep and that I had some tablets. I went to my dressing table. But he stopped me. No, it wasn't sleep he needed. If he did sleep it would only be worse when he woke. Then he said, would I come with him into the study? (That was what we called the room where Father used to do his business.) He said that there was someone there. He knew there was. Did I think him mad? Well, he wasn't. This had been going on for weeks and weeks. . . . Someone was there. . . . He'd seen him a number of times. If I went with him I would realize that it wasn't nonsense what he was saying.

My father's room had been locked for a considerable time. In the weeks immediately following his disappearance Mr. Symon and Leggett had been there, looking through papers and so on. But, after they had finished with it, no one had been there except Uncle Michael.

To reassure him I said I'd go with him. Down the passage we

went. He unlocked the door and we went in. I stood there in the
dark while he fumbled for a match. He lit the gas. The globe was
dusty and the light dim.

There was now very little furniture in the room: the roll-top
desk, the green safe, a table, two chairs. The blinds were up,
which always gives a room a desolate and abandoned air at
night. The place was very dusty and there was a sheet of newspaper on the floor falling and lifting a little in the draught.
Uncle Michael stood, without moving, looking in front of him.
I was suddenly very frightened; I wanted to turn and run. I
had always hated this room, but now I was aware that Uncle
Michael's terrors were not groundless. This room was evil and
loathsome. It was not only the stale smell natural to a room that
had, for many weeks, been closed, nor was it only the kind of
cellar chill which some rooms have. Nor was it only the dim and
uncertain light and the slight hiss of the gas jet. All these things
and something more. . . .

The room was papered with a pattern that always looked
to me like grey lizards running between brown toadstools. My
father had chosen the paper himself. I was staring at the empty
wall opposite me and some of the wall-paper there was torn.

I fancied that I saw a shadow against the wall-paper. (I want
to allow for every possible explanation of what followed. I was
tired, I was impressed by the exhaustion and unhappiness of my
uncle, the gaslight was very dim, the air of the room musty and
oppressive, the torn wall-paper might easily have provided an
illusion. I am simply writing what I saw.)

Against the wall there was a shadow. As I stared I looked
into the empty blind eyes of a man—first the eyes, sightless,
dead, then the whole drawn parchment face, a *dead* face, then
a long thin body in a grey overcoat, hands in grey gloves,
hanging down. The whole figure was grey save for the yellow-
white face and the long white nose.

It was the face of my father.

I heard Uncle Michael draw in his breath with a hiss. I cannot precisely define my own impressions. I remember that I
heard the noise of the gas, the rattle of the newspaper on the

floor. I remember that the room was intensely cold with the cold of mould and damp brick and sprouting fungi.

I remember thinking that if the figure moved I would die of terror, then and there. My whole mind was concentrated, I think, into the determination that it should not move.

"Don't move! Don't move!" my frightened spirit murmured. The shadow seemed to look at us, through its sightless eyes, with bitter malevolence. Then the wall-paper was as it had been. No one, nothing, was there.

Michael had stumbled, half onto his knees. Then he slid onto the floor and lay there, huddled. He was crying. I could do only one thing. Whatever he had been, whatever he had done, only pity was possible here. I knelt down on the floor, put my arms around him, held him against my breast, kissing his forehead, stroking his hair—tried to comfort him. . . .

CHAPTER V

October 11th: Marlowe's Night Journey

On the afternoon of October 11th at 2:30 they held in the Cathedral the annual festival of St. Clare. This was a service attended by the children of all the girls' schools in Glebeshire. The girls filled the Nave, and their white dresses, seen from the steps of the Altar by the Bishop as he pronounced the Blessing, made the church brilliant as though with freshly fallen snow. The October sun, slanting through the great Rose Window, lighted the Bishop's Tomb, the delicate lacework of the stone screen, the shining black-marble recumbent figure; the green stone of the ring on the finger burned with a personal fiery glow. Kendon looked at the tomb; he looked far away to the hundreds upon hundreds of children. He had already preached to them from the pulpit in the Nave. He was not feeling well today—nothing more than weakness, weariness, a general feebleness of head and limb.

But, as he looked down on those many upturned faces, thought of all that was in store for those children, how, even now, their minds were filled, not with what he was saying to them but rather with a dress, a friendship, a game, a schoolmistress, a social snobbery, he felt for them an infinite tenderness and compassion. His own time was now drawing so very short; they had so much to bear and suffer and endure, were advancing so lightheartedly forward. Behind him, to the left, was Henry Arden. All history was in that place. He felt now, as he had felt once before when, on a visit to California, he had looked through the great hundred-inch telescope at Mount Wilson and seen Saturn, ringed, a blazing globe of silver, so near, so lovely, so superb in its certain grandeur; and now this little earth, this strife and agony, this unawareness, this false sense of security. . . .

". . . Children, as you grow older you will hear God questioned by very clever men. Don't let that disturb you. However clever those men, they cannot answer the questions. Your own answer, however simple, is as good as theirs. Now abideth these three— Faith, Hope, Love. And the greatest of these is Love."

They knelt for the Blessing. A fluttering as of birds, or a soft wind through grass, broke the silence as they all knelt down.

"The Blessing of God the Father . . ."

When he had ended and was kneeling in front of the Altar, he wondered whether he were going to faint. A great weakness swept over him. He seemed to hear, rising from all over the Cathedral, voices: "We are here. We are waiting. Have no fear . . ." and within his closed eyes he seemed to see a dark figure at his side, tall, erect, its hand raised as though to touch him on the shoulder.

But life surged back. He was aware of aches and pains, sharp as knives, in his back, his thighs. He had an almost irresistible impulse to cry out for Coniston. Where was Coniston? He would never reach safety without him. . . . But he was a courageous man, and with a fearful effort he pulled himself up from his knees.

He followed the Cross back to his throne and there he waited while the children filed out of the church. Now he could see directly across to the Black Bishop's Tomb.

"That was a near thing that time, my friend," he thought. "I nearly joined you."

The verger, standing there, waiting to precede him out of the Choir, thought to himself: "How white the old boy looks! They say he's pretty bad."

The Bishop moved on to the vestry, still thinking of Saturn. At the vestry door he saw Coniston waiting.

"Yes—it's all right, Coniston. I'm a bit tired." Then he

murmured a line from Coleridge: "'The alien shine of unconvincing stars.'"

"I beg your pardon, sir?" said Coniston, helping him on with his overcoat.

"It's nothing. Only poetry, which you don't appreciate. Tell Frank to drive slowly—it's such a lovely day. . . ."

Marlowe had been present at the service, and when he returned home he was told that someone was waiting to speak to him.

Going into the study he found Leggett waiting there.

"Excuse me, Mr. Marlowe," Leggett said pleasantly. "I thought I'd just like a word with you."

It is one of the strangest features of this sequence of events in Polchester that casual and apparently most unimportant incidents were of the first importance. Had Mr. O'Hara not gone to Mrs. Braund's party, had Mrs. Cronin not lived in the Precincts, had Mrs. Dickens not possessed a cat, had Romney not preferred a white dining room . . .

In any case nothing was, and remains, more mysterious than the behaviour and personality of Leggett. In this world there are no villains. Leggett was not one. He had simply allowed himself a surrender to certain tastes and indulgences that he had not strength enough to control. The most probable explanation of his behaviour on the 10th and 11th of October is perhaps hidden in this very interview with Marlowe. He came with the intention of terrifying the old man and glorifying himself. He saw himself, as Michael Furze had seen himself, as carrying on Stephen Furze's power. Now, in this short interview with Marlowe, he made the appalling discovery that he wasn't "up" to it—that he wasn't big enough or strong enough. He realized now perhaps for the first time what a really great man Stephen Furze had been, and that a really bad man or woman is one of the rarest of God's creatures because greatness is so rare. . . .

In any case he began with an attempt at bullying.

"Now, Mr. Marlowe, this has gone on long enough. What I've come here to know is—are you going to pay up or aren't you? I must say that it doesn't seem to me quite an honourable position for a clergyman——"

Marlowe blinked at him. He had had no proper sleep for months; he had reached so bewildered a state that he was clear about nothing except that God was ashamed of him. This conviction had grown, through these months, so strong that now at last neither Leggett nor Furze's ghost nor any other possible persecutor had any power over him any longer. He was face to face with his God.

So all that he said was, very simply:

"I don't owe you anything, Mr. Leggett. You know that as well as I do. I paid Mr. Furze far more than I ever borrowed from him. Moreover, I have no reason to suppose that you have any right over Mr. Furze's affairs. In the first place there is no evidence as yet that he is dead. In the second I have no reason to suppose that he has left you as his executor."

"Now look here——" Leggett began.

Marlowe's head was clear as it had not been for months. He had an odd notion that if he could play the Allgaier opening with Cronin this afternoon he would be certain to beat him. It was as though God were standing there with him in the room; he was concerned only with Him and had scarcely a moment to bother with Leggett. You may decide (and a great many intelligent people have apparently so decided) that God is all nonsense, but for those who believe that He exists no word of yours can have any weight. So Marlowe went on:

"So, Mr. Leggett, it's really of no use your coming here again. In fact I shall, from now on, give orders that you are not to be admitted. You can go to law or take any steps that you please. If you continue to disturb me I shall ask the police to interfere."

He, subconsciously, was recalling the opening moves of the Allgaier:

	White	Black
1.	P – K4	P – K4
2.	P – KB4	P × P
3.	Kt – KB3	P – KKt4
4.	P – KR4	P – Kt5

"Do you play chess, Mr. Leggett?" he asked.

"No, I don't," Leggett answered fiercely. The old fellow was crazy and ought to be locked up. Look here," he said, "do you realize what this means? Nice thing it would be, wouldn't it, if the Rector of St. James's appeared in the police court arrested for debt—a pretty scandal! What would your parishioners think?"

"The point is," Marlowe said, rubbing his hand through his hair, "what would God think? I don't suppose you believe in God. So many people don't—or think they don't. But I do, and after many months of distress I have discovered that this money matter is nothing compared with my own neglect of Him. . . . So you'd better go, Mr. Leggett. You can't do anything to me—nothing whatever. If Mr. Furze is not dead and returns and manages his own affairs—then I will talk with him. But to you I have nothing more to say, either now or at any other time."

It was then that Leggett discovered his impotence. This discovery involved very much more than old Marlowe and was simply overwhelming.

It was as though he could see Stephen Furze there in the room, over by the window, standing there and grinning at him. He was no use; he had never been any use. He couldn't frighten a fly. That swine, Lampiron, had knocked him down and he had left without a word. Even Michael Furze wasn't afraid of him—and now this flabby old clergyman with his blue eyes and untidy white hair ordered him to leave his house.

A desperate sensation of having reached the end of everything seized him. That old beast, Furze, was laughing at him, the old clergyman was laughing at him, everyone was laughing at him. What was he going to do? What would become of him if nobody was afraid of him any more?

"It's all very fine," he blustered. "You wait and see. If you don't pay what you owe within a week——" But he couldn't go on. Marlowe simply wasn't listening to him.

He went to the door. He thought of saying something shameful about Marlowe's daughter. But he couldn't. The words

wouldn't come. He hadn't the spirit of a louse. He went, banging the door after him. In the street he paused. He felt a dreadful emptiness, uncertainty, discomfort. Rather as though he
were standing on a platform in midair and the platform were
beginning dangerously to shake—rather as though someone
had whispered in his ear that he was condemned—condemned
for ineffectiveness.

Marlowe, after Leggett had gone, got his hat and started
out of the house. It was dusk now and a pale-violet colour
soaked houses and streets. The chrysanthemums in the garden
were a dull dusty gold and seemed to dissipate very faintly the
prophetic odour of smokily burning leaves. Marlowe took out
his key and let himself into his church. It was not a beautiful
church, St. James's. The glass was violently crude and there
was a very ugly reredos supplied by the Ladies' Guild of St.
James's "in memory of Emma Jane Courtois, a Worker Before
the Lord." The church smelt a little stale, as though somewhere
damp hay were stored, as though near the very ugly stone
font a great cheese were secreted and mice busily occupied
there.

Nevertheless Marlowe loved this church and it was his home.
He knelt in his own seat in the choir and prayed to God to forgive him. He thanked God for sending His servant in the shape
of a mean and vindictive usurer to wake him to a proper sense
of his own backslidings. He had wickedly neglected the service of
God, but it should be neglected no longer. His mind was not
entirely clear as he prayed. It had been in a state of confusion,
distress and unhappiness too long to be suddenly now sharp and
accurate. As he knelt there he felt in close touch with God, but
he was also pursuing the Allgaier with its breath-taking chances,
its surrender of a Knight, its exposure of the King, and he was
thinking of Penny, her sweetness and beauty, he was thinking
of his headaches and how suddenly they had left him.

His mind was cleared. He was in close contact with God.
He had the sensation of resting in His arms, of encirclement and
protection. There was no longer the presence of the stern In-

quisitor. That was over. "Save my children. Go forth, my son, and do your duty. . . ." Very clearly, as though actually he heard a voice, he remembered how Penny had told him that she had been to Seatown and helped some child and how they had told her that no parson came down there.

"And why don't they?" she had asked fiercely. "Is it no one's parish?"

He rose from his knees, went out of the church and started down the hill.

On that same evening Gurney and his men made two arrests in Seatown—Lanky Moon and Fred Ottley, the fat lazy son of the man who kept the billiard saloon.

It was said afterwards that they were really after Tom Caul, but he was not to be found that evening. The arrest of Lanky caused some trouble. He was serving drinks in the Dog and Pilchard. There were some five men in the place at the time, fat Fred Ottley being one. Gurney and his men entered and, almost at once, Moon hit Gurney in the face. A scuffle then began and Ottley kicked one of the policemen. There was a fine scene in the Dog and Pilchard. Men and women crowded the doors. The end of it was that both Lanky and fat Fred went their way to justice.

This happened about six-thirty. By seven an ominous and total silence had fallen on Seatown. Not a human soul was anywhere to be seen. The public bar of the Dog and Pilchard was deserted. The river flowed on its way, the mist came up as it often did on these autumn evenings. The chimes of the Cathedral came softly and gently from behind walls and windows.

There is no doubt but that the arrest of Lanky Moon was the decisive moment in this crisis of the town's history.

Gurney was slow and Gurney was placid, but he knew his duty. It was generally understood that night throughout the town, in the mysterious fashion of these things, that the problem of Stephen Furze's murder was at length completely solved. More arrests would follow. It was also understood that this Furze affair would be made the occasion for a clearing-up of the

Seatown situation. Once more the decent citizens of Polchester would wash Seatown white!

It is apparent enough now that Seatown was aware of this and was gallantly resolved on its own protection. The best method of defence is attack. Lanky's arrest gave Tom Caul and his friends what they needed.

At about eight o'clock on that evening Mrs. Murphy of the sweetshop in Bridge Street, coming down with Mrs. M'Canlis to the river to gather gossip, saw a strange sight.

Mrs. M'Canlis was a very thin woman of a fierce temper, and the arrest of her son ("poor lad, no one's enemy but his own, and a better son never drew breath"), after his attack on Gurney, had made of her a kind of prophetess virago. With all the easy mounting of passion that comes from continued ill-fortune and constant drinking, Mrs. M'Canlis was in a raging temper and longing to get her nails into somebody. Even Mrs. Murphy, who was a stout soft-bosomed body with a face like a crimson nutmeg grater, was angered, she scarcely knew why. She had never liked young M'Canlis, who had been a terror to the neighbourhood for a very long while and thoroughly deserved imprisonment—nevertheless weeks and weeks of propaganda had made her indignant. Indignant about what? She was herself comfortable. She had four trades—the sweetshop, fortune telling, sale of indecent pictures and postcards, and the use of her upstairs bedroom by lovers who wanted privacy and security. She was jolly, good-natured, let-live-and-ask-no-questions, by temperament. She still, herself, had a lover or two, stout though she was: "I've a loving 'eart, damned sight too loving," and she would laugh and roll her shoulders. Nevertheless, although she had not a grievance against anyone in the world, she was worked up now to a fine frenzy of feeling towards the "uppermost" of people in Polchester—them and their pageants and fat clergy and fine ladies. Things were wrong all the world over. Look at the unemployed, and the way they worried the poor fellows who were given the dole. Look at Russia! (In her imagination Russia was a cold place, north of

Scotland, where it always snowed.) They managed things better in Russia—no unemployed there. So, if the lads wanted to break the windows of a shop or two and light a bonfire on the Cathedral Green *she'd* no objection!

So she was saying to Mrs. M'Canlis when, reaching the riverside, they came on a very strange sight. A fat little clergyman, without a hat, his white hair ruffled by the evening breeze, was standing on the old stone step below the broken-down mill and talking at the top of his voice. It is probable that, as he was a clergyman, he was preaching. The very curious thing was that, at the moment when Mrs. Murphy and Mrs. M'Canlis arrived he was talking to empty air. There was no one present. The river behind him made at this point, as it tumbled over the old millstones, a considerable noise, but Mrs. Murphy noticed at once that the old man had an excellent voice, sweet and piercing.

"Why, it's the parson from St. James's!" Mrs. M'Canlis said.

The two ladies stood there listening, and very shortly they were joined by one or two more. Two young men stopped; two boys with a puppy on the end of a string; an old woman with a paper bag; two old men.

It seemed to be a matter of indifference to Marlowe whether he had an audience or no. The street lamp outside the little row of houses known as Canute's Row threw a light on him that was beneficent and kindly. Even the puppy sat down on its haunches and stared around as though it were settled there for the evening. The air was cold and damp, and Mrs. Murphy murmured, "'E'll be catching his death if 'e isn't careful."

"And it doesn't matter, dear friends, whether we wish it or no. We can no more change the conditions than we can alter the course of the stars. God's there, however we behave. I have myself been struggling against Him for the last year and more, and you really wouldn't believe how patient He's been. Struggling's no good. You may do without Him till you die, but that won't help you." He shook his head, thrust his hand through his hair and went on very confidentially. "All this hatred is no good. People have gone on fighting for hundreds of years, and really it's very childish. It's quite time we grew up and realized that we had better love one another. Because that's what it will come to in the end. God won't do it for us. We have to do it ourselves of our own free will and we'd better make up our minds to it."

"'E's balmy," Mrs. M'Canlis said. "All this talk about love. Parsons are all the same. They don't recognize facts. What about my boy? Lots of love they've shown *him.*"

The crowd was increasing. The news that the St. James's parson had gone mad and was preaching down by the Mill soon spread.

"I can tell you," Marlowe went on, smiling on everybody with great friendliness, "that I've had a miserable time myself lately hating someone—and all of us in the town have been letting our tempers go and quarrelling with one another."

A man interrupted, calling out: "Stow it, can't you, you old preaching windbag?"

That seemed to please old Marlowe. He threw up his head and called out: "I'm not a windbag—I've never talked in this place before, more shame on me. At home I do sometimes talk too much, but my wife's been married to me so long she's learnt not to listen. There's a fruit tree in our garden that has the most beautiful mulberries. Every year. It never fails. How old it is I don't know, but every year it's better. That tree——"

"To hell with you and your mulberries," a young man called out. "As you *are* here let's hear how much they pay you for preaching to people who don't want to hear you. It's you blasted parsons——"

Old Marlowe began to grow very excited. "No, no! You're wrong. Truly, you're wrong. It's not preaching that's my business but helping——"

At that moment someone pushed him from behind. He stumbled, waved his hands in the air and would have fallen had not a young man caught him. He rested his hand on the young man's shoulder.

"Thank you, friend——"

But the crowd came in closer, laughing, shouting, bent on mischief.

Penny Marlowe was finishing her supper. She was alone. She had asked about her father, been told that he went out about six. Had not said where he was going. The front-door bell rang. The maid said: "There's a little girl, miss." Standing in the hall was Fanny Clarke's child. She was wearing an old straw hat, a shawl over her shoulders.

She said: "You must come at once, miss. They're 'aving a game with your father." In the street she said: "Oh, miss, I do love you so. I do really. I 'ates everyone else."

"Hush," Penny said, hurrying along. "You mustn't say that. What were they doing to my father? Where is he?"

"Down by the Mill, miss. They're kiyiking and callin' 'im names and throwin' things. I thought you'd want to know."

Penny hurried on. The little girl (whose name was Christabel —her mother, very drunk one night, thought of the name: she'd seen it outside a pub somewhere, "The Christabel Arms" or something) said:

"I been in the police station, Miss Marlowe. They ask me questions. I know 'oo did it. I was there that afternoon 'iding and I see them both come in and——"

"Tell me," Penny said. "What are they *doing* to my father? What are they *doing?* Why isn't someone there? Hurry! Let's hurry!"

And the child, running along, her hat on one side, continued in a kind of chant:

"Oh, miss, I do love you so! I don't care *what* they does to me, I'll never love no one but you, and if you was to die I'd kill myself, so 'elp me God. And I 'ates all the others. Mr. Caul, I 'ates 'im the most, and Ratty Brown and Sally Beal and Mrs. Murphy and Ma M'Canlis and Dirty Mary and——"

Penny was running now. The child ran beside her.

"Oh, hurry! . . . Let's hurry! Let's hurry!"

And Christabel, running, chanted: "I know 'oo did it. I see them come in and it was thunder and lightenin' and I saw 'im take 'im by the throat and shake 'im. And there weren't nobody there but me, and I 'aven't said a word because I wouldn't, and then they said your gentleman done it, Miss Penny, so I told Mr. Gurney because I love you, Miss Penny, and I 'ates all the rest——"

"Oh, there!" Penny cried. "There! I see them. They're shouting."

She had arrived at the moment when the young man had put out his arm and supported her father.

She saw that he was neither unhappy nor dismayed. He stood there, bareheaded, smiling. He put up his hand and began to talk again. Then someone threw a stone. She ran across the street, crying out. In that moment she cared for nothing in the world—no, not for Lampiron himself—in comparison with her father. There was something in both his defencelessness and his happiness that stirred her very bowels of memory. Deeper than any other impulse was this stirring of love and pity springing from the old roots—a child ill and he softly opening her door lest he should wake her, she (small, in pigtails) stealing up to him as he played chess, nestling up against him but not speaking because, when he played chess, she must not. His childlike pleasure as they started out together to walk towards Carpledon or to the fields above Orange Street or to the Market. She was truly beside herself as she pushed through the crowd, ready to die with him, to be crucified with him, to be burnt at the stake with him.

But there was no melodrama. Everything ended very quietly.

Tom Caul had appeared from nowhere and as soon as he began to speak no one thought of the silly old parson any more.

"Come, leave the old man be," Caul said. "He's done no harm. There's others than him we're after." He spoke very quietly. There was great quietness everywhere. No sound but the distant hoot of a taxi and the chuckle-and-run of the river.

"It was me they wanted tonight, friends. Well, they didn't find me. I'm not one to skulk. Tomorrow night they shan't have no trouble. And you'll be with me. We'll all go together. We'll go and find *them* this time. Now quietly, friends. Go home and sleep a bit. Tomorrow you'll be up most of the night."

Everyone dispersed. Caul said to Marlowe: "Go home, parson. Come and preach to us another time. When we're ready to hear you."

He walked away, striding down the street, his head up, shoulders back. Mussolini at the very least.

Marlowe was trembling. He put his arm through his daughter's. They started up the hill.

The old man said very little, only that he was happy because now everything was clear. He saw where his work lay.

"It was very kind of you to come, Penny. We must stay together in future. I think we have work to do. Everything is quite clear to me."

"Your head's bleeding, darling." She stopped under a lamp and took out her handkerchief.

"No, it's nothing. Someone threw a stone. It shows they were interested." She could see that he was as excited and pleased as Daniel must have been when he found himself in the lions' den and that the lions were real.

At that moment she was granted a vision. This was the second step in her journey to maturity. Her love for Lampiron would not die but it would never be fruitful. That was not the road that she would go. But rather this. . . . Her father, her mother, Fanny's child, the endless claims. . . .

She felt his hand tighten on her arm, and for a swift rebellious moment knew a fierce, bitter antagonism. Then, very tenderly, under the lamp's light, she tidied him, putting his hat straight on his head, dusting his coat. She kissed his cheek.

"Yes, Father . . . and I'll tell you what. First we'll have a little holiday. We'll go to Lyme Regis."

"Oh, Lyme Regis! . . . Why, Penny, what a grand idea! I like Lyme Regis better than anywhere!"

CHAPTER VI

October 12th: Death of Anyone

THE TOWN WOKE, on the morning of October 12th, to a deluge of rain. The storm lasted from some early morning hour to eleven or eleven-thirty. The rain just thundered down, and Polchester, accustomed to wet mists and drizzles and short sun-shed showers, was frightened by all the new sounds, the gurgling of gutters, the garrulous chatter of water-pipes, and the thunder, as of horses' hoofs, stamping on the roofs. The sky was, for those hours, ebony black with little streakings of china-white clouds.

The Cathedral was grey, almost sulphurous. The water rushed down High Street. With the rain was a cold under-chill. It was the pared nail of the advancing finger of winter. It was not the lovely aggressive cold carrying in its arms chestnuts at brazier corners and snow drifting up the windowpanes, nor a roaring wind that's tactless with its careless youth—this was a niggardly, sly, and give-your-best-friend-away cold. The town knew the kind of cold it was and bent its back to the slashing rain with apprehension in its heart. No one moved about the town that morning. It was like a town that had been cleared for its next tenants. Mrs. Coole's old ladies huddled over the fire, and in Bellamy's the girls stood behind the counters waiting, and Godfrey Burdon took a secret nip at a brandy flask that he kept in a drawer among the socks and underwear. He looked shabby and unwell.

"You need a holiday, Mr. Burdon. That's what you need," Alice Coste, who had once thought of marrying him but now was glad she hadn't, said to him.

"What I want," Burdon said, "is to get away from this blasted place. They were at it again last night in Seatown. They say——" His voice sank into a whisper as his uneasy eyes wandered down the long passage between the departments.

Everyone was uneasy that morning. When the rain stopped about eleven-thirty everyone sighed with relief and then thought how still the place was. The nurse turned Mrs. Braund in her bed and made her more comfortable.

"There! That's better. . . . Why, I declare the rain's stopped!"

Mrs. Braund, out of one corner of her mouth, murmured something.

"Why, certainly, dearie. . . ." The nurse was very motherly. Mrs. Braund hated her more than any poison.

Mr. O'Hara was calling for Mrs. Carris to take her for a round of golf on the St. Leath Hotel course.

But Mrs. Carris declined. "No, Edward, thank you. I'm not going out."

He blustered a little. "No, it's no use your swearing. I don't like the look of things. It's cold. I'll stay in. What did you quarrel with Hattaway for last evening?"

The tall thin Irishman coloured angrily. "He was damned insulting. I'm clearing out. I loathe this town. Ever since that silly joke at the Braunds' I've been insulted right and left. You know I only stay here for you."

"Yes, I wish you hadn't done that." Mrs. Carris patted her hair. "I can't get the poor thing out of my head. . . . I shall never be comfortable again. *Was* it *really* you, Ted?"

"What do you mean?"

"You know what I mean. If it was you standing in the door-way it was the most wonderful impersonation I ever——"

"*Of course* it was me. . . ." But he moved about the room uneasily. "I'm clearing out though. I can't get that old man they murdered out of my head. I see him at every corner. I'm Irish, you know."

"Yes, I know you are," Mrs. Carris said drily. "Perhaps you *are* better away. People here don't seem to like you much. Try London, and I'll come and visit you."

"*What* a foul sky!" O'Hara said, staring out of the window. "Looks as though it were struck with leprosy."

About midday a pale watery sun came out, and Canon Ronder walked across the Cathedral Green and into the Cathedral. There he found Gaselee showing two friends, a fat clergyman and an exhausted spouse, the sights.

"Now," Gaselee was saying, "we come to the Brytte Monument—Henry, Eighth Marquis. Lovely babies—like Mino da Fiesole. Ever heard of Simon Petre? . . . Ha, Ronder! We came in from the rain. May I introduce you? Canon Ronder, Mrs. Bateson. Bateson, this is Canon Ronder."

(He is certainly stepping into my shoes, Ronder thought. That is just the way I showed off both myself and the Cathedral thirty years ago.)

He had wakened that morning feeling not at all well—apprehensive, depressed, very old. His mind was swept, as a beach is threatened by a high tide, with the surge and thunder of the past. Now, as he stood listening to Gaselee and old Broad, who had joined them, Gaselee became his own young self and Broad a little older now than the pompous and conceited Lawrence. He could hear Lawrence saying to Davray the painter: "No, you can't go up the Tower. It's forbidden." Then how polite Lawrence had been at sight of himself, Ronder! So now Broad was saying to Gaselee: "Afraid you can't go up the Tower today, sir. Been closed for some time. It's to be opened again this afternoon. Mr. Hattaway and the London gentlemen are to examine the woodwork tomorrow morning."

So, just as himself thirty years ago, Gaselee now answered: "Thanks, Broad. Another time will do. My friends are here for several weeks." Gaselee's manner was perfect. He patronized the Cathedral without offence, for he was clever enough to patronize himself at the same time. So—exactly—Ronder thirty years back!

Gaselee and his friends moved away. Broad and Ronder were left together.

"Cold this morning, sir," Broad said. "*Very* cold."

"Yes," Ronder said. "That was heavy rain we had."

The Cathedral indeed had an icy chill that struck upwards from the flagstones, clung to the vast pillars, had some being in the cold aloofness of the purple and green of the glass that was not friendly today nor comfortable.

Broad sniffed. "Excuse me, sir," he said. "Do you smell anything?"

Ronder sniffed.

"No, I can't say that I do."

"My imagination. But I know this place so well that I imagine things, I daresay. Only my boy—he thinks the same. No one else can detect anything. A kind of fishy tinned-food-gone-bad sort of smell, if you understand me."

"Your imagination, Broad, I expect," Ronder said.

"Very likely, sir."

But when he had left the Cathedral some kind of odour did seem to persist in the Canon's nostrils—an odour (very, very faint) of dried blood, corruption.

He was very conscious too of that threatening constriction about the heart—not actual pain as yet but something approaching, stealthily, on padded feet. His eyes too were a little dimmed. The sun still shed a watery light, but the wet, shining vigour of the grass after the rain seemed to pass into the lowering sky and be translated there into an unhealthy green shade.

As though he would stay the approaching enemy, Ronder, halfway across the Green, stopped and looked back.

"My eyesight's going," he thought. He had known this for some time but had not expected to find so dim a view as now, when the very walls of the Cathedral seemed to spread like the wings of a bird, when he could scarcely distinguish King Harry against the grey-white sky, when there was, he would have sworn, some figure standing motionless in the West Door, watching him.

Would he never see the Cathedral clearly again? Was he really going blind? Or was this some kind of spiritual recedence, as though the Cathedral were indeed only what you made of it, as though it slipped from your fingers at the very moment when you thought you had it firmly? His whole life had been spent in the effort to catch it, hold it, present it as his great prize, and now, that silent figure ironically watching, it turned into mist before his eyes!

"I must go up to London and see that oculist Dale was telling me about," he thought.

But there was that smell of dried blood in his nostrils. He would not go down to the town as he intended, but rather home, be warm by the fire and look at the new additions to his 'Nineties collection that had arrived from London.

But, strangely enough, within his room he did not feel any safer. Here in this house, Number 8 the Precincts, he had been for over thirty-six years. He remembered, as though it had been yesterday, how he had been driven up in the smelly cab (he remembered even the name of the cabman, old Fawcett, long, long since dead), polite Mrs. Clay at the door. . . .

The house itself had been his friend from the beginning. It had been owned, he remembered, by an eccentric old lady, the Hon. Mrs. Pentecoste, and it had been empty for a while because the ghost of Mrs. Pentecoste's cat (a famous blue Persian) was supposed to walk there. And was it not strange that even to this day, after all these years, he would pause for a moment at an unexpected sound and murmur, "Mrs. Pentecoste's cat?" How pleased he had been with the drawing room, its dark-blue curtains, the white furniture and white bookcases—the white Hermes, ready for flight, on his pedestal.

So it had been then: so it was now! There was the copy of Rembrandt's Mother, there on the round mahogany table the books of the moment. He remembered even what they had been, some of them, in those first days—Mrs. Humphry Ward's *Sir George Tressady*, Barrie's *Sentimental Tommy*, the *Works* of Max Beerbohm. Now they were Stella Gibbons' *Cold Comfort Farm*, Stephen Spender's *Poems*, Virginia Woolf's *Flush*,

Trevelyan's *Blenheim*. . . . Better or worse? It did not matter. Art was sure: the only passion that life could not conquer, the only lust that knew no satiety.

He moved into his study, but even there his discomfort did not leave him. He thought of ringing for his housekeeper, Mrs. Hepburn. She was always multiplied with comforts. But no. . . . He liked better to be alone. It must be near luncheon time. Had he been wise to live for so long alone? Why had he not married? Would it not be pleasant now to have someone to comfort him, to stroke his forehead, to . . . ? No, it would be odious!

He slowly undid the parcel on the table and looked at his new treasures. Where would he put them? No room, no room. Oh, Lord!

Poems by John Tabb, the American first edition of *The Green Carnation*, a fine first of *Cashel Byron*. . . . He turned away. For the first time in his life books seemed to have no interest for him.

Leaning over to his desk he picked up the letter from an American friend who was visiting Hollywood . . . an amusing, intelligent letter, not abusing Hollywood as is the fashion, but talking of the pale-green skies before sunset, the open-fronted fruit markets, brilliant with colour, fruit like jewels in Aladdin's Cave, and the censor saying to the producer of some picture that he hoped that he would take care that the baby's diaper was decently changed. . . . But he didn't care about America either. Still that scent of dried blood in his nostrils and, beyond the window, the tawny chrysanthemums quite unreal, bunches of ragged tissue paper.

"Mr. Romney would like to see you for a moment, sir." The maid (nice girl, Maude) stood a little timidly in the doorway.

Romney! Oh yes, he would see Romney. Romney might perhaps be real.

Romney came in, immaculate, bloodless, intelligent.

"Only a moment, Ronder. . . . I want your advice."

"Sit down. Have a cigarette. My advice? If this were the last piece of advice allowed me ever I'd give it, gratis and for nothing." (Why had he said that?)

Romney sat down, very elaborately selecting one of his own cigarettes out of a blue enamel cigarette case.

"It's only—that I'm a little nervous."

"Nervous—you? I thought you were imperturbable."

"Oh, well—in a sense I am. What does it matter *what* happens? It is only that they are about to lay Furze's murderer by the heels, and Seatown, I am afraid, means to celebrate the event."

"Oh, are they? Who's the murderer?"

"Does it matter? *That* isn't the important thing. What *is* important, Ronder, is the inartisticness of coming events. They might even try to burn the Cathedral down. That would distress me very much. What should I do to prevent them? Some of them are my friends. I feel a certain responsibility. What ought I to do?"

Ronder laughed. He could not see Romney very clearly. As he sat there he seemed to merge into the books behind him. This visit might be imaginary. Romney might not be real at all.

"What a strange fellow you are!" Ronder said. "I've known you all these years and yet to this day and hour I'm not sure whether you're real or no. In any case it's right that you should be worried. You are more responsible for the trouble in this town than any other."

"Yes, I suppose I am," Romney said, laughing. "Myself and the late Stephen Furze. The two trouble makers of the present world—selfishness and the lust for power. I suppose that's what the moralist would say. I don't, in fact, know why I've come in to see you, Ronder. Nothing that you can say will make the slightest difference. Nothing that anyone can say. You're right, Ronder. I'm as much a ghost as Furze is. I have no sex, no passions, only taste. I'm absorbed in myself as all ghosts are, I must be continually meddling in what is not my business as all ghosts do. I love beauty as ghosts must. I'm ruthless and conscienceless as ghosts are. I and Furze between us have created the apprehension in this town as ghosts do. One fine morning I shall be gone—there will be a white rose in a crystal vase on a white table in my white dining room. The rose will die. It will be swept away. A faint, humorous sigh will be heard in the wainscot. 'Do you believe in ghosts, Mr. Humpty-Dumpty?' 'Why, of course not, Miss Shakespeare.' Curling like smoke from a chimney above their heads I shall laugh and fade into eternity. . . . Well . . . I must go, like Puck, and put a girdle around the world. I don't know why I came in to see you, Ronder. Except possibly to make my apology to you. You are the most intelligent man in Polchester. You alone, when all the fuss is over, when the spirits have sunk into their graves again, when everyone has learnt their lesson and forgotten it, you only will understand how responsible I am, how dangerous I am, how, if they had their wits about them, all the justices of the world would order my instant execution. Do I flatter myself? I think not. For wherever I am there is trouble. . . . Good-bye, Ronder. Look after yourself. You are more like me than you know."

Romney rose, took Ronder's hand, looked at him with great affection and departed.

When luncheon came Ronder did not want it. He told Mrs. Hepburn that he was not hungry.

She looked at him with anxiety. He knew that she was a motherly soul, so motherly that people were to her not individuals but babies in a maternity home. He suddenly disliked very much to be a baby in a maternity home, so, rather irritably, he bade her go her way. When she was gone he wished he had not been irritable.

That showed well enough how old he was getting, for, in earlier days, it had been one of his first rules that he must never be irritable. He sat now at his desk, the desk that he had brought with him to Polchester.

On it were arranged with meticulous care the objects that had always been arranged there—a thin vase of blue glass now filled with two red roses, a Chinese figure of green jade, a small gold clock, a photograph in a silver frame of the Blind Homer from the Naples Museum. These had been here, exactly in their present places, since his first arrival in Polchester. The only addition to them was a photograph of his aunt, now dead, who had too many years kept him company. She understood me, he thought, better than anyone else has ever done, and she spoilt me because she allowed me to be as she wished me to be. But Aunt Alice! A fine observer. Like nations that have no history, a happy woman!

But here, too, distaste caught him. He disliked these things. They reminded him of a life that seemed to him now one long, lost and wasted effort. He remembered how he had taken orders because that career would give him, he thought, great power over men. He remembered how Aunt Alice had said to him that men thought clergymen fools and that this gave a man who was not a fool a great advantage as a clergyman. That had been his first mistake. His second had been to fight Brandon. He should have left Brandon alone because, whatever follies that man might have, he possessed a virtue that Ronder had not, he believed. Ronder had believed in nothing except his own cleverness and now he was clever enough to perceive that cleverness was not sufficient. As he had warned Gaselee that day in the Cathedral, he, Ronder, had missed it—and by a hair's breadth.

He had never known more clearly and surely that he had missed it than during these last months. Something had been astir in the town that was the very expression of the thing that he had missed. Forces had been moving before his eyes, the very forces that all his life he had been denying—the mystery of the survival of the spirit, its strength, even its fury, its determination *not* to be denied.

"God is a Spirit—and they that worship Him must worship Him in spirit and in truth."

He shivered, walked to the fire, just straightening, by an old mechanical habit, the books in the shelves—he had always disliked to see one book projecting in front of the others. Then he put on soft slippers of brown kid, slippers of the kind that he had worn his life long. He lay back in the big comfortable armchair of red leather, a chair made especially to suit his bulk. He looked out of the corner of his left eye at the drawer, locked, of course, where he kept his erotic books and prints. Had he better destroy these? It would not be a very fine thing if they were discovered after he was gone! A few intimates—Gaselee, Romney, Hattaway—knew of them and had seen them. Gaselee enjoyed looking at them. Himself, he had wearied of them long ago. He remained now, at this old age, a virgin as he had been at twenty. To think that he had reached the end without any experience of that deep intimacy that comes from the physical expression of spiritual love! He had never desired it. He had never wished to surrender himself to anybody. In his vigorous physical years he had been absorbed by his passion for power over men, and when that passion had weakened his bodily passions had weakened too. Moreover he had long felt a deep disgust of his own body. It was an idea horrible to him beyond any other that any human being should see him naked. No human being, since his maturity, save his doctor, had ever done so. He was ironically disgusted with his own obesity, ironically because he had not the strength of mind to diet or take physical exercise.

He remembered how that Dane, Harmer John (ah yes! *he* had seen him naked, a reason for his dislike of him!), how Harmer John had pommelled and smacked him with a sort of angry vindictive scorn! And how he was twice as fat as he had been in Harmer John's day! How revolting the body, how minute in scope the human brain, how meanly animal the bodily functions, how ugly and shabby nine humans out of ten after forty! He recalled a lithograph by George Bellows that he had seen somewhere—"Business Men's Bath"—a brilliant, savage impression of middle-aged men in a bath. His lip curled; nausea rose in his throat; there was again that scent of dried blood in his nostrils. . . .

What time was it? Had he been sleeping? He got up, padded across the thick, soft carpet and looked out of window. A grey, lowering sky, the Cathedral, the Green with no figure on it, the smug houses of the Precincts with their gardens, the Arden

Gate. Three birds, in triangle pattern, flew across the sky. He heard, from the far distance, murmurs which might be men shouting at a football game. How still the town was! How still and how unpleasant! What in the world was more unagreeable than an English provincial town on a dead humid autumn afternoon?

So they'd caught the murderer, had they? Not that it mattered very much. He did not even speculate very actively—old Furze's brother, perhaps, or one of the riffraff from Seatown. A usurer like that must have many enemies. A usurer! And suddenly he saw how closely allied in their passions Furze and himself had been.

Power over men! With both of them the same. Power simply for itself, not for anything grander or larger. Mussolini cared for Italy, Hitler for Germany, Einstein for knowledge. He, Ronder, hated despots, but at least these men were patriots. But all the others, the greedy snatchers at money, business tyranny, power over women, power *only* for the greedy pride in power—they were all lost men and he was among them.

He was back in his red-leather armchair. He snoozed. His head fell forward on his chest. He woke with a start and then snoozed again.

Where was he? Still in his room, but Miss Stiles, that ancient gossiping virgin, had entered. She was saying, "I suppose things have been smashed in the move; nothing valuable, I trust." But hoping, nevertheless, that something valuable had been broken —not because she was malicious or unkind but simply because she liked people better when they were unfortunate.

How well he knew her! But even while he told her that all was well she changed as they change in *Alice in Wonderland* into stout, dog-loving Mrs. Combermere, who was saying, in her hearty, masculine voice: "A great deal can happen in a year, Canon Ronder. You may be a bishop by then!"

A bishop! He woke to see the study filled, as it seemed, with smoke. It was only the autumn day that already was darkening beyond the window. A bishop! No, he had never become a bishop—not even an archdeacon or a dean.

"You are a worldling, Ronder—only a worldling." This was the voice of Canon Foster, a man he had always disliked. They were arguing as to whether the school should have a new garden roller. That had been his first victory. He heard the soft, gentle voice of the Dean:

"I fear that it is I who must give the casting vote. I think I decide *for* the roller. Ronder has satisfied me that it is necessary."

His first victory! That he should remember it after all these years! He was awake enough now to see the anxious face of Mrs. Hepburn in the doorway.

"Shall I bring you some tea now, sir?"

The woman irritated him; she was so very solicitous.

"No, thanks. I think not."

"But you had no luncheon."

"No. . . . I'm not hungry."

"Are you quite well? Is there anything I can do?"

"I'm perfectly well." Damn the woman!

"Very good, sir."

She had withdrawn. He was snoozing again and now he was back in Brandon's house, drinking tea. Mrs. Brandon was there and Morris, the man she ran away with, and the nice girl, Brandon's daughter, now Lady St. Leath. The door opened and there was Brandon's son, sent down from Oxford, and Brandon was in a rage and Ellen Stiles pricking up her ears with pleasure. They vanished into air. Only Brandon remained. They were riding together in a small wagonette. It was a very hot day and there was not room for their knees. They were quarrelling, ludicrously quarrelling, there in the open before the astonished driver!

Brandon was crying, "I refuse to drive with you another step. I refuse! I refuse!"

And out of the wagonette he got and there he stood in the hot, dusty road, looking ludicrous while the wagonette drove on.

And now they were in the Chapter House. Brandon was appealing to them all: "Don't do this thing! If you do, it will

mean the beginning of the end! ("The beginning of the end"—
what a ridiculous phrase!) Not this shame! Save the Cathedral!"

And there he was, poor old man, falling down before them
all, falling . . . falling . . . falling . . . dying . . . dying . . . dead.
Looking on Ronder to the last as his enemy. He lay there, poor
old man, at Ronder's feet and Ronder bent to pick him up and
it seemed to him that he himself was lying there and Brandon
standing over him.

"All waste, Ronder," Brandon said. "This hatred. Gets us
nowhere. We had better all be friends and see if we can't build
something together." But now he and Brandon *were* together,
huddled on the ground. The Cathedral loomed over them.
Someone came out of the Cathedral and Ronder waited in a
frenzy of apprehension. The figure came to him, bent down,
examined him. He felt that his innermost being was inspected.
He was opened up and everything that he was and had been
was laid bare. And the figure shook his head.

"Nothing here, I'm afraid. Nothing at all."

At those words Ronder shrivelled away. Only a little dust on
the ground that the wind blew idly. . . .

He awoke with a start. Someone was knocking on the door.
"Come in," he said testily, and at the same time raised himself
in the chair. As he raised himself he felt a sharp pain attack him
as though a sword had been driven into his stomach. The pain
went as quickly as it came.

It was Mrs. Hepburn at the door again.

"It's past eight o'clock, sir, and I was really getting anxious."

Now the pain was in his arm. He bit his lip to keep back a
cry. Then he heard a distant shouting and crying. He thought
of the footballers. But it was past eight. They would not be
playing football now. The shouts grew louder.

"What's that, Mrs. Hepburn? That shouting?"

He saw now that she was in a state of great alarm.

"Oh, sir. We don't know what to do! They say that it's a rising
of the unemployed. They say they're coming here to the
Precincts. They're throwing stones and breaking windows."

He stood up. He found it very difficult to move and the room was not clear before his eyes. He was by the window. It was very dark, but in the direction of the town he could see a flickering glow. Now he could hear very clearly the shouts of many men. He saw figures running across the Green.

"What——" he began.

Then the pain struck him. He was stabbed by the unseen enemy again and again and again.

"Oh! Oh! Oh!" he cried. There was a great roar of voices in his ears. The world was up in rebellion. They were coming to seize and destroy him, but he did not care, for already he was stabbed, he was killed, he was slain. . . .

"Oh! Oh!" he cried.

He screamed, flung up his arms, fell to the ground with a crash.

He lay there, dead, his mouth open, a dreadfully obese old man.

CHAPTER VII

October 12th: True Story of an Irresistible Impulse

Elizabeth Furze was wakened that morning of October 12th by the furious beating of the rain against her windows. She got up and stood in her nightdress, looking out. She shivered. How cold it was and with what relentless power the rain was coming down!

She dressed and went in to her mother.

"Did the rain wake you?"

"To tell the truth, darling, I don't think I've slept at all. . . . I was listening for Michael."

"Michael?"

"Yes. I went into his room. He was sleeping like a child. I want to get up now."

"Oh, Mother, why don't you stay in bed this morning? It's such a wet day and cold and horrible."

Mrs. Furze smiled. "No. I must be up and about today. I think perhaps if it clears later on I might go for a little walk." She looked about the room, her eyes seeming to take in everything as though her blindness saw further into her surroundings than did ordinary sight. "We shan't be here much longer. That's one good thing," she said, nodding her head.

Elizabeth, having made breakfast, knocked on her uncle's door. There was no answer. When she looked in there was no one there. She came downstairs to find her mother waiting.

"He's gone out—in all this rain," she said.

"He had a good night's sleep, anyhow," Mrs. Furze said.

Elizabeth, seeing that she had everything she needed, perceived how, with every day, her mother seemed to gain strength and vigour. Only a year ago what a shadow she had been, how pale and, apparently, submissive!

This morning she seemed to shine with some inner light and even happiness, as though she had had some excellent news. She asked for more bacon and then said, very quietly:

"When you marry Mr. Bird, Elizabeth, I hope his work will be in some nice place and as far away from here as possible. . . . I would like," she went on, "somewhere very bright so that I can feel the sun on my cheeks. A real garden and plenty of birds. . . . I know we're going to be very happy."

"And Uncle Michael?" Elizabeth asked. "What about Uncle Michael?"

Mrs. Furze shook her head. "Poor Michael. . . . Is that the marmalade, darling? No. I think after all I'll have some honey this morning."

Elizabeth had arranged to meet Mr. Bird at eleven o'clock inside St. James's Church. They had made that their meeting place quite frequently of late. It was close at hand, there was seldom anyone there of a morning, and if someone did come they were not noticed, sitting in a corner and talking.

Today their conversation was to be of great importance, for on the previous evening Bird was to have handed in his resignation to Porteous. As she hurried along the few yards to the church she worried as a mother might worry about her child. Jim was so gentle and small and Porteous was such a bully. She thought of Miss Camilla Porteous and her visit.

She saw herself standing at her Jim's side and joining in a by no means dignified battle. She could hold her own with Camilla very thoroughly if it came to it.

The rain had ceased and a gauzy sun gave an azure light to houses and trees. No one was about. She entered the ugly little church and found Jim Bird waiting for her. She saw at once that he had some very serious news.

They went to their accustomed place in the corner of the side aisle behind the pulpit. An old woman was kneeling on the altar steps scrubbing.

"What is it, Jim?" Elizabeth asked. "What's happened?"

"Terrible things. Elizabeth, you've got to be brave."

Her hand trembled in his.

"No. Not about us. Except that we must be married as soon as ever we can."

"You spoke to Mr. Porteous?"

"Oh yes, of course."

"What did he say?"

"What *could* he say? I think he's glad to be rid of me. He lectured for almost an hour—but listen, Elizabeth. That isn't an important thing. It's what I've heard this morning. Just now. The organist at St. Paul's told me. The whole town knows."

"Knows? Knows what?"

He put his arm around her. The old charwoman straightened herself with a groan, wiped her nose with the back of her hand, gave them a look, knelt down again and went on with her scrubbing, making a soft hissing noise.

"They know who murdered your father. They have all the evidence at last."

"Yes," said Elizabeth.

"It seems that there was some little girl—the daughter of a woman, Fanny Clarke, who lives in Seatown. She saw it all. She was in the Cathedral at the time."

"The Cathedral?"

"Yes. It happened there. She saw your father struck down. Then she slipped away. She doesn't know what happened after that, but she saw enough. She wouldn't speak for a long time, but it seems that Penny Marlowe had been kind to her and she got it into her head that Penny's friend, Mr. Lampiron, was suspected, so when she heard this, she told Gurney.

"They had been pretty sure for a long time but couldn't get the least bit of evidence." He held her a little closer to him. "They will arrest your uncle at any moment."

Elizabeth said quietly: "I think I've known for weeks."

He scarcely heard her.

"What a lucky thing that we're engaged. I have the right to stand by you. You mustn't mind what they say. You'll have to give evidence. You'll be before everyone's eyes. They may say that you and your mother knew of it, encouraged him or something dreadful. You mustn't care, you mustn't mind. We shall be married and go away——"

"Why, Jim," she said, "you don't know. I've been ostracized all my life long. You've no idea what it's been, for years and years. I've had no friend but Mother. Until you came no one spoke to me, no one asked me anywhere. And when I first knew that you cared for me I was so ashamed. I thought it horrible that anyone should join his life to a spoilt one like mine. I remember the shame that I felt at the Carol Service last Christmas when you came and sat beside me. Do you remember? But love changes everything. I came to understand that you loved me and that it was better for you to have me, whatever anyone thought or said. Besides, I couldn't help it. I belong to you and you to me.

"So for Mother and me this is nothing. But Michael . . . Oh, where is he? He went out in all this rain. Father drove him to it. Father persecuted him and starved him. . . ." Her face quivered. Her eyes were blurred with tears. "Have they found Father? Do they know what happened?"

Bird shook his head.

"It's only what they say in the town—that they haven't found the body. I don't know. The whole town's in a ferment. Last night old Mr. Marlowe went down to the river and began to preach in the street. They threw stones at him, and this morning they say Seatown's humming—they've forbidden the Town Guard to come out tonight lest it should lead to riots." He held her yet more closely to him. "They might come to your house, Elizabeth. The Seatown people, I mean. There's no knowing what they'll do."

They both stopped and listened. The old woman moved away from the altar steps and, picking up her brush and pail, went clop-clop down the aisle. The sun faintly shone in through an open window and they could hear two birds twittering on a tree in the graveyard.

Elizabeth got up.

"Michael. Uncle Michael. I must go and find him."

Bird drew her down again beside him.

"Listen, Elizabeth," he said. "Before you go there's one thing I want you to remember. The time will come—perhaps very soon—when we shall be away from here. All your life here will be forgotten. For months this town has been unreal. People have believed absurd things. You yourself in that horrible house have seen ghosts. To myself it's as though the town has been invaded by an invisible army. Haven't you felt that yourself? As though behind every person you met there was a shadow. Even in Porteous' house, which heaven knows is real enough, it's so ugly it *has* to be real—even there, even in that hideous drawing room, I've fancied absurd things, haven't wanted to be alone in there. . . . Soon the town will be normal again—bright sunshine, no ghosts, no ridiculous yellow-faced men with broken necks. And we'll be safe, happy in some place far away from here. You'll have children and I—I——" his voice broke. He bent down and kissed her hand. "I worship you next to God. You *are* part of God to me. You say that you have been alone all your life—so have I been. I didn't think anyone would ever love a commonplace scrap of a man like me. I'd determined *not* to want it, not to think about it, to make my life of other things, my duty and so on. But duty's never enough. It oughtn't to be. I longed for love. I prayed to God for it. For love and a home and children. . . . And you love me. I can't ever do enough for you to thank you—to show you what you've done. . . . So remember—if in these next weeks it all seems horrible and people seem cruel . . . you will remember, won't you, that *this* isn't our life. Real life is coming and it's going to be wonderful—both of us together. . . ."

In the early afternoon she began her search. The black clouds had come up again. The sun had gone. Even in certain shops the electric light was shining. People were walking about shivering.

Elizabeth went into one shop after another. No one told her anything. Everyone was busy on his or her daily affairs and yet it seemed too that everyone was listening.

At the bottom of the High Street was Miss Creed's shop. Miss Creed sold Irish linen. She was a little fat round jolly woman and had always been pleasant to Elizabeth.

"Good-afternoon, Miss Furze."

"Good-afternoon, Miss Creed. I wanted to see some table-cloths—small ones——"

"Certainly, Miss Furze. A horrible day, is it not? Only three o'clock and we've been forced to have the light. . . . Now I wonder if *this* is the kind of size . . ."

Through the window Elizabeth could see a piece of black cloud and the front of the Glebeshire Bank, which shone, under the cloud, with a dull dead light. She could see some leaves and a piece of newspaper blown along by the wind. At any moment Michael might pass down the street. . . .

"I beg your pardon, Miss Furze. . . ."

She recalled herself with an effort.

"Oh, thank you. . . . That's the kind of size. . . . I wonder whether I might look in tomorrow when I've spoken to my mother. . . ."

"Why, of course. . . ."

She hurried out. She knew that Miss Creed stood there, staring after her.

In Bellamy's it seemed to her that there was a large crowd of completely silent people. Everyone moved about as though in a dream, and this dream-like effect was increased by the electric light, which has always an unreal dead glitter in the afternoon. The passages between the counters were narrow, and women, stout and thin, children, a solitary man or two, walked slowly as though obeying some order from a director of ceremonies. It resembled a ceremony or one of those modern ballets satirizing daily affairs. The women hesitated, looking at things as they passed, stopping for an instant, then moving on again. But no voices could be heard. It had the effect of a cinematograph picture when the sound apparatus fails, when lips part and there is a ghastly, almost maniacal silence.

Among just such a crowd Michael might be moving, avoiding his pursuers. He would press from room to room, upstairs and downstairs, his hat crushed over his eyes, and perhaps when night came he would slip behind a counter and hide; then, after the doors were locked, he would be alone in the building, with the shoes and the ribbons and the hats and the costumes all waiting for him to surrender himself.

Elizabeth felt that she must break the silence. She stopped at a counter. A pale-faced, weary-looking woman with pince-nez attended on her.

"Excuse me" (and Elizabeth found that she too was lowering her voice), "I wanted some cherry-coloured ribbon——"

The woman produced spools of ribbons.

"What a horrible day, is it not? I am sure I don't know what our climate is coming to. . . ."

"Yes, isn't it dreadful?"

A man with a broad back, his head bent, was walking up the stairs to the next floor.

"I think," she said, "I'd better bring a piece of the stuff to match the ribbon with. If I may—tomorrow——"

She hurried towards the staircase. She knew that the woman with the pince-nez was watching her. But when she reached the next floor there was no man there but only the costume department, models with waxen faces, fur coats, sports costumes. Against the black sky that lowered beyond the high windows two models of young women with jet-black hair and ghastly faces of shining wax stared at one another relentlessly. There was no one there. Nothing moved. Not a sound to be heard save the stealthy footsteps of those passing up the stairs beyond.

The models stared at her like the images of the dead. She thought that one yellow head bent ever so slightly. The neck twisted and the lips moved.

Anything was safer than this. Even home.

Then she heard the Cathedral bells begin to ring for Evensong, and at the same time rain began to fall again, spattering the windows with little sharp spiteful flicks. The bells sounded very loud in that long room inhabited only by the wax models. She knew the chimes by heart, of course, and very often she had thought them friendly, reassuring. But now the very idea of the Cathedral was horrible to her, and alone there with those electric-shining waxen faces she seemed to see for the first time that the Cathedral had been responsible for all these events—for Uncle Michael's coming to Polchester, her father's death, the misfortunes of the Pageant, the recent "nerves" of the whole town.

She saw her uncle as someone pursued relentlessly, driven on to a certain course of action from the moment of his arrival in Polchester, and the wish that she had had before to protect him was now doubly strong.

She hurried down the stairs, through the shop (and here she had the impression that it was full of ghosts who all, turning their yellow necks, stared after her, while the Cathedral bells rang from counter to counter as though summoning everyone present to an urgent examination). Down the hill, through the Market, into the quiet of the little streets that border the Rock, she still heard through the rain that pattered on her umbrella the urgent clatter of the bells. "*Come* along—we want you. *Come* along—we want you. *Come* along—we want you," and then, as she went up the little gritty garden path, they fell into a more dangerous, menacing monotone, "Come—Come—Come —Come . . . You—had—better—You—Had—Better." When she was inside the house she sighed with relief as though she were safe from some danger.

For the next hour she read from Wilkie Collins' *Armadale* to her mother. She sat there, reading on, and subconsciously she was living in a world strangely compounded of love and fear. She thought of James Bird's words over and over again. "You are part of God to me. . . . I never thought that anyone could love me. . . . We shall be away from here and life will be real again. . . ." And although she was in actuality leaning forward, holding the book in one hand, her other resting on the table edge, her arms were around him, her lips caressed his eyes, she heard the little sigh of contentment with which he laid his head against her heart. Love was not a light thing for someone who had longed for it but never hoped for it, whose very act of resignation had so deeply redoubled its strength and truth. They were neither of them spoilt people. Because they had been poor so long they knew that gifts, when they come, are not lightly to be regarded. So she knew what it was to be loved, as she sat reading *Armadale*. She knew what it was to be afraid also. Now that James Bird was not with her, fear of things inside the house and out of it increased with every beat of the clock. What might they not do to her mother and herself? Mobs were terrifying things. Justice too was terrible. No two human beings anywhere could have been more innocent of any crime than her mother and herself, but for years they had been hated, and now the town would want to be revenged on someone for the weeks of fear and silly apprehension.

The escape with her mother and the life with Jim, far away from here, now seemed so heavenly desirable that it must therefore be unrealizable. She would never, God helping her, see a cathedral town again. How quiet and peaceful they appeared with their chiming bells, their walled gardens, their kind old ladies like the Miss Trenchards, their sweet old clergymen; but the past was alive in them, not dead as people supposed—and it was restless, jealous, and could be roused to fury if it were neglected.

"That's the end of the chapter, Mother darling."

"Well, begin the next, dear. It's so very exciting. It will be tea-time in half an hour."

Later on they had tea. Darkness had come in, blinds and curtains were drawn, the room had even now a certain life and cosiness. Her mother sipped her tea.

"Mother," Elizabeth said suddenly, "they are going to arrest Uncle Michael. Perhaps they've done so already."

Mrs. Furze said: "Yes, poor Michael!"

"They may come here. We shall have to give evidence."

"We've already told them all we know," Mrs. Furze said. "But we can tell them all of it again certainly. How did they discover about Michael?"

"It appears a little girl saw them quarrelling in the Cathedral."

"Have they found Stephen's body?" Mrs. Furze asked.

"No. I don't know. Perhaps by now—I haven't heard anything since this morning. I went into the town thinking I might see Michael or hear something about him. No one told me a word. It was horrible. Everyone seemed to be looking and listening."

"It will be all quiet again," Mrs. Furze said, "when they have found Stephen's body. Although," she went on, "it will take more than that to put an end to Stephen. Ghosts aren't easy to settle with. I settled with him years ago. And he knew it. But evil spirits live long."

Then she asked for another cup of tea and half an hour more of *Armadale* if Elizabeth wasn't too tired.

She went to bed very early, feeling her way up the stairs; her door closed with that soft gentle firmness especially hers.

"Good-night, darling. I will see myself to bed. Now don't be anxious. Everything will be for the best."

In the passage Elizabeth listened, and as though at that very moment she had been expecting it, there was the sound of the hall door opening. Elizabeth stood at the top of the stair. Michael Furze stood in the hall. Behind him the door was open and Elizabeth saw the dark arms of a tree wildly waving and could hear the garden gate creaking. A motor horn blew in the distance.

"Shut the door," she said. She came down to him. "Are you wet?"

"Soaking." He was very calm. "Wait here. In the dining room. I'll change my clothes and come down to you."

"Are you hungry?"

"Ravenous. I've had nothing to eat all day."

When he came she had arranged for him a cold ham, some fried eggs, a cheese, tea. He sat down (he was in his shirt-sleeves). He had put on a clean shirt and his hair was wet as though he had been plunging his head in water. He had also shaved and had nicked himself just under the wing of the nose. This cut annoyed him. He put up his handkerchief to staunch it, but the blood always started to flow again and marked his cheek with a crimson line—a sharp contrast in colour with the damp pallor of his nose.

Elizabeth sat looking at him. She noticed the almost mad eagerness with which he ate and how he stopped between bites to turn his head and listen.

"They may come any time," he said suddenly, his mouth full of ham and bread.

"I know," Elizabeth said.

"And I'm going to tell you everything if they let me. By God, this cheese is good. Do you know where I've been all day, Elizabeth?"

"No."

"Up in the Harry Tower. It's open again. I expected they'd be up there this afternoon but they weren't. No one was there. It's the first time it's been open for weeks and they've had the door unlocked since three. That's why I expected they'd be there."

"Why have *you* been there, Uncle Michael?" Elizabeth asked.

He stared at her as though he couldn't conceive that she should ask so silly a question.

"Why, of course, because——" Then he nodded. "Ah, but you don't know. I've got to tell you. . . . Can you listen? . . . a long time maybe."

Elizabeth nodded. "Yes—as long as you like."

"All afternoon I've been up there. The bells roar in your ears, the dust gets up your nose. And then I would go out to the gallery and look down. Then I would go back to him and talk

430

to him, and tell him what I think of him and ask him how he likes it——" He broke off. "Haven't you any jam, Elizabeth?"

"Yes, of course." She got up and soon returned with it.

"Blackberry and apple—that's good."

He spread a chunk of the loaf thickly. He smacked his lips as he ate. He stroked the side of his nose, which gleamed now with sweat. Then he saw on his finger the blood from the cut, and he licked his finger like a child or a wounded animal. He had had enough. He leaned back in his chair, his hands in his trousers-pockets, his paunch protruding, and his round face glistening with the sweat that the meal had created. His eyes were sharp and restless, but the face, Elizabeth thought, was pathetic. The lines of the mouth were kind and weak—a misfortune for a man, from the very beginning of his life, to have so prominent a nose and no chin! Yes, he was kindly, amiable, asking to be liked. Also weak, furtive, shiftless.

And then she saw (for she was concentrated now entirely upon him) that he was in a rage—a fury of suppressed anger. His lips twitched, his eyes were angry, one hand on the table was clenched. Now that his hunger and thirst were satiated, this rage—a trembling, agitated weak man's rage—was uppermost again. Words poured from him as bubbles quiver on the surface of boiling mud. But between the words his mouth was slackly open, and continually he picked his teeth with his fingers and put up his hand to feel the thin dried streak of blood on his cheek.

"How long have you known, Elizabeth? It doesn't matter. Everyone's known, perhaps, and just hasn't spoken—not until now. Now they're all going to speak at once—only they're too late. Just a day too late."

She saw that with his rage and apprehension there was also a vainglorious boastfulness. These things were strange, all springing together in the heart of a weak amiable man.

"Listen, Elizabeth. I want you to know everything—all—everything, from the beginning. You're the only one who's been kind to me. I'm afraid of your mother, always was. The others are only fair-weather friends—round you while you've dough in your pocket—then, no use for you! You're the only one who's been kind—so listen."

He stopped for a moment, staring at her.

"You know, when I first came, I thought you were downright ugly. That's a plain girl, I thought. You don't mind, do you? But as time's gone on you've grown beautiful to me—you have, really. It's in your eyes. You're softer somehow than you used to be. When I first came you were like a woman policeman. Know what I mean? 'Get out of here. No loitering here.' Now, if you did your hair a bit differently you'd be mighty attractive. And *I* know. I've seen plenty of women the world over."

Elizabeth smiled. "That's all right, Uncle Michael. Don't mind me. Perhaps we haven't much time."

"No. You're right. Perhaps we haven't."

She was thinking: This man murdered my father. He's a hunted criminal. At any moment they'll be coming for him. But I'm calmer, quieter than I've been for weeks. Perhaps it will be the same with everybody now.

He leaned across the table and touched her hand with his.

"Listen, Elizabeth. You've got to get this right. I'm not a bad man. You don't think I am, do you?"

"No, I don't think you are," she said.

"It's religion has been the undoing of me. If I hadn't been a religious man I wouldn't be in the spot I am. I've always wanted to do good to my fellows. That's been my great idea. And I've believed in God. Churches and cathedrals—you can't *fancy* the appeal they've had for me. Stronger than women. Really. That doesn't sound natural, does it? But it's true.

"Where I did wrong was to come here at all. I ought never to have come to this town. And then to sell the crucifix. That was the other wrong thing I did." He paused and listened. They both listened.

"It's nothing," Elizabeth said.

"Is it raining?"

"No. I don't think so."

"That's good."

He went on:

"I want you to understand me, Elizabeth. I'm weak, I guess. Weak because I'm religious and want people to like me. As soon as you care whether people like you or no you're weak.

"And I came to this town thinking I was going to be liked. I'd been wandering around for years with no home and now I thought, I'll have a home—and maybe I'll marry and I'll have children and we'll all go to the Cathedral on a Sunday. That's the picture I had in my mind. Then I recollected that Stephen lived here, and although we hadn't loved one another when we were kids still I thought: Sure, it will be all right now.

"The mistake I made, Elizabeth, was having no money. You ought never to go to relations when you haven't any money. They don't respect you. And to get some money I sold the crucifix in the first hour I was in the town. That was the only wrong thing I did. Everything followed from that. Way I figure it is I was Judas-like, betraying the thing I cared for most in the world. Better I'd sold the shirt off my back than that crucifix, and there was the Cathedral just over the grass watching me as I did it. Nothing was right from that moment. . . . The way I look at it is that if you haven't any sense of religion inside you, why, you're not insulting anybody if you pay no attention to it, but if you *have* some of it, why, then you've got to act straight by it. Having it as I've always had it makes you different—different from ordinary people, I mean. *I* was different, and I ought to have behaved up to it. But I didn't. That was where I had to suffer. . . ."

The clock on the mantelpiece chimed.

"Quarter to eight," Michael said. "I'll be going out again later."

The house was so still about them that the tap of a branch against the window halfway up the stairs was very clear.

They had left the door of the dining room ajar so that they might know if anyone was at the hall door. Elizabeth went to the door and listened for her mother. Sometimes when her mother couldn't sleep she called to her to come up to her. There was something slightly ludicrous, slightly menacing about her mother's calm. Or was it only that the real world seemed so unreal to her now that she didn't think about it any more? She put out her hand and touched her uncle's, which was cold with damp perspiration.

"Don't go out again," she said. "Finish telling me and then go to bed. Don't go out again."

His rage with something or somebody (not herself) surged up again.

"Of course I'm going out. There are things to be done. You wait and see, Elizabeth. They shan't have it all their own way. So . . . listen. . . . You know what happened. I sold the crucifix, or rather I rented it to that man Klitch for fifty pounds. I had the money; if I'd got a job all would have been well. I'd have had the crucifix back, gone to live on my own, married a nice girl.

"But your father saw to that. He saw I didn't get a job. That was the second mistake I made—coming here to live. What I did it for I can't imagine. That first sight of your father told me everything—that we hated one another just as we did when we were kids—more—much more. I'm different from your father. I can't bear to be hated. I'm too soft-hearted altogether, I guess. There was a Norwegian captain I served under. He hated me. He was thin and brown with a cast in his eye. How he did hate me, that man! And how miserable I was! I used to cry in my bunk just because he hated me so. And I used to dream of killing him, strangling him, knocking him on the head, not because I hated him but because *he* hated *me!* To get him out of the way so I wouldn't be hated any more. Anyone who hates me has got a kind of power over me. I go weak inside. It was different with your father though. I hated him as much as he hated me—the mean, lousy, son of a bitch. But then he *liked* to be hated. It made him proud thinking I hated him. He'd rather I hated him than not. Then you know what he did. He waited till my money was gone. Then he caught me as a spider catches a fly. I hadn't any energy any more. I was ashamed to go about looking for jobs now, when only a week or two before I was treating everyone to drinks. And he kept me, starved me, possessed me. I couldn't get him out of my mind, Elizabeth. I reckon you don't know what it is to have someone on your mind, morning and night, never to be clear of them. I ought to have gone away. You told me to and offered me money. You were the only one who was kind to me. But I hadn't the pluck. I hadn't been eating enough and I wasn't sleeping and I couldn't get your father out of my head, and I knew, wherever I was, he'd *still* be in my head. So long as he was alive. If he was dead it would be better. That was the first time I began to think of how much better it would be if he was dead. There were plenty of others thinking the same thing.

"Then came the night of the service in the Cathedral. You know, Elizabeth, the carols. That was the third mistake I made. I was sitting there, listening to the carols, thinking how swell the Cathedral was, all the history that had gone into it, the artists and the saints and the soldiers—yes, and feeling pretty miserable too because I was hungry and knew none of them would lend me any money, although they'd been glad enough to be friendly when *I* had some." (This, Elizabeth thought, constantly irritates him. He returns to it again and again.) "So I sat there, loving the Cathedral and hating everything else, when I *knew* that he was telling me to come back to the house. That's when I ought to have fought him, Elizabeth! That's the mistake I made!"

He was shaking with excitement. He banged the table with his fat fist. The sweat stood out in beads on his nose.

"If I'd fought him then I'd never have had to fight him again. It would have been easy. I'd have known I could master him— I wouldn't have been frightened any more.

"But I couldn't manage it—it was too much. I left the Cathedral. I almost ran to the house, came in, went up to his room. He was waiting for me. He sneered, he baited me—then he showed me the crucifix. He had bought it from Klitch. I hadn't the money to redeem it. He bought it to tease me, to drive me mad, just to show me the power he had. It must have hurt him to pay so much for it. He can't have liked that, but that just shows how he enjoyed seeing me squirm.

"All the same, it was that evening, Christmas Eve, when he first began to be afraid of me. Oh, not very much. He was too conceited for anything, Stephen was, and he used to boast he wasn't afraid of anyone in the world. That was right. He wasn't. All the same after that evening he began to wonder whether he wasn't driving me too far. I could see him wondering. Knowing that made me want to do something to him. He had all that power over me—at the same time I could see him speculating about me and that stirred me a bit. 'I'll give you something to wonder about!' I'd say over and over in my own room, because I'd got the habit by that time of talking aloud to myself. . . . Yes, I had, Elizabeth, and a bad habit it is too."

"Yes, I know," Elizabeth said. "Mother and I often heard you."

"It's a kind of relief when you're shut off from other people as I was. I was shut off by *him*. I couldn't get into touch with anybody—he was always there, in between. That's why it's a relief to be talking like this now. I haven't really spoken to anyone for months. And there's plenty of time this evening. They won't be needing me yet.

"Well, the idea grew in me—of being rid of him. There was nothing wicked in that. Everyone in the town would be glad. I'd be doing a public service. Anyone would. I'd think about it and think about it, walking up and down my room. I guess my health was a bit undermined by this time. I used to wonder at first how you and your mother could live on eating so little. But now I understood. After a while you don't *want* it although you still *need* it.

"And then I couldn't sleep. That was the worst. I'd lock my door but all the same he'd be in my room—or I'd fancy he was. I got into the way of thinking that bars and locks and bolted doors meant nothing to him, and I still think it. Not till he's been properly buried . . . but that's for later. I'd talk to myself by the hour as to how I could get the crucifix back. It was driving me mad, just as he intended, because you see I'd thought all the time that I'd committed a kind of sacrilege selling it to Klitch, and now it was a sacrilege, a far worse sacrilege, Stephen having it, insulting it, mocking at it, and the crucifix there in his room, patiently suffering it all because *I'd* sold it. I tell you I felt like Judas, Elizabeth. I'd betrayed everything I believed in. As I said, it's nothing if you don't—it's everything if you do. If I did sleep I had terrible dreams. I'm not trying to make excuses for myself, but bad dreams pull a man down worse than anything. There was one dream I had that went all over the town after, about a yellow-faced man with a broken neck coming out of the Cathedral. It doesn't mean much as you say it—dreams don't mean anything anyway. But I had the feeling that some-one *had* come out of the Cathedral to punish me for selling that crucifix. I've imagined things all my life. I remember once in Monte Video—but never mind that now."

He stopped, clearing his throat. They both listened, but there was no sound save the ticking of the clock and the tapping, through the open door, of the branch on the window. That was louder now and Michael said: "The wind's getting up." He was much quieter now than when he had started and he was taking great pleasure in telling his story.

"Then there came all the talk about the Pageant. That seemed to me a worse kind of sacrilege than selling the crucifix. Most pageants don't matter. They're silly things at the best from the Flurry Dance to crowning a king in Westminster. But I tell you, Elizabeth (here he banged the table with his fist), "it's dangerous fooling with the past. I've never had many brains nor *any* education, but I know that much. You can't be sure enough whether anyone's really dead or not. There's plenty thought to be alive far more dead than those *supposed* to be dead! Anyway, the Pageant stirred me up and, strangely enough, it stirred Stephen up too! It offended his pride. He wanted to boss the town. There's no doubt he wanted that more than anything else in the world. And here was something with which he had nothing to do, had no power over. He had no power over the Cathedral if it came to that, and I think he was just beginning to realize that. That was why he liked to put the screw on poor old Mr. Marlowe and that assistant at Bellamy's who sings in the choir. While he was bullying them he could feel he was putting the Cathedral in its place, if you get me.

"He had a grandeur mania. It was growing stronger all the time. He knew that everyone hated him and that everyone feared him. That pleased him to death. But he knew too that one day, driven by an irresistible impulse, someone like Leggett or Lampiron or myself might do him in. That gave him pleasure too, but at the same time he didn't want to die. I know just how he felt. He liked people to hate him enough to want to kill him, but all the same he didn't want to be killed. At the same time I think his grandeur mania had come to this—that he didn't think he *could* be killed, and that even if he *was* done in he would still be there. And perhaps he's right. Who knows? . . . In any case nothing could have pleased him more than to dominate the town the way he *has* done these last months. I have done him *that* service!"

"Wait!" Elizabeth said. She got up and went to the window and opened it. Very clearly could be heard, brought up on the rising wind, the sound of human voices.

"Something is happening in Seatown," she said.

Michael jumped to his feet.

"Yes. Yes. . . . They've started. . . . It's as I planned——"

His fat body shook with excitement. He caught Elizabeth's arm.

"Here. Sit down beside me. There's not much time. I must tell you what happened. That day—it was the day before the Pageant opened—he did everything as I wanted it. And yet I hadn't planned a single thing. You must believe me in that, Elizabeth. I hadn't planned a single thing. That afternoon about four o'clock I was at Arden Gate: I was there watching the preparations, feeling bloody miserable, hungry; I saw Klitch there and one of the old women from Mrs. Coole's. Klitch asked me in to have a cup of tea, and I can't tell you, Elizabeth, how I wanted to go. Toast, crumpets, seed cake. I tell you my mouth just dribbled. But because he sold Stephen the crucifix I wouldn't have anything to do with him. I hung around, went into the Cathedral, saw Broad the verger and his boy. They were just finishing Evensong. When they'd finished I came out with the crowd. It must have been about a quarter to five then and thundershowers came on. It poured like the deluge. So I went into the Cathedral again to wait till it was over. There was no one there by that time—no one *I* could see—although I now know that that child, Fanny Clarke's little girl, was there and Ronder up in the Choir. I thought I was alone—until suddenly Stephen was there. Right there in front of me, his grey overcoat dripping with rain—soaked to the skin he must have been!

"He must have been as surprised to see me as I was him! He just stared. He'd come in for shelter I suppose—anyway, everyone knows that the last person who'd seen him was Klitch, seen him standing in the rain, staring in at his window.

"And there we were, quite alone as we thought in that Cathedral, staring at one another, and the thunder banging on the roof as though they were dropping cartloads of bricks.

"I tell you, Elizabeth, I hadn't had a thought in my head but just that I was miserable and lonely. All the same, as soon as I saw him I shook all over. It was an irresistible impulse. That was what it was, an irresistible impulse! His lip curled; he said, 'Praying again, Michael?' And those were the last words he ever uttered. We were in the side aisle near the King Harry door. No one could see us, not from the Choir nor the Nave. That little girl must have been so close to us we could have heard her breathing. Not that I'd have cared just then if there'd have been a thousand people. I just saw the figure of my dream, for Stephen's face was a kind of shiny yellow, wet with the rain, and his head was on one side, him sneering at me. I only saw that neck. I only knew that I hated him more than anything that ever was, alive or dead. I caught his neck in my hands. He gave one cry—and then I'd twisted it. . . . I can feel the hard thin bones yet and the skin dry but damp with the rain. His eyes went round in his head, showing the whites. His mouth opened and his tongue came out, a furry grey it was. I had my knee in his stomach and I squeezed and I twisted and I squeezed. His head lolled over just as it did in the dream, and his tongue stuck out, and his body was as limp as though all the bones had turned to putty. He crumpled to the floor and his old bowler hat was lying there. He was as dead, Elizabeth, as a dead dog."

Elizabeth said nothing. She sat as though she were listening for somebody or something.

"Do you hear anything?" he asked.

"Yes." The window was open and the air very cold. Neither of them felt it. To Elizabeth it was as though she were sitting in blazing heat.

"Well—there I was," he went on. "I'd no time to lose. My chief feeling was pride. He'd bullied and tortured me for months and now I'd wrung his yellow neck. That's all I felt, and a very pleasant feeling it was. But something had to be done. I saw the door of the Harry Tower right in front of me. I went and tried the handle. By a miracle the handle turned and the door opened. I say a miracle because it was always locked and Broad the verger kept the key. Perhaps he'd been taking some visitors up the Tower, gone home for his tea, forgetting to lock it. Or maybe they'd been having a last survey before they shut it up altogether—that very evening they closed it because of the dry rot and it's never been open since till today. No one's been up there yet though—or not until I left it this afternoon.

"I hadn't time to think of reasons. I just pulled dear brother Stephen through the door and up those stairs. *That* was a job, I can tell you! They're narrow and twisty and dark. But I bumped his head on the stone, Elizabeth! With every bump I paid him out a bit. I dragged him with one hand and carried his old bowler in the other. I was sort of drunk or mad. I fancy I was singing. I don't know, but I fancy I was. I dragged him past the Whispering Gallery up into the little room above. That's a strange little room, Elizabeth. I know because I've been living there ever since. It's small and empty, smelling of straw and mice. It's smelling of other things now too. I know, because I've been there all afternoon. Don't mind what I say, Elizabeth. Don't shrink from me. You've always been so kind. I'm not mad—only excited because the end's come at last—the end to me and Stephen and everything and everybody. It's time it did, because it's a rotten world—should be wiped out and started all over again. Well, it's a funny little room. No one ever in it till Stephen and I came there. One side is open and railed in so that you shan't fall over. A fine fall that would be! You can look down and see the Nave—miles below you, it seems, with the people like ants. Makes you think poorly of human nature seeing them so small. Fine when the lights are on and the pillars and buttresses rising out of the gold haze. Oh! the Cathedral's a grand place, Elizabeth, and proud too. It knows what to do if it's neglected or insulted. That's what I kept on telling Stephen today. 'Come and look, Stephen,' I said. 'Come and lean over and see the lights.' We could hear the organ and the choir singing, Stephen and I, although he can't hear as much as three months ago because there are ants now crawling in his ear, yellow ants—and worms in his eye. Don't you move, Elizabeth. You'd better not move because although you've been always kind to me, you've got to do what I tell you."

She didn't move, but her hands gripped the edge of the table. He never took his eyes from her face and yet he seemed not to see her. His eyes had a stare of pitiful appeal, but his face now was brutal and cruel. He looked at her as though he might, at any moment, spring at her throat. He seemed also as though he were now beyond brain control and knew it, and was in despair —also as though he were triumphantly, madly exultant.

"And now I must hurry—there's no time, no time at all. On the other side of the little room, up against the wall, there's a drop. The wooden floor doesn't come to the wall. There's a drop there. Down there I dumped Stephen. Yes. He piled up there like a sack of rubbish, his head where I'd twisted it all on one side. What I thought I'd do was, the next night I'd come along and pick him up and take him out and drop him into that well there is on the other side of the Cathedral. No one ever would have found him—no, sir—never and never. How was I to know they were going to shut the place up that very night, shut it up, too, without ever going up to see whether anyone had left anything? If I'd stayed there any longer I'd have been locked up there myself. A fine figure I'd have been, shouting down from the Whispering Gallery, asking them to come up and find me and Stephen. It was old Broad's mistake. I guess he was excited about the Pageant next day and forgot.

"So I just went home. I saw two people on the way, though. When I was in the Nave again, there was an old woman lodged at Mrs. Coole's—Mrs. Dickens I found out her name was afterwards. Well, she gave me a look. Don't worry, Elizabeth—I'm not going to move unless *you* move. Here we are, the two of us, and old Mrs. Dickens in Paradise. Don't be afraid. *She* won't come back.

"There was only one other thing. In the Market I stopped by the old man, Caul, that had a stall there. He was blind, you know, like your mother. But I wanted to stop. I was gay. I was happy, Elizabeth. Because now the crucifix was mine again and Stephen was dead, or I thought he was. So I stopped and spoke to the old man. So he touched my hand and he said: 'Where's your brother? What have you done to your brother? He was talking to me this afternoon.'

"That would give you a turn, wouldn't it, Elizabeth? Just after you'd killed a man. It happens that way sometimes. When you've killed one man you've got to kill another, just to keep him quiet. So, weeks later, I had to push him down the Rock— an irresistible impulse. Passing, seeing him standing there . . . Because what right had they to hunt me down? I hadn't done any wrong. They all hated Stephen. You know they did. If I'd known that little girl was going to talk . . ."

He rubbed his hands together.

"It's all logical if you look at it. One thing follows another."

It was very clear now, carried to them on the wind—the confused shouting of voices. Elizabeth half rose.

"Don't move, Elizabeth. I told you not to move. It's nearly ended. There's very little more to tell. What *is* there to tell? Stephen drove them on to hunt me—Lampiron, Leggett, Gurney, that fat Canon Ronder, Caul, young M'Canlis, Lanky Moon . . ."

He seemed to fall for a moment into a kind of trance, reciting the names.

"Lanky, Leggett, Lampiron. . . . No. It wasn't Stephen. He was used. The Cathedral used him to destroy me because I sold the crucifix. Do you understand that, Elizabeth? Do you understand that? That I'm not my own master, that we none of us are when the Cathedral takes a hand—that I must do what it says, when he comes out of the Cathedral door with his neck broken—*I* broke it, Elizabeth—*I* broke it—then we all run away and hide. We listen with bated breath. We dare not speak above a whisper. But he catches us just the same, and he strikes us down one by one—Stephen and the Braund woman and old Caul, and soon it will be my turn, and yours perhaps, Elizabeth—yours, my dear. . . ."

He had got up and come over to her side of the table. He knelt down, laying his head on her lap.

"I've been hunted. . . . They've never left me alone and I'm tired and worn out. I give it up. I'll show them where Stephen is. They're coming for him. Listen!"

They both moved to the open window, and as they did so the crowd turned the corner by St. James's Church. There was a thin watery moon, green-coloured. The clouds had cleared from the sky leaving it a smoky grey with a silver star or two. This faint opalescent light made it seem as though all the movement which was sharp and active in the wind, were under water.

They were marching in some kind of order. At the procession's head men walked four abreast, but as they passed they became more ragged, wilder, and soon the air was filled with shouts, fragments of "The Red Flag." There were many women, a number of children.

Suddenly Michael climbed the window sill and dropped into the little garden. He stood there, swaying on his feet. He rocked like a drunken man, as though he might pitch over and lie prone. But he steadied himself.

He turned towards the room and very quietly said, "Good-bye, Elizabeth." Then he went to the gate, unlatched it and was lost in the crowd, making towards the town.

That was the last glimpse of him she was ever to have.

CHAPTER VIII

October 12th: Climax to the Crucifix

There was no meeting of any public kind that evening in Seatown as Gurney and his men had been expecting! They had been waiting for something all the last week. Extra police had been drafted into the town, the "Specials" had been warned; even the Town Guard, which Gurney had forbidden to meet, had been told that they might, in a crisis, be needed.

On that day, October 12th, Gurney felt that the crisis to everything had arrived. The murderer of Stephen Furze would have been arrested on the afternoon of that day were it not that there were still a few investigations to be made in the Cathedral and elsewhere. The body of Stephen Furze had not yet been discovered. Nevertheless for himself, Gurney, the damnable weeks of suspense were over. He would be able to speak to Lord St. Leath on friendly terms again.

He was a slow man but sure, and, as he told Mrs. Gurney, "Let them try their games. I only wish they would. This thing's like a boil. It's got to burst"—which Mrs. Gurney thought a very handsome parable.

It did burst, but not at all as Gurney expected. At seven o'clock that evening there was not a soul stirring either in Riverside or Daffodil streets. By seven forty-five the whole of the Seatown district was crowded with people.

The moon was out by then, the sky was clear, and there

was a boisterous wind. The policemen on duty in Seatown reported that there was a big silent crowd of men, women and children in Riverside Street, most of them armed with sticks and rough weapons. These policemen were ordered to report at once at headquarters, which they did.

It was as though the Pol had overflowed into Riverside Street transforming itself into human beings, so closely packed, so silent was that crowd. Presently Tom Caul and a number of his friends appeared. He addressed the crowd from the front of the Dog and Pilchard. He spoke very much more quietly than was his custom. He said that for a long time past the real citizens of Polchester had received great injustice. Who were the real citizens? Not the parsons nor the society swells nor the shopkeepers in the High Street but the men and women who lived in humble homes and did the drudgery and bore the burden and heat of the day. What was their lot? They searched for work and found none. They had a bare subsistence thrown at them like dogs and were expected to go on their knees for it. Meanwhile the clergy spent thousands of pounds on a show which ended by their being the mock of the whole of England.

If the money that had been wasted on that blasted pageant had been spent on the Polchester unemployed, how many women and children might now have enough to eat, a comfortable place to sleep?

They had been very patient and what had they received in return? Some among them had been arrested for no rhyme or reason. On the other hand there had been two, possibly three, murders in the town within a few weeks and no arrests made. One of the victims had been his own brother, but he would say nothing about that here. He could deal with that little matter himself. They all knew that the town was in a bad way, everyone at loggerheads, the Cathedral people old and doddery, police obsolete, townsmen squabbling, that no one knew who would be murdered next, and of course all the disorder was charged on Seatown. What had Seatown to do with it? Exactly nothing. Seatown sat quietly, obediently waiting while its most respectable citizens, like the landlord of the public house in front of which he was standing, were ruthlessly seized and carried off. Well, they had been patient long enough. It was time that they made a protest, and tonight they would show that in one town at least in England men and women refused to be enslaved, beaten, imprisoned, starved without a struggle.

They were law-abiding, decent people. All they wished was to state their case, and that they now would do on the steps of the Town Hall, at the door of the Cathedral itself if need be.

They would dig out old Stephen Furze's ghost and get it to show some of the swells in Polchester where they got off. Anyway, they were tired of all the nonsense of the last months. They would show the people of Polchester that Seatown meant something and that in future the wishes and needs and sufferings of Seatown people must be attended to. . . .

No one apparently knew it at the time, but it became clear after that Romney was present in the crowd. Some weeks later he described it to Mary Bassett.

"What were you doing there?" she asked him suspiciously. "How did you know that anything was going to happen?"

"Darling, it's my business to know. My only use in this world is to be a kind of news carrier."

"Not a very honourable job."

"Oh, honourable, darling! What an old-fashioned word! I'm surprised at you. Nevertheless, I *was* there. It was a strange enough sight too. They were all so quiet. There was scarcely a murmur while Tom Caul was speaking. I've seen him drive them into a frenzy, but on that night they didn't want to waste their breath. The moon looked sick and the river looked sicker, and there they all were, packed as tight as sardines."

Where did they all come from? No one knew—not even Romney. The last riot in Polchester—the only other one within anyone's living memory—had been on that night nearly thirty years before when Harmer John had been killed. That had been a small affair compared with this present one, but on that occasion as on this men and women had appeared from nowhere.

Under that opalescent moon it did not seem too unreal to

suppose that old long-dead ruffians of the past Seatown life were mingling in that crowd—restless, rebellious ghosts, always ready for a tussle again, so that it seemed to them only a moment of time since the river battle of the pirate ships, the fight for the Rock, the smugglers' battles in King George's day, the riots of the Reform bill.

Once the margin of the river had run with blood and the bodies had been piled so high where the old mill is now that the stench from them had reached the none-too-fastidious nostrils of the Cathedral monks.

Over and over again it had been the battle between the Seatown outlaws and the Cathedral priests. Tonight once more that old warfare was renewed. When Tom Caul had finished speaking, the crowd slowly began to move. Very definite arrangements must have been made, for soon they were marching in pretty good order, four abreast, up Bridge Street. Another proof of the power that Tom Caul exercised was the wonderful silence. Coming up from the river, in that faint moonlight, it was as though a big scale-backed mastodon raised its head from the marshy banks and began to coil up the hill towards the Rock. The Cathedral bells chimed eight o'clock just as the head of the procession reached the small square with the Queen Victoria monument. This was apparently their first work of destruction. The Queen was represented, as she so often was, seated on a stone chair wearing her crown and carrying a sceptre. It was a very ugly and misshapen statue. In a very short time Victoria's head was in the road, her squat but dignified body tumbled to pieces. It was at this moment that the crowd began to express a kind of indignant life, and it was at this moment that the town awoke to what was occurring.

At eight o'clock most citizens were in their own homes. Queues had formed outside the Arden and the Grand cinemas for the programme that began at eight-fifteen. At the Arden they were showing *Henry VIII* with Charles Laughton; at the Grand *Tugboat Annie* with Marie Dressler and Wallace Beery. At the Old Philharmonic in Queen Anne Street the Polchester Choral Society were giving a performance of *Iolanthe*. At

the Y.M.C.A. in Pontippy Square there was a concert for the
Young Women's Friendly, and Porteous was in the chair.
The only other gathering of any note was the meeting of the
Shakespeare Society at Canon Cronin's. They were to read
Julius Cæsar. Gaselee was to be Brutus, the Archdeacon Mark
Antony, Dale Cæsar. They were all gathered together in the
Cronin drawing room, standing about, chatting and looking
at their parts once again to make sure that no tiresome in-
decencies had escaped their attention, when Mrs. Cronin's
maid, Bertha, forgetting for once her careful training, ran into
the drawing room exclaiming: "Oh, mum! . . . we're all to be
murdered! They're rioting down at the Market something
fearful!"

Up at the Castle, Lord and Lady St. Leath had been at
dinner some quarter of an hour—a very quiet and domestic
meal, the two of them alone in the great dining room, the
candles on their small table illuminating one patch of polished
floor and panelled wall.

It happened that at that moment when eight struck on the
chiming clock in the hall, St. Leath was speaking of Gurney.

"I don't know what's come to the feller. I always knew he
was slow, of course, but then I'm slow myself. But the months
have gone by and the murderer still at large. It's damned uncomfortable having somebody hangin' around ready to cut
your throat. I don't know what's *happened* to Gurney. A good
bird this, Joan—and cooked to a T."

"I'm sure Gurney's doing his best, Johnny. They can't find
the body, that's the trouble."

The telephone rang. The butler went, and returning murmured:

"Inspector Gurney on the telephone, my lord."

"Well, I'm damned," St. Leath said.

He was away for some time.

"Your food's getting cold, darling."

"Never mind the food! What do you think? It's come at
last!"

448

"What's come?"

"Russian Revolution. Stalin is in the Market-place surrounded by a yelling mob. The ghost of old Furze is hanging from a lamp-post!" He bent down and kissed her cheek. "Seriously, dearest, I must go. The Seatowners have broken out, as everyone expected they would. We'll have that fellow Caul in jail in an hour's time."

"A riot! Here! In Polchester!"

"Yes—it's happened before, you know, and will happen again—so long as we leave Seatown standing. I must be off! Old Gurney sounds quite elated. I'll ring up from the Town Hall."

After he was gone Joan St. Leath sat—waiting and listening. So before she had waited, all those years ago on Jubilee night. She was thinking of her husband, not her father—seeing, in the town library, an indignant young man with a bulldog and he was crying out: "But this is scandalous, Miss Milton! If Miss Brandon ordered the book she must have it! My mother can wait!"

She smiled. What a wonderful success their marriage had been! What a lot she had to be thankful for! She went to the window, opened it, and stood there listening.

At the St. Leath Hotel, as the gong sounded for the eight o'clock dinner, Bellamy, Aldridge (completing his second year as mayor), Crispangle and Carris were sitting down to a men's four at bridge. They had played bridge together at the St. Leath once a week for years.

"So it's Mike Furze," Bellamy said, lighting his pipe.

"I always knew it," Crispangle said.

"Well, it clears poor old Lampiron. That was always fantastic anyway! The only thing is, they haven't found the body yet. You can't try a man for murder without the body, can you?"

"No." Crispangle stretched his arms and yawned. "The damnable part of all this nonsense is that it's bad for business. I've never had a worse beginning of a season, what with these twopenny libraries springing up in March Street and Denver

Street, and the foul book societies, and novelists writing a million words a day! Books have gone to the devil."

Aldridge, who looked very green about the gills, said: "What I say is that all this nervousness murders the digestion! There's my boy goes out every night with the Town Guard, and his mother not sleeping because she's expecting him to be killed every minute. And I'm weak, weak as butter. There I was last night knowing pork plays the devil with me. And what do I go and do?"

Someone was standing in the doorway. "You're wanted on the phone, Mr. Aldridge."

The Mayor got up and left the room.

Carris said: "I'm taking the wife and girls for a cruise. I'm sick of the way things have gone here this summer. That trick of O'Hara's—well, I don't mind confessing to you boys that I'd have cut off my right hand . . ." He stopped and began to shuffle the cards.

Carris is not the man he was, Crispangle thought—got Mrs. Braund on his conscience. I bet he had a few words to say to his lady wife on the subject.

Aldridge was in the room again. He was breathless with his news. "I've got to go. They're rioting down in the Market. . . ."

Bellamy and Carris jumped up.

"Rioting? . . . Who are?"

"Who do you think? A mob come up from Seatown. I've got to be at the Town Hall."

"My God!" Crispangle said. "So it's come."

Carris laughed. "Something definite at last, thank the Lord. We'll go with you and support you, James."

They all hurried out together, leaving the cards deserted on the green cloth.

The town was stirring.

From the dignified houses in the Precincts, Orange Street, Arden Square, to the old survivals of Pontippy Square, Canon's Yard, Norman Row, through the now dark empty shops of Bellamy's, Smith's, Polrudden's the genteel hairdresser's,

Mellock's the pastrycook's, Cooper's Art Gallery, the Library, to the slums and degradations of Bridge Street and Tontine Bridge, Daffodil Street, Myre Street, the brick and mortar, the worm-eaten boards, the flaky plasters, the iron-and-steel doorknobs, and window ledges, old brick chimneys and the fine panelled walls of eighteenth-century elegances—everywhere the whisper ran:

"We are in danger again. There is trouble once more. Fire and smoke are abroad. Hold on. Hold fast. We are in danger— in danger."

If you listened you could hear strange murmurs carried by the rising wind. For example, it was remembered afterwards by many people that the bells of St. James's began to ring at eight o'clock. St. James's had a very musical peal, and this was simply the weekly evening practice of the bellringers; but it was known that old Marlowe had been found preaching like a madman in Riverside Street, so it was supposed at once that he had ordered the peal as a kind of crazy danger signal to the town. The wind rose to almost gale force on this particular night. This was the night when the *Vesper* was wrecked off Hester Point and nine lives lost.

A romantic imagination might suppose that many of the old houses in Pontippy Square and Canon's Yard were creaking and groaning in fear, but in actual fact two chimney-pots came down in Pontippy Square and a number of tiles were blown off the roof of Miss Bennett's "Cathedral Shop," No. 3 Norman Row. Klitch himself afterwards said that never in the whole of his life before had he known houses quiver and shake in the wind as the Norman Row buildings on that stormy night. They were very ancient, some of them going back to the sixteenth century. It may well be believed that the old ladies in Mrs. Coole's, No. 10, were frightened, especially when the mob reached the Cathedral Green. Mrs. Coole herself, very far from terror, played a marked part in the last stages of the affair.

When the crowd reached the Market-place it was clearly astonished at meeting no opposition. There was not a sign of a policeman anywhere. The mob, which had now the concerted emotions and passions of one person, had to make up its mind as to what it was there to do. One impulse had been an appeal to the Mayor at the Town Hall, another to release Lanky Moon and young M'Canlis from the gaol, yet another to burn down Hattaway's house as a warning to him to leave Seatown alone, yet another was to be some kind of assault on the clergy, and it was here, in the Market-place, that two effigies were produced, one a clumsy and insulting attempt at Mrs. Braund riding a stuffed clothes-horse, the other the image of a clergyman in a white stiff collar and gaiters.

But it was here also that three men suddenly stood up on a board raised on trestles and held aloft an image of Stephen Furze. Seen there in the moonlight the resemblance was almost horrible. The usurer had been thin enough in real life, and there he was, his head on one side under his soup-plate bowler, his long grey overcoat flapping against the stake on which the head was stuck. The effigy was blown hither and thither by the wind and seemed to have a ghastly life of its own. Against this was fastened a board on which was printed in capital letters:

WE DEMAND THE MURDERER

The unexpected sight of this effigy seemed to rouse the crowd, which now filled the whole of the Market-place, to riotous energy.

Tom Caul jumped onto the board beside the other men and cried out:

"Friends! In this Market-place my brother for many years quietly carried out his peaceful business. He was foully murdered. No steps have been taken to avenge him. They threaten to pull down our homes, to destroy our livelihoods. They take our savings to fill the paunches of the lazy greedy parsons up there on the hill. You know that old man in front of whose image I'm standing. He was the wickedest and greediest old swine this town has ever known. He tried to bleed many of us to death. Well, someone has done him in, but until his murderer is caught and hanged his ghost refuses to be laid. As the police are incompetent I suggest we go and catch the murderer for them. It's time we stood up for our rights, and old Furze shall see that we get 'em!"

A great roar of laughter went up at this, and then shouts and cries of rage. The crowd was quite suddenly violently alive. It had gone so far that it must now go further.

It also now became clear for the first time that much liquor had been distributed. Several old women were dancing about, quite shamelessly drunk, and the leader of them, the noisiest and most violent, was Mrs. M'Canlis, the mother of young M'Canlis—a very unpleasant sight, an old skinny woman, holding up her skirts, a bonnet on one side of her head, dancing about, singing and shouting about her son and screaming for murder.

It was now beyond question that the more serious men in the affair saw that they must go the whole way. Whither that would lead them they could not know, and it is probable that one or two of the fanatics, Ottley of the billiard saloon, and Sandy Lugge, a half-crazed old-clothes man who had once been a local Methodist preacher, really fancied that this might be the beginning of a rising all over England. Why not? Stranger things had happened. One thing led to another. What could Gurney and his policemen do against numbers like these? Once fire the Town Hall and one or two other important buildings and they would frighten everyone into some sort of surrender.

There is no doubt that the effigy of Furze had a great effect on the crowd. They had hated that figure so violently when he was alive that hatred, roused again by the sight of him, passed on, wave after wave, to other objects—Hattaway, Mrs. Braund, Lampiron, Gurney—anyone you pleased.

The destruction of that night actually began with the breaking of the windows of Cooper's Art Gallery, and it was here that Leggett, of all people in the town, was the first unexpected victim.

THE INQUISITOR

In many later summaries of these events—the entire sequence from the arrival of Michael Furze in Polchester to the climax of the riots—a quite disproportionate amount of importance was given to Leggett. Had he but known it his vanity would most certainly have been flattered! This little ugly baldheaded vicious rat of a coward! The theory was that first he had been behind Stephen Furze in everything, and secondly, he was, afterwards, the principal inspirer of Lanky Moon and Caul. This all unquestionably ranks him too high.

Leggett was an important element in this story, not because he was himself effective, but because, in his vanity, eagerness for power, jealousy, meanness and viciousness he stirred up everywhere the passions of his neighbours.

It is not the strong who are dangerous in this world but the weak. It is the weak who inspire strong men to attempt what the weak have not strength to accomplish. Had Leggett lived in Russia he would have been a useful member of the Ogpu. As it was, Stephen and Michael Furze, Tom Caul and Lanky Moon, Marlowe, Elizabeth—many another—behaved as they did partly because Leggett failed to behave as he wanted to. In any case his hope of cutting an important figure in the world ended abruptly, there and then, in front of Cooper's Art Gallery.

There is no doubt, from what he said to Caul on the afternoon of that same day, but that he had lived in a considerable state of terror during that last week. It seemed that he had for some obscure reason suddenly become convinced that Stephen Furze had not been murdered but was almost at once returning from a hiding place in the country. This thought of Furze's return convulsed him with terror. He would have left Polchester that same afternoon were it not that Symon, Furze's lawyer, kept him there with some threat or another. There was no dirty work of Leggett's of which Symon was not aware. Or it may have been that Leggett could not bear to leave Polchester without bringing off some kind of revenge against Lampiron. That moment when Lampiron had knocked him down had done something final to Leggett—the beginning of a finality which his conversation with Marlowe completed. He knew that any man now might, if he had only the spirit to venture it, stamp on him, spit on him, drive him at the cart tail.

At any rate he certainly went to Tom Caul on that last afternoon and did his best to prove to him that Lampiron had pushed Caul's brother over the Rock. Tom Caul believed it all right. He didn't need proofs, he said.

And then it may be that Leggett sniffed death. Fear of death had been his companion his life long. Those who have an extravagant fear of death savour it in their nostrils. In any case Leggett was seen by Fanny Clarke and another woman hurrying up Bridge Street, after his visit to Caul, panting, his hand at his side, his face white-streaked, just as though old Furze were really behind him.

If one dignifies this Polchester episode with the name of history, any observant chronicler of it might remark that there are Leggetts and Romneys in every revolution. They are perhaps two of the most important figures—the ambitious coward and the sexless diplomat—the despot's two forerunners.

Again, speaking historically, it was about eight-fifteen when the mob smashed the Art Gallery windows. The glow here was very uncertain. There was one lamp post outside the Gallery, and to the left could be seen the lights of High Street, but it was at this point that a number of lighted tarred stakes and sticks appeared blazing above the heads of the crowd. The mob was now for the first time really vocal.

Being now one entity it spoke with one voice, an animal voice, the low thunderous growl that rises sharply to a scream but is more menacing in its undertones. It was Leggett who provoked the next move. The Art Gallery was once one of Polchester's most beautiful eighteenth-century houses, standing alone, with gardens at the back of it, and there is still a stone mounting block to the left of the fine carved doorway. Leggett was suddenly seen, standing on the mounting block, gesticulating and shaking his gloved fist at the swaying effigy of Furze.

In the high wind his words were lost. No one will ever know what Leggett's last words on this planet were—not, in all probability, words of wisdom. It may be that, confronted un-expectedly by that image of his ancient enemy, maddened by the thought of the injustices, frustrations, tyrannies that he had suffered at that old devil's hands, he attempted some kind of last futile defiance.

He looked in any case sufficiently ludicrous there, his bald head gleaming in the lamplight, his ugly distorted visage, his gesture of frustration and failure as he shook his fist at a scarecrow.

What followed may have been also his own doing—he may, so to speak, have ordered his own funeral or chosen his manner of suicide.

Some fools in the crowd may have felt his gesticulations as a kind of order to action. In any case it was then and there that the first stones were thrown—a whole volley of them. The glass went crashing and one of the stones caught Leggett on the side of the head. He fell and the crowd surged forward, already forgetting him, for he was one of those men who, once their needful act is committed, are at once forgotten.

The crowd surged forward and he was trampled to shape-lessness. He was stamped to death without any living soul realizing that he was there. At that moment when, half stunned, he struggled to rise and a boot kicked his eyes, he must have known one instant of frantic horror—a sudden cry of his soul: "It has come. It is as terrible as I feared!" When, afterwards, he was found, his eyeballs were crushed, his nose stamped flat, his chest ripped open. On his right hand there was still a dirty lavender-coloured glove.

At Carpledon, Bishop Kendon was just finishing his dinner —drinking with great satisfaction his glass of hot water which was all the stimulating beverage he was allowed.

"It is strange, Coniston, what the imagination can do. Hot water can become . . ." He broke off. "Isn't that the telephone?"

"Yes, my lord. Walter is answering it."

"And now for a few records." He raised his long thin arms

above his head and smiled. "There is something very satisfying about that roaring wind. I hope those two birches near the orchard gate stand it, though. It's a real gale. . . . We'll have a little music. Come and put on the records, Coniston. I'm lazy—and then in bed a few chapters of that new book on Hans Andersen. Where is it? I hope I didn't lend it to Miss Merdstone when she came about the Women's Guild this afternoon. I'm so weak when someone wants to borrow a book. And Miss Merdstone, Coniston. Such an unfortunate name. Whenever we meet I want to talk to her about donkeys. . . ."

He walked into the study where the gramophone was, his long thin body moving slowly, as though keeping guard on itself quite apart from its owner.

At the door of the study young Walter appeared:

"You're wanted on the telephone, my lord. . . ." Then he added breathlessly: "There's rioting in the town."

A minute later Kendon called out to Coniston:

"The car . . . I must go at once."

Coniston said: "What is it, my lord? . . . But you shouldn't. Really you should not . . . You know what . . ."

But the Bishop was in the hall, wrapping his muffler round his throat. He listened to the wind.

"Perhaps it will happen this way," he said to himself.

The blowing torches thrust their faces into the black abysses left by the broken windows. The lower rooms of the Art Gallery suddenly flared into life and you could see plaster casts of Julius Cæsar, the blind Homer and Æschylus, while, lonely in his splendid endurance and symmetry, in the middle of the floor, was a bad reproduction of the Dying Gladiator. There were drawings pinned on the walls—drawings of the nude, of the Cathedral, and a number of baskets of flowers. The mob peered in but it did not stay. The breaking of those windows had done something to its spirit—acted as a kind of fire water. Someone, without knowing it, gave Leggett's muddied cheek a last kick and passed on. They all passed on.

The Town Hall was not far distant, facing St. Leath Square

above the Market and to the left of the High Street. This is a charming old square with cobblestones, a fountain presented to the town by the widow of Sam Hooker, Mayor of Polchester in 1882–87. There are some trees, a bench or two; the Town Hall itself is one of the best architectural things in Polchester, with a broad flight of stone steps, a simple dignified façade, and, in the hall, an enormous oil painting of Dido Forsaken by Æneas. All these minutiæ had on this occasion their importance, for the benches were destroyed, the fountain lost its charming figure of Boy with Flute, and before the mob moved on, the famous Dido picture had been stoned, Dido herself torn asunder.

The mob filled the Square, and on the steps to meet them were Aldridge and a number of town officials, Lord St. Leath and Gurney.

One of the things that will never be truly known was the amount of liquor distributed among the rioters—also by whom distributed? It is certain that in the crowd outside the Town Hall many were drunk, but at the same time it was here and now that the more serious element in the movement became manifest. And a very serious element it was! Lord St. Leath said afterwards that it was only when he looked down on the mob from the steps of the Town Hall that he knew that these people meant murder. *Why* they meant murder he will never be able to understand. Johnny St. Leath had no imagination and has been the happier for not having it, but he loved, and loves, this town like his own child. The angers, mistrusts, fears of the last months had altogether bewildered him; his final state of exasperation was reached by the trick played on Mrs. Braund and now he was a very angry man. He said afterwards the very sight of that ridiculous image of Furze swaying in the smoky light "turned his stomach"—and the first thing he shouted at them was: "What's that damned scarecrow doing here? I won't talk to you until you throw it away." He was Lord Lieutenant of the County, and that was often quite a lot —it was nothing tonight. He knew at once that it was not. He knew that he and Aldridge and the rest of them, his beloved

town as well, were in very real and actual danger. Later he
told Joan, his wife, that you'd have thought Furze was waving
them on. He seemed to gesticulate in the wind. "If I'd had
anything to throw I'd have had a pot at the thing."

They had, however, determined—he and Aldridge and
Gurney—that nothing provocative should be done on their side
until the Riot Act had been read. First the mob would be asked
to disperse. This St. Leath now did.

He was immensely popular in Polchester. He had been born
there; they had known him as a chubby snub-nosed boy home
from Eton, as a thickset bulldog-attended undergraduate;
they had watched the tenacious patient love for Joan Brandon
and approved, to a woman and a man, when he had married
her in spite of all the family scandal and the protests of a
cockatoo of a mamma; they had admired and loved and trusted
him, his honour, his fidelity, his courage, his love for his king,
country, town and family through all these years of war and
change and uncertainty. They knew that he was not very
clever, Johnny St. Leath, but they liked him all the better for
that. They were not very clever either. He had no side: he and
Lady St. Leath were generous and tactful in their charities.
Everyone in Polchester knew that Johnny St. Leath stood for
something very valuable to England, a type, often mocked
and derided, not to be found anywhere else in the world. . . .

And now he did not know them! As he stood on the Town
Hall steps looking at them, he felt a kind of confirmation of
all his bewilderment of the last months. There *was* some evil
influence abroad in this, his town. He was simple enough to
believe in evil. He had known "fellers" at school, college, in
the war, who were "damned rotters, you know—had a sort of
stink." Well, now in this town there was "a sort of stink."
And it must be got rid of.

He looked at them and his indignation grew. There were
many faces that he did not know. Tom Caul, standing over
there on the bench near the fountain, was their leader—but
there were many worse than Caul. Where had they come from?

Well, no matter, he would tell them where they could go to!
. . . And he did. He asked them what they wanted, why they
were there, what they were after. Then he warned them that
they were breaking the law. He told them that if they dispersed
now no further action would be taken, but that if they remained after the Riot Act had been read, their blood would
be on their own heads. Then he became their own familiar
colloquial Johnny St. Leath. What the hell were they doing,
behaving in this absurd manner? Who had told them to?
What did they hope to get from it? What after all *were* their
grievances? These were hard times, as he himself knew, but
that was not the fault of the Polchester authorities. He himself . . .

And at this moment someone threw a stone and caught him
on the forehead above the left eye. Being hit by that stone
was perhaps the very worst, most wounding thing that ever
happened to Johnny St. Leath. That in his own beloved town
where he had lived for years surrounded by friends he should
be stoned! should be hissed and struck on the very steps of
the Town Hall. . . . He put up his hand and felt the blood
dripping into his eye. His rage convulsed him.

"By God!" he said, turning to Aldridge. "Give me the Riot
Act."

He read it to them.

Riots and revolutions, like pestilence, wars and love, must,
when started, run to their climax. In front of the Town Hall
members of that mob began to discover themselves. Some
wished to go home: many wanted to remain what they had
been at the beginning, observers. Very many translated their
own personal grievances—an ulcer, a debt, a rent unpaid, a
quarrel, a headache, a general malaise, a bad wife, a frustrated
lust, hunger—into a determination on revenge. Men throw
stones in riots because their wives think poorly of them.

There were some who followed a definite plan. Tom Caul
had been waiting for this moment his life long, ever since he
and his blind brother had, as children, been beaten within an

inch of their lives by a sadistic coal heaver whose mistress their mother was. Caul was part fanatic, part swollen with pride, part enraged at his brother's death. He did not see to the end of this, but, whichever way it went, there would be, he thought, glory and self-justification for himself in it. Self-justification! He wanted that, perhaps, more than anything else in life. At certain times when the world was silent and he alone in it he mocked, with bitter contempt, at himself and all that had made him.

Lastly, there were the fanatics who saw stars and thrones and crowned martyrs blazing through the sky. There were only a few of them.

While St. Leath read the Riot Act at the Town Hall these separate elements became one element. When more than twelve persons are gathered together there is seldom sense talked. Twelve persons become one person obeying the lowest denominator.

And now this mob was suddenly one person, a shrill, screaming, brainless maniac carrying a torch in one hand and a scarecrow in the other. This imbecile, directed by a cold, determined power, wished to destroy. It brandished the torch, it followed the scarecrow. St. Leath, Aldridge, Gurney, seen through smoke, were puppets, and before the eyes of this screaming silly creature were wood and plaster to be burned, walls of glass to be broken and whirling circles of human faces to be hammered.

"All right—they shall have it," Johnny St. Leath said to Gurney.

A moment later the Square was surrounded by the police. But they were not fast enough at Abbot's Lane. Gurney said afterwards that Abbot's Lane, which led straight through Kirk Street to the High Street, was to have been the first to be blocked, but in surrounding the Square the policemen had filed in from the east end instead of the west. Caul had seen this at once—he had many of the qualities of a true leader. He had waved his arm, and a second later they were pouring through Abbot's Lane to the High Street.

"Bloody fool, Gurney," St. Leath murmured. There was nothing to be done. There in the St. Leath Square the police were moving slowly forward, marshalling what remained of the mob towards the Market. What remained, however, were simply those pacific elements who thought they would like to go home. Quite a number but not an important number.

"Quick, Gurney," St. Leath shouted. "Get your men up to the Cathedral." But Gurney, poor Gurney, whose life's tragedy this night was to be, was not born to be quick. This was his first experience of a riot and, as unkind fate in the shape of higher authorities afterwards decided, his last.

Tom Caul and his friends had, for an appreciable five minutes, the High Street altogether to themselves.

A number of citizens—the Bennett family, the Mellocks, Crispangle's wife, the assistants at Bellamy's who lived in—will, as long as life lasts, take pleasure in describing that mad rush up the High Street, as, terror in their souls, they watched it from behind window blinds.

The very heart of the town was now invaded as it had never been since the Middle Ages. Once again from the very face of the Rock, from the heart of the river, the Goths, the Huns, the gipsies, the Heathen, assaulted the Cathedral, not knowing that it was the Cathedral itself that had, for its own purposes, roused them up.

"God help us," said old Mrs. Mellock, whose plump body seemed always to smell faintly of flour.

Mrs. Crispangle, whose heart must be filled with men or it scarcely beat, knew suddenly that she loved her large cynical husband. Where was he? Out in the town somewhere. He had gone to play bridge at the St. Leath. He might be there still. She moved into the back office and telephoned. No. He'd left for the Town Hall with Mr. Aldridge.

Scarcely knowing what she was doing, she put on her hat and coat. She must go out and find him.

The mob roared up the street, shouting it knew not what. Behind the windows they all whispered: "The Cathedral! They'll go for the Cathedral."

The mob itself was aware that the climax of the affair was approaching it. At the top of the hill, in front of Arden Gate, it paused. Behind it were the police, in front of it the Cathedral. Up here the wind was raging. The lighted stakes flourished in the wind, but across the Cathedral Green all was dark. Only the mass of the Cathedral was black against the oyster-pale sky, the thin moon behind swathes of tenuous cloud. The Cathedral waited. The mob waited.

The mob waited, in fact, for it knew not what. It knew only that it wished to show that it was an important mob with a character of its own and to do that thoroughly it must destroy something.

So it set fire to the Library. No one will ever know how, or by whom that was done. Nor will anyone ever understand why, on that night of raging wind, the whole of the High Street was not burnt down and much else with it. The police and the fire brigade together did some noble work, but later, when the mob was scrambling on the Cathedral Green, why, in that first ten minutes, had the whole of Polchester not started to blaze?

Enough for the moment that that old room, historic in the lives of so many of us, blazed to the heavens, and Clara Reeve, Bage, Godwin, Cooper, and all the others with it! Never again would a young Jeremy Cole slip in and borrow a new Haggard, the most recent Pemberton! Is the skeleton of Miss Milton there crackling in the flame? Where now is that untidy schoolboy, his black cap with its yellow lettering sideways, dust on his cheeks and nose, astride the ladder, his begrimed fingers turning the pages of *The Wandering Jew?*

The ghosts, broomstick riding, fly with the flames into the vaporous sky. . . . The mob is aware for the first time that it has done something. The noise now is the echo of the sea through trees. Men and women scream like gulls. The wild unsteady glare of the burning library lights up the whole High Street; the sky is glittering with sparks and jets of gold. The Cathedral now sails forward, all its windows glowing. . . . Then someone started the cry of "The soldiers!" and no one ever knew where *that* call came from. It was enough in any case to bring to a point of madness the panic, confusion, and uncertainty of that rebellion.

"By God!" said Caul. "If it's the soldiers we'll fight them"—but that was absurd because they had nothing to fight real soldiers with! They had, however, their sticks, knives, hatchets and a pistol or two, and now, with the thought that the soldiers were at the bottom of the street pressing up on them, with the fierce independent life of the Library burning in their eyes, they rushed forward to Arden Gate, under it and on to the Green.

It was here and now that the first real battle occurred, for Gurney had managed at last to bring some of his men up, through Green Lane and out to the top of the High Street along Norman Row. And a fine sight it was for Mrs. Coole's old ladies, for the Fowlers, father, mother and son, of the Glebeshire Tea-shop, for Broad the verger, his wife, his son Timothy, for Mr. Doggett the organist, above all for the Klitch family, from behind their window curtains, to see the marching policemen, the sky illuminated with the Library fire, and to hear the roaring shout of the mob, to look across the Green and admire the Cathedral so calmly facing its enemy.

"I'm going out," said Mrs. Coole.

"I'm going out," said Klitch.

But the first actual fighting occurred just inside the Arden Gate. Caul, followed by some of the more desperate spirits, started in the direction of Mrs. Braund's house.

(Mrs. Braund, lying flat on her bed, sees the sky flare, hears shouts, sees the trees rock in the wind.

"It's all right," says the nurse consolingly. "They won't be coming here, the ruffians."

But Mrs. Braund moves not a muscle. She had known that this would occur. Perhaps after this Lady Emily will be satisfied.

"Go on with your book, please," she murmurs out of the corner of her crooked mouth.)

Caul and his friends may have vaguely thought they would have at some of the "blasted clergy." By this time the plan of campaign had fallen into an untidy wantonness.

Caul lifted his stick and a policeman's eye was laid open.

"Take that for a bastard," Caul, suddenly berserk, shouted. Soon everywhere the Green, chequered with the dancing reflection of flame, was thick with fighters. Fighters for what? By this time no one knew. . . .

It was now that Lampiron appeared.

His legs stretched in front of him, the studio dark behind him, he had been reading Santayana's *Character and Opinions in the United States* when Bridget, his old servant, cried from the doorway: "They are murdering and burning all over the town."

He finished what he was reading. It was a key for him for the remainder of the evening. He read:

"Veritable lovers of life, like Saint Francis or like Dickens, know that in every tenement of clay, with no matter what endowment or station, happiness and perfection are possible to the soul. There must be no brow-beating, with shouts of work or progress or revolution, any more than with threats of hell-fire. What does it profit a man to free the whole world if his soul is not free? Moral freedom is not an artificial condition, because the ideal is the mother tongue of both the heart and the senses. All that is requisite is that we should pause in living to enjoy life, and should lift up our hearts to things that are pure good in themselves, so that once to have found and loved them, whatever else may betide, may remain a happiness that nothing can sully. . . ."

"Veritable lovers of life. . . ." Yes, he was that. Indeed, he was that!

He looked up. "What do you say, Bridget?"

"They're burning the town down. Killing and slaying. Something awful."

"Who are?"

"Seatown roughs—and foreigners."

He smiled at her. Oh, he was a handsome old man, she thought, with his black hair and shoulders like an ox, his face so brown, his eyes so blue—a clean strong old man whatever they might say! *He'd* never murdered anybody, not he! And now as like as not they were coming to do him a harm.

"Sir . . ." she repeated it. He appeared not to be listening. "Sir . . . maybe they'll be coming this way."

"Veritable lovers of life. . . . What does it profit a man to free the whole world if his soul is not free?" *There* was something for the propagandists, the lecturers, the preachers! But his own soul *was* free at last, for the first time. He got up and stretched his arms, yawning.

"All right, Bridget. I'll go out and have a look at them. More words than deeds, I expect."

He looked about the room. He was quite radiantly at peace. After all the turmoil, passionate lusts and temptations, futile effort to conquer some kind of beauty, this last love for a child, this last tournament against his fellow men's abuse, now these words . . . ". . . We should pause in living to enjoy life." Ah, but he had enjoyed life if anyone had and now he was ready to go. Someone had shown him in these last months where true values lay—in that inner, secure, vitalizing life of the spirit. Who had shown him? What company had he been keeping? Had he come close in some way to the spirit of Arden? Or was there even now in the room with him a dark companion? . . . No matter.

"Thanks," he said aloud.

He went out.

The first thing that, standing in the street, he noticed was the reflection of the fire in the sky. About him everything was quiet save for the rushing of the wind, the bending and creaking of the boughs, the running of the river under the bridge.

He decided to make for the Cathedral and, moving very quickly, he climbed Orange Street, cut through into Green Lane and then by Canon's Yard and Norman Row reached the Green. Here for a moment he stayed amazed. There is nothing more astonishing to the observer than the instant's transformation of a well-known tranquil street or town into destruction and danger. It is as though some old pipe-smoking book-collecting bachelor friend produced from his pocket a rattlesnake.

And yet, Lampiron thought, this scene is familiar to me. It is even more familiar than it is in its ordinary tranquillity. He had seen it once when all the buildings to the west of it were blazing and the sky was a sheet of trembling gold. He had ridden under the Gate and stood at the hill-rise shouting. . . . But this was absurd. There was more immediate business than romantic dreams. He was at the edge of the Green not far from the trees that bordered the Braund house, and the next thing of which he was really aware was that Gaselee was at his elbow.

"Why, Gaselee!"

Gaselee peered.

"Oh, it's you, Lampiron! I say, isn't this awful! They're crazy. They'll be doing the Cathedral damage."

"What's it all about?"

"I don't know. No one knows. It's been brewing for months."

"Well, what are *we* going to do?" Lampiron was impatient. He had never cared for Gaselee very much anyway. "We can't leave them to burn the Cathedral down."

"There! . . . The police are moving forward."

"Time they did."

Gaselee made no reply. This old man, Lampiron, was a bore and, in any case, he felt uncomfortable, a kind of sickness in his stomach. This was not *his* world. *His* world must be ordered, with planks across the ditches and walls above the precipices . . . and Ronder was dead.

"Do you know," he said, "Ronder's dead——"

But Lampiron was gone.

Black figures, like puppets, began to run across the grass. There was a pistol shot. Mounted police came sweeping over the Green. Gaselee hurried, then he trotted, then he began to run. . . .

Lampiron also was running, but he was running towards the fighters, not away from them.

As he ran he waved his arms and shouted. He knew only one thing, a pagan overmastering impulse to fight. The shadowy troubles of the last months were over. While it was his own private history that was attacked he was too proud to move, but now he was urged to defend something beyond himself.

The mob was frenzied with panic and rage. It was frightened

of the soldiers in the rear (there *were* no soldiers) and frightened of the Cathedral in front of it.

For now that they were face to face with the Cathedral what could they do about it? For months they had been threatening but they had not expected such a demand for an answer. There it was, couched and brooding in the darkness, only its long windows flaming in answer to the fire. What were they to do? It was stronger than they!

Some of them turned back, but with a great number that worst rage of all, the rage born of helplessness, leapt beside them like a wild unthinking animal. They'd have their money's worth! They'd destroy something before they went to gaol for it! Someone had passed the word that a man had been killed, his face stamped out by the crowd, and the Library was burning. They'd have to pay for these things. Let them give something in return.

But one of them afterwards described the fighting on that Green as the most terrifying experience. Only for one brief period or so, ten minutes at the most, did the crowd and the police come into real conflict. Then heads were broken and arms smashed. For the rest, young Eddie Callender told Cronin a week or two later:

"You'd have thought the Green was crowded with people. Believe me or believe me not, it was as though you couldn't move for people pressing in on you. I was feeling pretty angry myself by that time although I can't rightly say why. I don't know what I ever joined in the silly thing at all for, if you ask me. Anyway, they said the soldiers was coming up the High Street, and there was the Library burning and we'd been cursing the clergy for months down in Seatown, *and* the police, and here we were, so I just wanted to hit someone. But I couldn't. I give you my word, I could hardly breathe for the crowd, and yet there wasn't a crowd. There wasn't a lot of us left by that time. Plenty of the boys was running away down the High Street. All the same that Green was full of people that night, I give you *my* word, and I ain't telling lies either."

Tom Caul and his friends got almost to the West Door before

the mounted police rounded on them. It wasn't more than fifteen yards from the West Door that Lampiron met them. He charged right into the middle of them, shouting, waving his arms, and at once he had caught two men, one after another, with his fists and down they went. That in fact was glorious—he had been thirsting for it for years; he achieved with it something his bad sculpture could never do. He was calm enough to realize, all the same, that he'd need a weapon of some sort, and as the second man fell (he himself nearly falling over him) he bent and took a rough nailed stake from his hand.

He shouted something like "Get back! Get back! . . . The Cathedral isn't for *you!*" or some nonsense of that kind, or were they the old words: "God's servant! Beware of God's servant!"

It mattered nothing. He felt that he was equal to a world of enemies and rebels. The whole affair can have lasted no more than two or three minutes and yet he felt as though all his life had been intended only for this—not so much for the joy of fighting as for the good clear common sense of his purpose. Life had so often been clouded in its purpose. So much frustration, disappointment of the flesh, blindness of the spirit, but at last he was defending something well worthy of defence. He could hear singing in his ears, the chanting of some old psalm, and in his nostrils there was the sweet stench of incense, armour clashed, and against flame-light he saw a sword raised. No; rather what he saw was young Dawlish who drove round crying vegetables and boxed a bit in his spare time; Lampiron had taken an interest in him once until he stole some suits and shirts and tried to seduce a little kitchenmaid Lampiron had at the time. So now Lampiron (the sweat was pouring down his face, his heart was pounding, his belly was cold and pressed by the shirt of mail he wore under his vestments) cried to young Dawlish, "Look out, Dawlish! . . . Get back, you young fool." But young Dawlish aimed a kick at his sensitive places, so he raised his nailed stake and brought it down on young Dawlish's head.

They were beginning to give way then. The mounted police were no joke. Men were running across the Green for their

lives. But Tom Caul wasn't. He wasn't running away for anyone.

And suddenly he saw Lampiron. This was a rich moment for
him. It was the thing he'd prayed for. "Here's for my brother."
Filth poured from him. Every obscenity at his command
obeyed. His cheek was cut, blood trickled into his mouth, cold
like a slug, he was bare to the belt round his waist. But he
dropped his stick. He went for Lampiron with his fist. A second
later they were locked in one another's arms. Lampiron hadn't
a chance. He was sixty-eight years of age. Caul was the strong-
est man in Glebeshire. Nevertheless those shoulders worked one
last time for their master. Lampiron broke Caul's arm-lock,
slowly heaved himself up, stood with Caul's arms about his
thighs. With a kick he was free for a moment of eternal time,
and in that moment, remembering all the glory of love and creation and the day when he watched the sunlit sea spread like a
fan over the hot earth, he cried, his arm raised (he felt his ringed
mail press against the nipples of his breasts and the cold edge
of the fine steel at the point where it met the bare thigh):

"God's servant! . . . God's servant!"

Then they fell on him; Caul had him round the waist, and it
was Eels Braddock, they said afterwards (but it was never
proved), who brought the iron spike down on his head. Some
one or other leapt at his head and he fell to the ground with
him; Lampiron's blood blinded him.

That was the way Lampiron died. Leggett one way, Lampiron
quite another. . . .

That was the moment, just when the mounted police turned
the skirts of the mob, that the Cathedral blazed and Kendon
stood in the West Door.

Kendon's orders. When he reached the Cathedral (this was
about the time when the mob rushed up the High Street) he
sent for Dale, Cronin, Doggett, poor old Broad. He put on his
vestments and himself switched on the electric light. Then he
stood in the West Door with Dale and Cronin beside him.

That sudden illumination of the Cathedral was a stroke of

genius. It sprang to life. The Green, the Town, the little puppet figures of men, sank to shadow-dimness. There was no reality save one.

But Kendon (old Mordaunt, sleeping in front of the empty fire grate, his drawings scattered on the floor, might see now in plain fact his watching, guarding figure) had no need for action. The riot was not ended, but its true climax was not as he could have expected it.

Caul had turned to run. The sudden burst of light, the springing into life of that building above him, around him, inside him, the huddled figure at his feet with the blaze from the door on the bloody shoulders, a fear of something more desperate than man (he saw the horses riding his way and never cared), started his running. He did not know where he was going, but the pressure here, crowding in on him, choking him, blinding him, catching at his knees—he must break that as you break a spider-mesh!—this turned him and, as he turned, his arm was caught and held. It was Michael Furze.

"Let go, you fool!"

Michael let go. But he ran to the Cathedral. He ran like a madman, as though he had not a minute to lose. He ran as though he were blind, his hand before his face.

He was through the West Door and inside the church as the police horses cleared the Green from end to end. Lampiron lay quite alone, his arm broken about his head.

But Michael stopped and gasped. This blazing church was the last thing that he had expected. He had been with his friends and brothers (for he loved all living things) all night, marching with them, cheering them on, laughing and singing, seeing the pretty places burn, talking, talking, talking, leading them all with him (friends and brothers: they had been unkind to him a week or two, but now they were all comrades again) to show them where all the trouble lay. The only thing that puzzled him was that dear brother Stephen, broken and mangled, yellow flies crawling out of his nose, up there in the Cathedral, was also here in this happy procession (all friends and brothers together marching to freedom) waving and bending and bowing, there in his bowler hat and old grey coat. Nothing odd in that, though. Had not brother Stephen a genius for being in two places at once? But he told them all, he told them again and again, anyone who would listen he told, that they would soon behold the sight of their lives, such a pretty sight, such a handsome sight. There they were, all marching together, and soon . . .

But they stopped, they paused. What was the matter with them? He urged them on, he implored, he beseeched. But they wouldn't listen. They ran. They ran as though Stephen himself were after them. So he went on by himself. There was nothing else to be done. He called to people as he ran. They wouldn't listen. So he ran on alone—out of darkness into this blaze of light.

For the account of what followed, Dale was the best witness. He saw and heard everything from Michael's first entrance to the last terrible moment. Young Dale was one of the best clergymen who ever served Polchester. He was fearless, a fanatic about his beliefs, but otherwise humorous, tolerant and wise. About this whole episode in Polchester he spoke, a few months later, the truest of all summaries.

He was the last man in the world to exaggerate in his account of anything. He did not rule out the possibility of miracles; he knew that insanity is as common as sanity, that the words are often interchangeable, that there are a thousand worlds and all of them true. Then he adored Kendon. Of anyone else he might have said that lighting the Cathedral was melodrama. (He did not object to melodrama. He knew that it was often the truest poetry for the occasion.) But whatever the Bishop did was right. So now he stood at his side, looking out onto the dark Green, seeing the glare fade above the Library; he went out and bent down over Lampiron's body. He looked up and saw the horses charging the Green, figures flying through the Arden Gate. A dog was howling. The wind was falling and a thin fine rain began to spatter the grass. He helped to carry Lampiron into the Cathedral. He was dead of course.

It was then that he heard Michael Furze shouting:

"Honestly that was as queer a sight as I shall ever see. The Cathedral was blazing with light and you could feel a stir everywhere. This wasn't an exaggeration, a kind of poetic licence. You people" (it was in Cronin's drawing room a week later) "can laugh if you like, and of course all our nerves were on edge by that time, but I wasn't the only one to notice it. It was like a mist when light should be clear, like faint music when there oughtn't to be a sound, like a dream when you're alone but know that you are surrounded by a thousand unseen listeners.

"All I can tell you is that the Cathedral seemed to be packed although, save for the little crowd of us by the West Door, there wasn't a soul to be seen.

"Lampiron, poor old boy, was lying there dead, his head smashed in. I was going over to him when this man Furze ran through the door, shouting something. I'd heard a lot about that old man's murder. Like everyone else in the town I'd been made uneasy by it, restless, disturbed. But so far as I know I'd never set eyes on this brother of his before. For any of you who hadn't seen him he was a fat, flabby, red-faced, sweaty fellow with a long protuberant nose. That was the only time I ever saw him and I can best describe him by saying that he seemed to me jointless, fat and loose, with sweat running down his nose.

"I hadn't of course at first the slightest notion of what he was saying. I didn't even know who he was. He seemed simply a lunatic.

"For a moment he had me by the arm. I'm thin and bony, not very muscular. I can only tell you I thought he'd break my arm. He seemed tremendously strong, flabby though he looked. There was something rather touching and pathetic about him. Well, a crazy man is always pathetic anyway.

"As he shook my arm he shouted in my ear, as the young man shouted to Father William. I can't tell you exactly what he said. It was to the effect that I must come with him and see what he had to show, that this was the end, the conclusion, the finale. He kept shouting: 'This is the end . . . We'll finish with

473

him! We'll finish with him! . . .' Naturally, I hadn't the slightest idea what he meant.

"Then he left me—as suddenly as he had come to me—and went for poor old Broad. Broad was almost off his head with fear and terror. He couldn't keep his eyes from Lampiron. I doubt whether he'd ever seen a dead man before and he'd known Lampiron very well. He was simply an aguish jelly from head to foot. His little boy was there, far less disturbed than his father was. He seemed to have a kind of protective eye on him.

"This all happened in a very few minutes, you must understand. I am trying to remember every detail.

"At any other time it might have been comic to see these two stout men, one of them shaking the other who was already shivering like a jelly. Poor Broad saw nothing to laugh at. Furze shouted: 'Open that door! Open that door! . . . Give me the key!'

"I didn't know what he meant until I saw Broad with a trembling hand unlock the little door of the Harry Tower. I learnt afterwards that this was the first day it had been opened. It had been closed, as you know, for repairs. Furze started through the door and up the stone steps like a madman. I didn't know what he was after, but I had an idea, I think, that he meant some mischief to himself. In any case I followed. Doggett was close behind me. By this time, I heard afterwards, numbers of people were pressing in through the West Door. The whole town was bordering the Green very shortly after this, the mounted police guarding it. The riot was over. The fire-brigade held the High Street. Caul and a number of others were already in the lock-up.

"Those King Harry stairs are narrow and twisty and dark. Furze was talking at the top of his voice all the way up. I was now persuaded that he was as mad as could be, and my great idea was to get to him before he could throw himself from the Gallery. But when Doggett and I reached the light and air again there was Furze standing there as quietly as could be, his finger on his lip. I don't know why, but for a minute or so both Doggett and I were dominated by him. Doggett will tell you the same. It was as though he had something very important to say to us, like the Ancient Mariner.

"What he *had* to say was really nonsense as far as I remember it. It was something about a crucifix—all the trouble had come from a crucifix. He'd offended the Cathedral in some way or another. It didn't do to play tricks with God. God was always stronger than you were. Sacrilege was the worst crime of all. He caught hold of Doggett's shoulder. Doggett said his eyes were full of tears. He was like a fat overgrown baby about to cry. What he wanted to say was that things would be all right now . . . once he and his brother were out of the way . . . but let it be a warning, a warning to everybody . . . not to commit sacrilege . . . and then something about the crucifix again. It was to Doggett he was speaking and I daresay I'm reporting him wrong. He *did*, however, use the words 'sacrilege' and 'crucifix' many times. The strange thing was that we should be standing there so quietly talking, the Cathedral fiery below us with the pillars and the arches, and someone calling up to us from the bottom of the stairs. I must tell you again—it all happened very quickly, not more than a few minutes in all.

"He broke away from us and ran up the stairs to the little room above the Gallery. We followed him quickly and, just as we got there, he turned to us, smiling excitedly, and cried, 'Look! Look! Here he is! Here he is!'

"He bent down over a hollow against the wall. He dragged something up. He pulled something across the floor. Then he bent down again and, turning to us (he was on his knees), threw something into the air with a cry like a triumphant child. It was an old dusty bowler hat. The heap on the floor looked like a pile of dirty clothes. It was a mass of corruption.

"He dragged this after him; the old dirty boots bumped against the wooden floor. I'm ashamed to say that, for that moment, neither Doggett nor I could move. We heard him bumping the thing down the stairs. We saw the tail of a shabby grey overcoat move round the corner as though it were alive. All the time Furze was shouting, talking to himself—'Come along, you old swine. Come along, you dirty old swine' and worse things. We heard the boots bump, bump against the stairs. Then we followed him. We must sound as though we were pretty useless. I can only say that it was like a dream—as though we were *forced* to be spectators. But then, too, you must remember that it all happened with very great speed.

"When we got to the Gallery he was standing by the rail. I had only a moment in which to look over, to see, as it seemed to me, a great crowd gathered in the Nave, all looking up. Then, a second later, he had gathered that filthy corpse up in his arms, raised it and flung it out, away, down into the light and haze and the waiting crowd. It spun, it circled, it fell.

"Furze, as you know, himself followed it. I remember that Doggett ran to him, caught him, I think, by the coat, but he had clambered onto the rail edge, kicked with his foot at Doggett, shouted once, twice. I hear his cry often still. It was triumphant as though he were bringing off the coup of his life. Then he fell. His legs bent, his arms stretched. I saw his nose shine. Funny the things that you notice at a crisis like that.

"I don't know, I can't tell you what happened afterwards. There were plenty of people there. I've not asked any of them. I felt very sick. I was standing in the West Door breathing the air. One thing I remember was the rain. It was coming down, softly, steadily, determinedly as though, like a word from Heaven, it were falling blessedly to wash from the earth all the stains, all the fear and blood and confusion. You know the hiss that rain gives as it falls, the gentle, beautiful, rhythmic sound. That was all. Everywhere there was quiet. I put my hand before my face and prayed."

CHAPTER IX

Outside Impression

The Times (London)
October 13, 1933

UNEMPLOYED IN POLCHESTER

A NUMBER OF UNEMPLOYED *caused a disturbance in the Cathedral town of Polchester last evening. They advanced in considerable force to the Town Hall, where they demanded to see the Mayor. The Town Library was set on fire and the windows of several buildings were broken. A conflict with the police occurred on the Cathedral Green. The rioters were quickly subdued. Three persons were killed and nineteen injured, eight of whom are in the local infirmary.*

It is reported today that everything in the town is quiet.

CHAPTER X

Epilogue: Return of the Same Music

IT WAS ON AN AFTERNOON late in January 1934 that Bishop Kendon preached his last sermon. The occasion was the Festival of St. Margaret—one of the oldest of all the Cathedral ceremonies.

The weather on that day was halcyon; the town lay soaked in that honey fragrance of a too precipitate Southern warmth; tomorrow the gales will blow in across the shivering fields and hail wil' rattle the farm windows, but today the sun lies like a warm hand on the stones of the High Street; the lanes above Orange Street are scented with almost the flower and leaf fragrance of May. Peace and stillness are iridescent in the haze of shadow and sun-shot chimney smoke. As the bells ring for the St. Margaret service Crispangle finds a purple leather prayer book for two old ladies; Bellamy stands, legs straddleways, talking to Aldridge on the sunny pavement; the bright red-brick building rising on the ruins of the old Library catches the sun and blushes perhaps for its newness; two clergymen, their hands behind their backs, walk slowly up the street, very seriously discussing their golf handicaps.

Here is Gaselee walking now a little as though the town were at his command, raising his hat to Mrs. Cronin and hoping that she won't stop him, reaching Arden Gate and pausing an instant to look down the hill of the busy street, savouring it with his nostrils, feeling the warm sun on his cheeks, sniffing that scent so especially Polcastrian, of cakes newly baked, primroses washed with rain, the salt of waves purling over crystal-shining sand, the warm brick walls of gardens, tang of Market-day dung and straw, the sudden chill of stone and brass on first entering the Cathedral—all these merging into that deep eternal odour of flowers, of rose and carnation, sweet William and dark-scented musk.

Yes, he loved this place that was to be now his home, loved it as it was today—so safe, so tranquilly merging past and present into one lovely security.

The bells pealed as though they were summoning all the countryside to the festival of that good saint who washed the feet of the beggars, cared for little children, and died, at the time of the first church, at the hands of the marauding Danes.

This would be, he reflected, one of the last sermons that the old Bishop would preach.

A pity, a pity that good men must die! But then, he happily reflected, there were always other good men coming on.

Then, halfway across the Green he encountered old Mordaunt, bent and shrivelled, almost invisible beneath his grey shawl.

"Well, Mr. Mordaunt." (There was developing in him quite naturally an agreeable and hearty manner to everyone. You never know who might, after all, be important.) "How's the drawing?"

Mordaunt looked up and showed him a grey, wizened face like a monkey's. He said something about being always "at home."

"At home? Don't you draw the Cathedral any more?"

He shook his head. "Nothing to draw. . . ." Then muttered something about "No activity . . . gone to sleep." But, whether he meant himself or the Cathedral, Gaselee could not be sure. The old man shuffled away.

Near the West Door Gaselee encountered Porteous.

"Ha! Gaselee! Good-day. Good-day to you! Glorious DAY! Superb!"

"It is indeed," Gaselee said, smiling. He detested Porteous, but why not be amiable? They stood for a moment, watching the people passing in.

"Very probably the last time we shall hear the Bishop preach. Oughtn't to be out. Lucky it's a fine day."

"By the way," said Gaselee, "I heard, oddly enough, of your erstwhile curate, Bird, yesterday."

"Indeed!" said Porteous, stiffening.

Porteous, thought Gaselee, can never hide his feelings.

"Yes. It was Hornblower. You remember? He was a curate at St. James's. He's got a church quite near Bird's—somewhere Eastbourne way. He was lunching with him only last week. Likes him extremely—and his wife. Such an intelligent woman he thought her. Says they are a devoted couple, never saw two people so happy."

"Really!" said Porteous, "very interesting." Then added: "We'd better go in. Time's getting on."

Now why, thought Gaselee, as he walked up the Nave towards the Choir, did I do that? Why did I have pleasure in annoying Porteous by telling him that Bird is happy? Not a very pleasant trait in me. But I did. I enjoyed it extremely. Porteous is such a fool . . . All the same these private pleasures are expensive. Porteous would make a bad enemy.

He found his seat in the Choir. He knelt down and prayed. Then, seated again, he looked at the "Service," the Anthem— "Love is the key of life and death"—Doggett.

Why, when had he heard that last? And then he clearly remembered. That afternoon, his own confused thoughts about himself, his childhood, his ambitions, his odd sense of shame, of shyness at the things he might discover in himself if he went deep enough. . . . Then! How long ago in experience if not in time! On that day, he remembered, although it was but an ordinary afternoon service with a small gathering in the Choir alone, he had felt that the Cathedral was thronged with unseen presences. Now today the Cathedral was thronged indeed with a human congregation and yet he felt it to be empty—still sleeping, tombs and chapels, brasses and stained glass, all unstirring. The Great Church asleep.

MICHAEL FURZE

And himself? The strange events of last year had done much for him. Ronder, Moffit, soon the Bishop, going, gone. Poor old Braund so deeply changed by his wife's illness that he was good for little more. Dale, in reality, his only rival. And Dale did not want the things that he, Gaselee, wanted. It might be that soon he would be the most powerful churchman in Polchester. . . .

He remained, throughout the service, in a kind of dream of power. Ronder had warned him . . . of what? He could not remember.

He had felt like everyone else, last year, danger in the air. But that was over, that episode closed. On the night of the riot he had run away. . . . Foolish. His nerves had been unstrung. And how fortunate! For he might otherwise have taken his place with the Bishop and seen what Dale saw . . . the spinning corpse. . . . He turned his mind away. These were nightmares. He was a man for daylight, common sense. That new committee . . . He would ask Romney to serve and possibly Cronin. . . . Who would be the new Bishop? . . . He was almost asleep— so still, so quiet. . . . There, in the choir stall opposite him, was Penny Marlowe with her mother. Pretty girl. He himself must marry one day. Every man ought to marry. She looked older. They say she was greatly upset at Lampiron's death, a man old enough to be her grandfather . . . a good girl . . . a good girl . . . good to her parents.

Across the spider web of his misted consciousness came the anthem:

> "Love is the key of life and death,
>   Of hidden heavenly mystery:
> Of all Christ is, of all He saith,
>   Love is the key."

And then the boy's voice (young Klitch, wasn't it?):

> "As three times to His Saint He saith,
>   He saith to me, He saith to thee,
> Breathing His Grace-conferring Breath:
>   'Lovest thou me?'"

481

Then (very distant it seemed, as across a lighted gulf) the choir:

> "*Ah, Lord, I have such feeble faith,*
> *Such feeble hope to comfort me:*
> *But love it is, is strong as death,*
> *And I love Thee.*"

"Love as strong as death"—that wasn't true. That was nonsense. One mustn't allow oneself to be cheated, to be sentimental. . . . One mustn't be cheated. . . .

And, as though in answer, came the frail bell-clear voice of the Bishop.

Had he been asleep, thought Gaselee? Had anyone seen him? He sincerely trusted not. He sat up in his stall very straight and looked sternly about him, as though calling the others to order. He heard the Bishop very plainly:

"My friends, I may not be here with you very much longer. I cannot have anything at this time of day very new to say to you. Only to give you all my love and beg you to believe in God's love and go to Him when you are in trouble. . . ."

(Sentimental, thought Gaselee, but that's always been the Bishop's weakness.)

". . . One thing I would say, however. I preached to you, some of you may remember, on Christmas Day and spoke of the year just passing as one of the most troubled in all Polchester's modern history. I need not remind you of those events. On this beautiful sunny day we are all at peace. Those incidents of last year must seem to us now unreal, incredible. And yet they were not unreal. They were very real indeed. You may remember how we all felt a disturbance, a disquiet, an apprehension. That apprehension is gone now, but I hope that you will not forget it. I believe, as you know well, that man is a spirit. I believe that he may be tempted to forget his spiritual self and, when that forgetfulness has hardened in him, it may be necessary for the spiritual powers to be active, to call him to consciousness of what is his only true reality. So I think they were active in this town last year and even used the powers of evil to stir our sleeping consciences.

"Now that we are all at peace again, do not let us sink back into security again. We are never secure. We shall never, in the conditions of this world, *be* secure. Our power is nothing against those other powers. We have only one weapon and that is love.

"Last year, as you all know, there was hatred, distrust, jealousy, even murder in this town. And now that we can look back and reflect, let us take courage. Do not despair of the world. Out of this confusion I believe in all sincerity that a great new brotherhood of man may come."

The old man seemed to be growing very feeble.

Platitudes, Gaselee thought. Platitudes. . . . It's of little use to most of us, I'm afraid, to talk about those vague things— vague . . . vague . . . His head nodded. He was almost gone. . . . He thought that he saw the recumbent Black Bishop put up his mailed fist and hide a yawn. . . . He woke with a start to see the old man walking, Broad carrying the Cross in front of him, back to his throne. He still carried himself superbly, his shoulders were scarcely bent. His face, as he looked forwards at the High Altar, had the beautiful serenity and happy calm of one of the saints.

He stood on the steps of the Altar to bless the people.

Halfway across the Green in a misty purple twilight through which silver stars were already burning, Gaselee encountered Klitch.

"Ah! Klitch! Happy to see you!"

"And you, Mr. Gaselee."

"Been at the service?"

"Why, yes. I always like to hear the boy, you know. His voice will be breaking soon."

"He sang well. That's a nice anthem of Doggett's."

"Very tuneful, very tuneful. . . . And the Bishop, bless him. He doesn't say anything new, but I always like to hear him. And he won't be long with us, I fear."

"No, I fear not."

They were in Norman Row. Klitch said:

"Excuse me, Mr. Gaselee. There's a thing in my shop I'd like to show you. It won't take you a minute."

"Why, certainly."

They went into Klitch's shop. There was a fine smell of frying onions.

Klitch apologized. "She's a good cook, my old woman. I look forward to tea, I can tell you. But this was what I wanted to show you."

He made a proud gesture towards a crucifix of black marble on a small table by itself.

"That's magnificent," said Gaselee.

"Yes, isn't it?" Klitch was beaming. "And that's not for sale—not whatever was offered for it. Funny story connected with that. I won't bore you with it now, but the fact is it was sold to me by Michael Furze. Then his brother Stephen bought it. Then, after all the trouble, the widow sold it back to me again."

"Dear me—what an extraordinary story!"

"Yes, isn't it?"

Gaselee stroked the marble. A beautiful piece—but he too was hungry. He was dining with Lady Mary, Romney, and a young poet friend of Romney's from London.

"Fine indeed! Fine indeed!" he said with a friendly heartiness that had, although he did not know it, an echo of Porteous' good fellowship.

He gave the crucifix another pat, said good-night and went.

Klitch stood there, sniffing the onions, admiring the crucifix.

He was about to switch off the lights and go upstairs to his tea when he suffered a strange hallucination.

In the shine of the shop illumination he thought he saw, staring in at him from the street, a figure. He saw a bowler hat, a long white nose, thin mean lips, a shapeless overcoat. The oddest thing was that he could swear there was the dim vapour of human breath on the windowpane.

Klitch stared. There was nothing and no one there.

He turned away, switched off the lights, started up the

stairs. Halfway up the stairs he paused, shook his head. Then went on again.

Cheerfully he called up:

"Well, old lady, what have you got for us tonight? I'm famished!"

THE END